WHERE RAINBOWS END

Before embarking on her writing career, Cecelia Ahern completed a degree in journalism and media studies. Her first novel, *PS, I Love You*, was one of the biggest-selling debut novels of 2004, reaching no. 1 in the *Sunday Times* bestseller list and being selected for the *Richard and Judy* Summer Read campaign. A film adaptation is currently in production with Warner Brothers.

Cecelia lives in County Dublin where she is currently working on her next novel. For more information on Cecelia Ahern, please visit www.ceceliaahern.ie.

By the same author

PS, I Love You

CECELIA AHERN

Where Rainbows End

HarperCollins*Publishers*

This novel is entirely a work of fiction.
The names, characters and incidents portrayed in it are
the work of the author's imagination. Any resemblance to
actual persons, living or dead, events or localities is
entirely coincidental.

HarperCollins*Publishers*
77–85 Fulham Palace Road,
Hammersmith, London W6 8JB

www.harpercollins.co.uk

Published by HarperCollins*Publishers* 2004

6

A catalogue record for this book
is available from the British Library

ISBN 0 00 718995 8

Set in Sabon by Palimpsest Book Production Limited,
Polmont, Stirlingshire

Printed and bound in Great Britain by
Clays Ltd, St Ives plc

There are so many special people who have been instru-
mental in helping this happen for me.

A huge thank you to my editors Lynne Drew and Maxine
Hitchcock. And to Amanda, Jane, Kelly, Fiona, Moira,
Damon, Tony, Andrea, Lee and the rest of the fantastic
team at HarperCollins for all your hard work and constant
support and belief in me.

Thank you:

Marianne Gunn O'Connor, super-agent and friend.

Mom, Dad, Georgina, Nicky and Keano for your love,
support, advice, laughter and friendship. You all mean the
world to me.

David, for taking every single step of this incredible
journey with me. I share it all with you.

After the year that I've had, everyone near and dear to me
deserves an even bigger thank you than ever. I'm lucky to
be surrounded by such a huge support group, so special
thanks to:

Fairy godmother Sarah & Lisa, Olive & Robert, Enda & Sarah, Rita & Mark, Colm & Angelina (ABCD), Dominic & Catherine, Raphael, Ibar, Ciaran & Carmel, Ronan & Jennifer, Eileen & Noel, Maurice & Moira, Kathleen & Donie, Noel & Helen (and families of all!).

Thank you Susana, Paula pea & SJ for keeping me sane (or for at least trying), Adrienne & Roel, Ryano & Sniff – I couldn't have done this without you both, ha ha! Neil & Breda and the Keoghans, Jimmy & Rose, Lucy, Elaine & Joe, Gail, Eadaoin, Margaret. Big thank you Thrity, Gerald & Clodagh, Daithi & Brenda, Shane & Gillian, Mark & Gillian, Yvonne, Nikki & Adam, Leah BH, Paul & Helen, Drew Reed, Gary Kavanagh (you're not in this one either!), Pat Lynch, Sean Egan, Madeleine Jordan, Michael Ryan, Sarah Webster and her good friend Sister Mary Joseph, Lindy Clarke and the Chinese Chess Team and a huge thank you to Doo Services.

Big thank you to super sub-agent Vicki Satlow.

My very special grandparents Olive, Raphael, Julia and Con who must be pressing magical buttons way, way up there and thank you God who must be helping them.

To everyone who has welcomed my books into their hearts. You've all put a smile on my face and a lump in my throat so I thank you with all my heart.

And finally, thank you, Rosie Dunne, for nagging me all night, every night until your story was told.

For Mimmie

PART ONE

Chapter 1

To Alex

You are invited to my 7th birthday party on Tuesday the 8th of April in my house. We are having a magician and you can come to my house at 2 o'clock. It is over at 5 o'clock. I hope you will come.

From your best friend Rosie

To Rosie

Yes I will come to your brithday party on Wensday.

Form Alex

To Alex

My birthday party is on Tuesday not Wednesday. You can't bring sandy to the party because mum says so. She is a smelly dog.

From Rosie

To Rosie

I do not care wot your stupid mum says sandy wants to come.

Form Alex

To Alex

My mum is not stupid you are. You are not aloud to bring the dog. She will brust the baloons.

From Rosie

To Rosie

Then I am not going.

Form Alex

To Alex

Fine.

From Rosie

Dear Mrs Stewart,

I just called by to have a word with you about my daughter Rosie's birthday on the 8th of April. Sorry you weren't in, but I'll drop by again later this afternoon and maybe we can talk then.

There seems to be some sort of little problem with Alex and Rosie lately. I think they're not quite on talking terms. I hope you can fill me in on the situation when we meet. Rosie would really love if he came to her birthday party.

I'm looking forward to meeting the mother of this charming young man!

See you then,

Alice Dunne

To Rosie

I would be happy to go to your brithday party next week. Thank you fro inviting me and sandy.

Form Alex your frend

To Rosie

Thanks for the great day at the party. I am sorry sandy brust the baloons and ate your cake. She was hungry because mum says dad eats all our leftovers. See you at skool tomorrow.

Alex

To Alex

Thanks for the present. Its ok about what sandy did. Mum says she needed a new carpet anyway. Dad is a bit mad though. He said the old one was fine but mum thinks the house smells of poo now, and its not baby Kevin.

Look at Miss Casey's nose. It is the biggest nose I have ever seen. Ha ha ha.

Rosie

To Rosie

I no and she has a big snot hanging down too. She is the ugliest alien I have ever seen. I think we should tell the police we have an alien as a teacher who has a really smelly breath and—

Dear Mr and Mrs Stewart,

I would like to arrange a meeting with you to discuss how Alex is progressing at school. Specifically, I would like to talk about the recent change in his behaviour along with the problem of his note writing during class. I would appreciate it if you called the school to arrange a suitable time to meet.

Yours sincerely,

Miss Casey

To Alex

I hate that we dont sit together anymore in class. I'm stuck beside stinky Steven who picks his nose and eats it. It is gross. What did your mum and dad say about Miss Big nose?

From Rosie

To Rosie

Mum did not say much because she kept laffing. I dont no why. It is reall boring up the front of the class. Smelly breath Miss Casey keeps on lucking at me. Have to go.

Alex

To Alex

You always spell know wrong. It is KNOW not NO.

From Rosie

To Rosie

Sorry miss prefect. I no how to spell it.

Form Alex

Hello form Spain! The weather is really nice. It is hot and sunny. There is a swimming pool with a big slide. It is cool. Met a freind called John. He is nice. See you in 2 weeks. I broke my arm coming down the slide. I went to the hopsital. I would like to work in a hopsital like the man that fixed my arm because he wore a white coat and had a chart in his hand and was really nice and he helped me to feel better. I would like to make people feel better and wear a white coat. My freind john signed my cast. You can too when I get home if you like. Alex

To Alex. Hello from Lundin. My hotel is the one in the picture on the front. My room is the one that is 7 up from the ground but you cant see me in the post card. I would like to work in a hotel when I grow up because you get free chocolates everyday and people are so nice that they tidy your room for you. The buses here are all red like the toy ones you got last Christmas. Everyone talks with a funny voice but are nice. Have met a frend called Jane. We go swimming together. Bye. Love from Rosie

To Alex

Why amnt I invited to your birthday party this year? I know all the boys from the class are going. Are you fighting with me?

Rosie

Dear Alice,

I'm sorry about Alex's behaviour this week. I know that Rosie is upset about not going to the party and she doesn't understand why she hasn't been invited. To be honest I can't quite understand it myself; I have tried to talk to Alex but I'm afraid I can't get inside the mind of a ten-year-old boy!

I think it's just a case of his not being able to invite her because the other boys don't want a girl to go. Unfortunately, he seems to be at that age ... Please give my love to Rosie. It seems so unfair and when I spoke to her last week after school I could see how hurt she was.

Perhaps George and I can take the two of them out some other evening during the week.

Best wishes,
Sandra Stewart

To Rosie

The party was not very good. You did not miss anything. The boys are stupid. Brian threw his pizza in Jameses sleeping bag and when James woke up he had tomato and cheese stuck in his hair and everything and my mum tried to wash it and it would not go away and then Jameses mum gave out to Brians mum and my mum went real red and my dad said something I didn't here and Jameses mum started to cry and then everyone went home. Do you want to go to the cimena on Friday and go to McDonalds after? My mum and dad will bring us.

Alex

To Alex

Sorry about your party. Brian is a weirdo anyway. I hate him. Brian the Whine is his name. I will ask my mum and dad about the cinema. Look at Miss Casey's skirt it looks like my grannys. Or it looks like sandy puked up all over it and the—

Dear Mr and Mrs Dunne,

I was hoping to arrange a meeting with you to discuss Rosie's recent behaviour in school and her note writing during class. How does Thursday at 3 p.m. sound?

Miss Casey

Alex,

My mum and dad won't let me go to the cinema tonight. I hate not sitting beside you. It's so boring. Frizzy Lizzys hair is blocking my view of the blackboard. Why does this happen to us all the time?

Rosie

TO ALEX
HAPPY VALENTINE'S DAY!
MAY THERE BE SEX IN YOUR LIFE AND . . .
LIFE IN YOUR SEX!
LOVE FROM YOUR SECRET ADMIRER XXX

To Rosie
  You wrote that card didn't you?
  From Alex

To Alex
  What card?
  From Rosie

To Rosie
Very funny. I no it was you.
From Alex

To Alex
I really don't know what you're talking about. Why would I send you a Valentine's card?
From Rosie

To Rosie
Ha ha! How did you no it was a Valentine's Card! The only way you could no is if you sent it. You *love* me, you want to *marry* me.
From Alex

To Alex
Leave me alone I'm listening to Mrs O'Sullivan. If she catches us passing notes again we're dead meat.
From Rosie

To Rosie
What happened to you? You've turned into such a swot.
Alex

Yes Alex and that's why I'll go places in life, like going to college and being a big successful business person with loads of money . . . unlike you.
From Rosie

Chapter 2

Dear Mr Byrne,
   Alex will be unable to attend school tomorrow, the 8th of April, as he has a dental appointment.
   Sandra Stewart

Dear Ms Quinn,
   Rosie will be unable to attend school tomorrow, the 8th of April, as she has a doctor's appointment.
   Alice Dunne

Rosie,
   I'll meet you round the corner at 8.30 a.m. Remember to bring a change of clothes. We're not wandering around town in our uniforms. This is going to be the best birthday you ever had, Rosie Dunne, trust me! I can't believe we're actually getting away with this!
   Alex
   PS. Sweet 16 my arse!

St James's Hospital
10 April

Dear Mr and Mrs Dunne,
  Enclosed is the medical bill for Rosie Dunne's stomach pumping on 8 April.
  Yours sincerely,
  Dr Montgomery

Rosie,
  Your mum is guarding the door like a vicious dog so I don't think I'll get to see you for the next ten years or so. The kind big sis you love so much (not!) has agreed to pass this on to you. You owe her big time . . .
  Sorry about the other day. Maybe you were right. Maybe the tequila wasn't such a good idea. The poor barman will probably be closed down for serving us. Told you that fake ID my mate got would work, even though yours did say you were born on the 31st of February!
  Just wondering if you remember anything that happened the other day . . . write to me. You can trust Stephanie to pass it on. She's mad at your mum for not letting her drop out of college. Phil and Margaret have just announced that they're having another baby so it looks like I'll be an uncle for the second time round. At least that's taking the attention off me, which makes for a change. Phil just keeps laughing at what you and me did because we remind him of himself ten years ago.
  Get well soon, you alco! Do you no I didn't think it was possible for a human being to go *so* green in the face. I think you have finally found your talent, Rosie, ha ha ha ha.

Alex/Mr Cocky,
  I FEEL AWFUL. My head is pounding, I have never had such a headache, I have never felt so ill before in my life. Mum and Dad are going ape shit. Honestly, you never get

11

any sympathy in this house. I'm gonna be grounded for about thirty years and I'm being 'prevented' from seeing you because you're 'such a bad influence'. Yeah right, whatever.

Anyway, it doesn't really matter what they do because I'm gonna see you at school tomorrow, unless they 'prevent' me from going there too, which is absolutely fine by me. Can't believe we have double maths on a Monday morning. I would rather get my stomach pumped again. Five times over. See you on Monday then.

Oh by the way, in answer to your question, apart from my face smashing against that filthy pub floor, flashing lights, loud sirens, speeding cars and puking, I can't remember anything else. But I bet that just about covers it. Anything else I should know about?

Rosie

To Rosie

Glad to hear everything is as normal as usual. Mum and Dad are driving me crazy too. I can't believe I'm actually looking forward to going to school. At least no one will be able to nag us there.

From Alex

Dear Mr and Mrs Dunne,

Following the recent actions of your daughter Rosie, we request a meeting with you at the school immediately. We need to discuss her behaviour and come to an agreement on a reasonable punishment. I have no doubt you understand the necessity of this. Alex Stewart's parents will also be in attendance.

The scheduled time is Monday morning at 9 a.m.

Yours sincerely,

Mr Bogarty

Principal

From   Rosie
To   Alex
Subject Suspended!

Holy shit! I didn't think that old bogey would go ahead
and suspend us! I'd swear we were axe murderers from the
way that he was carrying on! Oh, this is the best
punishment *ever*. I get to stay in bed for a whole week
nursing a hangover instead of going to school!

From   Alex
To   Rosie
Subject I'm in hell

Glad life is going so wonderfully for you these days. I'm
emailing you from the worst place in the world. An office.
I have to work here with Dad for the entire week, filing
shit and licking stamps. I swear to God I am NEVER
EVER going to work in an office in my life.
    The bastards aren't even paying me.
    A very pissed off Alex

From   Rosie
To   Alex
Subject A very pissed off Alex

Ha ha ha ha ha ha ha ha ha em . . . I've forgotten what I
was going to write . . . oh yeah . . . ha ha ha ha ha ha ha
ha ha ha ha ha ha ha ha ha.
    Lots of love from an extremely comfy, snuggy, warm and
happy Rosie typing from her bedroom.

From   Alex
To   Rosie
Subject Lazy

I don't care. There is an absolute babe working in this office. I am going to marry her. Now who's laughing?

From   Rosie
To   Alex
Subject Don Juan

Who is she?
    From a non-lesbian so am therefore NOT jealous.

From   Alex
To   Rosie
Subject To non-lesbian

I will for the time being humour you by calling you that although I have yet to see any evidence to suggest otherwise.
    Her name is Bethany Williams and she is seventeen (older woman!), blonde, has a massive pair of boobs and the longest legs I have ever seen.
    From the sex god

From   Rosie
To   Alex
Subject Mr Sex God (puke puke gag vomit)

She sounds like a giraffe. I'm sure she is a really nice person (not!). Have you even said hello to her or has your future wife yet to acknowledge your existence? (Apart from handing you memos to photocopy, of course.)

You have an instant message from: ALEX.

Alex: Hey there, Rosie, got some news for you.

Rosie: Leave me alone, please. I'm trying to concentrate on what Mr Simpson is saying.

Alex: Hmmm wonder why . . . could it be those beautiful big blue eyes all you girls are always going on about?

Rosie: Nope, I have a great and growing interest in Excel. It's so exciting – I could just sit in and do it all weekend.

Alex: Oh, you're turning into such a bore.

Rosie: I WAS JOKING, YOU IDIOT! I hate this crap. I think my brain is turning to mush from listening to him. But go away anyway.

Alex: Do you not wanna hear my news?

Rosie: Nope.

Alex: Well, I'm telling you anyway.

Rosie: OK, what's the big exciting news?

Alex: Well, you can eat your words, my friend, because virgin boy is no longer.

Alex: Hello?

Alex: You still there?

Alex: Rosie, c'mon, stop messing!

Rosie: Sorry, I seem to have fallen off my chair and knocked myself out. I had an awful dream you said you are no longer virgin boy.

Alex: No dream.

Rosie: I suppose that means you won't be wearing your underwear over those tights any more.

Alex: I have no need for underwear at all now.

Rosie: Uuuugh! So who's the unlucky girl? Please don't say Bethany please don't say Bethany . . .

Alex: Tough shit. It's Bethany.

Alex: Hello?

Alex: Rosie?

Rosie: What?

Alex: Well?

Rosie: Well what?

Alex: Well say something.

Rosie: I really don't know what you want me to say, Alex. I think you need to get yourself some male friends because I'm not gonna slap you on the back and ask for gory details.

Alex: Just tell me what you think.

Rosie: To be honest, from what I hear about her, I think she's a slut.

Alex: Oh, come on, you don't even no the girl, you've never even met her. You call anyone who sleeps with anyone a slut.

Rosie: I've seen her around and, eh, SLIGHT exaggeration there, Alex. I call people who sleep with different people every day of the week sluts.

Alex: You no that's not true.

Rosie: You keep spelling KNOW wrong. It's KNOW not NO.

Alex: Shut up with the 'know' thing. You've been going on about that since we were about five!

Rosie: Yeah, exactly, so you think you would listen by now.

Alex: Oh forget I said anything.

Rosie: Oh, Alex, I'm just worried about you. I know you really like her, and all I'm saying is that she's not a one-man kind of girl.

Alex: Well, she is now.

Rosie: Are you two going out with each other?!

Alex: Yes.

Rosie: YES?????

Alex: You sound surprised.

Rosie: I just didn't think Bethany went out with people, I thought she just slept with them.

Rosie: Alex?

16

Rosie: OK, OK, I'm sorry.

Alex: Rosie, you need to stop doing that.

Rosie: I no I do.

Alex: Ha ha.

Mr Simpson: You two, get down to the principal's office now.

Rosie: WHAT??? OH, SIR, PLEASE, I WAS LISTENING TO YOU!

Mr Simpson: Rosie, I haven't spoken for the last fifteen minutes. You are supposed to be working on an assignment now.

Rosie: Oh. Well, it's not my fault. Alex is an awful influence on me. He just never lets me concentrate on my school work.

Alex: I just had something really important to tell Rosie and it just couldn't wait.

Mr Simpson: So I see, Alex. Congratulations.

Alex: Eh . . . how do you know what it was?

Mr Simpson: I think you two would find it interesting sometimes if you listen to me every now and again. You can really learn some useful tips, like how to keep an instant message private so everyone else can't see.

Alex: Are you telling me other people in the class can read this?

Mr Simpson: Yes I am.

Alex: Oh my God.

Rosie: Ha ha ha ha ha ha ha ha ha ha ha ha ha ha ha

Mr Simpson: Rosie!

Rosie: Ha ha ha ha ha ha ha

Mr Simpson: ROSIE!!!

Rosie: Yes, sir.

Mr Simpson: Get out of the class now.

Alex: Ha ha ha ha ha ha ha

Mr Simpson: You too, Alex.

Chapter 3

From   Rosie
To   Alex
Subject   Julie's house party

Hiya, long time no see . . . I hope they're not working you
to death down there at 'the office'. I've hardly seen you at
all this summer. There's a party at Julie's house tonight so
was just wondering if you wanted to go. I don't really
want to go on my own. Anyway, I'm sure you're busy
doing whatever it is you do so just ring me when you get a
chance or email me back.

From   Alex
To   Rosie
Subject   Re: Julie's house party

Rosie, this is just quick email. Real busy. Can't go out
tonight, promised Bethany would go to cinema. Sorry! You
go and have fun.

Rosie, hello from Portugal! Weather here really hot. Dad got
sunstroke and all Mum does is lie by the pool, which is really

boring. Not much people here my age. Hotel quiet (on front of postcard) and it's right on the beach, as you can see. You would love to work here! I'm bringing home a collection of those little shampoos and shower caps and stuff that you love. The bathrobe is too big to fit into my bag. See you when I get back. Alex

From   Rosie
To   Alex
Subject   Catching up?

How was the holiday? Haven't heard from you since you've been back. Fancy going out tonight to catch up?

From   Alex
To   Rosie
Subject   Re: Catching up?

Sorry have been so busy since I got back. Got you pressie. Can't go out tonight but will drop your pressie by before I head out.

From   Rosie
To   Alex
Subject   Re: Catching up?

Didn't see you last night. I want my little shampoos, ha ha.

From   Alex
To   Rosie
Subject   Re: Catching up?

Heading to Donegal for the weekend. Beth's parents have a little 'hideaway' there. Will drop your pressie by when I get back.

To the most inconsiderate asshole of a friend

I'm writing you this letter because I know that if I say what I have to say to your face I will probably punch you.

I don't know you any more. I don't see you any more. All I get is a quick text or a rushed email from you every few days. I know you are busy and I know you have Bethany, but hello? I'm supposed to be your best friend.

You have no idea what this summer has been like. Since we were kids we pushed away every single person that could possibly have been our friend until there was only me and you. It's not that we didn't *want* anyone else, it's just that we didn't *need* them. You always had me. I always had you. Now you have Bethany and I have no one.

Sadly it looks like you don't need me any more. I feel like those other people that used to try to become our friends. I know you're probably not doing it deliberately just as we never did. Anyway, I'm not moaning on about how much I hate her, I'm just trying to tell you that I miss you. And that, well . . . I'm lonely.

Whenever you cancel nights out I end up staying home with Mum and Dad watching TV. Stephanie's always out and even Kevin has more of a life than I do. It's so depressing. This was supposed to be our summer of fun. What happened? Can't you be friends with two people at once?

I know you have found someone who is extra special, and that you both have a unique 'bond', or whatever, that you and I will never have. But we have another bond: we're best friends. Or does the best friend bond disappear as soon as you meet somebody else? Maybe it does, and I just don't understand that because I haven't met that 'somebody special'. I'm not in any hurry to either. I liked things the way they were.

In a few years' time if my name ever comes up you will probably say, 'Rosie. Now there's a name I haven't heard for ages. We used to be best friends. I wonder what she's doing now; I haven't seen or thought of her in years!' You will sound like my mum and dad when they have dinner parties with friends and talk about old times. They mention people I've never even heard of when they're talking about some of the most important days of their lives. How could Mum's bridesmaid of twenty years ago be someone she doesn't even ring up now? Or in Dad's case, how could he not know where his own best friend from school lives?

Anyway, my point is (I know, I know, there is one), I don't want to be one of those easily forgotten people, *so* important at the time, *so* special, *so* influential and *so* treasured, yet years later just a vague face and a distant memory. I want us to be best friends for ever, Alex.

I'm happy you're happy, really I am, but I feel like I've been left behind. Maybe our time has come and gone. Maybe your time is now meant to be spent with Bethany. And if that's the case I won't bother sending you this letter. And if I'm not sending this letter then what am I doing still writing it? OK, I'm going now and I'm ripping these muddled thoughts up.

Your friend,
Rosie

From   Alex
To   Rosie
Subject   Buttercup!!

Hey, Buttercup, you OK? (Haven't called you that for a *long* time!) I haven't heard or seen you in a while. I'm sending you this email because every time I call by your house, you're either in the bath or not there. Should I begin to take this personally? But knowing you, if you had a problem with me you wouldn't be too shy to let me know all about it!

21

Anyway, once the summer is over we'll see each other every day. We'll be sick of the sight of each other then! I can't believe this is our last year in school. It's crazy! This time next year I'll be studying medicine and you will be hotel manager woman extraordinaire! Things at work have been frantic. Dad kind of gave me a promotion so I've more to do than just filing and labelling. (I answer phones now too.) But I need the money and at least I get to see Bethany everyday. How's your job as chief dishwasher at The Dragon? I'm amazed you turned down baby-sitting for that. You could have stayed in all night and watched TV instead of turning your hands to prunes while you scrape egg noodles from woks. Anyway, email me or call me back or something.

From   Rosie
To   Alex
Subject   Moonbeam!

It's not because I hate Bethany that I'm not seeing much of you (although I do hate her) it's just that I think Bethany dislikes me just a little. It could have something to do with the fact that a friend of hers told her what I wrote about her in that (not so) private instant messaging thingy in computer class last year. But I suppose you already know that. I don't think she liked being called a slut, I don't know why . . . some women are just funny like that. (Speaking of computer class, you know Mr Simpson got married this summer? I'm gutted. I'll never look at Excel in the same way again.)

Anyway it's your birthday soon! You will have finally reached the grand old age of eighteen! Want to go out and do some legal celebrating (well, legal for you, anyway)? Let me know.

PS. Please STOP calling me Buttercup!

From   Alex
To   Rosie
Subject 18th Birthday

Good to hear you're alive after all. I was beginning to worry! I would love to celebrate my 18th with you but Bethany's parents are taking me and my parents out for dinner to the Hazel. (How posh is that?) It's so we can all get to know each other. Sorry, another night definitely.

~~Dearest Alex,~~
   ~~Well whoopdeedoo for you.~~
   ~~Fuck Bethany.~~
   ~~Fuck her parents.~~
   ~~Fuck the Hazel.~~
   ~~And fuck you.~~
   ~~Love your best friend Rosie~~

From   Rosie
To   Alex
Subject Happy Birthday!

OK then. Well, enjoy the meal. Happy birthday!

From   Rosie
To   Alex
Subject DISASTER!

I can't believe this is happening! I was just talking to your mum; called over for a chat and she told me the bad news. This is the *worst* news *ever*! Please call me when you can. Your boss keeps telling me you can't take calls during working hours – QUIT, Mr I never EVER want to work in an office.

   This is so terrible. I feel awful!

Chapter 4

Dear Mr Stewart,

We are delighted to inform you that you have been accepted to fill the position of Vice President of Charles and Charles Co. We are thrilled that you will be joining the team over here and we look forward to welcoming you and your family to Boston.

I hope the relocation package we are offering is to your satisfaction. If there is anything further that Charles and Charles Co. can do for you, please do not hesitate to ask. Maria Agnesi, personnel executive, will call you to discuss a suitable date for you to begin work.

We look forward to seeing you at the office.

Welcome to the team!

Yours sincerely,

Robert Brasco

President, Charles and Charles Co.

From   Alex
To   Rosie
Subject Re: DISASTER!

I'll call you when I get home. It's true. Dad was offered a job doing something that sounds incredibly boring . . . I don't really know, I wasn't listening when he told me exactly what. I can't understand why he has to go all the way over to Boston to do a boring job. There's plenty of them right here. He can have mine.

I'm so pissed off. I don't want to go. I only have a year left in school. This is such the wrong time to leave. I don't want to go to a stupid American high school. I don't want to leave you.

We can talk about it later. We have to think of a way that I can stay. This is really bad, Rosie.

From   Rosie
To   Alex
Subject Stay with me!

Don't go! Mum and Dad said that you could stay here for the year! Finish school in Dublin and then we can both decide what to do after that! Please stay! It will be so brilliant, us living together. It'll be just like when we were young and we used to keep each other up all night with those walkie-talkies! We used to hear more static than our voices but we thought we were so cool! Remember that time on Christmas Eve absolutely *years* ago when we had a 'Santa' watch? We planned it for weeks, drawing little diagrams of the road and maps of our houses just so we could cover every angle and not miss him. You were on the 7–10 p.m. watch and I was on the 10 p.m.–1 a.m. watch. You were *supposed* to wake up and take over from me, but – surprise, surprise – you didn't. I stayed awake all night, screaming down into that walkie-talkie, trying to wake you up! Ah well, it was your loss. I saw Santa and you didn't . . .

If you stay with us, Alex, we'll be able to talk all night! It would be so much fun. When we were kids we always wanted to live together. Now's our chance.

Talk to your mum and dad about it. Convince them to say yes. Anyway, you're eighteen so you can do what you like!

Rosie,

I didn't want to wake you so your mum said she would pass this on to you. You no I hate goodbyes, but anyway, it's not goodbye because you're going to come over and visit all the time. Promise me. Mum and Dad wouldn't even let me stay with Phil, never mind you. I couldn't convince them. They want to keep their eye on me for my final year of school.

I have to go . . . I'll miss you. Ring you when I get there.

Love,

Alex

PS. I told you, I *was* awake that Christmas Eve. My battery just went dead on my walkie-talkie . . . (and I did see Santa, I'll have you no).

Alex,

Good luck, little brother. Don't worry, you'll enjoy yourself once you get there and I can't wait to come and visit. Despite having Margaret and the kids, I still feel like moving over with the lot of you. I'll miss you all. It won't be the same without you. Stop worrying about Rosie. Her life's not going to fall apart just because you're in different countries. But if it'll make you feel any better I'll look out for her for you – she does almost seem like my little sister. By the way, if Sandy doesn't learn how to control her bladder in this house then I'm sending her over to you on a plane.

We'll miss you,

Phil (+ Margaret, William and Fiona)

From   Rosie
To   Stephanie
Subject   Urgent sisterly advice needed

I can't believe he's gone, Steph. I can't believe you're gone. Why is everyone leaving me? Surely you could have 'found yourself' a little closer to home? But France? Alex left only a few weeks ago but I almost feel like he's dead . . .

Why did he have to break up with Slutty Bethany just two weeks before he left? Then I wouldn't have gotten used to him being around so much again. Things really got back to normal, Steph. It was brilliant. We spent every second together and had so much fun!

Brian the Whine threw a going-away party for Alex just last week; I think it was just an excuse for Brian the Whine to get permission from his parents to have a party, to be honest, because the two of them *never* liked each other. Not since that pizza in James's hair incident. But anyway, Whine held the party in his house and invited all of his friends, and me and Alex knew hardly anyone in the entire place! The people we did know we can't stand, so we left and headed into town. You know O'Brien's where we held your surprise 21st? Well, we went there and Alex had the bright idea of standing outside the pub door and pretending to be the bouncer. (There was none on the door that night because it was only a Monday.) Well, he pulled it off anyway because he's really tall and muscly – you know Alex! Anyway, we stood there for ages turning people away; I don't think he let one person in. Eventually we got bored and headed inside to the empty pub. Of course, the more drinks we had, the more me and Alex ended up getting all weepy about him moving away . . . Apart from that the night was brilliant. I miss the times we had, just us together like that.

You can't imagine how lonely it is at school these days.

I'm just short of getting down on my hands and knees and begging for someone to be my friend. How pathetic. No one really cares. I spent the last few years ignoring them so they don't feel like they really have to talk to me. I think some of them are even enjoying it. The teachers are loving it. Mr Simpson called me back after class to congratulate me on how well I'm doing lately. It's shameful; Alex would be appalled if he found out I was actually working at school. I'm horrified that things have gotten so bad that I actually pay attention to the teachers. They're the only people who even talk to me from one day to the next. How depressing.

I wake up in the morning and I feel like I'm missing something. I know that there's something not right, and it takes me a while to remember what it is . . . then I remember. My best friend is gone. My only friend. It was silly of me to rely so much on one person. It's all coming back on me now.

Anyway, sorry for whinging on and on all the time. I'm sure you have enough problems of your own to worry about. Tell me how my sophisticated big sis is doing over in France. Strange you're over there – you always hated French class. At least it's only for a few months, right? And then you're coming back? Dad's still not happy about you dropping out of college. Why you had to go away to find yourself is beyond me. Just look in the mirror. What's the restaurant like? Have you dropped any plates yet? Are you going to work there for long? Any nice men? There must be; French men are yummy. If there are any spare men that you don't want, send them my way.

Love,

Rosie

PS. Dad wants to know if you have enough money and if you've found yourself yet. Mum wants to know if you are eating properly. Little Kevin (he is so tall now you wouldn't believe!) wants to know if you'll send him some video game or other over. I don't know what he's talking about so just ignore him.

From   Stephanie
To   Rosie
Subject   Re: Urgent sisterly advice

Hello, my darling little sister.

Don't worry about Alex. I've thought long and hard about it and I've come to the conclusion that it's a good idea he's not there for your final year of school because at least for the first year EVER you may not get suspended. Think of how proud you would make Mum and Dad. (Oh, by the way, tell them I'm broke, starving and currently looking for myself in an internet café in Paris.)

I definitely know how you feel right now. I'm alone here too, but just stick the year out and when you're finished maybe Alex will move back to Ireland, or you can go to college in Boston!

Aim for something, Rosie, I know you don't want to hear it, but it will help. Aim for what you want and the year will all make sense. Go to Boston if that will make you happy. Study hotel management like you've always wanted.

You're only young, Rosie, and I know that you absolutely hate to hear that but it's true. What seems tragic now won't even be an issue in a few years' time. You're only seventeen. You and Alex have the rest of your lives to catch up together. After all, soulmates always end up together. Silly Bethany won't even be remembered then. Ex-girlfriends are easily forgotten. Best friends stay with you for ever.

Take care. Tell Mum and Dad I said hi and that I'm still looking for myself but may have found someone else in the process. Tall, dark and handsome . . .

Chapter 5

Dear Ms Rosie Dunne,

Thank you for your application to study Hotel Management with us at Boston College. We are delighted to inform you that you were successful in your application . . .

From   Rosie
To   Alex
Subject   Boston here I come!

I GOT IN!! Boston College, here I come!!! WAHOOO! The letter arrived just this morning and I am soooo excited! You'd better not move a muscle, Mr Stewart, because I am finally coming to see you. It'll be great, even though you and I won't be studying at the same college. (Harvard is far too distinguished for the likes of me!) But I think it's just as well because I don't think we can really afford to get suspended again . . .

Email or call me as soon as possible. I'd call you but Dad put a block on long-distance calls, as you know, after the last bill. Mum and Dad are so proud, they're phoning all the family to tell them. I think they're hoping I'll be the first Dunne child to go to college and actually finish the course. Dad keeps warning me not to go trying to 'find myself' anywhere like Stephanie did. By the way, it doesn't look like Steph is coming home anytime soon. She met some chef that works at the restaurant she's waiting at, and she's officially 'in love'.

The phone hasn't stopped ringing all day with congratulations! Honestly, Alex, the house is buzzing! Paul and Eileen from across the road sent over a bunch of flowers for me, which was really nice. Mum's getting the house ready for a get-together tonight, just a few sand-wiches and cocktail sausages, that kind of thing. Kevin is happy I'm leaving so he can be even more spoiled than usual. I'll miss the brat even though he never talks to me. I'll miss Mum and Dad even more, but right now everyone is just so excited I've been accepted to think about the fact that I won't be living here any more. I suppose the enor-mity of it will hit me the day I wave goodbye, but in the meantime we'll continue to celebrate!

PS. One of these days I can run a hotel and you can be the doctor-in-the-house who saves the lives of the guests I poison in the restaurant, just like we always planned. Oh, this has all worked out wonderfully . . .

From   Alex
To   Rosie
Subject Re: Boston here I come!

This is *brilliant* news! I can't wait to see you too! Harvard isn't too far away from Boston College (well, in comparison to being a whole ocean apart – can you believe Harvard accepted me? It must be the intellects' idea of a hilarious joke). I'm too excited to type – just get over here. When are you coming?

From   Rosie
To   Alex
Subject September

I won't be over till September, only a few days before the
semester starts, because I have got so many things to sort
out you wouldn't believe!

The debs are at the end of August – will you come over
for them? Everyone would love to see you, and I need
someone to go with! We will have so much fun and we
can annoy all our teachers, just like old times . . . Let me
know.

From   Alex
To   Rosie
Subject Re: Debs

Of course I'll come home for our debs. I wouldn't miss it
for the world!

Where r u??? I'm waiting at airport. Me & Dad have been
here for hours. I tried ur house phone & mobile. Don't know
where else 2 call. Hope everything's ok.

Hi Rosie. Just got ur text. Sent u an email explaining. Can u
check email at airport? Alex

From   Alex
To   Rosie
Subject Sorry!

Rosie, I am so sorry. This whole day has been an absolute
nightmare. There was a foul-up with the flight. I don't no
what happened, but my name wasn't in the system when I
went to collect my ticket. I've been here all day trying to

33

get another flight. They're all booked because of people flying home from holidays and students returning home, etc. I'm on standby, but so far there's been nothing. I'm just hanging around the airport waiting for a flight. This is a nightmare.

From   Rosie
To   Alex
Subject   Flight tomorrow

Dad's talking to the lady at Aer Lingus ticket desk. She says there's a flight that leaves Boston tomorrow at 10.10 a.m. It takes five hours to get here so that will make it 3 p.m., then we're five hours ahead, which will make it 8 p.m. We could collect you from airport and go straight to ball? Or maybe you'd prefer to go to my house first? You can't wear your tux on the plane because you'll get all crumpled. What do you think?

From   Alex
To   Rosie
Subject   Flight

Rosie, bad news. That flight is fully booked.

From   Rosie
To   Alex
Subject   Flight

Shit. Think, think, think. What can I do? It seems that we can get you here every other bloody day except tomorrow. Somebody up there really doesn't want you to get on that plane. Maybe it's a sign?

From   Alex
To   Rosie
Subject My fault

It's my fault, I should have double-checked with the airline yesterday – they always say you should reconfirm your flights but whoever does? I no I've messed up your night but please go to the debs anyway. You still have the whole day to find someone else to go with you. Take loads of photos for me, and enjoy yourself. Sorry, Rosie.

From   Rosie
To   Alex
Subject Re: My fault

It's not your fault. I'm disappointed but let's be realistic, it's not the end of the world. I'm gonna be in Boston in a little over a month and we'll be seeing each other EVERY DAY! Make sure you get your money back for that flight, the eejits. We'll have a brilliant time. I better go searching for a man now . . .

From   Alex
To   Rosie
Subject Manhunt

Any luck finding a man?

From   Rosie
To   Alex
Subject Man found

What a stupid question!! Of course I found a man. I'm insulted you even needed to ask . . .

From   Alex
To   Rosie
Subject   Mystery man

Then who is it?

From   Rosie
To   Alex
Subject   Secret man

That would be absolutely none of your business.

From   Alex
To   Rosie
Subject   Invisible man

HA! You didn't find a date!! I knew it!

From   Rosie
To   Alex
Subject   Big strong man

Yes I did.

From   Alex
To   Rosie
Subject   No man

No you didn't.

From   Rosie
To   Alex
Subject   Yes, man!

Yes I did.

From   Alex
To   Rosie
Subject What man?

THEN WHO IS IT?

From   Rosie
To   Alex
Subject Almost a man

Brian.

From   Alex
To   Rosie
Subject Brian?

BRIAN? BRIAN THE WHINE?

From   Rosie
To   Alex
Subject Re: Brian?

Maybe . . .

From   Alex
To   Rosie
Subject HA HA!

Ha ha ha ha ha ha, you're going to the debs with Brian the Whine?! Talk about scraping the barrel! Brian who lifted your skirt when you were six, in front of everyone in the school yard, to reveal your knickers? The Brian you were stuck sitting beside for all of second class, who ate fish sandwiches every day for lunch and picked his nose while you ate your sandwiches? The Brian who followed us home from school everyday singing 'Rosie and Alex up a tree, K-I-S-S-I-N-G?' and made you cry and ignore me for a week? The Brian who spilled his beer all down your new top at my going-away party? The Brian you absolutely can't stand and was the one person you actually hated all throughout school? And now you're going to the last school dance ever, *with Brian?*

From   Rosie
To   Alex
Subject   No, the other Brian

Yes, Alex, *that* Brian. Now may I ask that you please stop emailing me as my darling mother is currently tying knots in my head trying to make me look half decent? She has also been reading your emails and wants you to know that Brian the Whine won't be lifting up my skirt tonight.

From   Alex
To   Rosie
Subject   Re: Brian

Well, it won't be for lack of trying. Have fun! May I suggest that you wear your beer goggles tonight?

From   Rosie
To   Alex
Subject   Re: Beer goggles

The beer goggles will be well and truly on! Brian was the only person I could get last minute, thanks to you. All I have to do is stand in with him for the photos so that Mum and Dad can have lovely memories of their daughter going to the debs all dressed up with a man in a tuxedo. The tables seat ten so I won't even have to talk to him at dinner. You're enjoying this, aren't you, Alex?

From   Alex
To   Rosie
Subject Re: Re: Beer goggles

Not really. I'd love to be there instead. Don't do anything that I wouldn't do . . .

From   Rosie
To   Alex
Subject Re: Re: Re: Beer goggles

Well, that doesn't rule out much. Hair's done now, have to get the rest of me ready. I'll let you know how it went tomorrow.

From   Alex
To   Rosie
Subject Debs

How were the debs last night? No doubt you're nursing a hangover. I'll wait to hear from you tomorrow but I'll wait no longer! I want to know *everything*!

From   Alex
To   Rosie
Subject Debs

Did you get my last email? I keep calling and there's no answer. What's up? I hope you're busy preparing for the big move over to me!
Email me soon, please.

Steph: Rosie, stop avoiding Alex and tell him how the debs
went. Alex is even emailing me wondering what
happened, and I'm certainly not going to tell him! The
poor guy missed out and all he wants to know is who
did what, where and when.
Rosie: Well, I certainly won't be telling him who did
who.
Steph: Ha ha.
Rosie: It's not funny.
Steph: I think it's hilarious. Come on, it's been three weeks
now!
Rosie: Are you sure it's three weeks?
Steph: Yeah, why?
Rosie: Holy shit.
Rosie has logged off.

From   Alex
To   Rosie
Subject Hello??

Rosie, are you there? Are you having problems with
your email? Please reply. You should be getting on a plane
soon to come over here – you'll miss the start of term.

From   Alex
To   Rosie
Subject Please, Rosie?

Are you mad at me? I'm sorry I couldn't go to the debs
ball, but I thought you understood. Things with whiny
Briany can't have gone that badly, can they? What have
you been doing all month? This is ridiculous. Why doesn't
anyone answer the phone at your house when I call?
    Answer me,
    Alex

Dear Alice,

Hi, it's Alex here. I'm just writing to see if Rosie's OK. I haven't heard from her and I was getting a bit worried, to tell you the truth. It's unusual for me to not hear from her in so long. Every time I call the house it just goes on to answering machine. Are you getting my messages? Maybe you've all gone away? Please let me no what's happening, and tell Rosie to call.

Best wishes,
Alex

Dear Sandra,

Alex has been leaving messages with us all week and he's terribly concerned about Rosie. I know you're worried about him worrying about Rosie so I'm just writing to let you know the situation . . .

From   Alex
To   Rosie
Subject   You're not coming to Boston?

My mum told me today that you're not coming to Boston. Please tell me what's happening. I'm so worried. Did I do something wrong? You no that I am always here for you when you need me.

Whatever it is, Rosie, I will understand and will always be here to help you. Please let me no what is happening. I'm going out of my mind here. If you don't get in touch with me, I'm booking a flight back to Ireland to see you myself.

Love,
Alex

From   Stephanie
To   Rosie
Subject   I'm coming over

Rosie, my sweetie, don't worry. Just take deep breaths and try to relax. Everything happens for a reason. Maybe this is the correct path for you; perhaps Boston wasn't. I'm booking a flight and I'll be home as soon as I can. Hang in there, little sis.
   Love,
   Stephanie

Dear Miss Rosie Dunne,
   Thank you for your recent letter. Boston College acknowledges that you will not be accepting your position this year.
   Yours sincerely,
   Robert Whitworth

Rosie, can't believe this is the decision u have made. You know I am not in support of it. I'm moving away as I had already planned. Hope everything works out well 4 u.

From   Rosie
To   Alex
Subject   Help

Oh God, Alex, what have I done?

Chapter 6

Alex,

It was good to see you again. Please don't be a stranger – I'm really going to need all the friends I can get right now. Thank you for being so supportive last week. I honestly think I would go mad without you sometimes.

Life is funny, isn't it? Just when you think you've got it all figured out, just when you finally begin to plan something, get excited about it and feel like you know what direction you're heading in, the paths change, the signs change, the wind blows the other way, north is suddenly south, and east is west and you're lost. It is so easy to lose your way, to lose direction.

There aren't many sure things in life, but one thing I do know is that you have to deal with the consequences of your actions. You have to follow through on some things.

I always give up, Alex. What have I ever had to do in my life that really *needed* to be done? I always had a choice, and I always took the easy way out – *we* always took the easy way out. A few months ago, the burden of double maths on a Monday morning and finding a spot the size of Pluto on my nose was as complicated as it ever got for me.

This time round I'm having a baby. A baby. And that baby

will be around on the Monday, the Tuesday, the Wednesday, Thursday, Friday, Saturday *and* Sunday. I will have no weekends off. No three-month holidays. I can't take a day off, call in sick or get Mum to write a note. *I* am going to be the mum now. I wish I could write myself a note.

I'm scared, Alex.

Rosie

From   Alex
To   Rosie
Subject   Baby talk

No, it's not double maths on a Monday morning. It will be *far* more exciting than that. Double maths on a Monday morning is boring: it makes you sleep and gives you headache. You will learn masses more from this experience than a maths class can ever teach you.

I am here for you for whenever you need me. College can wait for you, Rosie, because you have far more important work to do now.

I no you will be just fine.

From   Rosie
To   Alex
Subject   Re: Baby talk

You KNOW I will be fine. Watch the spelling, Mr Stewart!

From   Alex
To   Rosie
Subject   Re: Re: Baby talk

Rosie, you're already acting like a mother – you're going to be fine! Take care. Alex

You have received an instant message from: ALEX.

Alex: I thought you said you'd keep an eye on her for me, Phil.

Phil: I told you, if she didn't learn to control her bladder she'd be out of here. She's fine in the garden.

Alex: Not the *dog*, Phil, I'm talking about *Rosie*.

Phil: What about Rosie?

Alex: Stop pretending you don't no. I heard Mum and Dad tell you over the phone.

Phil: How do you feel about it?

Alex: Everyone keeps asking me that and I have no idea. It's weird. Rosie is pregnant. She's only eighteen. She can barely take care of herself, let alone a baby. She smokes like a chimney and refuses to eat greens. She stays awake till 4 a.m. and sleeps till one o'clock in the day. She chose to take a job washing pots and pans at the Chinese takeaway for less money than her neighbours were offering for baby-sitting because she couldn't stand the hassle. I don't think she's changed a nappy in her life. Apart from when Kevin was tiny, I don't think she's ever held a baby for more than five minutes. What about college? What about working? How the hell is she going to manage? How will she ever meet someone? How will she make friends? She's just trapped herself into a life that's her worst nightmare.

Phil: Believe me, Alex, she'll learn. Her parents are supporting her, aren't they? She won't be alone.

Alex: Her mum and dad are great but they will be at work all day, Phil. She's an intelligent person, I no that. But as much as she tries to convince me, I'm not quite sure she's convinced herself that when the crying starts, she can't hand this one back. If only I'd gotten on that flight and made it to the debs . . .

Dear Stephanie,

Let me help you find yourself. Allow my words of wisdom, from the sister who greatly loves and respects you and wishes for nothing but happiness and great fortune in your life, to rain down on you and shower you with knowledge. Please take my advice. Never get pregnant. Or *enceinte*, as you would say over there. Look at the word, say it out loud, familiarise yourself with it, repeat it in your head and learn to *never ever* want to be it.

In fact, never have sex. Might as well try to completely eradicate the odds.

Trust me, Steph, pregnancy is not pleasant. I'm not feeling at all at one with nature, I'm not radiating any sort of magical motherly signals, I'm just fat. And bloated. And tired. And sick. And wondering what on earth I am going to do when this little one is born and looks at me.

Glowing, my bum. Smouldering is more like it. Alex has started his wonderful life in college, people who were at school with me are out tasting what the world has to offer and I'm just expanding by the second, wondering what I have got myself into. I know it's my own fault but I feel like I'm missing out on so much. I've been going to these antenatal classes with Mum where they teach me how to breathe. All around me I'm surrounded by couples, and they're all at least ten years older than me. Mum tried to start me chatting with them but I don't think any of them are too interested in becoming friends with an eighteen-year-old just out of school. Honestly, it's like being back at playgroup and Mum trying to teach me how to make friends. She told me not to worry because they were just jealous of me. I don't think the two of us have laughed so much for months.

I'm not allowed to smoke and the doctor says I have to start eating properly. I'm going to be a mother yet I'm still being spoken to like a child.

Lots of love,
Rosie

Mr Alex Stewart,

You are invited to the christening of my beautiful baby daughter, Katie. It's on the 28th of this month. Buy a suit and try and look presentable for a change, seeing as you're the godfather.

Lots of love,
Rosie

From   Alex
To   Rosie
Subject Re: Christening

It was great to see you. You look amazing! And you are NOT fat! Little Katie was a girl of few words but I am already besotted with her. I almost felt like stealing her and bringing her back over to Boston.

In fact that's a lie. I really felt like staying in Dublin. I almost didn't get back on that flight. I love it here in Boston and I love studying medicine. But it's not home. Dublin is. Being back with you felt so right. I miss my best friend.

I've met some great guys here, but I didn't grow up with any of them playing cops and robbers in my back garden. I don't feel like they are *real* friends. I haven't kicked them in the shins, stayed up all night on Santa watch with them, hung from trees pretending to be monkeys, played hotel or laughed my heart out as their stomachs were pumped. It's kind of hard to beat those sorts of experiences.

However, I can see that I have already been replaced in your affections. Little Katie is your whole world now. And it's easy to see why. I even loved her when she threw up on my (new and very expensive) suit. That must mean something. It's weird to see how much she looks like you. She has your twinkling blue eyes (I sense trouble ahead!) and jet-black hair and a little button nose. Though her bum is slightly smaller than her mother's. Just joking!

I no that you are incredibly busy at the moment but if you ever need a break from it all, you're welcome to come over here and relax. Let me no when you want to come – the invitation is always open. I realise things are tricky for you financially so we could help out with the cost of the flights. Mum and Dad would love you to come over too. They've got photos of you and Katie from the christening all around the house already.

There's also somebody I would like you to meet when you come over. She's in my class in college. Her name is Sally Gruber and she's from Boston. You would both get along.

College is a lot tougher than I thought it would be. There's just so much studying to do; so much reading. I barely have a social life. I've got four years here in Harvard altogether, then I've to do about five to seven years in a general surgical residency so I'm estimating that I'll be fully qualified in my specialised field (whatever that will be) by the time I'm one hundred years old.

So that's all I do here. I wake up at 5 a.m. and study. Go to college, come home and study. Every day. Not much more to report really. It's great that Sally and I are in class together. She takes away from the feeling of dread I get every morning at having to face another day of study, study, study. It's tough, but then I don't need to tell you that. I bet it's a hell of a lot easier than what you're doing right now. Anyway, I'm going to sleep now, I'm shattered. Sweet dreams to you and baby Katie.

Note to self:
　　Do not bounce Katie on knee after feeding.
　　Do not breast-feed beside football pitch.
　　Do not inhale when changing nappy. In fact, allow Mum and Dad or even random strangers to change nappy as often as possible if they so wish.

Do not push buggy by old school for Miss Big Nose Smelly Breath Casey to see.

Do not laugh when Katie falls on her bum after attempting to walk.

Do not try to have conversation with old friends from school with whole lives ahead of them, as this will result in huge frustration.

Stop crying when Katie cries.

Bonjour Stephanie!

How's my beautiful sister doing? Sitting in a café drinking a *café au lait*, wearing a beret and a stripy top while stinking of garlic, no doubt! Oh, who says stereotypes are dead and gone?

Thanks for the present you sent Katie. Your goddaughter says she misses you very much, and she sends lots of drool and sloppy kisses your way. I think I could make those words out of the screaming and wailing bellowing out of her tiny little mouth, anyway. Honestly, I don't know where all the noise comes from. She is the tiniest and most fragile little thing I have ever seen, so that sometimes I'm afraid to hold her, *but then* she opens her mouth and all hell breaks loose. The doctor says she's colicky. All I know is that she doesn't stop screaming.

It's amazing how something so small can be *so* smelly and *so* noisy. I think she should go into the *Guinness Book of Records* for being the smelliest, noisiest, smallest thing ever. What a proud mother I would be.

I'm so knackered, Stephanie. I feel like a complete zombie. I can barely read the words I'm writing (apologies for mashed banana on bottom of page, by the way – small breakfast-time accident). Katie just cries and cries and cries through the night. I have a constant headache. All I do is wander around the house like a robot, picking up teddy bears and toys that I trip over. It's hard to bring Katie anywhere because she just screams wherever we are; I'm afraid people think I'm kidnapping her or being a terrible mother. I still look like a balloon. All I wear are the most unflattering tracksuits. My bum is huge. My stomach is covered in stretch marks; there's all this flab that just won't seem to go away, no matter how much I shout at it, and I've had to throw all my belly tops out. My hair is dry and feels like straw. My tits are HUGE. I don't look like me. I don't feel like me. I feel like I'm about 20 years older. I haven't been out since the christening. I can't remember the last time I had a drink. I can't remember the last time a member of the opposite sex even looked my way (except the people who glare at me angrily in cafés when Katie starts to scream). I can't remember the last time I even cared about a member of the opposite sex not staring at me. I think I am the world's worst mother. I think that when Katie looks at me she knows that I haven't a clue what I'm doing.

She's almost walking now, which means I'm running around saying, 'NO! KATIE, NO! Katie, do not touch that! NO! Katie, Mummy says NO!' I don't think Katie cares about what Mummy thinks. I think Katie is a girl who sees something she wants and she goes for it. I dread the teenage years! But time moves so fast that she'll be grown up and moving out before I know it. Maybe then I'll have some rest. But then again that's what Mum and Dad thought.

Poor Mum and Dad, Steph. I feel so bad. They have been so fantastic. I owe them so much and I don't just mean money. Although, there's another depressing situation. I get benefits and all, and I'm paying them as much as I possibly can each week for our keep but it never feels like enough and you know the situation, Steph – things were always tight for us as it was. I don't know how I'm ever going to move out *and* work *and* look after Katie. Dad and me are going to some clinic during the week to talk to some guy about putting me on a list so I can get a place of my own. Mum keeps saying that I can stay with her and Dad, but I know Dad's just trying to help me get some sense of independence.

Mum has been fabulous. Katie loves her. Katie listens to her. When Mum says 'NO, KATIE!' Katie knows to stop. When I say it, Katie laughs and keeps going. When will I ever feel like a proper mum?

Alex has met someone over in Boston, she's the same age as me and has enough brains to be studying medicine at Harvard. But is she *really* happy I ask myself? Anyway, I have to go. Katie is wailing for me.

Write soon.

Love,

Rosie

To Rosie

I'm glad all is well with Katie; the photos you sent of her on her third birthday are beautiful. I framed them and they're on our mantelpiece in the house. Mum and Dad were delighted to see you when they visited Dublin last month. They can't stop talking about you and Katie. We're all so proud of you at having created such a perfect child.

Hope you had a happy 22nd birthday. Sorry I couldn't make it home to celebrate with you, but things have been crazy at college. Because it's my final year here there's just been so much work to do. I'm dreading the exams. If I fail I don't no what I'll do. Sally was asking after you. Although you've never met, she feels like she nos you from me talking about our old times so much.

From Alex

To Alex

~~Katie's teething is not as bad as it was.~~

~~Katie is starting playschool soon.~~

~~Katie said five new words today.~~

It was Dad's birthday last weekend and we splashed out

51

and went out for dinner to the Hazel restaurant where I believe you went with slutty Bethany and her rich parents all those years ago for your 18th. It was good to be able to let my hair down and relax without Katie. I hired a baby-sitter so that was my treat for the weekend.

Rosie

From   Alex
To   Rosie
Subject (none)

Ah come on, Rosie! You're letting the side down! You better have something wild to tell me about next time!

From   Rosie
To   Alex
Subject 3-year-old child

In case you didn't know, I have a three-year-old child, which makes it rather difficult for me to go out and drink myself silly, otherwise I wake up with an awful headache and a screaming child who needs me to look after her and NOT to be sticking my head down the toilet.

From   Alex
To   Rosie
Subject Sorry

Rosie, I'm sorry. I didn't mean to come across as insensitive. I just meant that you should remember that you need to enjoy life too. Look after yourself and not just Katie. Sorry if I hurt you.

From   Rosie
To   Stephanie
Subject   A moment to whinge

Oh, Stephanie, sometimes I just feel like the walls are closing in on me. I love Katie. I'm glad I made the decision I made, but I'm tired. So bloody tired. All of the time.

And that's how I feel with Mum and Dad helping me. I don't know how I'm going to cope on my own. And I'm going to have to do that eventually. I can't live with Mum and Dad for ever. Although I really want to.

But I wouldn't want Katie depending on *me* so much when *she's* older. Of course, I want her to know that I'm here for her always and that my love is absolutely unconditional, but she needs to be independent.

And I need to be independent. I think it's time for me to grow up now, Steph. I've been putting it off, running away from it for so long. Katie will be starting school soon. Imagine! It's all happened so quickly. Katie will be meeting new people and beginning her life and I have left mine behind. I need to pick myself up and stop feeling so sorry for myself. Life is hard – so what? It's hard for everyone, isn't it? Anyone who says it's easy is a liar.

As a result of all that, there's this huge divide between me and Alex right now because I feel like we're living in such different worlds, I don't know what to talk about with him any more. And we used to be able to talk all night. He phones once a week and I listen to what he's been up to during the week and try to bite my tongue every time I launch into another Katie story. Truth is, I have nothing other than her to talk about and I know it bores people. I think I used to be interesting once upon a time.

Anyway, I've decided I'm finally going to visit Boston. I'm going to finally face up to what my life could have been like had Alex gotten on that plane and made it to the debs with me instead of . . . well, you know who. I could have a degree by now. I could have been a career woman. I know it seems silly to put all that's happened down to the fact that Alex couldn't make it to the debs, but if he had come then I wouldn't have gone with Brian. I wouldn't have slept with Brian and there would be no baby. I think I need to face what I could have been in order to understand and accept what I am.

   All my love,
   Rosie

Chapter 7

Stephanie,

Honey, Mum here. I was wondering if you would be able to get in touch with Rosie and maybe have a word with her. She just returned from Boston a week earlier than we expected and she seems upset about something, though she won't say what it is. I was afraid this would happen. I know she feels that she has missed out on huge opportunities. I just wish she could see the positive side to what she has now. Will you get in touch with her? She always loves hearing from you.

Love you, sweetheart,
Mum

You have an instant message from: STEPH.
Steph: Hey, you, you're not answering your phone.
Steph: I know you're there, Rosie. I can see that you've logged online!
Steph: OK, I'm going to stalk you until you reply.
Steph: Hellooooo!
Rosie: Hi.
Steph: Well, hello there! Why do I get the feeling I'm being ignored?
Rosie: Sorry, I was too tired to speak to anyone.

Steph: I suppose I can forgive you. Everything OK? How was the trip to Boston? Was it as beautiful as it looks in the photos Alex sent us?

Rosie: Yeah, the place is really gorgeous. Alex showed me around everywhere. I hadn't a minute to spare while I was over there. He really took care of me.

Steph: As he should. So where did you go?

Rosie: He showed me around Boston College so I could see what it would have been like for me to study there, and it is so magical and beautiful and the weather was just fabulous . . .

Steph: Wow, it sounds great. I take it you liked it then?

Rosie: Yeah, I liked it. It was even better than the photographs I saw of it when I was applying. It would have been a nice place to study . . .

Steph: I'm sure it would have been. Where did you stay?

Rosie: I stayed in Alex's parents' house. They live in a very posh area, not at all like around here. The house is really lovely: Alex's dad is obviously making loads of money in that job.

Steph: What else did you two get up to? I know there has to be some exciting story here! There's never a dull moment when you two are involved!

Rosie: Well, we went looking round the shops, he brought me to a Red Sox game in Fenway Park and I hadn't a clue what was going on but I had a nice hotdog, we went out to a few clubs . . . sorry I've nothing that interesting to tell you, Steph . . .

Steph: Hey, that's a hell of a lot more interesting than what I did all week, believe me! So how is Alex? How does he look? I haven't seen him for ages. I wonder if I'd even recognise him!

Rosie: He looked really well. He's got a slight American accent although he denies it. But he's still the same old Alex. As lovable as usual. He really spoiled me for the entire week, he didn't let me pay for a thing, he brought me out somewhere new every night. It was good to feel free for a while.

Steph: You are free, Rosie.

Rosie: I know that. I just don't feel it sometimes. Over there I felt like I hadn't a care in the world. Things felt so good and it was almost as if every muscle in my body relaxed the moment I landed there. I haven't laughed so much in years. I felt like a twenty-two-year-old, Steph. I haven't felt like that much lately. I know this probably sounds weird but I felt like the me that I could have been.

I liked that I didn't have to look out for somebody else while I walked down the street. I didn't have the fifty near heart attacks per day that I usually get when Katie goes missing or puts something in her mouth that she shouldn't. I didn't have to dive onto the road and hold her back just in time from being hit by a car. I liked that I didn't have to give out, correct people on their pronunciation or make threats. I liked laughing at a joke without my sleeve being tugged at and being asked to explain. I liked having adult conversations without being interrupted to cheer and applaud a silly dance or the learning of a new word. I liked that I was just me, Rosie, not Mammy, thinking just about me, talking about things I liked, going places I liked to go without having to worry about what Katie was touching, or putting in her mouth, or sleepy-head tantrums. Isn't that awful?

Steph: It's not awful, Rosie. It's good to have time to yourself but it's good to be back with Katie, isn't it? And if things were so great then why did you come home so early? You weren't supposed to return for another week. Did something happen?

Rosie: Not really worth mentioning.

Steph: Oh, come on, Rosie. I know when something is bothering you, and you can tell me.

Rosie: It was just time to go, Steph.

Steph: Did you and Alex have a fight or anything?

Rosie: No, too embarrassing to explain.

Steph: Why, what do you mean?

Rosie: Oh, I just made a show of myself one night.

Steph: Don't be silly. I'm sure Alex didn't mind! He's seen you make a show of yourself plenty in your lifetime.

Rosie: No, Steph, this was a different kind of making a show of myself. Trust me. Not the usual kind of Alex and Rosie thing to do. I kind of threw myself at him and the next day I was mortified.

Steph: WHAT? Do you mean that . . . ? *Did you and Alex . . . ?*

Chapter 8

Rosie: Calm down, Stephanie!

Steph: I can't! This is too bizarre! You two are like brother and sister! Alex is like my little brother! You can't have!

Rosie: STEPHANIE! WE DIDN'T!

Steph: Oh.

Steph: Then what happened?

Rosie: Well, I'm hardly going to tell you now, Ms Overreactor.

Steph: Just stop trying to wind me up and tell me!

Rosie: OK, I realise that this was a very silly thing for me to do and I am extremely embarrassed so don't go mental at me . . .

Steph: Go on . . .

Rosie: Well, it's really far more innocent than you think but equally embarrassing. I kissed Alex.

Steph: *I knew it!* And what happened?

Rosie: He didn't kiss me back.

Steph: Oh. And did you mind that?

Rosie: The unsettling thing is that yes, I did.

Steph: Oh, Rosie, I'm so sorry . . . but I'm sure Alex will come round. He was probably just shocked. Oh, I'm sure he feels the same!! This is so exciting! I always knew something would happen between you two someday.

Rosie: I've been lying on my bed, staring at the ceiling ever since I got home, trying to figure out what came over me. Was it something I ate that made me feel light-headed and impetuous? Was it something he said that I could have misunderstood? I'm trying to convince myself that it was more than just the silence of the moment that changed my heart.

At first we had so much to catch up on we were talking a hundred words a second, barely even listening to the ends of one another's sentences before moving on to the next. And there was laughing. Lots of laughing. Then the laughing stopped and there was this silence. This weird comfortable silence. What the hell was it?

It was like the world stopped turning in that instant. Like everyone around us had disappeared. Like everything at home was forgotten about. It was as if those few minutes on this world were created just for us and all we could do was look at each other. It was like he was seeing my face for the very first time. He looked confused but kind of amused. Exactly how I felt. Because I was sitting on the grass with my best friend Alex, and that was my best friend Alex's face and nose and eyes and lips, but they seemed different. So I kissed him. I seized the moment and I kissed him.

Steph: Wow. And what did he say?

Rosie: Nothing.

Steph: Nothing?

Rosie: Nope. Absolutely nothing. He just stared at me.

Steph: So how do you know he didn't feel the same?

Rosie: At that very moment, Sally came bounding over. We had been waiting for her before going out. She was all excited. Wanted to know whether Alex had told me the good news or not. He didn't seem to quite hear her the first time. So she snapped her fingers in front of our faces. Then she repeated, 'Alex, honey, did you tell Rosie the good news?'

He just blinked so she wrapped her arms around him and she told me herself. They're getting married. So I came home.

Steph: Oh, Rosie.

Rosie: But what the hell was that silence?

Steph: It sounds like something I'd like. It sounded nice.

Rosie: It was.

Phil: What kind of a silence?

Alex: Just a weird silence.

Phil: Yeah, but what do you mean by 'weird'?

Alex: Unusual, not normal.

Phil: Yeah, but was it good or bad?

Alex: Good.

Phil: And that's bad?

Alex: Yes.

Phil: Because?

Alex: I'm engaged to Sally.

Phil: Did you ever have 'the silence' with her?

Alex: We have *silences* . . .

Phil: So do Margaret and I. You don't always have to talk, you know.

Alex: No, this was *different*, Phil. It wasn't just a silence, it was a . . . oh, I don't no.

Phil: Bloody hell, Alex.

Alex: I no. I'm all over the place.

Phil: OK, so don't marry Sally.

Alex: But I love her.

Phil: And what about Rosie?

Alex: I'm not sure.

Phil: Well then, I don't see a problem here. If you were in love with Rosie and not sure about Sally *then* you'd be in trouble. Marry Sally and forget about the goddamn silence.

Alex: Once again, you've put my life into perspective, Phil.

Dear Rosie,

I am so sorry about what happened. You didn't have to leave Boston so soon; we could have worked this out . . . I'm sorry I didn't tell you about Sally before you got here but I was waiting until you met her and had got to know her – I didn't want to tell you over the phone. Maybe I should have . . .

Please don't distance yourself from me. I haven't heard from you in weeks. It was wonderful seeing you . . . please write soon.

Love,
Alex

To Alex, or should we say Dr Alex!
CONGRATULATIONS!
GIVE YOURSELF A BIG PAT ON THE BACK . . .
YOU MADE IT!! WE KNEW YOU COULD DO IT!
Congratulations on graduating from Harvard, you genius!!
Sorry we couldn't be there,
Love Rosie and Katie

You have an instant message from: ALEX.

Alex: Rosie, I wanted you to be the first person to no that I've decided to become a heart surgeon!

Rosie: Great, does it pay well?

Alex: Rosie, it's not about the money.

Rosie: Where I come from, it's *all* about the money. Probably because I don't have any. Working part time at Randy Andy Paperclip Co. isn't really as financially rewarding as it sounds.

Alex: Well, in my world it's all about the lives you save. So

62

what do you really think? Do you approve of my choice
of employment?
Rosie: Hmmm.... my best friend, the heart doctor. You
have my approval.

From   Alex
To   Rosie
Subject Thank you!

The last time we spoke I forgot to thank you for the
congrats card you and Katie sent me. It's about the only
thing I actually have here in the new apartment. Sally and
I just moved in a few weeks ago. You and Katie are very
welcome to come over and see it whenever you like. It can
be Katie's first time on a plane to visit her godfather in
Boston! There's a nice park directly across the road and it's
got a playground for kids. Katie would love it.

The apartment is small but because I've such long shifts at
the hospital, I hardly get to be here anyway. I've got another
life-long sentence here at Boston Central Hospital before I
can actually call myself a heart surgeon. In the meantime I'm
being paid a pittance and slaving away till all hours.

Anyway, that's enough about me. I seem to be just
talking about myself these days. Please write to me and let
me no how things are going for you. I don't want there to
be any awkwardness between us, Rosie.

Keep in touch,
Alex

To Alex
Merry Christmas!
May the festive season be filled with love and joy for you
and your loved ones.
Love Rosie & kAtIe

Rosie and Katie,
HAPPY NEW YEAR!
May this year bring you lots of fun, love, and happiness!
Love,
Alex and Sally

Dear Stephanie,

You will not believe the card that just arrived through my door this morning. I was almost sick. I was just cleaning up the mess Mum and Dad made after their annual New Year party when it made its grand entrance on the doormat. I'm surprised the sound of trumpets didn't accompany it! 'Da da da! Announcing the arrival of the extremely sad coupley card!' (Our wonderful Uncle Brendan was at the party, by the way, and was looking down my top as usual. He was asking for you . . . lots. God, he's so creepy.) There was about ten million bottles of wine rolling around the floor when I came downstairs and I nearly tripped over a game of Trivial Pursuit (yes, it was one of those nights). There were those stupid paper hats strewn around the living room, hanging from the light bulbs, dangling in the gravy dish, looking extremely unappealing. There were Christmas crackers pulled apart with their crappy little miniature toys falling out that no one could possibly ever use, like little torches the size of your thumbnail and jigsaws with about two pieces, lying in the leftover food. *The place was a mess!*

Honestly, Steph, whenever Mum and Dad went away we held the *craziest* parties, but at least we still managed not to behave like farmyard animals. Plus they were screaming and singing (well, *trying* to sing) and dancing (or stamping their feet in some sort of crazy people ritual) *all night.* Poor Katie was terrified of all the noise (she obviously can't be my daughter!), and she spent the night in tears so I let her share my bed and she elbowed me in the face about ten times. Eventually everyone started to leave the house at about 6 or

7 a.m., and I was starting to fall asleep when I was jerked awake by a little monster jumping on me and demanding food.

So anyway, I think what I'm *trying* to say is that I wasn't in the greatest mood for what arrived on my doorstep. I had a pounding headache, I was so tired and after cleaning the mess downstairs (which is fine because it is Mum and Dad's house, after all, and they are kindly letting me stay rent free so I'm not complaining about them) I just wanted peace and quiet and a bit of sleep.

But the card came.

On the front was a lovely little picture of Alex and Sally all wrapped up warmly in their winter coats and hats and gloves, etc. They were standing outside in a park that was covered in snow with their arms wrapped around . . . a snowman. A bloody snowman.

They looked so sickeningly happy. Two little happy Harvard-heads. Uugh. How sad is it to send a photo of yourself and your boyfriend building a snowman??? Very, very, very sad. That's how sad. And to send it to me, especially!! The cheek! I should have sent them a photo of me and . . . me and . . . George (the lollipop man and the only fellow I seem to speak to these days), standing outside in the freezing cold, jumping in puddles. That's how pointless that would have been to them!

Oh God, I'm rambling. Sorry. I have to go before Katie finishes the last of that red wine in the bottle on the floor.

Oh, by the way, it was great to meet Pierre after all this time. He's a really nice guy. You two should come home more often. It was fun speaking to people closer to my age for a change.

Happy New Year. Whoever thought of that expression?

Love, your festive and extremely joyous younger sister, Rosie

To Rosie

Happy Birthday, my friend!

Welcome to the world of twenty-six-year-olds! We are getting old, Rosie!

Write to me more often!

Love, Alex

TO ALEX

YOU ARE IVNITED TO MY 7TH BIRTHDAY PARTY ON THE 4TH OF MAY IN MY HOWSE. WE ARE HAVING A MAJICIN. I CANT WAIT. IT IS ON AT 2 O'CLOCK AND YOU CAN LEAVE AT 5 O'CLOCK.

LOVE KATIE

Dear Katie,

I'm sorry I can't come to your birthday party. The magician sounds like he will be lots of fun. You will have so many friends you won't even no I'm not there!

I have to work at the hospital so they won't let me take a holiday. I told them it was your birthday but they still wouldn't listen!

However, I have sent you a little something so I hope you like it. Happy Birthday, Katie, and take care of your mummy for me. She is very special.

Lots of love to you and Mum,

Alex

To Alex

Thank you for my brithday present. My mummy cried when I opened it. I never had a locket before. The photographs of you and Mummy are very small.

The majicin was good but my best freind Toby said he new he was cheating and showed everyone where the man hid the cards. The man was not very happy and he got mad at Toby. Mummy laffed so loud I do not think the

66

majic man liked her eether. Toby likes Mum.

I got lots of nice presents but Avril and Sinead got me the same notepad. Mummy and me are moving howse soon. I will miss Grandma and Granddad so much and I no Mummy is sad because I heard her crying last night in bed.

But we are not moving too far away. You can get the bus form Grandma and Granddad to our new house. It does not take too long and we are nearer to all the shops in town so we can walk.

It is much smaller than the howse we are in now. Mummy is funny she calls it a shoe box! There are 2 bedrooms and the kitchen is tiny. Just a place to eat and watch telly. We have a balcony and it's nice but Mum wont let me stand on it on my own.

I can see the park. Mummy says the park is our garden and that we have the biggest garden in the world.

Mummy said that I can paint my room whatever colour I want. I think I'll paint it pink or purple or blue. Toby says we should paint it black. He is funny.

Mummy has a new job. She works only a few days a week so sometimes she can collect me from skool and other times she cant. I play with Toby until she comes home. His mum always brings him and collects him because they say we are too young to get the bus. I don't think Mum likes her job. She is always tired and crying. She said she would perfer to be back in skool doing dubble matts. I don't no what she means. Me and Toby hate skool but he always makes me laff. Mummy says she is tired of having to keep going back to my teacher Miss Casey. Grandma and Granddad think it is funny. Miss Casey has the biggest nose ever. She hates me and Toby. I do not think she likes Mum eether because they always fight when they see each other.

Mum has a new freind. They work in the same building but not in the same office. They met outside in the cold because they have to smoke outside. Mum says she is the best freind she has had for ages. Her name is Ruby and she is real funny. I like when she comes over. She and Mum are always laffing. I like it when Ruby is here because Mum doesn't cry.

It is real sunny now in dublin. Me and Mum have been to Portmarnock Beach a few times. We get the bus out and it's always full of people in their swimsuits, eating ice creams and with loud music. Upstairs in the bus is my favourite. I sit in the front and pretend to drive and Mum loves looking out the window at all the water on the way. I am learning to swim. But I have to keep my armbands on in the sea. Mum says she wants to live on the beach. She says she would like to live in the sea shells!

When are you coming to see us? Mummy says you are getting married to a girl named Bimbo. That's a funny name.

Love,
Katie

Chapter 9

You have an instant message from: RUBY.

Ruby: Hey, you, happy Monday.

Rosie: Oh, great. Hold on while I get the champagne.

Ruby: What did you do over the weekend?

Rosie: Oh, *wait* till you hear this! I was just *dying* to tell you all morning, it's *so* exciting! You'll *never* believe it, I—

Ruby: I sense sarcasm here. Let me guess: you watched TV.

Rosie: Introducing Ruby . . . and her psychic powers!! I had to listen to it with the volume blaring just to drown out the loving couple next door screaming their ears off. Some day they're going to kill each other. I can't wait. Poor Katie didn't know what was going on so I sent her down to stay at Toby's house.

Ruby: Honestly, don't some people understand the meaning of the word DIVORCE?

Rosie: Ha ha, well, it's a magic word for you.

Ruby: I would appreciate it if you wouldn't make fun of a devastatingly difficult time in my life that left me feeling shattered and emotionally distraught.

Rosie: Oh, please! Getting that divorce was the happiest

day of your life! You bought the most expensive bottle of champagne, we got pissed, went out clubbing and you snogged the ugliest man in the world.

Ruby: Ah well, people have their different ways of grieving . . .

Rosie: Have you finished typing up all that crap Randy Andy gave us?

Ruby: No, I haven't. Have you?

Rosie: No.

Ruby: Good. Let's take a coffee break as a reward. We really shouldn't overwork ourselves. I hear it's quite dangerous. Will you bring your fags? I forgot mine.

Rosie: Yep, meet you downstairs in five minutes.

Ruby: It's a date. Gosh, how exciting. Neither of us has been on one of them for a while.

You have an instant message from: RUBY.

Ruby: Where the hell were you? I waited for you in the café for half an hour! I had to force myself to eat *two* chocolate muffins *and* a slice of apple pie.

Rosie: Sorry about that. Randy Andy here wouldn't let me leave the office.

Ruby: Oh, he is such a slave driver! You should complain to Head Office, get the asshole fired.

Rosie: He is Head Office.

Ruby: Oh yeah.

Rosie: Well, in all fairness, Ruby, he may be a prick but we did just take a break an hour ago . . . and it was our third one in less than three hours . . .

Ruby: You are turning into one of THEM!

Rosie: Ha ha. I have a child to feed.

Ruby: As do I.

Rosie: That child feeds himself, Ruby.

Ruby: Ah, leave my little fatso alone. He's my baby and I love him regardless.

Rosie: He's seventeen.

Ruby: Yes, and old enough to have a baby of his own, going by your standards . . .

Rosie: Well, he'll be fine as long as he doesn't go to his school ball with the most uninteresting man in the world, with the ugliest face. That way he won't have to drink a sickening amount of alcohol to trick the brain into thinking that man is beautiful and funny and . . . well, you know the rest.

Ruby: Are you suggesting that my son could perhaps have a gay relationship at his debs?

Rosie: No! I was just saying—

Ruby: Oh, I know what you were saying, except I think that my poor darling son may be the exact person that girls will have to drink excess amounts of alcohol just to love.

Rosie: RUBY!! You can't say that about your son!!

Ruby: Why not? I love him with all my heart but, bless him, he wasn't born with his mother's looks. Anyway, so when are you going to *ever* go out with *someone, anyone*?

Rosie: Ruby, we are *not* having this conversation again. Everyone you have tried to set me up with has been a complete weirdo! I don't know where you meet these men and in fact I don't think I even *want* to know, but after last weekend I can assure you that I'm never going to Joys again. Anyway, you can't talk. When exactly was the last time you went out on a date?

Ruby: Ah, that's a very different matter altogether! I'm a woman ten years your senior who has just been through a very difficult divorce from a selfish little bastard of a man and I have a seventeen-year-old son who only communicates with me in monosyllabic grunts. I think he is the son of an ape (actually, I know he is). I have no time for a man!

Rosie: Well, neither do I.

Ruby: Rosie honey, you're twenty-six years old, you've got at least ten years of your life left before it's over. You should get out there and enjoy yourself, stop letting the weight of the world rest on *your* shoulders; that's my job. And stop waiting for him.

Rosie: Stop waiting for who?

Ruby: For Alex.

Rosie: I don't know what you're talking about! I am *not* waiting for Alex!

Ruby: Yes you are, my dear friend. He must be some man because nobody can ever measure up to him. And I know that's what you do every time you meet someone: compare. I'm sure he's a fabulous friend and I'm sure he always says sweet and wonderful things to you. But he's not here. He's thousands of miles away, working as a doctor in a great big hospital and he lives in a fancy apartment with his fancy doctor fiancée. I don't think he's thinking of leaving that life anytime soon to come back to a single mother who's living in a tiny flat working in a crappy part-time job in a paperclip factory with a crazy friend who emails her every second. So stop waiting and move on. Live your life.

Rosie: I am not waiting.

Ruby: Rosie—

Rosie: I have to get back to work now.

Rosie has logged off.

Dear Rosie and Katie Dunne,

Shelly and Bernard Gruber proudly invite you to the marriage ceremony of their loving daughter, Sally, to Alex Stewart.

I am so angered by your last letter! You cannot miss Alex's wedding! That would be completely unthinkable!

This is *Alex* we're talking about! Alex, the boy who used to sleep on a sleeping bag on your floor, the boy who used to sneak into my room and read my diary and look through my underwear drawer! Little Alex who you used to chase down the road and shoot at with a banana for a gun! Alex who sat beside you in class for twelve years!

He was there for you when you had Katie. He was so supportive throughout the entire thing when I'm sure it was difficult for him to adjust to the fact that little Rosie, who had slept in a sleeping bag on *his* floor, was having a *baby*.

Go over to him, Rosie. Celebrate this with him. Share in his happiness and excitement. Share it all with Katie. Be happy! Please! I'm sure he needs you right now. This is a huge step for him and he needs his best friend by his side. Learn to get to know Sally too, as she is an important person in his life now. Just as he has learned to get to know Katie – the most important person in your life. I know you don't want to hear it, but if you don't go you will be ending what was once and what still is one of the strongest bonds of friendship that I have ever seen.

I know you are embarrassed by what happened a few years ago when you visited, but swallow your pride, hold your chin up. You are going to be at that wedding because Alex *wants* you to be there for *him*; you are going to be there because you *need* to be there for *yourself*.

Make the right decision, Rosie.

Dear Rosie,

Hey there! I have no doubt you have received our wonderful wedding invitation that took Sally about three months to choose. Why, I don't know, but it seems that a cream-coloured invite with a gold border was so much more different than a white invite with a gold border . . . you women . . .

I don't no if I should be worried or not, but Sally's mom hasn't seemed to have received a reply yet! Now I no I don't need one from you because I'm just *presuming* you will be there!

The reason why I am writing and not ringing is because I want to give you time to think about what I'm asking you. Myself and Sally would be honoured if you would allow Katie to be our flower girl at the wedding. We would need to no quite soon so that Sally and Katie can pick out a dress.

Whoever thought this would be happening, Rosie? If someone had told us ten years ago that *your daughter* would be a flower girl at *my wedding* we would have just laughed at the ridiculousness of it all. Even though it has taken Sally and me so long to get round to actually getting married – what with doctors' mad schedules ruling our lives!

The second question I have to ask you is the one I'm sure you will need to think about. You are my best friend, Rosie; that goes without saying. I have no best friend over here, no one that measures up to what you mean to me, therefore I have no best man. Will you be my best woman? Will you stand beside me at the altar? I no I will definitely need you there! And I trust you will organise a better stag night than any of my male friends over here!

Think about it and let me no. And say yes!

Love to you and Katie,

Alex

You have an instant message from: ROSIE.
Rosie: You won't fucking believe it.

Ruby: You got a date.

Rosie: No, more unbelievable than that. Alex has asked me to be his 'best woman'.

Ruby: I don't suppose that means you'll be standing to the left of him in the church?

Rosie: Eh, no . . . to the right.

Ruby: What about his brother?

Rosie: He's an usher or something.

Ruby: Wow, so he really is going ahead with it?

Rosie: Yep. Looks like it.

Ruby: I think you should stop waiting for him now, honey.

Rosie: I know. I probably should.

Chapter 10

My 'best woman' speech.

Good evening, everyone. My name is Rosie and, as you can see, Alex has decided to go down the non-traditional route of asking me to be his best woman for the day. Except we all know that today that title does not belong to me. It belongs to Sally, for she is clearly his best woman.

I could call myself the 'best friend', but I think we all know that today that no longer refers to me either. That title too belongs to Sally.

But what *doesn't* belong to Sally is a lifetime of memories of Alex the child, Alex the teenager and Alex the almost-a-man that I'm sure he would rather forget but that I will now fill you all in on. (Hopefully they will laugh.)

I have known Alex since he was five years old. I arrived on my first day of school teary-eyed and red-nosed and half an hour late. (I am almost sure Alex will shout out, 'What's new?') I was ordered to sit down at the back of the class beside a smelly, snotty-nosed, messy-haired little boy who had the biggest sulk on his face and who refused to look at me or talk to me. I hated this little boy.

I know that he hated me too, him kicking me in the shins under the table and telling the teacher that I was copying his school work was a tell-tale sign. We sat beside each other every day for twelve years, moaning about school, moaning about girlfriends and boyfriends, wishing we were older and wiser and out of school, dreaming of a life where we wouldn't have double maths on a Monday morning.

Now Alex has that life and I'm so proud of him. I'm so happy that he's found his best woman and his best friend in ~~perfect little brainy and annoying~~ Sally.

I ask you all to raise your glasses and toast *my* best friend, Alex, and his new best friend, best woman and wife, Sally, and to wish them luck and happiness in the future.

To Alex and Sally!

OR SOMETHING TO THAT EFFECT. WHAT DO YOU THINK, RUBY?

You have an instant message from: RUBY.

Ruby: Gag gag puke puke puke. They'll all love it. Good
luck, Rosie. No tears and DO NOT drink.

Dear Rosie,

Greetings from the Seychelles! Rosie, thank you so much for last week! I had such a good time. I never really thought I could actually enjoy my wedding day but you made it so much fun. Don't worry, I don't think anyone noticed you were drunk for the entire ceremony (maybe they did for the speech – but it was funny), but I don't think the priest was too impressed when you hiccuped just as I was about to say 'I do!'

I can't quite remember the stag night but I hear it was a great success. The boys just keep going on and on about it. I think Sally is a little angry that she had to marry a man with one eyebrow and I don't care what anybody says, I no it was you who did it! All the wedding photos are of the left side of my face but it doesn't matter because Sally says it's my best side. Unlike you, who say my best side is the back of my head.

The wedding went really well, didn't it? I thought I was going to be a bundle of nerves all day but you just made me laugh so much I think it helped to get rid of the nervous energy. Although we shouldn't really have laughed when the wedding photos were being taken, I doubt we'll find any decent shots where my face and yours aren't distorted from laughter. Sally's family thought you were really terrific. They weren't really keen on the idea of me having a best woman, to be honest, but Sally's dad thought you were great. Is it true you made him knock back a shot of tequila?!

My mum and dad were *so* glad to see you and Katie. I'm glad Katie wore the locket I gave her on her last birthday. It's funny; Mum says Katie is exactly how you looked when you were seven. I think she kind of kept hoping that it *was* you and that I was that age again too. She was very teary that day! But they just wouldn't stop going on and on about how beautiful you looked in that dress! It's as if you were the bride!

But you did look beautiful, Rosie. I don't think I've ever seen you in a dress before (not since you were Katie's age, anyway). Well, I suppose I would have seen you in one had I made it to the debs all those years ago. God, listen to me. I sound like an old man reminiscing on years gone by!

Everyone agreed your best woman speech was brilliant. I think all my friends have a crush on you. And no, you can't have their phone numbers. By the way, Rosie, you *were* my best woman that day and you still are my best friend. Always will be. Just to let you no.

Married life is going well so far. We've only been married ten days so we've only had, let's see . . . ten fights. Ha ha. I'm sure somebody told me that was healthy in a relationship . . . I'm not worried. The place we're honeymooning in is fabulous, which I'm glad about because it's costing us an absolute fortune. We're staying in this little wooden hut-type building on stilts high up over the water. It's beautiful. The water is that turquoise-green colour that you can see through right down to the multicoloured fish below. It's paradise; you would love it. Now *this* is the hotel you should work at, Rosie. Imagine your office being the beach . . .

I would just love to laze on the beach and drink cocktails all day, to be honest, but Sally always has to be doing something so every second I'm being dragged into the sea or I find myself flying in the sky hanging out of some odd contraption. I wouldn't be surprised if she decides that we should have lunch underwater while scuba-diving.

Anyway, I've bought you and Katie presents so I hope they arrived at your house safely and that they weren't crushed in the post. They're supposed to be a kind of good-luck charm over here and I no you always loved collecting shells on the beach when we were kids so now you can wear the prettiest ones around your neck.

Well, I better go. Apparently people aren't even supposed to send postcards while they're on their honeymoon, never mind writing novels for letters (according to Sally – so I must go). I think she wants to do something crazy like be dragged around on water-skis by a dolphin.

God help me, what have I gotten myself into?!
Love,
Alex
PS. I miss you!

You have an instant message from: RUBY.
Ruby: I spotted you out the window coming into work – what the hell are you wearing around your neck? Is it shells?
Rosie: It brings luck.
Ruby: Uh-huh. Any luck yet?
Rosie: I didn't miss my bus this morning.
Ruby: Uh-huh.
Rosie: Oh, piss off.
Rosie has logged off.

From   Rosie
To   Ruby
Subject   You'll never believe this.

I'm faxing you over a letter Sally sent Katie. Let me know what you think.

Dear Katie,

Thank you for being my flower girl at my wedding last week. Everybody said that you looked beautiful, just like a real little princess.

Myself and Alex are now on holiday in a place called the Seychelles, just where your mummy wants to live. Tell her it is lovely, very hot and sunny, and you can show her the photograph of me and Alex lying on the beach so she can see what it looks like here. We are very happy and very much in love.

I am enclosing a photograph of you, me, and Alex on our wedding day so you can frame it and put it up in your house. I hope you like it.

Ring us soon.
Love,
Sally

You have an instant message from: RUBY.
Ruby: Sounds like the bitch is just pissing around her man to mark her territory.
Rosie: By sending a letter to a seven-year-old little girl??!!
Ruby: Well, she obviously knew that it would get into your hands. That's cruel alright. Don't let Sally worry you. She's just trying to let you know who the woman is in Alex's life now. Anyway, why is she doing this? Did you do anything to make her feel threatened?
Rosie: No way! As if!
Ruby: Rosie?

Rosie: Oh, OK then, maybe she felt just a little threatened by the fact that Alex and I had a better time at her wedding than she did.

Ruby: Bingo!

Rosie: Yes, but that's the way we always are, Ruby. It wasn't flirting, it wasn't anything. It was just happiness. However, she did not crack one smile for the whole day. She just kept sucking her cheekbones in and pouting at everyone.

Ruby: OK, I believe you, but millions wouldn't. Anyway, don't rise to her, just ignore it.

Rosie: Oh, don't worry, I won't respond. I'm just sorry that the stupid woman didn't have the common sense to leave my daughter out of her insecurities.

Ruby: Katie will be fine; she's a smart girl. Just like her mother.

Dear Sally,

Thank you for your letter. I'm glad you liked my dress, but if I were you I would have worn a pretty dress like my mum's for my wedding day. Everyone said that it matched Alex's tuxedo really well. They looked so nice together, don't you think? I showed Mum and Toby (my best friend) the photograph of you and Alex on the beach and Toby says that he hopes that your sunburn doesn't hurt too much. It looks really sore.

That's all for now. I have to go now because Mum's new boyfriend is coming to the flat soon. Tell Alex that me, Mum and Toby said hi.

Love from Katie xxx

Chapter 11

From   Alex
To   Rosie
Subject   Secret boyfriend

Back home from my honeymoon; you sly little lady, you never told me about this new boyfriend of yours! Sally couldn't wait to tell me, which I thought was rather sweet. I didn't realise Katie and Sally were writing to each other, did you?

Anyway, why didn't you say a word about this guy at the wedding? You usually tell me everything. So come on! What's he like? What's his name? Where did you meet him? What does he look like? What does he do for a living? I hope he earns loads of money and that he's treating you well, or else I'm coming over to throttle him.

I'll have to get back to Dublin to meet this guy; make sure he gets the best friend approval. Anyway, let me no all the details (maybe not *all* of them).

Hi Stephanie,

Just writing to see how you are, love, and to share a bit of good news with you. I'm sure Rosie hasn't told you this already because she's keeping pretty quiet about it, but she's met someone! We are all so delighted. She seems so happy, those big blue eyes don't look so sad any more and there's a spring in her step again. More like the Rosie we used to know.

Anyway, she brought him over to the house yesterday for dinner and I have to say he really is a charming man. His name is Greg Collins and he's a bank manager for AIB in Fairview.

He's a little taller than Rosie with a cute little face. He's thirty-something, I would guess, and he is absolutely wonderful with Katie. They spent the day teasing each other, which was very funny. It's been difficult, as you know, for Rosie to meet someone who she likes herself as well as taking into account that it has to be somebody that Katie feels comfortable with too. But there should be no compromises I keep telling her. Too often she ended up on dates with those other men just because Katie liked them. Anyway, as I said, Katie adores Greg. I'm so pleased Rosie seems to have found a nice fellow at last.

Anyway, how's work? Busy as always? Don't work yourself too hard in that restaurant, love; you need to enjoy life too. Your dad and me were thinking of coming over to you for a little holiday soon – would that be OK? Let us know when you're free and we'll work around it. Say hello to Pierre for us. Looking forward to seeing you.

Love,
Mum

From   Rosie
To   Alex
Subject   Re: Secret boyfriend!

Oops, my little secret is out now, thanks to Katie and her big mouth! Well, I didn't say anything about Greg (that's his name) at your wedding, because at that stage we hadn't even gone out yet! We met in the Dancing Cow nightclub (it's a very long story!) just before I went over to you in Boston, and he took my number and asked me out but I said no! So I must have gone all gushy after your wedding because when I came back I rang him up and asked him out!

Oh, Alex, I've been wined and dined like never before! He's taken me to restaurants I've only read about in magazines and he's terribly romantic, but you said not to give you *all* the details so I won't tell you about our weekend away down the country . . . OK, so you wanted to know all about him, here goes. He is thirty-six, works at the bank in Fairview. He's not exactly tall (my height), which isn't exactly small either, but . . . OK if he was to stand beside you, you would have a fantastic view of his scalp. But he has sandy-coloured hair and wonderful twinkling blue eyes.

He is always bringing Katie little gifts when he comes, which I know he shouldn't do, but I love seeing her being spoiled, especially as I haven't exactly been able to do that myself over the years. I can't believe I have finally met a man who doesn't mind that I have a daughter; all the others looked at me like I was diseased when I told them, and would suddenly think of a great excuse to have to leave the dinner table. I also can't believe that Katie and I have finally agreed on the same man. She seemed only to like the young, pretty ones that she fancied herself, probably. We need to be realistic here, though. I can hardly afford to be picky!! Her idea of a great partner for me was someone who would play games with her all the time, pull silly faces, put on unattractive voices and wear brightly coloured clothes that should only be worn on Saturday morning TV.

Anyway, I seem to have found him. He is a very

generous, caring and thoughtful man, and I think I am very lucky to have met him. It may not last for ever but I'm enjoying myself, Alex. I know I've been such a misery guts for the past, oh, I don't know . . . ten years or so (!) but now I have realised that Katie and I are a team and if they can't love us both then they can get lost.

But I *think* I may have met a man who does. Fingers crossed.

PS. I notice you have stopped referring to Ireland as home. Your heart must finally be in Boston now.

From   Alex
To   Rosie
Subject Oooh Rosie's in love!

Oooooh! Rosie sounds like she's in love!

With a bank manager who goes clubbing in a place called the Dancing Cow? What kind of bank manager (or any man, for that matter) goes to the Dancing Cow? Fair enough, you and your friend Ruby seem to have gone off the rails altogether, so therefore I wouldn't expect anything more from you. But I don't no, I'm not yet convinced this man is the right one for you.

And I have to say I was slightly insulted by your last letter. What do you mean by the statement, 'I have finally met a man who doesn't mind that I have a daughter'? I think that I have always been supportive of you and Katie – in fact I no I have. Whenever I can, I visit you and bring you out to all your favourite restaurants and bring my goddaughter presents.

Anyway, I'd better go. Just worked a double shift at the hospital so I'm feeling really tired.

From   Rosie
To   Alex
Subject Thanks, Mr Supportive

Well, thank you, Mr Supportive, for being so happy for me. In case you haven't noticed, you and I are not involved in a romantic relationship. Yes, you are a wonderful friend (supportive and generous), but you are not here every day with me. I'm sure you will understand when I say that finding a friend and finding a partner are two very different things. You accept me warts and all, some men don't. But you're not here.

OK, well, that's all. Hope married life is going wonderfully!

You have an instant message from: RUBY.

Ruby: Katie told Sally what??

Rosie: I know, it's crazy, isn't it? And Katie wrote that letter after I had only been on *one* date with Greg!

Ruby: Wow, she must really like him to be telling people about him so soon. Ah well, maybe Sally won't feel like you're trying to get your grubby little mitts on her husband now.

Rosie: Ah, who cares anyway? I have my Greg!

Ruby: Ugh, you make me sick. You've turned into one of those sickening couples that we hate. You two are carrying on like love-struck teenagers; I think I'll have to find a new single friend so that I don't feel like a *complete* gooseberry the next time we go out.

Rosie: You're such a liar! You were having a great time with all those guys every time I looked at you. You were the centre of attention!

Ruby: Oh, a girl does what she has to . . . Anyway, you must have spotted me only on the rare occasion you detached your lips from Greg's. Oh, by the way, that guy called me last night so I'm thinking of—

You have an instant message from: GREG.

Greg: Hello, gorgeous. How's your day going?

Rosie: Oh, hello! Oh, it's the same as usual . . . better now, though!

Ruby: Hello? Are you still there or has Randy Andy attacked you?

Rosie: Sorry, Greg, just a second. I'm chatting to Ruby online too!

Greg: Do you two ever do any work?!

Rosie: Enough to keep ourselves from getting fired.

Greg: I'll try you again later.

Rosie: No, no! Don't be silly! I'm perfectly capable of carrying on two conversations at the same time.
Besides, I want to chat to you and if I tell that to Ruby she'll be even more angry at me for becoming one of *them* . . .

Greg: Who's 'them'?

Rosie: Part of the secret couple élite.

Greg: Oh, *them*! Of course, silly me . . .

Rosie: Sorry, Ruby, Greg is messaging me too, so bear with me for a few minutes.

Ruby: Can you two not live without each other for a few hours?

Rosie: No!

Ruby: Oh, I miss Rosie. Who are you and what have you done to my man-hating friend?

Rosie: Don't worry, she's still here, just taking a well-deserved break. So what were you saying about this guy you met the other night?

Ruby: Oh yeah, his name is Ted (a real teddy bear), he's overweight but then again so am I so who cares; we can bounce off each other. He's a truck driver and he seemed like a nice guy because he kept buying me drinks, which puts him up pretty high on my Decent Man scale. Plus he was the only person who wasn't ignoring me in the pub that night.

Rosie: Oh, I'm so sorry, but you know what it's like when you meet someone new: you want to get to know *everything* about them.

Ruby: No, I don't quite want to know everything about Ted . . . I don't want to be put off him.

Rosie: So, Greg, what are you doing tonight?

Greg: Rosie, my dear, I am all yours! Why don't we get a bottle of wine, some takeaway and stay in? We can get Katie a DVD or something.

Rosie: Yep, that sounds like a great idea! And Katie will be really excited to see you.

Ruby: So should I call him?

Rosie: Call who?

Ruby: TED!

Rosie: Oh, yeah, of course! Ask him out. I can get Kevin to baby-sit and then we can all go on a double date. I've always wanted to do that!

Ruby: Oh, please, the innocence of the young and inexperienced. Ted and Greg will have absolutely nothing in common. They're like chalk and cheese: a bank manager and a possible bank robber. They will hate each other, the atmosphere will be awkward, no one will talk, all you'll hear is the munching of food in our mouths over the deafening silence like some kind of weird Chinese torture, we'll all refuse dessert, skip the coffee, pay, leg it out the door and feel relieved and promise ourselves never to meet up again.

Rosie: How does next Friday sound?

Ruby: Friday's fine.

Greg: I hope Ruby is OK with us after the other night; we were kind of in a world of our own.

Rosie: Don't be silly, she didn't mind at all. She met some guy called Teddy Bear. Oh, and by the way, are you free to go out on a double date thingy for dinner on Friday night? That's if I can get a baby-sitter for Katie.

Greg: A dinner date with Ruby and a man named Teddy Bear. Sounds interesting.

Rosie: Greg said he's free for dinner on Friday.

Ruby: Well, that's all very well but I haven't asked Ted yet. What did Alex say about you and Greg being *in love*?

Rosie: Well, I didn't say I was *in love*, Ruby! Greg and I haven't even said that to *each other* yet! But Alex sent me some weird letter telling me that he thinks that Greg sounds like a freak of nature and that he's insulted that I don't think that he's supportive of me and Katie. He just went on a bit of a rant, to be honest, but I won't take any notice because he had worked all night at the hospital and he was tired.

Ruby: Uh-huh.

Rosie: What's that supposed to mean?

Ruby: This is just as I suspected. He's jealous.

Rosie: Alex is *not* jealous!

Ruby: Alex is jealous of your relationship with Greg; he feels threatened.

Greg: So what time should I call over to you tonight? Seven or eight?

Rosie: No, Alex is *not* jealous of my relationship with Greg! Why should he be? He's married to perfect pretty little Sally – happily, might I add (at least according to Sally) – *and* I have a lovely photograph of the two of them lying on the beach together looking *very* much in love just to prove it. I gave him a chance to be part of Katie's life and mine and he chose to remain my friend, which I have now come to terms with. It's fine. Now I am in a relationship with Greg, he's wonderful and I no longer care about Alex in that way *at all whatsoever*! So that's all I have to say about that, thank you very much! I am over Alex, he is not interested in me and now I am in love with Greg! So there!

Greg: Well . . . thank you for sharing all that with me, Rosie. I can't tell you enough how thrilled I am to hear that you are no longer in love with a man named Alex *'at all whatsoever'*, as you so articulately put it.

Rosie: Oh my God, Ruby!! I just sent Greg the message that was supposed to be for you!! Fuck fuck *FUCKETY FUCK!* I TOLD HIM I *LOVED* HIM!!!!

Greg: Em . . . that, eh . . . went to me again, Rosie. Sorry . . .

Rosie: Oh . . .

Ruby: Oh what?

Chapter 12

Rosie: OK, so that has to be the singularly *most embarrassing* thing that has ever happened to me, without any doubts, NO exceptions!!!

Ruby: What about the time you wore that white dress out to a club with no underwear on, and someone spilled water all over you and it was suddenly completely see-through?

Rosie: OK, so that was pretty embarrassing.

Ruby: And what about the time you were in the super-market and you grabbed another little girl's hand by mistake and started dragging her out to the car while Katie waited inside crying her eyes out?

Rosie: That little girl's mother said it was fine and she dropped the charges.

Ruby: And what about the time—

Rosie: OK, that's enough, thank you! Maybe it was not *the* most embarrassing thing ever, but it's pretty much up there with the all-time classics. The number-one embarrassing moment being the time I kissed Alex.

Ruby: Ha ha ha ha ha ha ha

Rosie: Oh, come on, you're supposed to make me feel better.

Ruby: Ha ha ha ha ha ha ha ha

Rosie: The joy of having supportive friends. I'm going now; Randy Andy is glaring at me like a schoolmaster over the rim of his incredibly sexy brown-rimmed spectacles.

Ruby: Maybe he wants you to be the naughty schoolgirl.

Rosie: Well, he's just a few years too late for that. I think he wants to kill me. His nostrils are flaring and he's breathing quite heavily.

Ruby: Are his hands above the desk?

Rosie: Uuugh! Ruby, stop!

Ruby: What? You don't think they call him Randy Andy for nothing, do you?

Rosie: I hate open-plan offices. He can see me from every corner of this room, and my legs underneath the desk. Oh my, now he's staring at my legs.

Ruby: Rosie, you really need to get out of that office. It's not healthy.

Rosie: I know, I'm working on it, but I can't quit until I get another job and that's proving to be rather difficult. Apparently no one really cares about whether or not you work as a secretary in a paperclip factory.

Ruby: How odd . . . and it *sounds* so glamorous.

Rosie: Oh my God, he has now moved his chair over so he can get a better look. Hold on a minute while I send him a message. I've had enough!

Ruby: Don't!

Rosie: Why not? I'll just send him a polite message asking him to stop looking at me because I find it distracting while I'm trying to work.

You have an instant message from: ROSIE.
Rosie: Stop staring at my tits, you pervert.

Rosie: OK, Ruby, I sent it.
Ruby: Oh, you are so fired. Randy Andy doesn't take

too kindly to brash young ladies who stick up for themselves.

Rosie: Screw him! He can't fire me for that!

Ms Rosie Dunne,

Andy Sheedy Paperclip & Co. will no longer be requiring your services, which means that your contract will therefore not be up for renewal next month as was previously discussed.

You are, however, entitled to remain as an employee of Andy Sheedy Paperclip & Co. until the end of the month, i.e. 30 June.

Andy Sheedy Paperclip & Co. thanks you for the work you have put into the company over the past few years and we wish you luck in the future.

Yours sincerely,

Andy Sheedy

Owner of Andy Sheedy Paperclip & Co.

You have an instant message from: ROSIE.

Rosie: I faxed the letter over, did you see it?

Ruby: Ha ha ha ha ha ha.

Rosie: Do you know what? The more I read it, the more I'm glad that I'm leaving. The name Andy Sheedy Paperclip & Co. says it all really, doesn't it? I wonder who wrote the letter for him, seeing as I'm his secretary and that's my job. I probably did it myself and didn't even realise it. Ah well, so what do you think?

Ruby: This is the best way to leave. Rosie Dunne, you will go down in history in this building as the woman who told Randy Andy to eff off. I will spread the word, Rosie; you being fired will not have been in vain. I'll miss you! Where will you go?

Rosie: I have absolutely no idea.

Ruby: Why don't you apply for a job in a hotel? Ever

since I met you you've been going on and on about
hotels.

Rosie: I know. I have a slight obsession with them. Before I
had Katie all I ever wanted to do was run a hotel. I
don't think that will ever happen now but we all need
dreams. We all need hope, that something more than
what we have is possible to achieve.

Perhaps it's the huge furniture that makes me feel so
safe in hotels, like oversized vases the size of people, and
couches that wouldn't fit in my living room and kitchen
put together. I feel like Alice in Wonderland in hotel
lobbies. At least I have a month to find somewhere. It
shouldn't be *that* hard. I'd better start writing up my
CV.

Ruby: That shouldn't take long then.

From   Rosie
To   Alex
Subject   Is my CV OK?

Attachment: CV.doc
Please, please, please help me with my CV or my poor
daughter and I will starve to death. How do I make all my
crappy jobs look impressive? Help! Help! Help!

From   Alex
To   Rosie
Subject   Re: CV

Attachment: CV.doc
As you can see (by the attached document) I have been
over your CV. The one you sent me was practically perfect
as it was, of course, but I just fixed the grammar and a
few spelling mistakes . . . you no how great at spelling I
am!

By the way, Rosie, you haven't been doing a 'crappy job', as you so nicely phrased it. I don't think you understand the difficulty of what you are doing. You are a full-time *single* mum who has a job as a personal secretary to a very successful businessman. I only changed the words around; I didn't alter the truth in any way. What you have been doing day after day is incredible. When I come home from work I'm so shattered that I just collapse; I barely take care of myself, never mind another person.

Don't underestimate yourself, Rosie; don't play down what you do. When you go into your interviews keep your head held high and feel confident that you are an incredibly hard worker (when you want to be), you have the wonderful ability to work with other people as you are always well liked (except that time when we had to do a group project in school on the planets and you insisted on drawing little men on Mars and little women on Venus over Susie Corrigan's picture that took her weeks to do in art class, which ended up causing everyone in the group to walk out in protest, leaving just the two of us having to start another one all by ourselves. God, what is it about you and me being together that makes everyone hate us?). You are wonderful, beautiful, smart, and intelligent, and if you knew anything about coronary heart diseases I'd hire you myself.

I've suggested adding that you were offered a place in Boston College, which is impressive, so everything will be fine. Just be yourself and they'll love you.

Just one more thing. I *strongly* suggest that you apply for a job that you actually *like* this time. You would be surprised at how easy it is to get out of bed in the morning when you're going to do something that doesn't make you want to jump off the top floor of the bus (I was a bit worried when I got that email). How about finally trying to find a place in a hotel? You've wanted to do that since you stayed in the Holiday Inn in London when you were seven, remember?

Go for it and let me no how you get on.

Chapter 13

From   Alex
To   Rosie
Subject Boston visit?

Just taking a sneaky break from performing 'lobotomies' to send a quick email to see how you're getting on with the job search. You have one week left till Randy Andy throws you out of his paperclip empire, so there's still plenty of time, and if by any chance something hasn't caught your eye by then, I can send a cheque to help tide you over for a while (but only if you *want* my help).

I would love to go home right now and go to bed, I am so tired. I've worked a double shift so I don't have to get my hands bloody tomorrow; I have the day off, such bliss ... The problem is that when I get home Sally will be getting ready to go on her shift. We don't have the most sociable hours in the world – well, not unless you count talking to people who are rolling around in agony on hospital beds. Sorry, that wasn't funny.

I'm just tired, and Sally and I don't really get to spend a lot of time together, and when we do we're usually so tired we just pass out.

Here's a good idea. If you come over with Katie and whatshisname then I'll take a few days off and we can see all the sights, eat out, enjoy ourselves and I can *sleep*. And I'll finally get to meet whatshisname. I've had a lousy few weeks; I really need your comic relief! Work your magic, Rosie Dunne, and make me laugh.

From   Rosie
To   Alex
Subject   Rosie is here!

Hello there, misery man. Have no fear, Rosie is here! Sorry things have been shit for you lately. I think life likes to do that every now and again: it does a dip and when you feel like you can't take any more it smooths out again. But until then, my dear friend, I will try to humour you by explaining the events of my life.

OK, firstly you are a bad, bad influence on me. After I read the masterpiece that was my CV, and after I read your letter I felt so motivated and hyped up that I donned my tracksuit, headband, wristbands and jogging shoes (not really) and I raced around Dublin city like a woman on a mission.

You horrible, horrible man. You made me feel like I could do anything, like I could take on the world (never *ever* do that again) so I proceeded to drop my CV into every single hotel I've ever wanted to work in but was always too afraid to try. Shame on you for giving me strength, because it quickly disappeared and I found myself faced with a million billion interviews with a million billion snotty companies that hated me and my cheek for even *thinking* I could work for them.

So let's see, which embarrassing interview should I tell you about first? Hmm . . . there are so many to choose from. Well, let's start with the most recent, shall we?

Yesterday I had an interview to work at the reception in the Two Lakes Hotel – you know, that really posh one in the city? The front of the building is made entirely of glass so you can see the big bright glistening chandeliers dripping down from miles away. At night-time the building looks like it's on fire, it's so bright. The restaurant is on the top floor so that you can look out over the entire city. It really is very beautiful.

But it's also one of those places where there's a guy (actually, more of a gentleman) dressed in one of those cloak things and a top hat who stands at the door and refuses to let anyone in. It must have taken me about ten minutes just to get inside the door. He just wouldn't listen, just kept saying that I needed to be a resident. Honestly, how could anybody ever get to be a resident if they don't let you in the door? Anyway, finally he let me in and I nearly slipped on the marble floor that was *so* shiny.

The place was so quiet you could hear a pin drop. No, I mean it literally: the woman at reception actually *did* drop a pin. I heard it. Well, I suppose the hotel wasn't *that* quiet: there was the tinkling sound of a piano filtering out from the lounge, there was a water fountain trickling down through the lobby area – the sounds were just so calming. It even had all those giant pieces of furniture that I always loved as a child, like huge mirrors, gigantic chandeliers, doors the length of my apartment wall. When I stepped onto the carpets I thought I was going to bounce up to the balcony, they were so spongy.

I was seated at The Longest Table Ever for the interview. Two men and a woman sat at one end – at least I think that's what they were; I was so far away I could barely see (I almost felt like asking them to pass the salt).

So I thought that I would try and make myself sound interested in the company, just like you told me to, so I asked them how the hotel got its name as I wasn't aware of any lakes in that part of the city. The two men started laughing and introduced themselves as Bill and Bob Lake. They own the place. How embarrassing.

So I basically just kept talking about what you told me to say: how I like working as part of a team, that I'm good with people, how I'm very interested in the running of a hotel and about how I'm such a hard worker and always put my mind to working on tasks and always finishing off what I start . . . bla bla bla. And then I waffled on for what felt like an hour about how I've loved hotels since I was a child and have always wanted to work in one. (Well, the luxury is in *staying* in one but we both know I can't afford *that*.)

And then they go and spoil it all by saying something stupid like: 'So, Rosie, from the time you spent working at Andy Sheedy Paperclip & Co. what have you learned that you think you can bring to the table here at the Two Lakes?'

Please, like that's even worth asking.

OK, I have to go now, actually, because Katie just got home from school with the look of evil on her face and I haven't made dinner yet.

From   Alex
To   Rosie
Subject Two Lakes Hotel

It's a shame you had to rush off. I was enjoying that email. Glad to hear your interviews are going so well – it's cheered me right up!

But I'm dying to no, what was your answer to that question they asked you?

From   Rosie
To   Alex
Subject   Re: Two Lakes Hotel

Alex, isn't it obvious?

   Paperclips!

(They just laughed so I got myself out of that one easily.) OK, so I'm really going now. Katie is shoving pictures that she drew in school in my face. Oh, by the way, she drew one of you . . . you look like you've lost a bit of weight. I'll scan it to you . . .

Dear Ms Rosie Dunne,

It is our pleasure to inform you that we are offering you the position of head receptionist at the Two Lakes Hotel.

On a more personal note, we are very excited about having you here following the success of your interview last week. You come across as a bright, intelligent and witty young woman; the kind of person we like to have working at the hotel.

We take pride in hiring people we ourselves would like to be greeted by in a hotel and we have great faith that the smiles you brought to our faces when we met will also be brought to the customers of the hotel when they arrive at reception. We are pleased to have you as a member of the team, and hope our working relationship will develop successfully over many years in the future.

We ask that you get in touch with Shauna Simpson at reception with regard to your work uniform.

Yours sincerely,

Bill Lake   Bob Lake

PS. We would also appreciate it if you would bring those paperclips with you – office supplies are rather low!

You have an instant message from: ROSIE.

Rosie: My God, Ruby, could it be possible that I'm actually going to have a *nice* boss/bosses? I think everything is finally falling into place.

Ruby: And then she goes ahead and jinxes herself. She will never learn . . .

From   Rosie
To   Stephanie
Subject   Congratulations

I'm delighted to hear that you and Pierre got engaged! I know we spoke on the phone for hours last night but I wanted to send you this email too. Congratulations! By the way, have you heard from Kevin lately? He never calls or emails me – I think he's afraid I'm going to ask him to baby-sit again.

Something rather bizarre is happening in my life, Stephanie. I have a boyfriend who loves me, and who I love back, I'm about to start work in the hotel of my dreams, Katie is beautiful and healthy and funny, and I finally feel like a good mum. I feel happy. I want to enjoy this feeling and revel in my good fortune but there's something niggling at me in the back of my mind. There's a little voice whispering to me, 'Things are too perfect.' It almost feels like the calm before the storm.

Is this how normal life is supposed to be? Because I'm used to drama, drama, drama. I'm used to things refusing to go my way. I'm used to having to struggle, moan and whinge my way into getting something that's not exactly what I want but that will *just do*.

This is not something that will 'just do', this is perfect; this is exactly what I wanted. I wanted to feel loved by someone, I wanted Katie to stop wondering if it was all her fault that she didn't have a daddy like all the other kids, I wanted to feel that the two of us not only belong together but that someone else would accept us in his life too, I wanted to feel important, I wanted to feel like *somebody*, I wanted to know that if I called in sick to work that I would be *missed*. I wanted to stop feeling so sorry for myself, and I have.

Things are going great. I'm feeling really good about myself and I'm not quite used to that. This is the new Rosie Dunne. Young and confused Rosie is gone. Phase two of my life now begins . . .

PART TWO

Chapter 14

Dear Ms Dunne,

I am hoping that you can come to the school to discuss Katie's rapidly deteriorating behaviour in class.

How does Wednesday after school sound? You can reach me at the school. You know the number.

Miss Casey

To Katie

What do you mean, your mum just laughed?

From Toby

From   Rosie
To   Alex
Subject   Flight details

Hey there, OK our flight is landing at 1.15 p.m. – flight number is EI4023. I'll be the woman dragging a terrified-looking man by the hair through arrivals, carrying a hyperventilating child by the other arm and pulling twenty suitcases along by my toes. (Greg hates flying, Katie is so excited I'm really very concerned that she's going to explode, and I couldn't decide what to bring with me so I've packed my entire wardrobe.)

Are you sure Sally knows what she's got herself into, allowing me and my mad family to stay with you?

From   Sally
To   Alex
Subject   Re: Rosie's stay

Of course it's not OK, Alex. You couldn't have chosen a worse time to invite her and you know it.

From   Alex
To   Rosie
Subject   Re: Flight details

Of course Sally doesn't mind. I can't wait to see you and Katie, and to meet whatshisname. I'll be waiting at arrivals for you.

Dear Alex,

Thank you so much for the holiday! I had such a fantastic time. Boston was even more beautiful than I remembered, and I'm glad I didn't have to run home early in embarrassment this time round. Katie just loved the whole experience, and the child will just not stop talking about you!

Greg really enjoyed it too. I'm glad you finally got to meet him and also learn that his face isn't usually the greenish colour that it was when he first got off the plane. It was such a treat to finally have my two favourite men in the same country, never mind in the same room! So what do you think of him? Does he get the best friend seal of approval?

So apart from the fact that your wife absolutely hates me, everything else was very comfortable and enjoyable. But I actually don't mind, Alex; I'll just accept it. It just makes it official and confirms what I've already thought: for some unknown reason, any girlfriend or wife of yours will forever hate me. And that's fine with me. I'm over it.

I just hope she lets me see your son or daughter when he or she is born. Now there's something else I never imagined would happen! Alex Stewart is going to be a daddy! Every time I think about it I just have to laugh out loud. God love your child to have a father like you! Just joking – you know I'm thrilled! Although I can't believe you kept it a secret from me for so many months. Shame on you.

By the way, I'm really sorry Katie spilled her drink over Sally's new dress. I don't know *what* got into her; she's usually not so clumsy! I've told her to write a letter of apology to Sally. Hopefully she won't hate us all so much then.

Anyway, my few weeks of fun are over now; it's back to reality again. I start work at my new job on Monday. All my life I've wanted to work in a hotel and I've put the thought away, with the rest of my dreams. I just hope it isn't hell, or all my little dream bubbles will burst in an instant.

There's one more thing I forgot to tell you. Greg has asked me and Katie to move in with him. I'm not quite sure how I feel about it. Things are going so well at the moment between us but it's not just me that I have to think about. Katie really likes Greg, and she loves to spend time with him (it may not have been that obvious in Boston because she was so excited to see you), but I don't know if she would be ready for such a huge change in her life. We're only in the flat together less than two years now and we're learning to live our lives with just the two of us. I'm not sure if uprooting her *again* would be the right thing. What do you think?

Well, I suppose all I need to do is ask her. But what if she says no? Do I say to Greg, 'Eh . . . sorry, I love you and all, but my eight-year-old daughter doesn't want to live with you?' Do I tell Katie, 'Tough luck you're moving house,' or do I do what she wants? I clearly can't just do what *I* want because there's two other people involved. I'm going to think about it for the next while anyway.

Thanks again for the break. I really needed it. I'll make sure Katie sends on that letter to Sally.

Love,
Rosie

Dear Rosie,

Welcome to your first day at the Two Lakes. I hope everyone has helped you to settle in so far. I'm sorry I'm not there to greet you but I am currently in the States finalising a few things at our new Two Lakes Hotel in San Francisco.

In the meantime, Amador Ramirez, the hotel assistant manager is there to show you the ropes. Let me know if you have any problems.

Once again, welcome!
Bill Lake

You have an instant message from: RUBY.
Ruby: Remember me?
Rosie: I'm sorry, Ruby, it's just that I don't get to spend much time on the computer like the last job. It's a bit difficult to pretend I'm doing work here.
Ruby: I give you one month . . .
Rosie: Thank you for your support; it's always very much appreciated.
Ruby: No problem. So how's life with Greg?
Rosie: Great thanks.
Ruby: So you don't hate each other yet?
Rosie: No, not yet.
Ruby: I give you one month . . .
Rosie: And once again, thank you.
Ruby: Just doing my duty as a friend. Any news with you?
Rosie: Well, actually I have a bit. I've told only Alex so far, but you're not allowed to tell anyone.

Ruby: Ooh, I love it! The most magical words you'll ever hear in a sentence. What is it?

Rosie: Well, a few weeks ago when I came home from work Greg had a beautiful dinner cooked, the dining table was set, candles were lit and the music was playing . . .

Ruby: Go on . . .

Rosie: Well, he asked me—

Ruby: To marry you!

Rosie: No, actually, he asked me if I was interested in moving in with him.

Ruby: Interested?

Rosie: Yeah.

Ruby: Were those his exact words?

Rosie: Eh, yeah, I think so. Why?

Ruby: You think that's romantic, do you?

Rosie: Well, he went to a lot of trouble to cook the meal, and set the table and—

Ruby: Jesus, you do that every day, Rosie. Do you not think it sounds a bit like a business proposition?

Rosie: In what way?

Ruby: If I wanted to open a joint bank account with Teddy I would say, 'Teddy, would you be interested in opening a joint bank account?' If I wanted to move in with Teddy, I would not say, 'Teddy, would you be interested in moving in together?' Do you see what I mean?

Rosie: Well, I suppose I—

Ruby: That is not the way to broach the subject. And what about marriage? Did he say anything about that? Or about Katie? If you and he get married, will he want to adopt Katie? Did you discuss any of those things?

Rosie: Well, actually . . . no, we didn't even discuss marriage. Anyway, I thought you were anti-marriage.

Ruby: I am, but I'm not the one who wants to get married and who is in a relationship with a man who doesn't. There lies a problem.

111

Rosie: I never said that I wanted to marry him.

Ruby: Well then, if neither of you feels comfortable marrying each other, go ahead and move in together; that sounds like a fabulous idea!

Rosie: Look, I don't recall hearing anyone saying that Greg doesn't want to marry me, and anyway, that's exactly what you and Teddy are doing!

Ruby: I've been married before and so has Teddy. We both don't want to go through it again. I've already been there, done that, while this is just the beginning for you.

Rosie: Anyway, it doesn't matter because I told him that I wasn't ready to move in with him right now. It's a bad time, with me trying to settle down in the job and everything, and Katie settling down in the flat. I need to allow a little more time to pass so that Katie can adjust to the whole situation. It's been a huge change in her life.

Ruby: So you keep saying.

Rosie: What's that supposed to mean?

Ruby: You've been in the flat for well over a year now, you've been in that job of yours for a few weeks now, I've seen Katie and she's fine, Rosie, she's very happy. She's adjusted to this 'huge change'. I think that maybe it's *you* who needs to adjust.

Rosie: Adjust to *what*?

Ruby: Alex is married now, Rosie. Move on and make yourself happy!

Rosie has logged off.

Steph: Why didn't Greg ask you to marry him?

Rosie: I wasn't aware that he had to.

Steph: Would you have liked him to?

Rosie: You know me, Steph: if anyone got down on one knee and proposed (on the beach with a four-piece orchestra in the background) I'd like it. I'm an old romantic.

Steph: Are you disappointed he asked you to move in with him and not marry you?

Rosie: Well, I presume if he had proposed it would mean I'd be moving in with him anyway, so I'm really not that heartbroken. I'm lucky to have met someone like Greg.

Steph: Come on, Rosie, you're not just 'lucky' to have met Greg. You *deserve* to be happy. It's OK to want more than you're offered.

Rosie: I've decided to move in with him. We'll take it one step at a time.

Steph: If that makes you happy.

Rosie: *Then* if things are still as perfect between us as they are now, I'll expect the room filled with roses and lit with candles.

Dear Sally,

Sorry I spilled my orange juice on your new dress when we visited a few weeks ago. It is just that when I heard you slagging my mum's new dress I got a shock and my juice went all over you. Just like you laughed to your friend the next day about my mum having me, accidents happen.

I hope your dress doesn't stain, seeing as it was so expensive and all. I hope you will come to visit us sometime in our new house. We are moving in with Greg. It's bigger than your apartment. We had so much fun in Boston when Mum and Alex got new passport photos done for my locket. I'll keep the two of them together in it for ever.

Love,

Katie

PS. My friend Toby says hi and says that he spilled orange juice on his school shirt and it wouldn't come out when it was washed. His mum had to throw it out. It was white too. But lucky for him, the shirt was not as expensive as your dress.

You have an instant message from: ALEX.

Alex: Hi, what you up to?

Phil: I've been surfing the net for hours, looking for the original chrome exhaust pipes on a 1968 Ford Mustang. And do you think I could find the original badges as well as two-tone leather seats for the 1978 Corvette?

Alex: Eh . . . no?

Phil: Exactly, but I don't suppose you want to hear about my problems. How was the Rosie trip? Any more silences?

Alex: Oh, drop it, Phil.

Phil: He he. What's the boyfriend like?

Alex: He's OK. Nothing special. He's not the kind of man I'd have put Rosie with.

Phil: He's not you, you mean.

Alex: No, that's not what I mean. He's not exactly the life and soul of the party.

Phil: Should he be?

Alex: For Rosie, yes.

Phil: Maybe he's a calming influence on her.

Alex: Yeah, maybe. He's polite and friendly, but he doesn't talk much about himself. I couldn't quite figure him out. He's one of those people that don't seem to have an opinion on anything. He would just agree with absolutely everything everyone is saying. It's hard to get a sense of him. Sally and he got along very well, though.

Phil: Maybe he just had a problem with you then.

Alex: Thanks, Phil, you always have such a good way of making me feel better.

Phil: And isn't that why you discuss all of life's little problems with me?

Alex: Yeah. How are Margaret and the kids?

Phil: Great. Maggie thinks she's pregnant again.

Alex: Jesus, another one?

Phil: I'm one fully loaded man, Alex.

114

Alex: Good to no, Phil.
Alex has logged off.

From   Alex
To   Rosie
Subject Moving in with Greg?

So I take it you're moving in with Greg? Sally got a letter from Katie during the week, but she wouldn't let me read it. She just said that they have an understanding between them now. I'm glad. Whatever that means.

In answer to your question about Greg, yes, he's a nice man. Not the kind of person I expected you to settle down with, he's very quiet and reserved. A lot older than you as well. He's what . . . thirty-seven? And you're twenty-seven. That's ten years, Rosie. How will you feel when he's old and decrepit and you're still young and beautiful? How will you ever look into those faded watery eyes and kiss those wrinkly dry cracked lips? How can you rub your hands over the varicose veins in his legs and go running through fields holding hands while all the time secretly worrying about his weak heart?

These are the things you need to worry about, Rosie.

You have received an instant message from: ROSIE.
Rosie: Are you on drugs???
Alex: Only the little pink ones . . .
Rosie: You're a doctor, help yourself. OK, I take it from that attempt-at-being-humorous-but-meaning-every-word-of-it reply that you don't like Greg. I've had enough of your snide comments about Greg. Well, to let the truth be known, I can't stand Sally. Ta-da!

I hate Sally and you hate Greg. Now we have learned that we all can't love each other. Katie and I are moving

in with Greg next week. Everything is wonderful. We are blissfully happy. I've never been so in love in my life, blah blah blah. Now stop annoying me and get over it. Greg is here to stay. So what have you got to say to that?
Alex has logged off.

Rosie, Katie, and Greg,
    Merry Christmas and a Happy New Year!
    Love from Alex, Sally, and baby Josh

To Alex, Sally, and baby Josh!
    Warm wishes for the New Year!
    With love,
    Katie, Rosie, and Greg

Chapter 15

Hello, sis,

Stop worrying! You have me more stressed out than you! Rosie, for the last time, it is absolutely normal for friends not to get along with each other's spouses/partners. Pierre's sister drives me up the wall but that's neither here nor there. Anyway, it doesn't mean that you and Alex are never going to speak to each other again.

The problem with you two is that you're too honest. I can't think of one friend of mine that I would feel comfortable saying, 'I hate your husband/wife' to, and if I even say one minuscule thing to Pierre about how frustrating his sister is then he jumps down my throat and defends her. There's never going to be anyone good enough for your best friend, Rosie. Alex is probably thinking that you could do far better than Greg and you think the same of Sally. Sally and Greg aren't stupid; they probably sense that. Greg knows that Alex was the most important man in your life (he also knows that you once had a crush on him, which doesn't make things any better). And Alex knows that he's been replaced. So both Greg *and* Alex are going to be a bit competitive with each other. This is all quite natural.

Anyway, stop giving yourself a headache with all this stuff, just ring the man or email or write or whatever it is that you two do. By the way, if you don't like Pierre, I don't care. I love him, so keep your opinions to yourself!

Send me your measurements over, will you? And don't lie, Rosie. This is for your bridesmaid dress and if you pretend you're two stone lighter than you actually are and the dress doesn't fit, tough, you have to wear it because I can't afford to get you another one. Do you prefer red or wine? Let me know.

Love,

Your agony aunt

PS. By the way, will you ring Alex and tell him that he and his wife are invited to the wedding? Now there's your excuse to talk to him.

To Rosie,

Birthday wishes from us to you!

Happy 28th – you're catching up on me!

Love,

Alex, Sally, and Josh

To Katie,

YOU ARE 9 TODAY!

Best wishes! I hope you can buy something nice with this!

Love,

Alex, Sally and Josh

From   Rosie
To   Alex
Subject   Great news!

Alex Stewart, why don't you ever answer your phone? I have become best friends with Josh's nanny now and we have both come to an agreement over the fact that you and that wife of yours work far too much. Does poor little

Josh even know who Mummy and Daddy are, or are you both happy with him thinking you two are just the nice people who pick him up and cuddle him a few times every day?

Anyway, the reason why I'm emailing you is because I have something brilliant that I really want to tell you and I refuse to announce it to you on a computer! So ring me when you get this message. Your good advice may have been helpful after all, and I thank you for it!

Ring me, ring me, ring me!

From   Alex
To   Rosie
Subject Re: Great news!

I am refusing to ring you on the grounds that I am far too angry over your attacking my parental skills. If one more person tells me how to be a father to my son I will explode.

Things are tough at the moment because of my and Sally's working hours. The majority of the time we arrive home when Josh is asleep and I have to stop myself from waking him up just to say hello. We never have the same days off together and we just can't seem to spend any quality time together. It's like we're passing each other in the halls and grabbing quick moments of forced happiness before we run out the door.

It's not the greatest situation for Josh to be in but we just simply can't afford to stop working to be there for him all of the time. And by the way, *never ever* get married.

From   Rosie
To   Alex
Subject Surprise!

Oh, shucks, you've gone and spoiled my surprise.

From   Alex
To   Rosie
Subject Re: Surprise!

Rosie Dunne, are you getting married?!

Chapter 16

From   Rosie
To   Alex
Subject Surprise!

Surprise! What a lovely, lovely way to tell you. I can't have imagined a better way of sharing my delightful news with my best friend.

From   Alex
To   Rosie
Subject Marriage!

Oh, I'm so sorry, that's great news. Don't mind what I say, I'm just tired and whinging. So how did it all happen? When's the big day? I thought whatshisname didn't want to get married.

From   Rosie
To   Alex
Subject Re: Marriage at last!

Oh, Alex, you don't have to pretend to be interested in all

the little details, it's OK. And his name is Greg, by the way. You've plenty on your mind now so I'll bore you another time. I just want to let you know that the 'big day' won't be so big. It's only going to be a small gathering with close friends and family. Greg doesn't really want anything too OTT and I'm happy enough to go along with that.

Katie is my flower girl/bridesmaid-type person and I want you to be my best man. If Greg is allowed to have one then so should I. Please say yes. Sally and Josh are more than welcome too. Make it a family holiday. I bet you haven't had one of those yet. You can relax and enjoy yourselves because you all deserve it. You can finally spend a few days together as a family.

I won't go into any detail about the proposal; I knew it was going to happen so it wasn't that amazing . . .

From   Rosie
To   Stephanie
Subject   So romantic!

Oh, Stephanie, it was *so* romantic. I had absolutely *no* idea he was going to propose! He took me away for the weekend to this tiny little village in the west that I've never even heard of so I won't even attempt to spell it. We stayed in this charming little B&B and we ate in a restaurant called the Fisherman's Catch. We had the entire place to ourselves. The atmosphere was magical and then Greg proposed over dessert! Then we went for a stroll around the lake and headed back to the B&B. It was low key and quiet but so romantic!

From   Stephanie
To   Rosie
Subject   Re: Romantic

That's funny, Rosie, because I always thought you said you wanted fireworks and romance, rose petals and violins while your man went down on one knee and proposed in front of a gasping and tearful crowd. Greg's proposal sounds *nice* and all, but whatever happened to that dream?

From   Rosie
To   Stephanie
Subject   Fireworks and rose petals . . .

Well, that kind of thing just isn't Greg's style; you know the way he is. It would have seemed silly if Greg hung from a chandelier singing Sinatra while showering red velvety petals over my head (although what a wonderful thought). Besides it's not the proposal that counts, it's the marriage . . .

Ruby: He proposed to you in Bogger-reef?
Rosie: Yes, it's a cute little village—
Ruby: You HATE cute little villages! You like towns, cities, noise, air pollution, bright lights, rude people, and tall buildings!
Rosie: But we stayed in this sweet little B&B owned by the nicest—
Ruby: You HATE B&Bs! You are obsessed with hotels. You work in one. You want to run one, own one, live in one and quite possibly be one. The biggest treat for you is staying in a hotel and he took you to a crappy B&B in the middle of nowhere.
Rosie: Oh, but if you had just seen the little restaurant. It

was called the Fisherman's Catch and it had these fishing
nets all draped around the ceiling—

Ruby: You starved Katie's goldfish until it floated on top
of that stinking bowl and then you flushed it down the
toilet. You gag whenever you see people eating oysters
(which, by the way, is very embarrassing in restaurants).
You block your nose whenever I eat tuna, you think
smoked salmon is the work of the devil, and prawns
make you vomit.

Rosie: I had a nice salad, thank you very much.

Ruby: You always say salad is for rabbits and supermodels!

Rosie: Anyway, we finished the evening by strolling hand
in hand in the moonlight alongside the lake—

Ruby: You LOVE the SEA. You want to live on a beach.
You secretly want to be a mermaid. You think lakes are
boring, you say they lack the 'drama' of the sea.

Rosie: Oh, please, *stop* it, Ruby!

Ruby: No! You please stop *lying* to yourself, Rosie Dunne.

Rosie has logged off.

From   Rosie
To   Alex
Subject SOS

Alex, please save me from my family and friends. They are
driving me absolutely demented.

You have received an instant message from: ALEX.

Alex: Snap. What's the problem?

Rosie: I don't really want to talk about it. I want to take
my mind off them.

Alex: That's fair enough, I can understand that. This is a
nice distraction for me too. So why don't you tell me
about whatshisname's proposal?

Rosie: OK . . . here I go again. *Greg* took me to a quiet little village down the country. We stayed in a gorgeous little B&B. We ate in a lovely restaurant called the Fisherman's Catch. He proposed while I had my mouth full of chocolate profiteroles, I said yes, we took a walk along the lake and watched the moon shimmering along the water. Isn't that romantic?

Alex: Yes, romantic.

Rosie: That's all you have to say?? Two words on one of the most important nights of my life?!

Alex: Could have been better.

Rosie: How much better? What would you have done to make it so much better? I'm just *dying* to know! Everyone seems to think they know me so much better than I know myself, so go ahead, humour me!

Alex: OK, that sounds like a challenge! Well, firstly, I would have brought you to a *hotel* along the coast so that your *suite* would have the best possible *sea view*. You could fall asleep listening to the waves crashing against the rocks, I would sprinkle the bed with red *rose petals* and have *candles* lit all around the room, I would have your favourite CD playing quietly in the background.

But I wouldn't propose to you there. I would bring you to where there was a huge crowd of people so they could all gasp when I got down on one knee and proposed. Or something like that. Note I have italicised the all-important buzz words.

Rosie: Oh.

Alex: That's all you can say? One word for the most important night of our lives? I get down on bended knee and ask that you'll spend eternity with me and you say, 'Oh'? You have to do better than that!

Rosie: OK, so that would *also* be a very nice proposal. Did I go on about proposals so much, Alex?

Alex: All the time, my friend. All the time. Anyone who nos you half well would realise that is more or less the kind of thing you have always dreamed about. But a weekend in a B&B sounds fine too.

To Alex, Sally and baby Josh
DENNIS & ALICE DUNNE
Proudly invite you to the marriage of their beloved daughter
ROSIE TO GREG COLLINS
on July 18th of this year

Chapter 17

Dear Rosie,

So you went ahead and did it. You married whatshisname. You looked beautiful, Rosie, I was proud to stand beside you at the altar, and I was proud to be there with you on your special day. I was proud to be your best man, but just as you said at my wedding, I wasn't the best man that day, whatshisname was. You both looked great together.

I got the oddest feeling when you turned your back to me to walk down the aisle with Greg. Could it have been a pang of jealousy? Is that normal? Did you get that feeling on my wedding day, or am I going completely crazy? I just kept thinking over and over in my head: everything is going to change now, everything is going to change. Greg is the man for you, now *he* gets to hear all your secrets, and where does that leave me? It was a weird feeling, Rosie, though it did eventually pass.

I didn't dare talk about it to anyone, especially Sally, because then she would be only too delighted to think that her little theory of men and women being unable to be 'just friends' was correct. It's not like I was jealous because I wanted to be your husband, it was just . . . oh, I don't no how to explain it. I suppose I just felt left out, that's all.

I'm glad Josh finally got to put his feet on Irish soil – well, actually mostly his bum but he's almost there. I meant to bring him home a long time ago but work got in the way. That's funny, I just referred to Ireland as home; I haven't done that for quite a while. It felt like home last week. Anyway, it was good for Josh to be there, and I think Katie was happy enough to mind him all week.

She is you, Rosie. The little girl with the raven-coloured hair and pale skin is the girl I used to go to school with. It was amazing. Even talking to her I felt like young Alex again. Toby kept a watchful eye over me, though; I think he was afraid I would steal his friend away. I felt like I was keeping a watchful eye over him too, because *he* was stealing *my* friend away. I had to keep reminding myself that she wasn't you.

I'm not quite sure how your plan to unite me, Sally, and Josh went. As you could probably tell, Sally wasn't in the friendliest of moods during the few days. I thought the break away would help us, but apparently not. It just gave us a chance to talk to each other too much. And that's not the best thing when neither of you have anything nice to say. I think I can safely say that the honeymoon period is over. We're together nine years now.

Anyway, I hope you and Greg are enjoying your honeymoon and I'm sure this letter will be lying on the mat at home awaiting your arrival. I always thought you wanted to go to an exotic beach location for your honeymoon, I never new you were interested in seeing all the sights around Rome. Although I'm sure they are beautiful, I just thought you were too shallow to care! Just teasing.

Get in touch with me when you get back. Prove to me that at least some things never change.

Love,
Alex

Greetings from Rome!

Hi, Alex. Weather warm, buildings beautiful. But, more importantly, fabulous hotels!

Love,

Rosie x

From   Rosie
To   Alex
Subject I'm baa-aack!

Just got home a few minutes ago from our honeymoon and I read your letter. You sounded down so I called and guess what? Surprise, surprise, you weren't there. So I'm emailing you once again.

I know I never really liked Sally much, but I want you two to get over whatever it is that's bothering you. It's a big change when a baby comes along – I know that only too well – and I can understand that it's difficult for two people who work harder than anyone I know to deal with a new addition in their lives.

You probably just need time to adjust, but maybe you should go see a counsellor or something. God knows, it took me long enough to accept that Katie was here to stay, as much as I love her. It was, and still is, hard work. So do what you do best and get to work on it.

I certainly don't pretend to be a know-it-all but just stop talking to me about how you feel and start telling Sally. I am always here for you, Alex, married woman or not.

Dear Alex,

I hope you are well. It was good to see you at the wedding. Josh is really cool. Mummy looked lovely and so did you. Me and Toby are fighting. He is ten next week and he thinks he is so cool just because he is a little bit older than me. He didn't invite me to his birthday party and I didn't even do anything wrong. We had a fight last week about whose turn it was to go first on the computer and I went first even though I remembered I went first the last time but I don't think he remembered so he is not mad at me about that. I did not do anything else wrong.

Mum called round to Toby's mum to see why but she does not no either. Toby will not talk to me. I hate him. I will make a new best friend. Mum told me to write to you and tell you because you are my godfather and no stuff about this.

Mum thinks that it is really, really mean of Toby and that I will be motionally scared when I grow up, from the xperience of not being invited to a birthday party. She says you no what she means.

Love,
Katie

Dearest Katie,

Your wise and extremely intelligent mother is correct, as always. I agree that Toby is being terribly cold and calculative. It is an awful thing for anyone to do to a person, to not invite your best friend to your tenth birthday party. I do believe it should be a crime. He is selfish and it is an unforgivable act that will haunt him for years to come, no doubt – maybe even until he is nearly thirty years old, in fact.

I think that there is no punishment bad enough to inflict on him and he should not get away with this. Toby has shown no mercy, has been immature and very very . . . bold. So tell your mother and tell Toby that I shall do my best to make sure that he and I redeem ourselves so that we can walk down the road with our heads held high.

Love,
Alex

Dear Alex,

That was a weird letter. I don't know what it meant but Mum says that Toby is even worse than all the things you said. But she was laughing when she read the letter so I don't no if she means it. I don't think Toby is *that* bad.

You two are weirdos.

Love,

Katie x

Dear Toby,

It's Alex here (Katie's mum's friend from America).

I heard that you're going to be ten next week. Happy birthday! I no you probably think that me writing to you is really weird but I heard that you didn't invite Katie to your party and I couldn't believe my ears.

Katie is your best friend! I no for a fact that your party won't be much fun without Katie there. It once happened to me. You will be watching the door like a hawk, just hoping that she will walk into the room so you can enjoy yourself. Who cares if your best friend is a girl? Who cares if the other guys laugh? At least you have a best friend and, trust me on this, it's really hard to live your life without a best friend, especially if you're in boring school with Miss Big Nose Casey giving out to you all day. If you don't invite Katie then you will really hurt her feelings and that's not very nice.

It's the best thing in the world to have a best friend – even if she is a girl. Let me no how you get on.

Alex

PS. Hope you can buy something nice for yourself with this present . . .

131

From   Toby
To   Katie
Subject KNOW not NO

Your mum's friend spells 'know' wrong, just like you. He
says NO instead of KNOW. By the way, do you wanna
come to my party next week?

From   Rosie
To   Alex
Subject Dunne women

Very clever, Mr Stewart, but you haven't quite redeemed
yourself yet. Us Dunne women are pretty hard to please,
you know . . .

From   Alex
To   Rosie
Subject Done woman

So I see. You're a done woman alright. Well, I have a
theory that I wish to share with you. Shall I?

From   Rosie
To   Alex
Subject Theory shmeory

If you must. I might read it if I have time.

From   Alex
To   Rosie
Subject My theory

Yes I must, and you *will* read it. OK, if I *had* invited you to
my tenth birthday party then Brian the Whine wouldn't have

been invited. If Brian hadn't gone then he wouldn't have thrown pizza all over James's sleeping bag and if he hadn't done that and completely ruined my party then you and I wouldn't have hated him so much. If you and I hadn't hated him so much then you wouldn't have had to drink so much in order to be able to accompany him to the debs. If you hadn't have done that . . . well . . . perhaps you wouldn't have been quite so drunk and your darling little Katie wouldn't have been born. Therefore I did you a favour!

And that, Rosie Dunne, is my theory.

From   Rosie
To   Alex
Subject   *My* theory

Very clever, Alex, very, very, clever. But you needn't have gone that far back to accept responsibility for Katie. Here's my theory.

Had I not been stood up by you at the debs, I wouldn't have had to go with Brian the Whine at all. Had you showed up at the airport that day our lives could have turned out very differently.

From   Alex
To   Rosie
Subject   Life

Yeah, that's something I'm beginning to wonder about.

Ruby: They WHAT? They *split up*??
Rosie: Yeah, they're finished. Sad, isn't it?
Ruby: Well, not really, actually. Why did they split up?
Rosie: Irreconcilable differences. Isn't that what people always say?

Ruby: Not in my case. Mine was lazy cheating bastard. So who has Josh?

Rosie: Sally took him and went to stay with her parents.

Ruby: Oh, poor Alex. So come on, spill the beans.

Rosie: Well, I don't know everything—

Ruby: Liar. Alex tells you everything, which is probably the reason in itself.

Rosie: Excuse me; please do not accuse me of being the reason for his marriage break-up. That is very insulting. It was a million little things that all finally blew up in their faces.

Ruby: So when are you going over to him?

Rosie: Next week.

Ruby: Are you planning on coming back?

Rosie: RUBY! QUIT IT!

Ruby: OK, OK. It's sad, though, isn't it?

Rosie: Yes, it is. Alex is devastated.

Ruby: No, I didn't mean that. The irony of it all makes *me* sad; I can't even imagine how *you* must feel.

Rosie: What irony?

Ruby: Oh, you know . . . you wait and wait for years for him until you finally give up and move on with your life. You eventually decide to marry Greg and weeks later, Alex splits up with Sally. You know, you two have the worst timing ever. When will you ever learn to catch up with each other?

Chapter 18

You are one today!
  May your special day be lots of fun,
  It's not every day a boy is one!
  We love our little special boy,
  Because you bring us so much joy!
  To Josh (and your daddy),
  We love you both and hope you have a very happy birthday
and Thanksgiving together.
  Lots of love,
  Rosie and Katie

Dear Rosie and Katie,
  Thank you for the teddy you sent me for my birthday. I call him 'Bear'. Daddy made the name up all by himself. He is very clever. I love to chew on his ear and drool all over him so that when Daddy hugs him, it leaves my slobber all over his face. I also like to throw Bear out of my cot in the middle of the night and then scream at Daddy until he picks him up for me. I just do it for the laugh. Daddy doesn't need to sleep. He's only here to feed me and clean my diapers.
  Anyway, I'd better go now. I have a very busy weekend with Daddy, I'm being fed at nine o'clock, followed by a

burping and then I'm going to try to take a few steps across the living room. I no I can do it. One of these days I won't land on my bum . . .

Thanks for Bear.

Love you and miss you both,

Josh (and Daddy)

From   Rosie
To   Alex
Subject   Happy 30th

I can't believe you're not having a thirtieth birthday party! Or are you having one and you're just not inviting me? I know you've been inclined to do things like that in the past. Jesus, imagine that was a whole twenty years ago. I never thought we would reach the time when we could remember anything happening that long ago. Anyway, Happy Birthday. Have a slice of cake on me.

From   Alex
To   Rosie
Subject   Thanks

Sorry I haven't been in touch, I'm almost ready to finish up my residency here so I can move on to do two more years of cardiothoracic residency program. My one hundred years of study are almost up! No celebrations for me this year, too busy trying to pay back my million-dollar student loan.

You have an instant message from: GREG.

Greg: Hi, honey, how's your day going?

Rosie: Oh, it seems to be one of those neverending days.

The hotel is completely booked out this weekend

because of the St Patrick's Day parade. There's been a steady flow of big groups arriving all day so I've been constantly checking them in. It has quietened down now, so I'm pretending to be really busy on the computer with reservations, so don't make me laugh, whatever you do, or my cover will be blown.

Well, when I say 'quiet' I mean no one is bothering us at reception. The noise level of the hotel is a completely different story altogether. There's a huge group of Americans in the bar singing along to old Irish songs. Would you believe they got the Paddy Band into the hotel as a special treat? I've never seen so many green faces and dyed red hair in my life.

Unfortunately some of Bill Lake's family have flown in from Chicago. There are thirty of them so I'm on my best behaviour. Apparently his nephew is a trombone player in the Chicago high school marching band that's taking part in the parade on Sunday.

I'm just dying for the day to end. My face is sore from smiling and my eyes are stinging from staring at this bloody computer screen. I'm thrilled Bill gave me the weekend off! He's such a sweetie. I can't remember the last time I had a Saturday off, or two days in a row, for that matter. Well, it means that for once we can go out tonight and I won't have to worry about getting up in the morning. We can meet up with Ruby and Ted. I was thinking of bringing Katie and Toby to the parade on Sunday – what do you think?

Sorry for rambling on, but I feel like I'm back at school on a Friday afternoon, waiting for the final bell to ring for the weekend.

Greg: Oh, Rosie, I'm sorry to dampen your good spirits but I have to head up north to Belfast tonight. I only found out this morning so it's completely last minute. I'm sorry.

Rosie: Oh no! Why do you have to go to Belfast?

Greg: There's this seminar that's on that I have to go to.

Rosie: What kind of a seminar?

Greg: A financial one.

Rosie: Well, of course it's a financial one. I hardly expect it to be on French cuisine. Do you *have* to go? Will they even notice if you're there?

Greg: No, they wouldn't notice, to be honest, but I want to go. They're quite interesting, you know, and I have to stay ahead of my game.

Rosie: How much more could you possibly learn about bloody banks? They give you money and ask for ten times more back. That's about it.

Greg: I'm sorry, Rosie.

Rosie: This is so annoying. Of all the bloody weekends Bill gives me off, it's the one you have to go away for. You do know that I will not get a weekend off for another year, don't you?

Greg: I love the way you never exaggerate, Rosie. Listen, I have to go, OK? Talk to you later. Love you.

Rosie: Oh, hold on, before you go, did you see the phone bill this morning?

Greg: What was it like, high?

Rosie: Guess.

Greg: Damn. That's you and all that time you spend on that internet sending emails, you know. I don't understand why you and Ruby can't just arrange to *meet* like normal people.

Rosie: Because no establishment allows us to sprawl across their couches in our pyjamas and smoke. It's far more comfortable at home. Anyway, the price of the bill couldn't have *anything* to do with all those hours a week you spend on the phone to your mother, convincing her she's perfectly capable living on her own, by any chance?

138

Greg: I somehow think you don't really mind me spending
   those hours convincing her, my darling!
Rosie: True! Oh, if only we knew a bank manager who
   could give us a loan . . . how simple life would be . . .
Greg: Unfortunately it doesn't work like that, Rosie.
Rosie: And imagine my disappointment when I found that
   out after I married you.
Greg: You stuck with me all the same – thank you for
   that. I have to go now and refuse to give a mortgage to
   someone, you know how it is. Love you.
Rosie: Love you.

From   Kevin
To   Rosie
Subject   My favourite sister

Hello, my most favourite big sister in the whole entire
world. It's Kevin here. Email me back when you get a
chance. I'm on the college computer so the internet is free
and I wanna ask you something.

From   Rosie
To   Kevin
Subject   Re: My favourite sister

Why do I only ever hear from you when you want
something?

From   Kevin
To   Rosie
Subject   Re: Re: My favourite sister

You sound like my ex-girlfriend. What makes you think I
want something? Maybe I just want to catch up with my
sister and see what's going on in her life. How's Katie? Tell

her I was asking for her. How's Greg? Tell him I was asking for him. How's Alex? Tell him I was asking for him. See how interested I am in your life? If you ever need a baby-sitter for Katie just let me know, I'd be only too delighted to help out. Anyway, that's all from me, take care of yourself and keep in touch.

PS. Any chance you could ask your boss for a job for me?

From   Rosie
To   Kevin
Subject A-HA!

A-HA! I knew there had to be a catch! You never usually care about what's going on in my life. Katie is fine, thank you, so is Greg, and so is Alex. You could see how they are with your very own eyes if you ever bothered to call round. Yes I would love you to mind Katie, thank you very much, but I'm not sure I could trust you after what happened the last time.

From   Kevin
To   Rosie
Subject Six years ago!

Oh, come on Rosie! That was at least six years ago, I was only seventeen! How could you give a seventeen-year-old male an apartment of his own and not expect him to invite round a few friends? It's only normal.

From   Rosie
To   Kevin
Subject Normal!

Kevin, you trashed the place. Poor Katie was terrified and I

didn't appreciate finding you asleep in my bed with that . . .
whatever she was . . .

From   Kevin
To   Rosie
Subject Water under the bridge

Well, you said make yourself at home . . . anyway, that's
all water under the bridge, we're both sensible adults now.
(You're getting on a bit – thirty next month!) I would
really love if you could help me out. I would be forever
grateful and I honestly, truthfully mean that.

From   Rosie
To   Kevin
Subject You owe me!

Oh, OK, but I'm not promising any miracles. Don't mess
this up, Kevin, or Bill will hold it against me and it'll ruin
my grand master plan of taking over this hotel.

From   Rosie
To   Alex
Subject Life!

Christ, Alex, who knew Kevin had learned to walk and
talk? I thought he was still at school. He just suddenly
grew up. Not that he was ever one for sharing his life
stories with me, anyway. He's so secretive. It's people like
him the world has to worry about.

Things change so quickly. Just when you get used to
something, zap! It changes. Just when you begin to
understand someone, zap! They grow up. The same is
happening with Katie. She changes every day; her face just
becomes so much more grown-up every time I look at her.

141

Sometimes I have to stop *pretending* I'm interested in what she's saying in order to realise that I *actually am* interested. We go shopping for clothes together and I take her advice. We eat out for lunch and giggle over silly things. I just can't cast my mind back to the time when my child stopped being a child and became a person.

And a beautiful person she is becoming too. I don't quite know where I'm going with this email, Alex, but I've been thinking about a lot of things lately and my head is a bit of a muddle.

Our life is made up of time. Our days are measured in hours, our pay measured by those hours, our knowledge is measured by years. We grab a quick few minutes in our busy day to have a coffee break. We rush back to our desks, we watch the clock, we live by appointments. And yet time eventually runs out and you wonder in your heart of hearts if those seconds, minutes, hours, days, weeks, months, years and decades were being spent the best way they possibly could.

Everything is spinning around us – jobs, family, friends, lovers . . . you just feel like screaming 'STOP!', looking around, rearranging the order of a few things and then continuing on. I guess you probably understand what I mean. I know you're having a really difficult time right now. Please remember that I'm always here for you.

Love, Rosie

Chapter 19

Dear Alex,

OK, so as you probably no, it's Mum's thirtieth next month, and me and Toby are arranging a surprise birthday party for her. So will you come?

So far we have invited Grandma, Granddad, Aunt Stephanie, Uncle Kevin (even though we didn't want to because he scares us), Ruby, Teddy, Toby's mum and dad, Toby and me. That's all so far. Oh yeah, and Greg too if he's here. He's always working and Mum is always giving out to him about it. The other weekend Mum was off work and she was real excited about it all week because she had stuff planned with Ruby and Greg. I no how she feels because I hate school and I love when the weekend comes. Anyway, Greg had to go away again, last minute. Then Ruby called her and said she was sick so Mum stayed in and watched TV with me and Toby, and she let him stay over.

Toby's got this cool new flashlight. It's like the best one you can get. When Mum went to bed we were shining it out our window and it reached all the way up to the clouds and everything, it was so strong. Well, we were shining it across the road and we could see Mr and Ms Gallagher in their house. Toby thinks they were playing leap frog. It was real funny except Ms Gallagher came across the road in her dressing gown real mad at us, and she was banging on the door shouting at Mum. Mum was so mad she said she wouldn't take us to the parade. But she did.

Me and Toby got our faces painted in town and it looked really cool. We even got Mum to get a little shamrock on her face as well and she did, but then she wished she didn't because it started raining and the green, white and gold face paints were running all over our faces. They looked like rainbow tears. Loads of Toby's got in his hair and I rubbed my eyes by mistake and all the green got in. They were stinging so much I couldn't keep my eyes open and I couldn't see, so Mum and Toby held my hands and brought me home. We had to leave before the parade even started.

We were soaking when we got home and Mum's new outfit was covered in the green stuff. The lady that put it on our faces said that it washes off clothes. It doesn't. Toby has had green hair for the whole week in school and Miss Big Nose Smelly Breath Casey isn't happy. Can you believe she is the principal now? Mum says the school must really be desperate. Anyway, when we got back from town we just watched the parade on telly but we only got to see the end because it took us so long to get home because of all the fucking tourists. That's what Mum said.

So will you come to the party? You can bring Josh too. We need more people anyway. Aunt Stephanie can't come because she is due next month and I don't think the pilot will let her fly because she's too heavy or something. Grandma and Granddad are going over to visit her, Pierre, and the new baby if it comes. Uncle Kevin can't come because he's starting his new job as a chef in a new hotel down the country. So it's just Ruby and Teddy, and Ruby says that she can't promise Teddy will be there, because she doesn't like to plan dates with him that far in advance. It's only two weeks, though.

I wanted it to be kinda special for Mum, because she's been really sad again this week. Things have been kinda weird these days. I think it's because the telephone is broken. Every time the phone rings and Mum answers it, no one is there. It happens when I answer it too. It doesn't happen when Greg answers it.

Greg said he would get someone to fix the phone and Mum just spilled her drink on him. I don't really think it's broken. I think that whoever is ringing just wants to speak to Greg and not me and Mum.

It would be good if you came over – you're loads of fun. You can even sleep here but you can't sleep in the spare room because that's Greg's room now, I think. You can sleep on the couch, or I have a pull-out bed in my room. Remember, don't ring because it's a secret and Mum just keeps hanging the phone up without saying hello anyway. Email me if you want.

Love,
Katie

From   Alex
To   Katie
Subject Re: Rosie's 30th

Thanks for the letter. That's a good idea of yours and Toby's but I won't wait until your mum's birthday, if you don't mind. I'll be over as soon as I can.

Happy 30th, Sister!
    Sorry we can't be there.
    Love, Stephanie, Pierre and Jean-Louis!

For our daughter
    Happy 30th.

Sorry we can't be there. Enjoy your day, love, and we'll see you when we get back.

Love, Mum and Dad

Happy 30th, Sis.

Sorry I can't be there but thanks for getting me the job. I owe you one.

Enjoy the night.

Kevin

Happy Birthday, Rosie.

Sorry we can't be there but we're stuck covering your shift!

Love from everyone at work xxx

To Rosie

I'm so sorry, please forgive me; I have been a complete fool. Please let's put this behind us and enjoy your birthday weekend.

Love,

Greg

Happy Birthday.

Let's get pissed.

Love, Ruby

Rosie,

I'm returning to Boston tomorrow but before I go I wanted to write this letter to you. All the thoughts and feelings that have been bubbling up inside me are finally overflowing from this pen and I'm leaving this letter for you so that you don't feel that I'm putting you under any great pressure. I understand that you will need to take your time trying to decide on what I am about to say.

I no what's going on, Rosie. You're my best friend and I can see the sadness in your eyes. I no that Greg isn't away working for the weekend. You never could lie to me; you were always terrible at it. Your eyes betray you time and time again. Don't pretend that everything is perfect because I *see* it isn't. I see that Greg is a selfish man who has absolutely no idea just how lucky he is and it makes me sick.

He is the luckiest man in the world to have you, Rosie, but he doesn't deserve you and *you* deserve far better. You deserve someone who loves you with every single beat of his heart, someone who thinks about you constantly, someone who spends every minute of every day just wondering what you're doing, where you are, who you're with and if you're OK. You need someone who can help you reach your dreams and who can protect you from your fears. You need someone who will treat you with respect, love every part of you, *especially* your flaws. You should be with someone who can make you happy, really happy, *dancing-on-air* happy. Someone who should have taken the chance to be with you years ago instead of becoming scared and being too afraid to try.

I am not scared any more, Rosie. I am not afraid to try. I no what that feeling was at your wedding – it *was* jealousy. My heart broke when I saw the woman I love turning away from me to walk down the aisle with another man, a man she planned to spend the rest of her life with. It was like a prison sentence for me – years stretching ahead without me being able to tell you how I feel or hold you how I wanted to.

Twice we've stood beside each other at the altar, Rosie. *Twice*. And twice we got it wrong. I needed you to be there for my wedding day but I was too stupid to see that I needed you to be the *reason* for my wedding day.

I should never have let your lips leave mine all those years ago in Boston. I should never have pulled away. I should never have panicked. I should never have wasted all those years without you. Give me a chance to make them up to you. I love you, Rosie, and I want to be with you and Katie and Josh. Always.

147

Please think about it. Don't waste your time on Greg. This is *our* opportunity. Let's stop being afraid and take the chance. I promise I'll make you happy.

All my love,

Alex

Chapter 20

Ruby: I've decided. I'm putting my Gary on a diet.

Rosie: *You're* putting *him* on a diet? How on earth can you control what your twenty-one-year-old son eats?

Ruby: Oh, it's easy. I'll just nail everything down to the floor.

Rosie: So what kind of diet is it?

Ruby: I don't know. I bought a magazine, but there are so many stupid diets out there I don't know which one to pick. Remember that ridiculous one that you and I did last year? The alphabet one where we had to eat foods beginning with a certain letter every day?

Rosie: Oh yeah! How long did we do that for?!

Ruby: Em . . . that would be twenty-six days of course, Rosie.

Rosie: Oh . . . right . . . of course. You *put on* weight on the third day.

Ruby: That's because the third day was the lucky letter 'C' . . . Cakes . . . Mmmm.

Rosie: Well, we made up for it on the last day. I was bloody starving on 'Z' day; I was practically chasing zebras with a kitchen knife around the zoo. Could have eaten the zoo, I suppose . . .

Ruby: Maybe I'll just invent a diet of my own and give those ridiculous magazines a run for their money.

Rosie: So what's your idea then?

Ruby: Hmm . . . OK, you should only eat . . . whatever food you look like.

Rosie: I bet those magazine diet experts are quaking in their boots.

Ruby: No, really! I think I'm on to something here! Teddy always reminds me of a tomato with his big ripe fat juicy red face. The two hairs on his head that stick up remind me of the stalk. I always feel the urge to stick his head in a blender and mix with vodka and Tabasco. A bloody Teddy. Simon from the office reminds me of a Brussels sprout. He's smelly and . . .

Rosie: Green?

Ruby: No, just smelly.

Rosie: What do I look like?

Ruby: Good question . . . hmm, I think you're a bit of an onion.

Rosie: Why, do I stink and make people cry? Why, do I stink and make people cry?

Ruby: Why did you just repeat yourself?

Rosie: Onions do that, don't they – they repeat on you?

Ruby: A funny onion too. No, I think it's because there are many layers to you, Rosie Dunne, and as the years go by, another one is peeled away. I think there's a lot more under there than people think. So what am I?

Rosie: Hmm . . . a cake. Sweet as sugar with a cherry on top.

Ruby: And fat and unhealthy.

Rosie: Look, Ruby, you invented this diet. If you look like a cake then all you can eat are cakes. Think about it.

Ruby: Yes, I take your point. I always thought secretly that I had a touch of the banoffi pie to me, alright. But it's not a proper diet unless you look like a vegetable or a fruit, and my Gary (although he may have the *qualities* of a vegetable) ain't no fruit or vegetable.

Rosie: What do you think Greg looks like?

Ruby: Ah, that's easy. A bull's testicle.

Rosie: HA! Since when did people ever eat bulls' testicles?

Ruby: It's a tribal thing . . . OK then, a slug. A slimy, disgusting, slow slug.

Rosie: I don't think Greg would eat a slug.

Ruby: Who cares what the cheating bastard eats? What do you think Alex looks like?

Rosie: A Skye.

Ruby: You think your six-foot-tall, brown-haired, brown-eyed, white-skinned friend looks like a chocolate bar with nougat inside?

Rosie: Yes.

Ruby: Now *that's* stupid . . .

Rosie: Well, excuse me, Ms I-Think-Teddy-Has-a-Tomato-Head.

Ruby: Look, all this talk of dieting is making me hungry. I'm taking an early lunch, OK?

Rosie: OK! You cheered me up, Ruby.

Ruby: Ooops, sorry, I wasn't supposed to do that, was I?

Rosie: No, but you're forgiven.

Ruby: Oh good. Bye, honey.

Rosie: Bye . . .

Ruby has logged off.

From   Alex
To   Rosie
Subject More time?

Alex here. It's been a while since I've heard from you . . . I was hoping you would have been in touch by now. If you need more time, I understand. Please let me no what's going on.

From   Rosie
To   Alex
Subject Re: More time?

Hey there, Skye! Sorry I haven't written in a while, I've been up to my eyes at work. It's been really busy round here for some reason. Probably because the sun is beginning to peek its big head up again; the country is so much nicer when the sun shines. What do you mean, do I need more time? It doesn't take very long to accept I'm thirty!

Thanks for coming over for my birthday, by the way. It was really sweet of Katie and Toby to organise it, even if you and Ruby were the *only* people there. Sorry I was a bit of a sour puss. I suppose I was just down because I turned thirty and most people were away. It just would have been nice if more people had come, but never mind, it's not the end of the world. You were there and that was good enough for me. I was so happy to see you. You are always there for me, Alex, and I appreciate that. You keep me strong when I don't feel like it.

Anyway, how are things with you? How's Josh? Give him a big huge sloppy kiss and a hug from me.

From   Alex
To   Rosie
Subject My letter

Didn't you get my letter?

From   Rosie
To   Alex
Subject Letter?

What's this about a letter? Maybe it's just delayed in the post; I'll probably get it soon. When did you send it?

Dear Alex,

Thank you for coming over for Mum's birthday party and thanks for my present too. She was real sad before you came over but I think you made her happier. I have to go because teacher is looking at me.

From Katie

Dear Katie,

Thanks for the letter. I hope you didn't get into any trouble at school for writing to me. I'm glad you liked your present. Tell Toby I said hi and that I'll send over that baseball gear for him soon.

How is your mum? How is everything at home? Do you no what a Skye is, by any chance?

Love,
Alex

From   Alex
To   Rosie
Subject   My letter

I didn't post the letter; I put it on the kitchen table in your house just before I left to go to the airport. Didn't you get it?

Dear Alex,

Toby is real excited about the baseball stuff. Things are kinda getting back to normal again. Greg only sleeps in the spare room some nights now. Mum said he's there because of his snoring. I don't believe her because Toby and I put a tape recorder in the room and he doesn't snore. He sleep talks, though! He said, 'Don't send the horses to the rainbow!' It's true, we have it on tape.

Things are kinda OK but not like before. It was nice when

you were here. I prefer to stay in Toby's house now. By the way, a Skye is a chocolate bar. It's Mum's favourite. She loves them. She says she would love a diet of Skyes all day. The other day she said she was in love with a Skye then she started kissing it and laughing.

Why do you want to no? Do you want one too? I can post one over if you want, if they don't sell them in Merica. I did that before when I was in England on my holidays and I sent a chocolate bar in the post to Toby because they didn't sell them here and when he got it, it was all melted and stuck to the paper. He couldn't read my letter but I was glad because I missed him when I was away and I wrote some silly things and it was imbarrassing.

So should I get you the chocolate bar? Mum says she can't live without her Skye. She's a weirdo.

Love, Katie

From   Alex
To   Rosie
Subject My letter

Hi, Rosie. It's important that I talk to you right now. It's about the letter. I wrote some really important things in there and I would love you to read it if you can. Please try and find it.

From   Rosie
To   Alex
Subject Your letter

Hi, Alex. I searched the house from top to bottom yesterday when I got home from work. No sign of it. Is everything OK? Can you just email me what it said?

From   Alex
To   Rosie
Subject My letter

Jesus Christ. Rosie, I'll call you in five minutes.

From   Rosie
To   Alex
Subject Your letter

Alex! You can't call me at work, you'll get me fired! What is this about?

From   Alex
To   Rosie
Subject My letter

So pretend to be talking to a customer, Rosie! I'm serious, answer the phone.

From   Rosie
To   Alex
Subject Your letter

Oh, hold on, Greg is online. Before you have a heart attack, I'll see if he's seen the letter.

From   Alex
To   Rosie
Subject My letter

Don't bloody well ask *him*!

You have an instant message from: ROSIE.
Rosie: Greg, did you see a letter on the kitchen table for me?

Greg: A letter? No, I think there was just your mobile phone bill and the electricity bill.

Rosie: No, I'm not talking about this morning; I'm talking about two weeks ago, the weekend of my birthday.

Greg: But, Rosie you didn't want me around that weekend. I stayed on the couch in Teddy's flat, remember?

Rosie: Oh, you poor soul. Of course I fucking remember. I thought you might like it, seeing as you've been sleeping in everybody else's houses for the past while. I'm not stupid, Greg. Oh, but sorry, I forgot that you thought that I was.

Greg: Honey, I—

Rosie: Don't honey me. Did you see the bloody letter or not? You were home on the Monday just after Alex left.

Greg: No, I honestly didn't see it.

Rosie: Well, there's a reason not to believe you, Mr Honesty.

Greg: Look, Rosie, we can't move on if you don't forgive and learn to trust me again.

Rosie: Oh, go shove your forgiveness up your ass. I don't have time for another one of these conversations with you. This is very simple. I've got Alex online waiting for me. He left a letter for me. He wants to know if any of us found it. So I'm asking you one more time, Greg, did you see the letter or not?

Greg: No, I promise you that I didn't.

From   Bill Lake
To   Rosie Dunne
Subject Personal emails

I hope they're business emails you've been sending for the last half-hour, Rosie. We've got a group of eighty arriving in the next few minutes for the weekend business conference in the De Valera Suite. Lots to do, Rosie.

From   Rosie
To   Alex
Subject Your letter

Alex, Greg didn't see the letter. Maybe you can just write
me another one or ring me later when I'm at home and
not when Big Brother is watching me on this stupid bloody
security camera pointed right at me. Now both of you men
leave me alone before I get fired.

From   Greg
To   Alex
Subject Your letter?

I was told you were online so I hope I caught you in
time. I happened to have stumbled across something I
believe you're looking for. I would appreciate it if you
would stop sending my wife love letters. You seem to
have forgotten that she's a married woman. Married to
me, Alex.

Rosie and I have had our troubles like all marriages do,
but we are willing to put all that behind us now and give
it another chance. You need to understand that none of
your letters is going to change that. You said it yourself:
you had your chance but now the moment has passed you
by.

Let's be realistic here for a minute, Alex. You and Rosie
are both thirty. You've known each other since you were
five. Don't you think that in all that time, that if
something was supposed to happen between you two, if it
was so *meant to be*, that it would have happened by now?
Think about it. She is not interested.

I want no further contact with you again. If you set foot
in my house I will be only too glad to show you how
unwelcome you are. To save you the embarrassment, I

157

won't speak of the contents of your letter again. And you're wrong, by the way. I do fully appreciate the fact that Rosie is my wife. She is a wonderful woman, loving, warm and caring, and I am so glad she is the woman that chose to spend the rest of her life with *me*. So you can keep on watching her back walk from you at the altar because she won't be turning round.

From   Alex
To   Greg
Subject   Rosie

Do you think your ridiculous attempt to scare me off is going to work? You are a pathetic sad little man. Rosie has a mind of her own and she doesn't need you making those decisions for her.

From   Greg
To   Alex
Subject   Re: Rosie

So what are you going to do if she says yes, Alex? What are you going to do? Move to Dublin? Leave Josh behind? Expect Rosie to uproot Katie, leave the job she loves and move to Boston? *Think*, Alex.

You have received an instant message from: ALEX.
Alex: She didn't get the letter, Phil.
Phil: Oh, bloody hell, Alex. I told you not to put it in one of those damn letters. You should have just told her. I don't know why you can't just use your mouth like the rest of us.
Alex: Greg found the letter.
Phil: The idiot husband? I thought they were finished?

158

Alex: Evidently not. But it doesn't change anything, Phil. I still love her.

Phil: Yeah, but she's *still* married, isn't she? You're not going to like what I say, and this is just my opinion, Alex, and hell knows you never take any advice anyway, but I wouldn't touch another man's wife. That's just me.

Alex: But he's an asshole, Phil!

Phil: And so are you but you're my brother and I love you.

Alex: I'm serious. The guy cheated on her. He's all wrong for her.

Phil: Yeah, but the difference between now and before is that *now* Rosie knows he cheated on her. She *knows* he's an asshole. But she's still with him. She must really love him, Alex. I'd say back off. Just my opinion but I'd say back off.

Alex: I don't agree with that, Phil.

Phil: Fine! You're your own man; do as you wish. I know you want the best for Rosie but you're being a bit selfish here. Look at it from Rosie's perspective. She's just found out that her asshole husband cheated on her, it must have been hard and for whatever reason she has decided to work it out and stay with him. Then just as she's getting used to that idea, in waltzes you, the best friend in shining armour, proclaiming your love for her. Do you want to confuse the poor woman even more? Look, if the marriage is a disaster, then it's a disaster and in a few months it'll end and Rosie will come to you. Just don't be the prick that tries to break up her marriage. She'll never forgive you for that.

Alex: So you think I should let it happen naturally? Let her come to me when she's ready?

Phil: Something like that. I'm thinking of starting one of those shows that they have on telly. You know, one of those advice ones?

Alex: You'd have me on it every week, Phil. Thanks.

Phil: No probs. Now, while you go give someone a new heart, I'll go give a car a new engine. Off with you. Do what you have to do.
Alex has logged off.

Chapter 21

From   Rosie
To   Alex
Subject Letter?

Alex, I searched high and low in the kitchen for your letter, I left no stone unturned and Greg and Katie swear they didn't lay a finger on it so I don't know where else it could be. Are you sure you left it there? We were in such a rush to get you to the airport that morning, maybe you forgot. I checked the spare room you were sleeping in. All I found was a T-shirt you left behind, but it's mine now so you're not getting it back!

So what was in the letter? You didn't call me when I got home from work yesterday. You're really keeping me in suspense, Alex!

From   Alex
To   Rosie
Subject Letter

How are things with you and Greg? Are you happy?

From   Rosie
To   Alex
Subject Greg

Wow, talk about a change of subject. That's a very direct question.

OK, I know you can sense that he and I are going through a bad phase and you're worried. And I also know that you absolutely can't stand him, which is really difficult for me because I would really *love* you to see him how I see him.

Deep down, underneath *all* his layers of stupidity, he's a really good man. He may act out far too many selfish thoughts, says all the wrong things at all the wrong times but behind closed doors he's a best friend. I *understand* that he has idiotic tendencies and I can still love him for it. He may not be someone that you feel comfortable sitting next to at a dinner party, but for me, he's someone that I feel comfortable sharing my life with.

I know it's hard for other people to understand what he's like. All you see is an overprotective paranoid mess, but, God, does that make me feel safe and wanted. And his stupidity makes me laugh! We have a long way to go to being the perfect couple. We certainly don't live the fairy-tale marriage, he doesn't shower me with rose petals and fly me to Paris on weekends, but when I get my hair cut, he notices. When I dress up to go out at night, he compliments me. When I cry, he wipes my tears. When I feel lonely, he makes me feel loved. And who needs Paris, when you can get a hug?

Somewhere along the way, without me even noticing, I grew up, Alex. For once, I couldn't take advice from anyone around me about what I should or shouldn't do. I couldn't go running to Mum and Dad and I can't compare my marriage to anybody else's. We all follow our own

162

rules. Taking Greg back was my decision to make and I wouldn't have if I hadn't felt that Greg, and most importantly that I, had learned something. I *know* that what has happened will never happen again and I really, really believe it. Because if I didn't feel so sure about our future, there's no way that I could go through with this.

I have a feeling that's what was in your letter, Alex, but don't worry about me. I'm fine. Thank you, thank you, thank you, for caring about me so much. There aren't enough friends like you in the world.

From   Alex
To   Rosie
Subject Greg

And that's all I've ever wanted. For you to be happy.

Dear Stephanie,

So how's the new mummy? I hope you're coping well with everything. I know it's a big change – but a wonderful one. Are you getting any sleep? I hope you are. I always knew you would be a fabulous mother: you always knew just how to take care of your baby sister (and her baby!).

Thanks for all the gory details about his birth, by the way. You're even more wonderful than I thought you were! And no, I don't want Pierre to send over his video tape of the 'magical' experience. I recall what happens only too well . . . Remember they used to show us those videos at school when we were kids to scare us all out of having sex? Well, neither of us was obviously *that* scared. If they really wanted to deter us they should have just shown us the nappy-changing procedure. That would have sent us running off in our thousands to the convent.

You all looked so happy together in the photograph – like the perfect family. Is there such a thing any more, because if there is, my little unit was definitely not in the queue when the title was handed out.

I'm really not sure if I have done the right thing by taking Greg back. It's so difficult to know what decision to make. Christ, Stephanie, I was always the first person to shout out that if my husband was unfaithful there would be no way I would ever take him back in a million years. I always said that was the one thing I could never forgive (well, that *and* abandoning your unborn child) so what am I doing, taking him back?

What am I doing, allowing him to sleep beside me in bed? Why am I cooking him dinner and calling him when it's on the table? This is not what I said I would do. I need all my strength to stop myself from reaching out and slapping him across the face every time he smiles at me.

I thought that sending him packing would be the easiest thing in the world to do, but part of the reason for taking him back was because I couldn't face coping all by myself once more. I just kept imagining me and Katie alone again and I couldn't take it. Now I'm beginning to question my decision. Should I stay with him and learn to love him again, or should I leave and learn to survive on my own, to be independent? I just don't think I can face another tiny flat and one crappy wage for myself and Katie to survive on.

But if I could just *forgive* him . . . if I could just erase the image of his lips kissing someone else's every time he talks to me . . . His touch makes my skin crawl, and I feel so much hate for him it's unnerving. It's hard for my wounds to be healed by the very same man who put them there.

And he's so bloody gung-ho about everything. He's Mr Enthusiastic about us going to see a counsellor together, and he takes a few hours out of his day to talk to me, *really* talk to me. It's all just such a textbook solution of 'how to please your wife after shagging another woman'. Firstly you make an appointment to see the counsellor, being sure to make a song and a dance about the fact you're cancelling important meetings to go, then cook the dinner every day and fill the dishwasher, ask your wife a million times a day if she is OK and if there's anything you can do for her, do the weekly shopping, remembering to include thoughtful little gifts like her favourite chocolate cake or a book that you think she might like, spend a few hours during the day to sit in silence with your wife doing a summary of your day and then discussing in detail how you feel your relationship is going. Do this five hundred times a day, add water and then stir.

And the thing is, the Greg I married would never do all of those things. He would never bother replacing the empty toilet roll with the new one; he would never wash all the food off his plate before putting it in the dishwasher. Everything has changed. Even the small daily routines that make life so comfortable have changed.

If I could find the strength in me to leave him I would, but I'm stuck in this noncommittal limbo. I just want to make the right decision *now*. I don't want to be a bitter old woman in forty years' time, still making snide comments to Greg about what he's done. In order to make this marriage work I need to know in advance that I can, if not forget, then at least forgive. I need to know that the little bit of love I feel for him will grow again, back to the way it was. The one thing that's making me so much stronger is the fact that I know that he won't do this to me again. We've had too many long nights of tears and fights for either of us to want to go through it again.

If Alex lived in this country I would know what to do. All I need is back-up. He's the little angel that sits on my shoulder whispering in my ear, 'You can do it!' It's funny. I'm thirty years old now and I still feel like a little girl. I'm still looking around to check and see what other people are doing to make sure I'm not completely different; I'm still looking around for help, hoping for a quick nudge and a whisper of advice. But

I can't seem to be able to catch anybody's eye. Nobody else around me seems to be looking around and wondering what to do. Why is it that I feel like I'm the only person who is confused and concerned about the choices I've made and where I'm headed? Everywhere I look, I see people just getting on with it. Maybe I should just follow suit.

Love,

Rosie

Dear Rosie,

Please do not torture yourself with questions that you don't know the answer to. You are going through a really difficult time right now but you *are* getting on with it, and you do it time and time again. Every knock back makes you stronger.

I can't tell you whether to stay with Greg or not – only you can make that decision – but all I can say is that if there's any love there at all then you should work at it. Every small thing grows when you nurture it, Rosie. Love is just the same. But if that is making you miserable then leave and find something else that brings you the happiness you *deserve* to feel.

Just listen to what your heart is saying and go with your gut instinct and it will lead you the right way. I'm sorry I have no great words of wisdom for you, Rosie, but at least you know that you're *not* alone; other people don't have all the answers to the questions. Sometimes we're all just as confused as you are.

Take care.

Love,

Stephanie

From   Rosie
To   Stephanie
Subject Silent heart

My heart isn't saying anything and my gut instinct is telling me to go to bed, curl up in a ball and cry.

Note to self:
   Do not under any circumstances fall in love again.
   Do not under any circumstances trust another human being.
   Purchase special Kleenex with a protective balm containing calendula as will then not be mistaken for Rudolph's mother.
   Eat.
   Get out of bed.
   And, for God's sake, stop crying.

From   Mum
To   Stephanie
Subject Is this working?

I think I've just about figured out this email thingy. Anyway, I just wanted to see if our plans are still in place for your father's sixtieth. He thinks it's a few quiet drinks with Jack and Pauline, so don't email me back on this address because he can read it too. Call me on my mobile. I really would love you to come. It would be nice for us all to be together again and I think it would be good for Rosie. I'm worried about her, she's so upset about Greg that she's lost so much weight. Your father is only two steps away from punching Greg in the face, which won't do anyone any good. Especially not your father's heart. Kevin isn't talking to Greg either, which isn't making life any easier for poor Rosie. However, the more family around her, the better.

Chapter 22

Ruby: OK, whatever diet you're on, I want my Gary to go on it.

Rosie: I'm not on a diet, Ruby.

Ruby: But you look sick and unhealthy; that's exactly the way I want him to look. Unattractive, stick thin, exhausted . . .

Rosie: Thanks.

Ruby: I just want to help, Rosie. Please tell me what's going on.

Rosie: There's nothing you can do to help; Greg and I just have to work this out on our own. Well, me, Greg and Ursula the wonderful marriage counsellor. We've all become such a great team it really makes me weep.

Ruby: How nice for you all. How is the wonderfully helpful Ursula?

Rosie: Wonderfully helpful. Yesterday she told me I had problems discussing my feelings.

Ruby: And?

Rosie: And I told her that made me feel angry and that she could go fuck herself.

Ruby: Well expressed. What did Greg say about that?

Rosie: Oh, wait for this; it's prize-winning. My amazingly

intuitive husband thinks that I 'have problems communicating with and understanding Ursula'.

Ruby: Oh dear.

Rosie: Oh dear is right, so I suggested that Ursula and I attend relationship counselling in order to have good communication skills during my marriage counselling.

Ruby: So what did Greg say to that?

Rosie: Well, I couldn't quite hear what he said over the slamming of the car door. It can't have been very positive, though. His nose was flared and he was snarling at me. I'm also thinking of purchasing a larger bed so that there's room for Ursula. She may as well know absolutely everything about us. Maybe she could count how many times I fart during the night or something . . .

Ruby: Is it really that bad?

Rosie: I just can't see how counselling is helping *anything*. Ursula only makes us fight more by forcing us to discuss all the little things that bother us about each other. If we ever start to get along with one another, I can almost *see* her getting worried about her next month's rent. Last week we argued *for an hour* about how much I hate it when Greg leaves a milk moustache on his face purposely just to make me laugh, then when I don't laugh he follows me around the house, tapping me on the shoulder with it still on, until I do.

Yesterday we fought about how it annoys me when his mouth starts to twitch when I get something wrong. If I said the sky was yellow, his top lip would start to do this odd sort of Elvis twitch. It bugs the hell out of me that he can't just *let it go*. He *needs* to let me know in some form or another that I've gotten a piece of 'vital' information wrong. *Oh no*, the grass is green not pink! Oops-a-daisy, what a difference *that* statement makes to our life!

Next week I think I'll bring up the fact that he always wears the silly novelty socks his dear mother buys him.

169

He thinks they're hilarious. Sometimes he just calls her up to tell her he's wearing them. Yellow socks with bloody pink polka dots and blue ones with red stripes. I'm sure his colleagues at the bank think they're absolutely *hilarious*. The wonderfully cool and hip bank manager that wears pink socks, ooh let's all get a mortgage from him! Plus when he sits down, his trousers lift and you can see them from a mile away . . .

Ruby: Wow, and they say you have problems expressing yourself . . .

Rosie: My point is that they just love going into such irrelevant detail. It shouldn't matter whether Greg kisses me on the forehead or on the cheek every morning; the fact should be whether he kisses me at all.

Ruby: So is this bizarre counselling having *any* kind of a positive effect on your marriage?

Rosie: Not really. I think Greg and I would do better without her.

Ruby: Do you think you could both break up with her?

Rosie: Well, we should, otherwise I can't see us still being together by the time Greg turns forty . . .

For My Husband
  Happy 40th Birthday, sweetheart.
  Lots of love,
  Rosie

Happy 40th!
  You are now uglier and older.
  To Greg
  From Katie and Toby

Dear Alex,
  I think I'm going to organise a search party. Have you fallen off the edge of the earth? Are you still alive?

I called your mother the other day and she hasn't heard from you very much either. Is everything OK? Because if it's not, I have a right to know. You're supposed to confide in me because I'm your best friend and . . . it's the law. And if things are OK then contact me anyway. I need gossip. It's section two of the same law.

Everything here is as crazy and unpredictable as usual. Katie is eleven now, as you know. Thank you for her present. She is so grown up that she tells me that she doesn't need to inform me where she is going during the day or when she'll be coming home. Unimportant information like that, which a mother apparently doesn't need to know. I thought I had another few years left until she became a monster; saw me as being in the way, interfering and deliberately setting out to ruin her life. (OK, so *occasionally* I do.) The child wears lipstick now, Alex. Pink, glossy, glittery lipstick. She wears glitter on her eyes, glitter on her cheeks, and glitter in her hair; I am raising a disco ball for a daughter. I am now under instructions to knock on her bedroom door three times before I'm allowed to enter, just so she can identify the intruder. (I'm quite jealous because Toby only has to knock once. Greg, on the other hand, has to knock thirteen times. Poor Greg. Sometimes, most of the time, he loses count and Katie refuses to let him in for safety reasons. I mean really, who else could it be at her door knocking thirteen times, or at least *trying* to knock thirteen times?! Although I have become very clever and only knock once sometimes; that way she thinks I'm Toby and lets me in to see the inner sanctum of Katie Dunne. You would expect it to have black walls, no light, scary posters on the wall, but it's surprisingly neat and tidy.)

I'm not sure if she is still writing to you, but if she fills you in on any interesting aspects of her terribly busy and secretive life, please let me know. I'm her mother and that is *definitely* the law.

Everything at work is going well. I'm still at the hotel and

171

I'm the longest-serving employee they have there now. Funny, isn't it? But – and there's always a 'but' with me – I know I've always been obsessed by the inner workings of hotels, but I kind of feel, 'Is this it? Is this all there is to it?' Doing what I'm doing is fine and all, but I'd like to try to move up a bit. I won't rest until I'm managing the Hilton hotels.

Greg says I'm mad. He says I would be crazy to move on from a job with good pay, a good boss and good hours. He thinks I have it easy here and I should be satisfied with that. I suppose he's right.

How is Josh? I would love to see him again. We must make arrangements to meet up soon. I don't want him not knowing who I am. We always promised our kids would be best friends, remember? I don't want to be one of those strangers to him that visit and, once in a blue moon, squeeze money into his hands. Although I very much liked that kind of people myself, I would personally rather mean more to Josh.

OK, so I think that's all my very exciting news for you for now. Write to me, ring me, email me or fly over and visit me. Or you could do all of those things. Just do anything to let me know that you're still walking the earth.

Miss you.

Love,

Rosie

Dear Rosie,

Just to let you know I'm still alive – just about. Sally seems to be sucking all the life out of me these days. We're finalising the divorce . . . it's a nightmare.

So that's what's going on with me. Must go now; have to stick my hands in someone's chest.

Give my love to Katie.

Alex

From   Rosie
To   Stephanie
Subject   Re: Gossip!

Thanks for your letter, Steph. I am absolutely fine, thank you. Everyone is well and healthy; we have no complaints. I feel I've made the right decision about Greg, and from just listening to Alex about the divorce procedure I'm glad Greg and I didn't take that route. At least Sally and Josh haven't moved far from Alex so he can make arrangements to see Josh quite regularly.

My worst nightmare would be to lose Katie. I don't know what I would do. She may watch MTV all day, blare music from her room, ruin my days off by making me go into school to fight with Miss Big Nose Smelly Breath Casey, leave glitter all over the couches and carpets, worry me to death when she's one minute late for her nine o'clock curfew, but she's the most important thing to me in my life. She comes first all of the time. I'm so glad Alex missed the debs and I'm so glad that Brian the Whine was such a boring person. The men in my life may have let me down but the little girl in my life makes up for it every single day.

Dear Ms Rosie Dunne,

I was hoping you would be free on Monday the 16th at 9 a.m. to meet with me at the school. Toby Flynn's parents will also be in attendance. It is regarding the recent results of the summer maths exam. It appears that Katie and Toby have the same answers for all the questions. What jumped out at me was the fact that the majority of these answers are wrong. I have discussed this with Katie and Toby and they insist it is coincidental.

Cheating, as you well know, is considered to be a very

serious offence at St Patrick's Primary School. I seem to have a case of déjà vu, Rosie . . . Please ring to confirm your attendance.

Miss Casey

Chapter 23

From   Rosie
To   Alex
Subject Grown-ups

What are the two of us like? I was going to say who knew we'd be going through so much 'grown-up stuff', but I don't consider you going through a divorce and me trying to pick up the pieces of my marriage is necessarily grown up. I think we both had it pretty much sussed when we were playing cops and robbers in the back garden. It's all been down hill from there!

The weather has been beautiful over here for the past few weeks. I love June in Dublin. The grey buildings seem less grey, the unhappy faces seem brighter. It is so hot here at work, though. The entire front of the hotel building is built from glass and it feels like we're working in a greenhouse on days like today. It's such a contrast to our winter months when the sound of the fat raindrops hitting off the glass echoes around the quiet foyer. It's a pretty sound but sometimes the hailstones are so loud and forceful, threatening to smash through the glass. Right now I'm staring up at a rich blue sky dotted with white candy-floss grazing sheep. It is beautiful.

Convertible sports cars have their tops down and music is blaring, businessmen have been casually strolling down the street past the hotel, with their jackets slung over their shoulders and their shirtsleeves rolled up, reluctant to get back to the office. The college students have all seemingly decided to call off their plans to attend lectures to flake out in large circles in the park. The ducks are gathering by the edge of the pond, glad they won't have to search for their own food today. Mounds of soggy uneaten bread float on the surface of the water, waiting to be pecked at.

A flirting couple chase each other around the large fountain, catching its cool spray on their bare arms and legs in order to cool themselves. Couples in love stretch out together on the grass and gaze longingly into each other's eyes. Children use the playground while their parents relax in the sun, keeping one eye shut and one eye lazily focused on their excited offspring, who squeal with delight.

Shop owners stand at the entrance doors to their empty shops, watching the world go by. Office workers gaze dreamily out of the windows from high up in their clammy, stuffy offices, enviously watching the city throb with excitement.

The sound of laughter is in the air, everyone is full of smiles, there's a bounce in their step. The veranda of the hotel is busy with people taking drinks out in the sun: Long Island iced tea, gin and tonic, tangy orange with crushed ice, lime-green concoctions, fruity cocktails and bowls of ice cream. Clothes are being discarded and hung on the backs of chairs.

Cleaning ladies hum softly to themselves and smile while polishing the brass, feeling the sun's rays streaming down on to their faces. Days like this don't come often and you can tell everyone wishes they did.

And I sit here and think of you. I send you my love.

From   Alex
To   Rosie
Subject Happy!

You sounded happy and very poetic! I've just returned from a weekend with Josh. He's a feisty little thing now, Rosie. He's running around trying to grab anything and everything from left, right and centre. I was almost afraid to blink in case the room came crashing down around me. But he's in great form and I feel so happy and rejuvenated after the weekend. Seeing him always lights me up, as if a switch is flicked somewhere in my body. I could watch him for ever. Watch how he learns, how he teaches himself, how he eventually finds a way to do things without help from anyone. Josh takes chances; he's braver than I am. He always takes that extra step when he nos he shouldn't. He does it anyway and he learns. I think we adults have a lot to learn from that. Perhaps to be not so afraid and over-sensible about reaching for goals.

So I am taking Josh's advice. An eminent surgeon is giving a talk during the week. It's a few days of seminars about a new heart procedure he has developed. I'm going to try and meet him – me along with the other thousand or so wannabe heart surgeons who will be there. Rumour has it he's from Ireland and has moved over here to develop his studies further – and needs some help.

Cross your fingers and pray for a miracle.

From   Rosie
To   Alex
Subject   Mysterious meeting

I have a mysterious meeting with Bill, my boss, next week. I have no idea what it's about, but I'm quite nervous about it. He flew over yesterday in a not-so-good mood and has had a series of secret meetings all day. Lots of suspicious-looking people, dressed in dark suits, have been arriving to talk to him on the hour every hour. I have an awful feeling in the pit of my stomach.

What makes it even worse is the fact that his brother, Bob, is flying over tomorrow morning. They only ever get together to do the hiring and firing. I think that's all Bob does, really. Bill does all the work on their hotels around the world and Bob just spends his share of the money on houses, cars, holidays and women, so I hear. Why is it that people always put women in the same category as cars and holidays, as though we're prizes on a game show? If I had millions you'd hardly hear people saying, 'Jesus, would ya look at that Rosie Dunne. All she does is spend her money on shoes, clothes and men.' Doesn't sound quite right, does it?

I hope they don't fire me. I don't know what I would do. I think I would sleep with him to keep working here. That's how much I love it. Or how scared I am about having to search for a job elsewhere. Or how desperate I am to sleep with a man other than Greg for a change. I love him but, bless him, he's a sucker for routine.

Better go and look like I'm really busy so that they will have absolutely no grounds to fire me. Cross your fingers for me, and I'll cross mine for you.

From   Alex
To   Rosie
Subject Re: Mysterious meeting

Don't worry, it will all be fine! They have no reason to fire you! (Have they?) You have done nothing wrong since the day you started working there. In fact, you've hardly even called in sick! Everything will be fine. Just about to leave the apartment now to go to seminar. Good luck to the both of us!

From   Rosie
To   Alex
Subject Re: Re: Mysterious meeting.

You're right. They can't fire me. I'm just being stupid. I am a great employee. They have no reason to. At least no reasons that they know of. I mean, they could never find out about the time I brought Ruby up to show her the penthouse suite. And even if they do know that, there's no way that they could know that we ordered room service and stayed the night. Could they?

Maybe it was the missing bathrobes that they noticed. But they were so cosy and I had to take one home . . .

Or maybe it was the empty mini bar. But I distinctly remember asking Peter to restock the fridge and he owed me one after I gave his parents a Valentine's Day discount in the middle of May. So it can't be that . . . Oh God, this is killing me. I really don't want to go back to working for Randy Andy, and I don't think I have the energy for sending CVs out again. Nor the stress of another job interview.

They only want to meet with me. But Bill didn't smile at me when he said it and his eyes weren't as twinkly as usual. What do you think that means? Oh my God, the

179

new skinny girl has a meeting too next week. She's the worst worker ever. She's called in sick more times than she's been in. Probably because she never eats. Lunch breaks are wasted on her. She just stares across the table at your plate with a horrible face on her, as though food is the devil, and she sips on a bottle of water. Then halfway through her bottle she gets full, tightens the lid and leaves it behind.

I'd better start job-hunting, I think.

From   Alex
To   Rosie
Subject Chill out!

For Christ sake, Rosie Dunne, I love you with all my heart but you need to chill out!

You have an instant message from: RUBY.
Ruby: Oooh, so he loves you with all his heart, does he?
Rosie: Oh, stop reading my emails, Ruby.
Ruby: Well, get a less obvious password, 'Buttercup'. You two are being all flirty with each other lately.
Rosie: No we aren't! How on earth are we being flirty??!
Ruby: You know yourself.
Rosie: Oh please, I thought you were going to make a good point for once in your life.
Ruby: I have one and you know it.
Rosie: We're just getting along like we used to do, that's all. Alex has perked himself up. I think he's happy again.
Ruby: Because he's in lurve . . .
Rosie: He is not in love. Well, not with me, anyway.
Ruby: Oh, sorry, I was just misguided by the fact that he said in his email that he 'loved you with all his heart'.
Rosie: As a friend loves a friend, Ruby.

Ruby: You're my friend and I do not love you with all my heart. Hell, I hardly love Teddy with all my heart.

Rosie: OK then, Alex and I are madly in love and we're going to run away and have a passionate love affair.

Ruby: You see? It doesn't hurt to admit it, does it?

Rosie: Hold on, Ruby.

[Rosie is away from her computer.]

Rosie: Oh my God, celery stick just got back from meeting with Bill and Bob and she's crying her eyes out. They just fired her. I'm next. Shit. I better go. Shit. Shit. Shit.

Rosie has logged off.

Chapter 24

Kevin,

Hi, son. I know I'm not one to write letters, but I'm not sure if you gave your mother and me the correct phone number of the staff barracks. Whenever I call it just keeps on ringing and ringing and that's at all hours of the day and night. You either gave us the wrong number, there's something wrong with your phone, or everybody is working so hard they're not there to answer my calls. I wouldn't like the idea of having to share a phone with thirty staff members. Couldn't you get one of those mobile phones? Then maybe your family could get in touch with you every once in a while.

I hope you're not doing anything daft down there. Rosie really stuck her neck out to get you that job in the kitchen. Don't mess it up like all those other ones you had. This is an opportunity for you now to get a good start in your life. Your old man is sixty now; I won't be around for ever for you to rely on, you know!

It's a shame you couldn't make it home for my retirement party. The company invited the entire family. They really treated us well for the night – treated me well for over thirty-five years, in fact. Stephanie, Pierre and Jean-Louis made it over from France. Rosie, Greg and young Katie were there too. It was a good night. I'm not picking on you, son – just wished you had been there too, that's all. It was an emotional night all the same. If you had been there you would have seen your old man cry.

It's funny how life goes. I spent forty years working for them, remember my first day like it was yesterday. I was just fresh out of school, all eager to please. Wanted to start making money so that I could propose to your mother and buy us a house. In my first week of work we held a party in the office for one of the old guys retiring. I didn't give much notice to him. People were making speeches, giving him gifts, talking about old times. But all I cared about was the fact that they were making me stay late at work, unpaid, when I wanted to get out of there to propose to your mother. The old guy had been there all his working life, he had tears in his eyes, was really upset about leaving, took him a lifetime to make the speech. I thought he would never shut up so I could leave. I had the engagement ring in my pocket. Kept sticking my hand in my trousers to make sure the velvet box was still there. I couldn't wait for that guy to finish talking.

Billy Rogers was his name.

He wanted to take me aside and explain a few things to me about the company before he left, seeing as I was a new boy. I didn't listen to a word he had to say. He talked and talked like he never had any intentions of leaving the damn office. I rushed him. The company wasn't that important to me then.

He kept on coming back to visit us in the office every week. Would hang around our desks, annoying all the new guys, some of the old guys too, giving advice and checking up on things that were no longer his business. We just wanted to do our jobs. He lived and breathed for that place. We all told him to find himself a hobby. Keep himself busy. Thought we were helping him. Only suggested it out of the goodness of our hearts – that and the fact he was really starting to get up his pals' noses. He died a few weeks later. Had a heart attack on the golf course. He was taking our advice and having his first lesson.

I hadn't thought about Billy Rogers for almost thirty years. Had completely forgotten about him, to be honest. But that night and since I haven't been able to get the thought of Billy Rogers out of my head. Looking around with tears in my eyes, listening to speeches, accepting gifts, catching the new guys sneakily glimpse at their watches, wondering when they could slip away to get home to their girlfriends or new wives or children or whoever . . . I couldn't help but think about all the guys who came through those office doors. Thought about the guys who started off on the same day as me: Colin Quinn and Tom McGuire, guys who never made it to retirement like me. I suppose that's what life's about. People come and go.

So there are no more early mornings for me. I caught up on a whole load of sleep I never even thought I needed. The garden is spotless, everything in the house that was once broken is now fixed. I've played golf three times this week, visited Rosie twice, took Katie and Toby out for the day, and I still feel like hopping into my car, speeding down to the office and teaching the rookies a thing or two about how to do business. But they won't care; they want and need to learn it for themselves.

So I thought I would join the Dunne women in writing. It seems that's all they do. Keeps the phone bills down, I suppose. Let me know how things are going for you, son.

Did you hear about our Rosie's job?

From Dad

From   Kevin
To   Stephanie
Subject Dad

How are things? I just got a letter from Dad today. Dad
writing a letter is weird in itself but what he was writing
was even more bizarre. Is he OK? He was talking about
some guy called Billy Rogers who died over thirty-five
years ago. Make sure he's not losing it. Anyway, it was
good to hear from him but he sounded like another man
altogether. Not necessarily a bad thing. Sorry I wasn't there
for his retirement do. Should have made more of an effort
to be there.

    Tell Pierre and Jean-Louis I was asking for them. Tell
Pierre I'll beat his culinary skills hands down next time I
see him! Dad mentioned something about Rosie's job?
What has she done now?

From   Stephanie
To   Mum
Subject Kevin and Dad

Something must be in the water over there in Ireland
because I just received an email from your son, my little
brother Kevin – yes, Kevin, the guy who never keeps in
touch with family unless he needs to borrow money. He
was writing to tell me that Dad had written to him and he
was worried! Did you even know that Dad could lick a
stamp?

    Kevin mentioned that Dad was talking about Billy
Rogers again. He told me about him too. Is he OK? I'm
assuming he is just feeling very contemplative now that he
has entered a new era in his life. Now at least he has *time*
to think. The both of you have worked so hard all your
lives. Now Kevin your baby is gone, Rosie and Katie are

gone, I'm gone and the house is finally all yours. I suppose I can understand how it's difficult for Dad to get his head round it. You were both used to a house full of screaming kids and bickering teenagers. When we finally grew up along came a crying baby and you were so good to help Rosie out. I know it was hard for you financially too. Now it's time to treat yourselves.

Kevin mentioned something about Rosie's job; I don't want to call her until I've heard from you about it. She was so worried that she was going to lose it. Let me know.

From   Mum
To   Stephanie
Subject Re: Kevin and Dad

You're absolutely right. I think your father has a lot of thinking to do and enough time in the day to do it now. I love having him home! He's not rushing off all the time or thinking about a problem at work that needs to be solved while I'm trying to have a conversation with him. It's like he's all here with me now – body and mind. I felt that way too when I left my job but I suppose it was slightly different for me. I already went part time at work when Katie was born to help Rosie cope. It didn't seem like such a drastic change for me when I eventually left the job completely. But your father is trying to find himself again.

I'm amazed you didn't hear about Rosie's job. I thought you would have been one of the first people she'd have told (apart from Alex, of course), but perhaps she wasn't ready to discuss it yet. That girl has me so worried at times. Honestly, she kept telling me all week that she was going to lose her job, then finally she calls me to tell me that she had a meeting with her bosses and she's got a promotion!

Oh, Stephanie, we were so thrilled for her! I'm surprised

she hasn't told you the good news yet, but it was only a few days ago. Anyway, I'll let her tell you herself or else I'll be in trouble for spoiling the surprise. I'd better go now; your father's calling me. We're about to go down to the garden centre. If he plants any more flowers or trees in that garden, we'll have to apply for planning permission for a jungle!

Take care, love, and hugs and kisses to baby Jean-Louis from Grandma and Granddad!

Chapter 25

From   Stephanie
To   Rosie
Subject   Job promotion!

I know you're at work so I won't ring you. Received a letter from Mum today. What's this I hear about a job promotion? Email me ASAP!

From   Rosie
To   Stephanie
Subject   Job promotion

Can't believe Mum opened her big mouth! YES!! The news is true and I'm so excited to get started. The job title is 'Hotel Host', and before you get overexcited like our beloved parents did, it's not the manager's job. I will be the primary source of information for guests to ensure maximum client satisfaction (or so they tell me . . .)!

It was the surprise of *all* surprises. I literally had to *drag* my body into the long conference room where I had my first interview years ago, with my heart banging and my legs feeling like jelly. My body language was all wrong, my palms were sweaty, my knees were knocking and I just kept having visions of being forced to go back to work for Randy Andy until we both became old-age pensioners. I really had convinced myself that Bill and Bob Lake were going to ask me to quietly and calmly return to my desk, gather my belongings, leave the premises and never return.

But they were so generous to me. They pumped me full of confidence as they went through what the job would entail. They said that they were delighted with my 'performance' within the hotel over the past few years (and I really hope they weren't referring to the time when I lay across the piano and sang Barbra Streisand songs after all the residents had gone to bed. Well, you can't blame a girl for trying to live out a fantasy when she can . . .). There they were, telling me I had an abundance of charm and confidence, when deep down I was just waiting for the moment they would break into a smile, look at me as though I was a fool for believing them before telling me the promotion was all a joke. I kept looking round for the hidden camera.

But it seems that I will be moving to a new hotel that's yet to be built (hence all the secret meetings with men and women in dark suits, leather briefcases, gelled hair and no smiles, who have been masquerading through the hotel lobby; it was like there was some sort of bizarre *Matrix*-y thing going on). But if they *are* serious, then my job is to be solely responsible for the running of all aspects of the resort and I'll have to liaise with head office and provide weekly reports. I've never had to 'liaise' before. It sounds sexy and dangerous. Any job that tells me that I have to 'liaise' with the big boys in head office is a winner to me. I can picture myself all dolled up in a cocktail dress at a work 'do' standing in a circle with the other 'suits', speaking in hushed tones about graphs and pie charts and financial reports. If people ask us what we're doing, I can say dismissively, 'Oh, don't mind us, we're just liaising . . .'

189

Apparently I have a flair for organising and have good communication skills. Anyone who has seen me rushing to get all my Christmas shopping done in the last hour on Christmas Eve knows the truth. But we all have our different ways of seeing things.

From   Alex
To   Rosie
Subject Congratulations!

I am so proud of you! If I was there, I would twirl you around and give you a great big sloppy kiss! You see, Rosie, things *can* happen for you, all you need is a lot more faith and self-belief and to stop being so negative all the time!

So where is the new hotel? Tell me all.

From   Rosie
To   Alex
Subject Job promotion

Well, I'm not quite sure of the location of the hotel just yet but I have a sneaky suspicion it's along the coast. Can you believe that I will finally get to work in a hotel by the sea? It will take longer to commute to, but it's worth it to be able to leave the city behind for a few hours every day. I should be out there within the next few months. The resort they are referring to is based around the new eighteen-hole golf course they're building. There will be a gym and pool and more leisure facilities, unlike here, which is in the heart of the city and has nothing but bedrooms, a tiny gym and restaurants. I'm a bit hazy on all the details because they haven't fully informed me of everything yet. They just asked me if I was interested in this new job and of course I couldn't turn it down!

But this entire experience has taught me something. It's taught me that I'm ready to move on from this job. I'm ready to accept a new challenge and, without having any sort of game plan at all, I seem to be moving closer and closer towards my dream. Whoever thought those childhood dreams of running a hotel weren't quite beyond my grasp after all? It's funny because when you're a child, you believe you can be anything you want to be, go wherever you want to go. There are no limits. You *expect* the unexpected, you *believe* in magic. Then you grow older and that innocence is shattered. The reality of *life* gets in the way and you're hit by the realisation that you can't be *all* you wanted to be, that you just might have to settle for a little bit less.

Why do we stop believing in ourselves? Why do we let facts and figures and anything but dreams rule our lives?

But now my mind is changed again. Nothing is impossible, Alex. It was there all the time. I just wasn't reaching out far enough, that's all.

Nothing is impossible. Not a bad statement to come from the pen (or rather keyboard!) of a cynic. Thank you for your faith in me, Alex. I would love to return that hug and kiss to you now! But then again, perhaps *some* things just might be beyond our reach after all.

From   Alex
To   Rosie
Subject Dreams

Again, Rosie, you're just not stretching far enough. I'm right here. Always have been, always will be.

Note to self:
  Dream, dream, dream, Rosie Dunne!

You have an instant message from: RUBY.

Ruby: What on earth is Alex's last message to you supposed to mean?

Rosie: For God's sake, Ruby, *stop* reading my emails!

Ruby: Sorry, I can't help it, but I can assure you that I will continue to read them until you decide to change your password *and* until I find a job that interests me at all.

Rosie: Well, it looks like I'll be changing my password then . . .

Ruby: Ha ha. So come on, I've seen it now, what's he talking about? What's this about stretching far enough?

Rosie: What do you think it means?

Ruby: I'm asking you and I asked first.

Rosie: Oh, Ruby, don't be so childish. It's simply a friend telling me that he will always be there for me, no matter what, and that he's not that far away at all from me and all I have to do is call and he'll be here.

Ruby: Oh, right, OK.

Rosie: There you go again, Ruby, with the sarcasm! What's your theory now then? I suppose you think it's his secret way of telling me that he loves me and that he will always be there for me and if I just reached out to him then he would drop everything, his new life in Boston, his family life, his great big amazing job, to come rescue me, whisk me away to live in a beach house in . . . oh, I don't know . . . Hawaii, where we would live happily ever after away from all the stresses and complications of the world? I suppose that's what you would interpret it as. You and your sick mind always twisting things, trying to make out as though the two of us—

Ruby: No, Rosie, I really meant 'oh, OK'. That's fine, I believe you.

Rosie: Oh.

Ruby: Are you OK with that?

Rosie: Yeah, sure. I just thought you might have read into it a bit more, like you usually do, that's all.

Ruby: No, that's OK. I believe that he meant it in a supportive friend kind of way.

Rosie: Oh . . . OK.

Ruby: Why, did you *want* it to mean something else?

Rosie: *God no*, I was just expecting you to go on a rant, that's all . . .

Ruby: So you're not disappointed? You're OK with him being your friend?

Rosie: No, why should I be disappointed? That's all he ever was to me! I'm perfectly happy!

Ruby: And you don't want to be rescued and whisked off to Hawaii?

Rosie: Of *course* not! That would be . . . *awful*!

Ruby: Good then . . .

Rosie: Yep, it's great . . . everything's great . . .

Ruby: Good.

Rosie: And the new job will make everything better!

Ruby: Good.

Rosie: And my marriage has been saved and I truly believe Greg loves me more than ever . . .

Ruby: Good.

Rosie: And I'm going to be paid a lot more than before, which is good. They say money can't buy happiness but I'm a fickle person, Ruby . . . I can get that new coat I saw in the Ilac Centre yesterday . . . I'm thrilled!

Ruby: Good.

Rosie: Absolutely! So anyway, I'm going to head off now, got a bit of work to do . . .

Ruby: That's really great, Rosie . . .

Rosie has logged off.

From   Rosie
To   Stephanie
Subject   It's a wonderful life!

Life is wonderful, life is great! I have a good job, just got promoted to an even better one. I have a daughter who talks to me, a husband that doesn't. Only joking! Have a husband who loves me! I have a wonderfully supportive family – mum, dad, brother and sister. I've two brilliant best friends who would do anything for me and who I love with all my heart. I remember telling you years ago just before I started my new job at reception that phase two of my life was beginning. Well, this appears to be the beginning of phase three! Things are looking up for me and I am so happy! I am in a deliriously giddy mood today, high on the excitement of life, I suppose!

From   Ruby
To   Rosie
Subject   Cork?

What do you mean, the bloody hotel is being built down in Cork? And they only tell you now? Are you moving down to *Cork*? I thought you said it was along *the coast of Dublin*? Did they think that piece of information was *irrelevant* to you? For Christsake, Rosie, how are you going to drag your family down to *the other side of the country*?

Do you even want to move? Oh my God, I think I'm going to have a heart attack! Email me back ASAP!!!

From   Rosie
To   Ruby
Subject Re: Cork?

Oh, Ruby, right now I have a headache. I don't know what to do. I know that I want this job but there are two other people to think about. I'll have to have a chat with Katie and Greg about it tonight. Pray for me! Please God, if you're listening and not busy sprinkling gold dust on all the lucky people of the world, please do me this favour and brainwash my family into thinking of what I want for once. I thank you for your time and patience. You can continue gold-dust sprinkling now.

From   Ruby
To   Rosie
Subject God

Hello, Rosie, this is God. Sorry to bring you bad news but life doesn't work like that. You must be honest with your family and try to convince them yourself. Tell them of your lifelong dream to take the job that you have been offered and if they are unselfish people they will understand your desire to move to Cork. My popcorn's ready so I'd better leave. I'm already missing the first of this evening's entertainment. I'm watching your friend Ruby's life tonight. Good luck with the family.

Dear Mum & Greg,

    Don't worry about us, Mum. Me and Toby will be OK. We have run away because we don't want to be apart from each other. He is my best friend and I don't want to move to Cork.

    Love,

    Katie and Toby

From   Rosie
To   Ruby
Subject God

I couldn't help noticing that God logged on under your name yesterday. If you see him around please tell him that if he's looking for drama, he should tune into my family today.

Note to self:
  Stop dreaming, Rosie Dunne.

PART THREE

Chapter 26

Dear Alex,

I was so happy when I finally got round to shutting the door on this horrible day. 'It's only a job,' Greg said. Well, if a job is so unimportant then why is he so adamantly refusing to leave his own? It's not *only* a job, though. So they offered me a promotion, but with it they offered me confidence and a little bit of self-belief. To believe that my hard work was being rewarded and I was seen as competent and smart.

But this time I wasn't even given the choice to screw it up myself. That decision was made *for* me. Katie won't leave Toby and I'm not quite hating Greg enough to storm off to Cork in a huff on my own. Although, I'm pretty close to it. God, does that man make my blood boil! Everything is always so black and white to him.

In his opinion, he has a great job here that pays well and I have a good job that pays OK. Why on earth would he want to move to a city where his wife will have a brilliant job and earn great money? Oh, of course, I forgot, they don't have any banks in Cork so there's no way he could ever find a job or be transferred. People just save money under their beds in shoe boxes there.

Plus everything (well, a lot of things, like houses for one) is cheaper down there than it is here. Katie would be able to *begin* her first year of secondary school in a perfectly good school so it's not as if she's being taken out of school midway here. It could all be so perfect.

On the other hand, I can honestly say that her friendship with Toby is possibly the most important thing to her. He's a great supportive force in her life; he makes her happy and keeps the innocence in her eyes. Children need close friends to help them grow up, to discover things about themselves and about life. They also need close friends to keep them sane, and due to Katie's little disappearing act I now know that her being without Toby, at this stage of her life anyway, would lead to incredible insanity.

Do you realise that they had actually booked their flights to you over the internet with Greg's credit card? They were in the queue to check in at the airport when the gardaí found them! I can just picture them: a little girl with jet-black hair and vanilla skin with no luggage except for a cuddly teddy-bear bag on her back. Beside her, a little boy with messy blond curls, in charge of the tickets and passport details. A miniature honeymoon couple. Someday I will look back on this experience and laugh. After I get over the shock, horror, bitterness and resentment. Probably in my next lifetime.

So I can't accept the job of my dreams because my family won't move with me. Big deal. It's not as though I bend over backwards for them. It's not as though I arrange my life to revolve around them. It's not as though I come home from work tired and still have dinner on the table for them, it's not as though I perform wonderful supportive wifely chores when there's a million other things I could be doing. It's not as though I defend my daughter at school, constantly fighting with the teachers about how she is not Satan's daughter. It's not as though I tolerate Greg's mother for dinner every Sunday and listen to her whinge about how the food isn't cooked right, about my hair, about the way I dress, about the way I have chosen to raise Katie and then have to sit through hours of reruns of her favourite soaps. It's not as though I'm always the one to take a day off work when Katie is sick or drop whatever plans I've made to help people out.

Just as well I don't do any of those things.

But who cares? I get burned toast and milky tea one morning once a year on Mother's Day as thanks. And that should make up for it, shouldn't it? Greg always tells me I'm forever chasing rainbows. Maybe I should stop now.

Love,
Rosie

From   Alex
To   Rosie
Subject Rosie Dunne!

I hate to see you miss out on another opportunity. Isn't there anything you can do to convince whatshisname?

From   Rosie
To   Alex
Subject Family

Thanks, Alex, but no. I can't force my family to leave their home if they don't want to. They're important to me.

I have to respect Greg's wishes; I don't think I would be too happy about moving away from my job and friends if he had to move due to work. I can't live my life pretending it's just me in the world. But how much easier it would be! Anyway, it's just another missed opportunity.

So enough about me – how are all those lectures going? Find out who Mr Fantastic Surgeon is yet?

Thanks for your support, as always.

From   Katie
To   Toby
Subject   Grounded!

I can't believe we are grounded! *And* on our summer holidays! Our parents didn't have to go all psycho about it! It's not like we ended up going anywhere – we were less than an hour away from home. Hardly worth locking us in our houses for two weeks. I told you we should have taken a ferry over to France or something. In the films, the first places the gardaí always check are the airports. That was where we made our mistake. I've been looking into this and we should have gone to Bus Arás, and got a coach to Rosslare. Next time that's what we'll do.

What do you think Alex would have done when we arrived on his doorstep? Mum says he's not even home, that he's away at some meetings or something, but I think she's just lying to try to prove that our plan wouldn't have worked. I don't think he would have been mad. Alex is cool. But he probably would have called Mum and she would have sent ten million squad cars and rescue helicopters over to get us.

Poor Mum. I'm glad we're not moving away but I feel sorry for her. She was so excited about doing that job and now she's back stuck at that desk where she's been working for years. I feel kinda guilty. I no she would have made me go anyway if Greg had said yeah but I still feel bad for her. She's just wandering around the house looking real sad and she keeps on sighing as though she's real bored and doesn't no what to do next. Just like us on Sundays. She gets up from one couch and moves to another room to sit in another chair. Then she gets up again and moves room, and stares out the window for *ages*, sighs about three million times, moves to another room, in, out, in, out . . . she makes me dizzy just watching her. Sometimes I just follow her around, seeing as I'm not supposed to be allowed in the outside world and I've nothing better to do.

Yesterday I started following her again and she started to walk faster and faster, by the end of it I was chasing her round the house and it was so funny. She opened the front door and ran outside in her dressing gown, teasing me because I couldn't go outside (being grounded and all). But I ran out anyway and the two of us sprinted round the block in our night clothes, me in my blue pyjamas with the pink hearts and Mum in her yellow dressing gown! Everyone was staring at us but it was fun. We ran to Birdie's shop on the corner and Mum treated me to some strawberry ice cream, the highlight of my day. Birdie didn't look too impressed at the sight of us, especially seeing as Mum wasn't wearing anything under her dressing gown, but she flashed her legs at old Mr Fanning, who was there to buy his morning paper. He looked like he was gonna have a heart attack. So at least I got to go outside for a little while.

As soon as we got back inside she continued just walking around the house as if she was in a museum or something. Greg says she's got a feather up her arse. Mum said she'd love to shove a pole up his. He didn't say much for the rest of the day.

Toby, if we had made it to the top of that queue in the airport, do you think we would have gotten on the plane? I'm not sure if I could have left Mum, but I don't think she would believe that now if I told her. She would probably just think I was trying to get out of being grounded, *although* that's not a bad idea. OK, I gotta go!

Email me back before I die of boredom!

From   Alex
To   Rosie
Subject Family duties!

You and your 'duties' to your family. I just don't want you
to be the only person following the rules, that's all.
The lectures are going great. You will never believe who
the surgeon is! Your very favourite man – Reginald
Williams.

From   Rosie
To   Alex
Subject Reginald Williams!

Pass me a bucket while I puke. You mean Slutty Bethany's
father? Have they come back from the evil past to haunt
us??!!

From   Alex
To   Rosie
Subject Re: Reginald Williams

It's OK, Rosie, take deep breaths! He's not so bad. A very
intelligent man.

From   Rosie
To   Alex
Subject Re: Reginald Williams

What does he do now, hypnotism? Has he been tampering
with your brain? So that's why he's been all over the
papers here. I have refused to read them out of protest for
him and his family's existence. Oh my God – Reginald
Williams! So do you think you're in with a chance to be
one of the 'chosen few' to work with him, seeing as you

were an almost-son-in-law? There's nothing like a bit of nepotism to keep the world a just and equal place.

From   Alex
To   Rosie
Subject   Nepotism!

I think the chances of that happening are fairly slim. I think I sealed my own doom when I dumped his favourite and only daughter!

From   Rosie
To   Alex
Subject   Slutty Bethany

Oh, I don't know about sealing your doom. I think it may have been the *best* move you have ever made. Come to think of it, I haven't seen Slutty Bethany for about ten years! What is she up to, I wonder. Probably living in a mansion in the hills, counting diamonds and evilly laughing . . .

From   Rosie
To   Stephanie
Subject   Best friends stay with you for ever

Oh, wise and wonderful sister Stephanie, you were right! When I was seventeen you told me that girlfriends come and go but best friends stay with you for ever. I found myself saying today, 'I wonder what Slutty Bethany is doing these days . . .' The exact statement I never wanted Alex to have to say about me. I didn't believe you at the time but I sure do now!! Thanks, Steph. Best friends do stay with you for ever!

Chapter 27

You have an instant message from: RUBY.

Ruby: So you're still here, then?

Rosie: Oh, your words of support are like a breath of fresh air. Yes, I am still here.

Ruby: So you found your daughter, then?

Rosie: Yes, we have her trained to come running back after three whistles and a clap of the hands.

Ruby: Impressive . . .

Rosie: I reminded myself that Alex and I ran off together a few times when we were younger. The first time we ran away because Alex's parents refused to let him go to some theme park to visit Captain Tornado for the weekend. I now understand his parents' point of view because, well, the theme park was in Australia . . . in a cartoon. Anyway, we must only have been about five or six. We packed our school bags and ran away. We literally *ran* away. We thought that was what we were supposed to do, *run* down the road, which was extremely inconspicuous, of course.

We spent the entire day roaming streets we had never been to before, looking at houses and wondering if the pocket money we had saved up that week was enough to buy a house of our own. We even looked at houses that weren't for sale. We hadn't quite grasped that concept yet. As soon as it got dark the two of us became bored with our freedom and a little scared too. Eventually we decided to head back home to see if our protests had made a difference to the Captain Tornado situation. Our parents hadn't even noticed we'd been gone. Alex's parents thought we were at my house and my parents thought we were at Alex's.

I don't know if Katie would have gotten on that plane had she been given the opportunity. I would like to think that I've done a good enough job as a mother for her to know that running away isn't a way to solve anything. You can run and run as fast and as far as you like, but the truth is, wherever you run, there you are. In fact, she tried to tell me today that she loved me with all her heart and that she could never leave me. I thought I sensed sincerity in her eyes and voice but as soon as I reached out to cuddle her, her face brightened and she asked if that meant she didn't have to be grounded any more. I'm afraid she's a chancer like her father.

Ever run away from home when you were a child?

Ruby: No. But my ex-husband ran away from home with a child half his age, if that's any help to you.

Rosie: Right . . . well no, it's not, but thanks for sharing it with me all the same.

Ruby: No problem.

Rosie: So what are you doing for your fortieth, Ruby? It's coming up soon.

Ruby: I'm going to break up with Teddy.

Rosie: No! You can't! You and Teddy are an institution!

Ruby: Ha! That's my point. OK, I mightn't then. I was just thinking of new and exciting ways to change my life. Funnily enough, that was the first one that jumped into my head.

Rosie: You don't need to change your life, Ruby; it's just fine as it is.

Ruby: I'm going to be forty, Rosie. FORTY. I'm younger than Madonna, would you believe, and I look like her mother. Every day I wake up in a messy bedroom beside a man who smells and snores, I trip over mounds of clothes in order to find my way to the door, I stagger down to the kitchen and make myself a coffee and eat a slice of leftover cake. On the way back to my bedroom I pass my son in the hallway. Sometimes he acknowledges me; most of the time he doesn't.

I fight with him to use the shower and I don't mean about who's first to use it – I actually have to *force* him to wash himself. I fight with the shower in order to be neither scalded to a crisp nor frozen to death. I get dressed in clothes I have been wearing for far too many years in a size that makes me physically sick, but that has caused me to lose the will to care about doing something about . . . *anything* – or anything about *something*. Teddy grunts goodbye to me, I squeeze myself into my banged-up rusty old unfaithful Mini that breaks down almost every morning on the motorway that bears more of a resemblance to a car park than a road.

I park my car, arrive into work late again, and get given out to by someone I have been forced to nickname Randy Andy. I sit at my desk where I concoct stories which help me escape the office and I flee to the outside world for a sneaky cigarette. I do this various times a day. I speak to nobody all day, nobody speaks to me and then I return home at 7 p.m. feeling absolutely exhausted and starving, to a home that will never be cleaned and a dinner that will never prepare itself. I do this *every day*.

On Saturday nights I meet you, and we go out and I suffer all day Sunday with a hangover. This means that I turn into a zombie and lie on the couch like a piece of broccoli. The house still doesn't get tidied, and despite being screamed at, it refuses to tidy itself. I wake up on Monday morning to that awful horrible wailing sound of my alarm clock, just to begin the week all over again.

Rosie, how could you say I don't need change? I *desperately* need change.

Rosie: Ruby, we *both* need change.

For a special friend

May this be the beginning of a truly happy and successful year for you!

Sorry, Ruby, this was the only half-decent card I could find that didn't go on about how your life is almost ending. Thanks for always being there for me, even though you'd rather not be! You're a fantastic friend to have. Let's enjoy this birthday and good luck in your new year.

Love, Rosie

PS. I hope you like your pressie. Never complain of *change* ever again!

This voucher entitles the bearer to ten lessons in Salsa dancing.

Ricardo will be your teacher every Wednesday @ 8 p.m. in the school hall of St Patrick's Secondary School.

You have a message from: RUBY.

Ruby: I'm all salsa'd out! The last time I was in this much pain was when Teddy got that Kama Sutra book for Christmas from the lads at work. I practically had to be fork-lifted to work after the holidays, remember? Well, this time I actually had to take the morning *off* work. Can you believe it?!

I woke up suspecting that I had been in a very serious car accident; then I looked across at Teddy and was convinced we had been. But I forgot that the drooling, sweating and disturbing noises were all part of the Teddy package. It took me twenty minutes to wake him up so that he could help me out of bed. It took me a further twenty minutes to get out of bed. My joints were on strike. They were all just lazily lounging around with their little pickets pitched up, screaming, 'Joints on strike, joints on strike!' The hips were the leaders of this conspiracy.

So I rang my boss and held the phone to my hips so he could hear them too. He agreed with me and let me have the morning off. (Well, he claims *now* that he *didn't* but I'm sticking to my side of the story.)

I never knew pain could be so bad. Childbirth is *nothing* compared to exercise, and Gary was a *big* baby. This is what they should do to prisoners of war when they're trying to interrogate them. Make them take salsa classes. I knew I was unfit but, my God, driving the Mini today was horrendous. Every time I changed gears I felt like someone was hammering away at my arm. First gear – sore, second gear – pain, third gear – torture. I ended up driving to work in second gear because it hurt so much. Not safe or healthy for the car at all but she managed to cough and splutter her way into work, just like her owner.

By the way I was walking you would swear Teddy and I *had* worked our way through the Kama Sutra book. Even typing was a traumatic experience as I suddenly realised that my finger bone is connected to my arm bone, which in some way was pulling on my hamstring, which was giving me a headache. I should have known I would be this bad. When you dropped me off last night I was so stiff I practically had to crawl in the hall door, where my ears were greeted by Teddy and Gary having a mutual grunting session in the living room. I've learned it's their odd little method of communication.

So I left my wonderful intelligent family and soaked in the bath and considered drowning myself. Then I remembered I still had chocolate cake left over from yesterday so I came back up for air. Some things are worth living for.

But thank you for the gift, Rosie; we had fun in the class, didn't we? I can't remember ever laughing so much in my life, which on second thought is probably why my stomach is so sore. Thank you for reminding me that I'm a woman, that I have hips, that I can be sexy, that I can laugh and have fun.

And thank you for bringing the sexy Ricardo into my life. Can't wait to feel this way again next week. Now after all my whinging and moaning, how do you feel?

Rosie: Oh, fine, thanks. No complaints.

Ruby: Ha!

Rosie: OK, OK, so I feel a little stiff.

Ruby: Ha!

Rosie: Oh, OK, so the bus had to lower the wheelchair ramp for me this morning because I couldn't lift my legs.

Ruby: That's more like it.

Rosie: Oh, the beautiful Ricardo, Ruby!! I had a dream about him last night. I woke up with my top off and my pillow covered in drool. (OK, so, *not really*.) The sound of that sexy Italian voice shouting, 'Ros-ie!! Pay atten-see-on!' and, 'Ros-ie! Stup laffing!!' and, 'Ros-ie!! Get up ov ze floor!' just sends a shiver up my spine. But it was the sound of, 'Vell done, Rosie, *fantabulous* hip action!' that really got me. Mmm, yummy Ricardo with the hips . . .

Ruby: Yes! The hips! Although as I recall, it was *me* he was referring to about the '*fantabulous* hip action'.

Rosie: Oh, Ruby, can't a girl *dream*? I was surprised to see so many men there, were you?

Ruby: Yes! It reminded me of when I was younger at the

school discos or the ceilís; I was always one of those girls, stuck dancing with another girl as a partner. There were more men dancing with men last night than there were women with women.

Rosie: Yes, I know, though somehow I get the feeling that was due to personal choice. Although they took the wearing high heels a little too seriously, don't you think? Could you imagine Greg and Teddy coming with us to a class?

Ruby: Oh, that would be a sight for sore eyes! Teddy can't wrap his arms around himself, never mind hug me. By the time he'd get round to doing a twirl, it would be next year.

Rosie: Ha! Yeah, and Greg would probably become so obsessed with Ricardo counting the steps aloud that he would begin to calculate them in his mind, add them, multiply them, subtract the first count from the square root of the sixth or something. Greg, the bank manager and his love affair with numbers. It looks like it's just you and me, Ruby.

Ruby: Looks like it . . . So what's Alex up to these days?

Rosie: He's still hanging around Slutty Bethany's dad, trying to get a job chopping people's bodies up.

Ruby: Oh . . . kay, who is Bethany, why is she a slut and what business is her father in?

Rosie: Oh, sorry. Bethany is Alex's childhood sweetheart and first love, she's a slut because I say so, and her dad is a surgeon of some sort.

Ruby: How exciting – the return of one of Alex' ex-girlfriends. This will be a page turner.

Rosie: No, she's not around any more; Alex is just attending some lectures being held by her father.

Ruby: Oh, Rosie Dunne, expect the unexpected, for once. Maybe this time you won't get such a shock when things don't go your way.

Chapter 28

Aries

The heady combination of Uranus in Aries along with your ruler Jupiter opposing Venus and the sun squaring Pluto means, well, complications.

The new moon brings some light relief – but with a strange twist of fate.

IRISH SURGEON TO JOIN WILLIAMS
by Cliona Taylor

Irish surgeon Reginald Williams, who recently achieved success with his much-publicised new cardiac surgery, today announced he would be welcoming fellow Irishman Dr Alex Stewart to the award-winning team. The 30-year-old Harvard graduate says, 'I have always followed Dr Williams' studies with great interest and admiration,' and that he is both delighted and honoured to become a new member of this ground-breaking and, most important, life-saving new surgery.'

Dr Stewart is originally from Dublin, and moved to Boston at age 17 when his father accepted a post with the prominent US law firm Charles & Charles. Dr Steward completed five years in Boston Central Hospital on a general surgical residency training programme before joining with Dr Williams for further cardiac surgery studies. Pictured above (from left to right) are Dr Reginald Williams with his wife, Miranda, and his daughter, Bethany, who accompanied Dr Stewart to the Reginald Williams Foundation for Heart Disease charity ball last night.

See page 4 of the Health supplement for Wayne Gillespie's report on this new cardiac surgery.

You have an instant message from: ROSIE.

Rosie: Hey, Ruby, you'll never guess what I just read in the newspaper this morning.

Ruby: Your star sign.

Rosie: Oh, please! Give me a bit of credit; do you think I read those things *every day*?

Ruby: I know you read them every day. It helps you decide whether to be in a good mood or bad mood. I can't quite figure mine out today. It says: 'Take the fullest possible advantage of lively financial conditions to seize the initiative at the end of the month. Mars has moved into your sign and you should be feeling full of energy. Exciting new experiences forecast.'

I have never been so broke, exhausted and bored in all of my life. So that's all a load of crap. I'm really looking forward to our next dance lesson, though. Can't believe we're going to be finished this week and that soon we'll be moving into intermediate class. The weeks have just flown by. Anyway, what was in the papers if it wasn't your star sign?

Rosie: Read page three of the *Times*.

Ruby: OK on page three, scanning down through articles as I type this . . . oh my Lord, look at that. I take it that's Slutty Bethany?

Rosie: Should you even have to ask?

Ruby: Sorry, love, but she looks like a normal filthy-rich well-dressed thirty-year-old woman to me, but I'll call her Slutty Bethany if you insist.

Rosie: Humour me.

Ruby: OK . . . Oh look, Rosie, it's 'Slutty Bethany' in the paper with Alex. On page three. Looking . . . em . . . slutty.

Rosie: So I see. Anyway, she's thirty-two. My star sign said that—

Ruby: A-ha! I told y—

Rosie: Oh, shut up with the 'I told you so's' and listen. My star sign said that I would feel light relief but with a strange twist of fate.

Ruby: And . . . ? Mine tells me I'm rich – so what?

Rosie: Well, I'm delighted that Alex has finally got the job of his dreams that he has wanted for so many years, but it's just ironic that it was her he had to meet to get it.

Ruby: I told you to expect the unexpected, Rosie, *and* to stop paying attention to those horoscopes. They're a load of crap.

From   Rosie
To   Alex
Subject   Congratulations!

Heard about your good news. You've made it into every newspaper over here today (I've kept all the press cuttings for you), and I heard you speaking on the radio this morning. I'm not quite sure exactly what you were talking about, but you sounded like you've got a cold. So you can practically bring people back from the dead but you can't get rid of the sniffles.

How's Josh? I rang your mother the other day and he was over with her for the weekend. She put Josh on the phone and I can't believe I could actually have a conversation with him! He's very intelligent for nearly three, a bright lad just like his dad was, absolutely nothing like his mum. He was telling me all about the animals he had seen at the zoo and proceeded to make the noise of every single one of them. I suggested to your mother that she work on the gorilla sound with him as he wasn't saying anything, but she informed me that the gorilla is so depressed he just sits in his cage and doesn't make a sound. So Josh is an impressionist too as well as a clever clogs.

I would love to see him again sometime; I would love to see you. We need to catch up on each other's lives. Tell me something about yourself that the papers, television and radio can't tell me.

Dear Alex,

Rosie here again. I'm not quite sure if you got my email a few weeks ago. I just was congratulating you on your fantastic news. We're all so proud of you over here; Mum, Dad, Steph, Kev, Katie and Toby are all cheering for you. I think Toby wants to be a doctor when he's older, just like you because he'll get to be on the radio and have his photograph in the newspaper. (Plus he revealed he wanted to rip people's hearts out like they do in some movie. I was deeply disturbed by that thought.) Katie is now insisting she wants to be a dance club DJ. You've had no effect on her in that department whatsoever; she'll be in a business that *gives* people heart attacks.

I'm still at the Two Lakes Hotel. Still at reception; still providing the big bad public with a glass roof over their heads. My boss has headed over to the US where he has opened up yet another new hotel so I don't think either of the Lake brothers will be here for a very long time. In their stead they have arranged a series of very sad team-forming experts to come in and teach us how to be at one with one another. Next week the team leader, Simon, is taking us out canoeing so we can communicate outside of a work environment. We're supposed to learn how to discuss our problems.

How can I tell Tania, who also works in reception, that the reason I don't talk to her is because I can't listen to her unnaturally high-pitched voice, that I hate it that she says 'What do you think?' at the end of every sentence, that she wears perfume that is far too strong for a small office, and pink lipstick that sticks to her teeth and that does not and *never will* look good with her hair colour? Steven's morning breath smells of dirty nappies; I love it when he goes on his first coffee break because that means he comes back almost smelling of roses in comparison. Geoffrey has a serious underarm odour problem; Fiona has a serious problem with flatulence – I don't know *what* she's eating. Tabitha nods all the time I'm speaking to her, says 'right' after practically every single word and, even more annoyingly, tries to finish my sentences for me, or join in with my last few words. The really annoying thing is that she always gets it wrong. Henry wears white socks and black shoes, Grace hums the same Spice Girls song every single day, which drives me demented but I always end up singing it to myself when I get home, which causes Katie to despise her old-fashioned 'way-behind' mother, who has no idea of the chart positions of this decade.

They all drive me bloody mad. In fact maybe this canoeing thing is a good idea after all; I can just drown the lot of them. Alex, write back and let me know what's going on in your life.

Love,
Rosie

Rosie,

Sorry I've been so distant recently, but I've been so busy. Still, it's no excuse for not being in touch. You pretty much no all my work news, I suppose, so there's no need to go into that. Mum and Dad are both well, they're still framing every single photo you send them of you and Katie. The place is beginning to look like some kind of shrine to you two Dunne girls.

I have good news! I'll be coming back to Ireland to visit next month. Mum and Dad are coming back too, and Sally has agreed to let me take Josh for the fortnight, seeing as she had him last Christmas. It's been a long time since the entire family has been back together and Mum decided she wanted to be with Phil, his twenty kids and the rest of the family and all her friends, for their fortieth wedding anniversary.

Forty years – imagine. I barely made it to two; I don't no how they did it. You're doing well, though. How long have you and whatshisname been together? Long enough, I would imagine.

I can't remember when I last spent Christmas in Dublin. But soon we'll be reunited, Rosie.

Alex

From   Rosie
To   Alex
Subject Your visit

That's great news! I'm delighted you're coming home. Would you like to stay over at my house or have you and your parents made other plans?

From   Alex
To   Rosie
Subject My visit

No, no, I don't want to put whatshisname out. Actually, there's no need for me to be so polite; I hate your husband. So Josh and I are staying with Phil and Maggie

218

and I've booked Mum and Dad into a hotel. Thanks for the offer, though.

From   Rosie
To   Alex
Subject G. R. E. G.

Hmm . . . Alex, you're going to have to learn my husband's name before you come over. It's Greg. G. R. E. G. Try and remember it, please.

Did I tell you that Ruby and I are salsa dancing queens? I got the first batch of classes as a present for Ruby's fortieth a few months ago and we enjoyed it so much we kept it up. In fact Ruby has surprised me with her talents but I'm secretly sick and tired of having to be the man all the time.

Greg refuses to come to the classes with me but he doesn't mind being taught in our bedroom when Katie is out, our bedroom door bolted, a chair pushed up against it, the blinds down and the curtains drawn. Even the TV must be off just in case an actor or presenter happens to have the magical powers of seeing into people's houses. Well, the whole point is for us to do something fun together but seeing as I'm always the man in class it's hard for me to be the woman at home (and I've *never* been any good at being the woman at home). Then we end up stepping on each other's toes, kicking each other's shins, getting really frustrated with each other, having a screaming match about whose foot was where, whose foot should have been where but wasn't and then storm out on each other.

Ruby's started taking the classes twice a week now but I can't go on Mondays because I have to bring Katie to basketball practice. Ruby does insist that it's not as much fun without me, because she has to dance with tutu-wearing Miss Behave, a six-foot-tall drag queen with the longest legs and blond hair, who's trying to learn salsa for her show, which is on at the local gay club.

Anyway, Ruby and I are really enjoying ourselves, and I find myself looking forward to the next class the minute each finishes. Ruby's delighted because she's losing a bit of weight (she's losing pebbles apparently, not stones). It's nice to find a hobby that excites you and makes you *look forward* to the week ahead instead of constantly dreading days. I hope you're having some sort of life, Alex, and that you're not overworking yourself. Go on any dates recently?

From   Alex
To   Rosie
Subject Dating?

I might have . . .

You have received an instant message from: ROSIE.
Rosie: I'm all ears now. Anyone I know?
Alex: Then again I might not have . . .
Rosie: Stop it! Who's the unlucky girl? Do I know her?
Alex: Maybe . . .
Rosie: Oh, please tell me it's anyone but Slutty Bethany.
Alex: Well, I'd better rush off because I have to get ready for tonight. Take care, Buttercup.
Rosie: You got a date?
Alex: Maybe . . . then again . . .
Rosie: Yeah, yeah, I get it, maybe not . . . Well, whatever you're doing, enjoy it. But not too much.
Alex: I wouldn't dare dream of it!

You have received an instant message from: ROSIE.
Rosie: Was just instant messaging Alex a few seconds ago.
Ruby: Yeah? Did he say anything interesting?

220

Rosie: No. We were just catching up on old times, you know how it is.

Ruby: Good for you both. You and Greg have any plans for tonight, then?

Rosie: He's going on a date, Ruby.

Ruby: Who is? Greg is?

Rosie: No! Alex.

Ruby: Oh, are we still talking about him? Who's he going out with?

Rosie: I don't know. He wouldn't tell me.

Ruby: Well, he's allowed to have a private life, isn't he?

Rosie: Yeah, I suppose.

Ruby: And it's good that he's able to finally move on after having his heart broken and going through a divorce, isn't it?

Rosie: Yeah, I suppose.

Ruby: Well, it's good that you feel that way. You're a great friend, Rosie, always wanting the best for Alex.

Rosie: Yeah. Yeah, I am.

You have received an instant message from: ALEX.

Alex: Hi, Phil.

Phil: Hi, Alex.

Alex: What you doing?

Phil: Surfing the internet, searching for a crank hole cover for a 1939 Dodge Sedan. It's a rare car. A real beauty. Just ordered front bumper bar extensions for the 1955 Chevrolet Sedan. It's being shipped in.

Alex: Right.

Phil: Something on your mind, Alex?

Alex: No, no.

Phil: Well then, did you message me for any particular reason?

Alex: No, just seeing how you are. Wanted to catch up with my big brother.

Phil: Right. How's the job?

Alex: I'm going on a date tonight.

Phil: Really? That's good.

Alex: Yeah it is.

Phil: Good to see you moving on.

Alex: Yeah.

Phil: Finding happiness again.

Alex: Yeah.

Phil: Meeting someone new will stop you from working so bloody much.

Alex: Yeah.

Phil: Does Rosie know?

Alex: Yeah. Just was chatting to her there by instant message before I messaged you.

Phil: How's that for a coincidence? Well, what was her reaction?

Alex: Not much of one, actually.

Phil: She wasn't angry?

Alex: No.

Phil: Or jealous?

Alex: No.

Phil: She didn't beg you not to date other women?

Alex: Nope.

Phil: That's good then, isn't it? You've got a good friend there. One that wants you to move on, meet new people and find happiness.

Alex: Yeah. That's good. Good to have a friend like that.

Aries

You're still heavily under the influence of Neptune, the planet that brings you your romantic dreams . . .

You have an instant message from: ROSIE.

Rosie: You're right, Ruby, star signs are a load of crap.

Ruby: Attagirl.

222

Chapter 29

To Rosie, Katie and Greg

You are invited to my 4th birthday praty on November 18th. I am haveing a magicman. He can make aminals out of balloons. He will give you a aminal for keeps. My party starts at 11 in the morning and there will be lots of candy and then you can go home with your moms and dads.

Thanks.

Love,

Josh

You have received an instant message from: KATIE.

Katie: I look like a goofball.

Toby: You do not look like a goofball.

Katie: You don't even know what a goofball looks like.

Toby: What does it look like then?

Katie: Me. I look like some sort of futuristic human race that got messed up with robots.

Toby: You don't.

Katie: Oh my God, everyone is staring at me.

Toby: Katie, we're sitting in the back row of the classroom. Everybody in the entire room has their back to us. They are NOT staring at you unless they've got eyes on the back of their heads.

Katie: My mum does.

Toby: Look, they're only braces, Katie. It's not the end of the world. Anyway, I know how you feel. When I got my glasses I felt like everyone was staring at me too.

Katie: That's because they were.

Toby: Oh. Could you do me a favour?

Katie: What?

Toby: Just say sizzling sausages one more time.

Katie: TOBY! That is so not funny. You said you wouldn't laugh. I'm gonna be stuck with these stupid train tracks for years now, and it's not my fault they're giving me a lisp. I'll even have them for my birthday photos next week.

Toby: Big deal.

Katie: It's my thirteenth birthday. I don't wanna remember myself in photographs when I'm older as being the one with the two gigantic lumps of metal jammed in my mouth. Plus *everyone's* coming to the party, people I haven't seen for absolute yonks, and I want to look nice.

Toby: Let me guess, you'll be trying to look nice in black again.

Katie: Yep.

Toby: You're so morbid.

Katie: No, Toby, I'm sophisticated. The black suits my hair. It says so in my magazines. But you can wear your ratty tatty shorts and T-shirt, if you like. No point in changing the habit of a lifetime.

Toby: That's what *my* magazines tell me to do.

Katie: No, I *no* what your filthy magazines tell you to do and it's not anything to do with dressing. More like undressing.

Toby: So I'm invited anyway.

Katie: Maybe. Then again . . . maybe not.

Toby: Katie, I'm going whether you invite me or not. I'm not missing your thirteenth birthday just because you're in one of your moods. I just want to see your birthday cake getting all caught up in your braces, oozing out through the cracks in your teeth and then hitting people on their faces when you speak.

Katie: Whatever. I'll make sure I speak to you the most then.

Toby: Who's going, anyway?

Katie: Alex, Aunt Steph, Pierre and Jean-Louis, Grandma and Granddad, Ruby, Teddy and her weirdo son that never speaks, Mum, of course, and a few girls from basketball.

Toby: Well, yippee. What about your Uncle Kevin?

Katie: Does he ever come to anything? He's still working in that posh hotel down in Kilkenny. He said he's sorry he couldn't come but he sent me a card with a tenner inside.

Toby: Well, that's all you want anyway. What about Greg?

Katie: Nope, he's working in the States for a week. He gave me thirteen euro. A euro for every year.

Toby: Cool. You're gonna be rich. Just as well he's working, I hate when him and Alex are in the same room. It freaks me out.

Katie: I no. It's even worse when Mum's in the room because she just spends the entire time running from one to the other like she's a boxing match referee.

Toby: Alex would kick Greg's ass if they were in a boxing match.

Katie: Definitely. Mum would kick both their asses if they even dared. At least now I'll be able to wear the locket Alex gave me without Greg looking at it like he wants to rip it off.

Toby: Oh, he's just jealous his photo isn't in it.

Katie: His head's too big to ever fit in my locket.

Toby: So is there anyone under the age of eighty coming that's not on your crappy basketball team?

Katie: Alex is bringing Josh.

Toby: Josh is four years old, Katie.

Katie: Exactly. You'll have lots in common. Same brain power.

Toby: Oh ha ha, metal mouth. Do you think you'll have any 'sizzling cocktail sausages' at your party?

Katie: You're hilarious, Toby. Well, I suppose my situation could be a million times worse. I could be stuck wearing glasses for the rest of my life like you.

Toby: Hardy har har. I was just thinking, you might not be able to leave the country for the next few years because of the metal detectors at the airports. You could be a real danger to the public. They could be turned into deadly weapons.

Katie: Whatever.

You have an instant message from: ROSIE.

Rosie: My baby is going to be a teenager next week.

Ruby: Thank your lucky stars it's almost over now, sweetie.

Rosie: Isn't it just beginning? And if I had any lucky stars they would be well and truly sacked by now. What's so great about my beautiful baby growing up and become spotty and bitchy while I decay right in front of my very own eyes? The older my child gets, the older I become.

Ruby: Clever discovery.

Rosie: But that's not allowed to happen. Because I haven't even started my own life yet, never mind bringing another one into this world and helping her through her own. I haven't actually done anything of substance yet.

Ruby: Some may argue that creating life is of substance. Anything I should bring to the party?

Rosie: Just yourself.

Ruby: Damn it, anything else instead?

Rosie: You're coming whether you like it or not.

Ruby: Oh alright then. At least Greg won't be there wrapping a leash around your neck to hold you back from Alex.

Rosie: Yeah. I just might be able to hump Alex's leg in peace this time.

Ruby: Here's hoping. So what do I get for the teenage girl who wants everything?

Rosie: Straight teeth, magic spot removal cream, Colin Farrell and an organised mother.

Ruby: Ah, now the organised mother bit I can help out with.

Rosie: Thanks, Ruby.

From   Alex
To   Rosie
Subject   Flight details

My flight is landing at 2.15 p.m. tomorrow. Really looking forward to meeting up with you and Katie again. Will whatshisname be there to greet me too?

From   Rosie
To   Alex
Subject   MY HUSBAND

My *husband's* name is GREG. And no, he will not be there to collect you because he is away on business. He's in the States so you two have luckily swapped countries for the next few days. Let's hope that will be far apart enough for the both of you.

To my wonderful daughter
  You're a teenager!
  Happy birthday, darling.
  Lots of love,
  Mum

To Katie
  You're a teen today,
  Hip hip hip hooray!
  It's a joyous day,
  You're a teen today!
  Greg

You're a groovy Chick!!
  Happy birthday, pet.
  Love you lots like jelly tots!
  Love, Grandma and Granddad

Happy birthday, Glitter Girl!
  Take this money and buy yourself an item of clothing that's
not black. I dare you.
  Love, Ruby, Teddy and Gary

For my niece
  Happy 13th, Beautiful!
  Bon Anniversaire!
  Love, Stephanie, Pierre and Jean-Louis

To my Goddaughter
  Happy 13th, you little adult!
  I'm so happy to share the day with you.
  All my love,
  Alex

You may be a teenager but you're still ugly.
From Toby

From   Kevin
To   Rosie
Subject   Secret visit!

Kevin here. I can't get through to your phone so I thought I'd send you an email seeing as that seems to be all you do every day.

Sorry I couldn't be home for Katie's birthday, but it's absolutely crazy at work. The golf open is being held here this week and all the world's greatest golfers and their dogs and goldfish have booked in. I've been rushed off my feet but they'll thankfully be gone by the weekend. I seem to keep missing the family do's (or family don'ts).

Anyway, the reason I'm emailing you is because I can't believe you kept it a secret from me that you were coming down here for the weekend! Don't even ask what I was doing checking the reservations but it seems that you have the honeymoon suite booked out for the weekend!

Good ol' Greg's a bit flash, paying for all that, isn't he? Anyway, I'm glad you're finally coming down to see me. It's about time. Don't think I've seen you since Christmas. I'll make sure all the staff treat you extra specially, and I'll even tell the lads in the kitchen not to spit into your food.

From   Rosie
To   Kevin
Subject   Secret visit

Sorry, my baby brother, but it must be another Rosie Dunne. I wish it *was* me!

From   Kevin
To   Rosie
Subject Secret visit

There's only one Rosie Dunne! No, the booking is actually under Greg's name. Shit! I hope I haven't spoiled a surprise. FORGET I said anything. Sorry.

From   Rosie
To   Kevin
Subject Secret visit

Don't worry, Kev – what day is the booking for?

From   Kevin
To   Rosie
Subject Secret visit

Friday until Monday. Oh, please don't tell him I told you. It was stupid of me to say anything. I should have used my head first. I really shouldn't have been looking at the reservations anyway. What an idiot Greg is. He should have known I work here.

From   Rosie
To   Kevin
Subject Secret visit

And in order for him to know where you work you two would need to have a conversation with each other once in a while. Don't worry! Greg's away in the States for the week so I'll be able to hide my excitement from him! I'd better go shopping for a few outfits. That hotel of yours is very classy!

From   Kevin
To   Rosie
Subject   Secret visit

Enjoy it and I'll see you at the weekend. I'll have a look of
pretend shock on my face.

Ruby: I have to admit that I'm surprised. That's very
    romantic of him!
Rosie: I know! I'm so excited, Ruby. I've dreamed of
    staying in that hotel for years. Oh, I bet the little
    shampoos and shower caps in the bathrooms are just the
    most beautiful things.
Ruby: Christ, Rosie, you could open your own shop with
    the amount of hotel products you've stolen.
Rosie: It's not *stealing*. They're not just there to be *looked*
    at. Although, they do seem to be nailing down the hair
    dryers a lot more these days.
Ruby: Just as well you're not strong enough to drag the
    beds out of the rooms.
Rosie: They'd see me at reception. Although the bed sheets
    I got from the last hotel I stayed in are by far my
    favourite.
Ruby: Rosie, you have a problem. Swiftly moving on,
    when are you being whisked away to the lap of luxury?
Rosie: Friday. I can't wait! I completely maxed out my
    credit card buying a few outfits for the weekend. I'm so
    pleased that he's made this effort. Things with me and
    Greg have reached an all-time high the last while. It's
    like we're back at our honeymoon stage. I am really,
    really happy.

From   Rosie
To   Greg
Subject Coming home?

It's Friday and I was just wondering what time you'll be home? You must be on the plane because your phone's going straight to answer machine. Maybe you can reply via your laptop from the clouds!

From   Greg
To   Rosie
Subject Re: Coming home?

Hi, love. I told you I'd be here in the States until Monday. I should be home in the evening sometime. Can I call you from the airport for a lift? Sorry if there was some confusion. I'm sure I told you it was Monday and not Friday. I wish it was today, darling, I really do.

    How's Katie after her first wild teenage party? I haven't heard from her. I thought she might have thanked me for the present by now.

From   Rosie
To   Kevin
Subject *This* weekend?

Do you think you could be mistaken about that booking for *this* weekend?

From   Kevin
To   Rosie
Subject Re: This weekend?

It's definitely correct, Rosie. Greg checked in this morning. Aren't you here?

Chapter 30

From   Rosie
To   Alex
Subject Whatshisname

Whatshisname is gone. For good.

From   Alex
To   Rosie
Subject Re: Whatshisname

I'll book flights for you and Katie to come over here immediately. I'll let you know the details within the next hour. Don't worry.

From   Rosie
To   Alex
Subject Please wait

Just give me a little time before you book those flights. There are a few things I want to tie up here before I leave. And once I go over to you in Boston I'm *never* coming back here. Just please wait for me.

Hi, it's me, Alex.

Look, I'm really sorry but I'm not going to be able to make it out for dinner tonight. I'm sorry to tell you in a letter but it's the best way I no how. You're a wonderful, intelligent woman but my heart lies with someone else. It has done so for many, many years. I hope that when we meet we can remain friends at least.

Alex

Chapter 31

Dear Bill Lake,

It is with great sadness that I submit my resignation. I will remain working in the Two Lakes Hotel for the next two weeks as I'm contracted to do so.

On a more personal level, I would like to thank you for five great years of allowing me to work in your company. It has been an honour.

Yours sincerely,

Rosie Dunne

From   Toby
To   Katie
Subject Disaster!

YOU WHAT?? You CAN'T be moving away! This is awful! Ask your mum if it's OK for you to stay with me for a while. I'll ask my mum and dad too. They'll definitely say yes. You can't leave.

What about school?

What about the basketball team?

What about wanting to DJ for Club Sauce?

What about your grandparents? You can't just leave them. They're old.

What about your mum's job and the house and everything? You can't just leave it all behind.

What about me?

From   Katie
To   Toby
Subject   Re: Disaster!

I can't change her mind. I can't stop crying. This is the worst thing that's ever happened to me in my whole entire life. I don't even want to go to Boston. What's so good about Boston? I don't wanna make new friends. I don't want anything 'new'.

Oh, I hate Greg so much. You no he hasn't even come home because he's so afraid of Mum. She's scary she's so mad. Even I'm afraid to talk to her sometimes. She screams down the phone at him like a crazy woman. No wonder he's not coming home. She said that if he did, she'd cut off his you-no-what. I'm kinda hoping he'll come home just for that.

It's all his fault we have to move away. It's all his fault Mum is upset. I hate him, I hate him, I hate him.

At least Alex and Josh are in Boston. That's something. I think we're gonna stay with them for a while. So we're really going, Toby. She's not just threatening. She told Greg she couldn't stand to be in the same country as him, never mind the same house. I suppose I no how she feels. I feel sorry for her but I really don't want to go. I just cried all night, Toby. It's so unfair.

Grandma and Granddad keep trying to talk her out of it. We're staying with them tonight because Mum can't stand to be at home. Every time she touches something of Greg's she shudders and wipes her hands. Ruby keeps

236

telling Mum to go because it's where her heart is or something. It's the first time I've ever seen Ruby cry. And Mum cries down the phone to Stephanie for hours every day. Last night I could hear her throwing up in the toilet so I got up and made her a cup of tea. She stopped for a while. She slept in my bed last night. It's only a single bed and we were kind of squashed but it was sort of nice. She squeezed me like I was a teddy.

Mum has started packing her bags now. She's gonna help me do mine in a while. She says she's sorry about moving me to Boston and I believe her. I don't blame her because she's so sad. It's Greg's fault but I haven't really seen him do much to make her feel better.

Mum said you can visit us all the time. Promise me you will. You may annoy the hell out of me, Toby, but you're my best friend in the whole entire world and I'll miss you so much. Even if you are a boy.

We can write to each other all the time. That's what Mum and Alex did when they were younger and he had to move away.

Love,
Katie

You have an instant message from: RUBY.
Ruby: So you're leaving in two weeks.
Rosie: Yep.
Ruby: You're doing the right thing, you know.
Rosie: Funny. You're the only one who seems to think that.
Ruby: I'm the only one who knows how you feel about him.
Rosie: Oh no, I'm not in the mood to go jumping into another relationship. I don't have the energy. My heart feels like it's been ripped out of my chest and tap danced on. I hate all men right now.

Ruby: Including Alex?

Rosie: Including Alex, my father, George the lollipop man, and my brother for telling me.

Ruby: You would have wanted to know, though.

Rosie: Yes, and I'm not blaming him. He hadn't a clue Greg was messing around. Again. The lying little . . . aaaah! I just feel like punching the shit out of him. I don't think I've ever been so angry in my life. The first time he did this I was hurt; now I'm just plain pissed off. I can't wait to get out of this country. I'm glad Kevin told me because I will be the fool no longer.

Ruby: I heard Kevin's in trouble at work. Is it for checking the reservations?

Rosie: No, it's for marching through the hotel restaurant during dinner and punching Greg on the nose in front of his lady friend and the rest of the hotel guests.

Ruby: Good for him. I hope he broke his nose.

Rosie: He did. That's what he's in trouble for.

Ruby: So who am I going to go to salsa lessons with now?

Rosie: I'm sure Miss Behave will be only too delighted to be your partner.

Ruby: I finally get to dance with a man and he wears tights. Oh, I'll miss you so much Rosie Dunne. It's not often in life a woman finds a friend like you.

Rosie: And I you, Ruby, but as much as Greg has hurt me, he's given me an opportunity to start from fresh. I'll be free of him and I'm stronger from it.

I'm leaving next week, Greg. Don't try to contact me, don't try to visit me, I want nothing more to do with you. You have betrayed me just when I had learned to fall in love with you all over again. This won't be happening again. You have thrown it all away but I thank you for it. Thank you for letting me see what it is I married and for freeing me from you.

Whether Katie wants to continue seeing you is completely her decision. You must accept what she says.

Alex: You were right, Phil. She's coming over to me. I just had to leave it and let her come at her own pace.
Phil: Lucky for me I was right! It was a good guess, wasn't it? So did she tell you that she loves you, that she never should have married that idiot and that she only wants to be with you and all that other stuff that they say in the movies?
Alex: No.
Phil: She didn't tell you she loves you?
Alex: No.
Phil: Did you tell her?
Alex: No.
Phil: Then what's she going over for?
Alex: She just said that she wanted to get out of Dublin and that she needed a change of scenery and a friendly face.
Phil: Oh.
Alex: What do you think that means?
Phil: Probably exactly what it says. So you've no idea how she feels about you?
Alex: No. Phil, her marriage has just ended. There's plenty of time when she comes over here to talk about our future.
Phil: Whatever you say, bro. Whatever you say.

From   Alex
To   Rosie
Subject   You and Katie

I'm so excited that you'll be here so soon. Josh is practically running up the walls with excitement. He loves Katie and is delighted about your decision to come live with us for a while. I've a friend who has a friend who owns a hotel and they are looking for a manager. You are more than qualified for the job.

I can help you through this, Rosie. Remember I've been in your shoes. I no how it feels to go through a marriage break-up. I'm here for you one hundred per cent. Moving to Boston may be fourteen years later than you planned but it's better late than never. Josh and I will be here waiting. See you next week.

You're moving away!

Good luck, Rosie. We'll all miss you here at the Two Lakes. From Bill, Bob, Tania, Steven, Geoffrey, Fiona, Tabitha, Henry and Grace

Sniff, sniff.

I'll miss you Rosie Dunne.

Good luck with your new life. Send us an email every now and again.

Lots of love,
Ruby

Rosie and Katie,

We are so sorry that you feel you have to go. We are so sorry that you have reason to go. We are so sorry this has happened. We will miss you both so, so much, but we hope you can find eternal happiness. No more tears for our two girls. Let the world be good to you. Phone us when you land.

Love, Mum and Dad

Good luck with the move. My fingers are crossed for you and Katie. We're all here for you if you need us.

Love,
Stephanie, Pierre and Jean-Louis

Sorry you had to go. Good luck.
    Kev

Katie,
    Good luck in your new home. I'll miss you.
    Love,
    Toby

Dear Mum and Dad,
    It's not like I'm disappearing for ever. We're only a few hours away. You can visit all the time! We love you so much and thank you for your constant support. This time we need to find the way by ourselves.
    Lots of love,
    Rosie and Katie

Chapter 32

Dear Rosie,

Before you rip this up please just give me a chance to explain. Firstly, I sincerely apologise from the bottom of my heart for the years gone by. For not being there for you, for not supporting you and giving you the help you deserved. I am filled with regret and disappointment with myself for the way I have behaved and chosen to live my life. I know there is nothing I can do to change or make better the years I acted so foolishly and mistreated the two of you.

But please at least give me a chance to build a better future, to make right what's wrong. I can understand how you must feel so angry, betrayed and hurt, and you must hate me so much but there's not just yourself to think of. I look back on my life and I wonder what have I to show for all these years? I haven't done many things in my life that I'm proud of. I have no stories of success to tell, I haven't made a million. There is only one thing in this life that I'm proud of. And that's my little girl.

The fact that I have a little girl, who isn't even 'little' any more. I'm not proud of the way I've treated her. I woke up one morning a few weeks ago on my thirty-second birthday and suddenly it was as if all the sense that's been missing for the past thirty-two years came to me in an instant. I realised I had a daughter, a teenage daughter who I know nothing of, and who knows nothing of me. I would love the chance to get to know her. I'm told that her name is Katie. That's a nice name. I wonder what she looks like. Does she look like me?

I know I haven't shown any signs of deserving this, but if you and Katie are willing to let me into your lives I can prove to you it won't be a waste of time. Katie will meet her father and I will see my daughter – how could that ever be considered a waste? Please help me fulfil my dreams.

Please contact me, Rosie. Give me a chance to undo all the mistakes of my past and to help create a new future for Katie and me.

Best wishes,

Brian

Rosie: No no no no no no no no no

Ruby: I know, honey, I understand. But at least just look at the other options.

Rosie: Options? BLOODY OPTIONS? I have none. NONE! I have to go. Staying here is not an *option*.

Ruby: Rosie, calm down. You're upset.

Rosie: Too right I'm upset! How on earth am I supposed to try and get my life together when everyone around me keeps fucking it up? When is it *my turn* to live *my life* for *me* instead of for everyone else? I'm sick of it, Ruby. I'm fed up. I have had enough. I'm bloody going. Who is this man? Where the hell has he been for the past thirteen years? Where did he disappear to for the most important years of Katie's life – or *my life*, for that matter?

Who stayed up all night breast-feeding, pacing the halls and singing fucking lullabies so the constant screaming would stop? Who changed shitty nappies, wiped snotty noses and cleaned sick from their clothes every day? Who's got stretch marks and scars, saggy tits and grey hairs at the age of thirty-two? Who went to parent teacher meetings, brought her to and collected her from school, made dinner, put food on the table, paid the rent, went to work, helped with homework, gave advice, wiped tears, explained the birds and the bees, explained why Daddy wasn't around, unlike most of the other kids' daddies? Who stayed up all night and worried when she was sick, taking temperatures and buying medicine, making trips to the doctor or the hospital in the middle of the night? Who missed going to college, took days off work and stayed home at the weekend to care for her? Fucking me, that's who. Where was the bastard then?

And *he* has the cheek to stroll back into our lives after thirteen years when all the hard work has been done, with a little shrug of the shoulders and a pathetic little sorry, just after my husband cheats on me, my marriage is over, I finally decide to move to Boston where I should have been anyway had it not been for that sly little prick ruining my plans, turning my life upside down and legging it off to another country with his dick between his legs.

Fuck him.

This time it's about me, Rosie Dunne, and no one else.

Ruby: But, Rosie, you're wrong. It's about Katie too. She needs to know he wants to see her. Don't punish her for the mistakes in your own life.

Rosie: But if I tell her, then she's going to want to see him. She'll be so excited to meet him and he'll probably let her down again and break her heart all over again. And who'll be the one who cleans up the mess? Me. I'll be the one who tries to mend my daughter's broken heart. I'll have to pick up the pieces and wipe away the tears.

I'll have to put on the happy face, shrug and say, 'Ah well, don't worry, my thirteen-year-old daughter, not all men are shits – just all the ones you've ever known.'

Ruby: But, Rosie, it could turn out really well. He may have really changed. You never know.

Rosie: You're right, you *never* know. EVER. And another thing, how can she get to know her father when we're halfway across the other side of the world? I don't want to stay here, Ruby. I want *out*. I want out of this entire mess of a life.

Ruby: It's not a mess, Rosie. Life is far from perfect, for everyone. You're not the only one. There isn't a great big black cloud just hanging over your head and no one else's. It just feels that way. But it feels like that for a lot of people. You just have to make the most of what you've got and you are *lucky* because you have a beautiful daughter who is healthy, intelligent and funny and who thinks the world of you. Don't lose sight of that. If Katie wants to get to know Brian then you should support her. You can still move away, he can come to see you – or if you think it's important enough to stay for, stay.

Rosie: Katie is going to want to stay. Last month, I *thought* I was living in paradise. Life changed in an instant.

Ruby: Well, that's the problem with paradise. Nothing attracts a serpent quite like it.

Dear Stephanie,

Congratulations on the pregnancy! I'm thrilled for you and Pierre. I'm sure baby number two will be a joy as Jean-Louis has been. I'm assuming Mum has told you the news. She's delighted I'm not moving to America any more. Alex isn't. He cursed and swore and screamed every bad word under the sun at me. He thinks I'm giving in again and letting everyone walk all over me so now he's in a huff and won't speak to me. I may have let people walk all over me before but not this time. Katie is number one in my life and my reason for being is to ensure she gets the best chance at happiness possible.

She's been through a lot lately, with Greg, having to move back in with Mum and Dad and then preparing to move again to America. She's been under plenty of unwarranted stress. She's supposed to be worrying about spots, bras and boys, not adultery, moving continents and her father doing a magic reappearing act. None of this is her fault and seeing as I brought her into this world the least I could do is continue the good work I've been doing. She isn't a drug addict, isn't rude, is doing fine in school, has all the right limbs in all the right places and hasn't managed to do anything really stupid with her life. So, with all the awful stories you hear, I think I'm doing a great job.

I'm expecting Alex to burst through the door any minute. I'm sure he has hopped on the first plane to get over here and beat up Brian. I suppose that's what best friends are for. I can't even think about what life 'could have been' like in Boston, without crying. I don't quite know where I should go from here. I have no job, no home and I'm back living with Mum and Dad again. Everything about this house brings back a time when I wasn't happy. I had a wonderful childhood but the years with Katie were so difficult, they're the strongest memories I have of this house – the smells, the noises, the wallpaper, the bedrooms all remind me of late nights, early mornings and worrying.

Anyway, forgive me for not being in contact over the past while but I've been trying to get my head round all of this. I'm trying to make some sense out of the phrase 'everything happens for a reason', and I think I've figured out what the reason is – to piss me off.

When I started school I thought that people in sixth class

were *so* old and knowledgeable, even though they were no older than twelve. When I reached twelve I reckoned the people in sixth year, at eighteen years of age, must have known it *all*. When I reached eighteen I thought that once I finished college then I would really be mature. At twenty-five I still hadn't made it to college, was still clueless and had a seven-year-old daughter. I was convinced that when I reached my thirties I was going to have at least *some* clue as to what was going on.

Nope, hasn't happened yet.

So I'm beginning to think that when I'm fifty, sixty, seventy, eighty, ninety years old I still won't be any closer to being wise and knowledgeable. Perhaps people on their deathbeds, who have had long, long lives, seen it all, travelled the world, have had kids, been through their own personal traumas, beaten their demons and learned the harsh lessons of life will be thinking: God, people in heaven must *really* know it all.

But I bet that when they finally do die they'll join the rest of the crowds up there, sit around, spying on the loved ones they left behind, and *still* be thinking that in their next life-time, they'll have it all sussed.

But I think I have it sussed, Steph. I've sat around for years thinking about it and I've discovered that no one, not even the big man upstairs, has the slightest clue as to what's going on.

Rosie

From   Stephanie
To   Rosie
Subject   Re: Life

Well, isn't that one thing you're all the wiser for? Age has taught you something. That *nobody* knows what's going on.

247

Hi,

My sincerest apologies for that ridiculous note I sent you last week. Just put it down to a momentary lapse in concentration, I'm a complete fool (as you're already aware) and I have absolutely no idea what I was thinking. But you'll be pleased to no (I hope) that I've landed back on earth with a thump and I'm willing and able to give us another go. So let's not waste any more of our valuable time but get down to the important stuff. Are we back on for tonight?

Alex

Chapter 33

You have a message from: RUBY.

Ruby: So you're still here then?

Rosie: Oh, not today, Ruby, please. I'm really not in the mood.

Ruby: I'm getting rather tired of you, Rosie Dunne. First you say you're moving to Cork, then you don't, then you say you're moving to Boston (again) and then you don't. Then I expect you to finally profess your love to Alex and you don't, so he still has absolutely no idea. I can't keep up with you and your 'leaving the country/ changing jobs/ leaving your husband'-type activities. Sometimes I think you just need a good kick up the behind for wasting all these good opportunities. You're an incredibly frustrating person, Rosie.

Rosie: Well, I'm an incredibly frustrated woman right now. And I'm not 'wasting' good opportunities; it's called 'presenting my daughter with new ones'.

Ruby: You can put whatever name you like on it but at the end of the day a missed opportunity is a missed opportunity. But don't worry; I think there's a lesson to be learned in all this.

Rosie: Please tell me there is *some* sort of reason for all this. What's the lesson?

Ruby: That you needn't bother trying any more, because you're going nowhere. So really, how are you?

Rosie: OK.

Ruby: Are you sure? Oh, come on, Rosie, if my heart can't take what's happening to you then I can't imagine how you must be feeling.

Rosie: Oh, my heart is broken; stopped beating two weeks ago.

Ruby: Well, it's a good thing you know a man who can heal it.

Rosie: No, no, no, it's the unspoken rule. He heals other people's hearts, not mine. I understand that's the way it is to be now.

Ruby: Here's an idea, Rosie. Why don't you just *tell* Alex how you feel? Why don't you just finally get all of those feelings out in the open, and clear your messed-up little head? At least then he'll know that you're not going over *not* because you don't care about him, but that in fact you love him, more than he knows, but that you need to stay here for Katie. Then that will put the ball in his court. He can make the decision whether to come to you or not.

Rosie: But what about his job? And what about Josh?

Ruby: That's *his* decision.

Rosie: Ruby, I can't. How do I tell him? If we had moved over to Boston I could have sussed things out a little, seen how he felt about me and then told him. He was just out on a date last week, for Christsake – how stupid would I look telling him I love him when he's seeing someone? It'll just be the whole Sally situation all over again. It's too complicated and right now the last thing I'm worried about is which man to fall in love with next. Anyway, he's not even returning my calls. He thinks I've made a stupid decision.

Ruby: Just give him time. He's disappointed how things worked out.

Rosie: I'm sorry – he's disappointed? *He's* disappointed? I think me and the rest of the world seem to be having a communication problem here. Does everyone think that I'm *ecstatic* at these new revelations? I mean, I'm really not looking for sympathy or anything but—

Ruby: Yes you are.

Rosie: Excuse me?

Ruby: Sympathy. Looking for it. Yes, you are.

Rosie: Thank you for decoding that for me. OK, so maybe it would be nice if at least some people acknowledged the fact that my husband has had an affair, my marriage has ended, I'm still a million miles away from Alex and will never know how I feel about him, my child's runaway father is back in Ireland and I HAVE NO JOB! A pat on the back, a sympathetic smile and a bit of a cuddle would be quite nice actually. A few months spent in my bed curled up into a ball, smothered by blankets, in a room darkened by drawn curtains, dressed in a pair of big pyjamas would be my idea of heaven, but unfortunately I can't do that right now because I have a daughter who is hyperventilating over the fact that her father, who she's never met, has come into her life and I need to forget about me and be strong for her. But a bit of sympathy would be nice too.

Ruby: Breathe, Rosie.

Rosie: No, that's how all my problems happen. If I wasn't breathing then everything would be fine.

Ruby: Don't talk like that.

Rosie: Oh, shut up. I haven't got time to kill myself; I'm too busy having a nervous breakdown.

Ruby: Well, I suppose that's good news, kind of. How was your meeting with Brian?

Rosie: OK. He booked a flight over here as soon as he got

off the phone from me so it seems he is very serious about his new role of fatherhood. He tells me he's been living in Ibiza for the past thirteen years, where he now owns a nightclub. Providing the highly sexed under-age drinkers of Ireland with a few good binge-drinking memories.

Ruby: Is he all tanned and gorgeous?

Rosie: Never before would I have put the words 'Brian the Whine' and 'tanned and gorgeous' all in the same sentence. He's pretty much the same, with less hair and more belly.

Ruby: How did you feel when you saw him?

Rosie: I had to muster all my strength to stop myself from punching him. Katie was so nervous about meeting him that she was shaking like a leaf and clinging to me. She was expecting me to be the strong one. Imagine – someone was relying on me. We met him in the coffee shop in Jervis Street Shopping Centre and, I have to admit, as we were approaching his table I felt sick. Sick with anger that the miserable little man who I was going to have to force myself to be nice to for the next hour, and help to become a part of my daughter's life, was the very same person who had caused me so much heartache in the past. *I* had to help *him*. It also felt odd that, as weak as I felt bringing Katie into town on the bus that morning, and as tired, nervous, angry and disappointed as I was to be doing that at all, I realised that these two people needed me to bring them together. So for the sake of Katie's relationship with Brian, whatever feelings of resentment I have for him need to be kept to myself.

Ruby: You've done a good thing, Rosie. It must have been difficult. It will probably be difficult for a long time, watching them grow closer.

Rosie: I know. I have to bite my tongue to stop myself from telling Katie just how much of a hero her father

252

isn't when she tells me about some of the things he has done in his life.

Ruby: What was he like with her?

Rosie: He was even more nervous than Katie so it was up to me to get the conversation started between them. You know, being the strongest out of the three really helped me to see that the decision I made about not moving to Boston was the right one. Katie needed me. They both needed me. He seemed genuinely interested in my life and in Katie's. He wanted to know everything about her and I quite enjoyed sharing our stories from over the years. At first I was telling each story with anger because he wasn't around for any of those situations, and then I realised I was bragging. It perked me up, in a strange sort of way, and made me realise how lucky I've been, as much as I moan and whinge about the responsibility of motherhood. It also helped me see the 'specialness' of Katie's and my situation; we're the only two to share all these memories together. And what we choose to let other people know is completely up to us. If Brian messes up absolutely everything else in my life at least he's inadvertently helped me realise that.

However, unfortunately it's not exactly the best time in my life to have an ex back again. In these situations you're supposed to have become so much more since the last time you've seen them – happy and successful in your life so you can say, 'Nah nah na-nah nah, look what I've done since you've been gone.' A failed marriage, no job and living with my parents did not have the desired effect.

Ruby: None of that stuff is important, Rosie. You should just be glad he's grown up a bit. How long will he be around for?

Rosie: A few weeks and then he'll have to head back to Ibiza for a little while. The summer months are obviously when he's at his busiest. He'll be back a few times to visit Katie, of course, and then he's going to hire someone else to run the club so he can stay in Dublin for the winter. He really seems to be taking this seriously and I'm glad for Katie's sake. Having Brian hanging around isn't exactly wonderful for me, but if it puts a smile on her face then it's worth it.

Ruby: Any luck finding a job?

Rosie: Well, I had just switched on the computer to search the internet when you messaged me.

Ruby: Oh, OK, well, I'll go now and let you become the responsible parent you should be. By the way, I'm making my Gary come to salsa dancing classes with me. Miss Behave drank one too many sangrias at the summer party last week and went over on her ankle in her twelve-inch platforms. All we could hear was a big CRACK! I turned round and she was on her back with a run in her tights and her wig beside her on the floor.

Rosie: Oh God, did you have to rush her to hospital?

Ruby: Oh no, she broke only the heel of her shoe, and seeing as they are her 'only dancing shoes' she refuses to come to class until she replaces them. Unfortunately they're only available in a store in New York so she has to wait until they're restocked and delivered. So I am without a partner and I won't even ask you because I know you'll say no.

Rosie: You're right. But how on earth did you get Gary to agree to go to dance classes with you? Did you threaten his life or something?!

Ruby: Yes.

Rosie: Oh. Well, I hope he enjoys it.

Ruby: Don't be silly, he'll hate it and shout at me for weeks, but at least he'll be talking to me again. Alright, I better go; I have to buy him a leotard and tights on my lunch-break. I know we don't actually have to wear them but it will be worth it just to see the look on his face when I pull them out of my bag.

Rosie: You evil, evil woman.

Ruby: Thank you. Now go find a job. In a hotel. After all this nonsense in your life, I want you to become the most successful hotel-worker person in the world. No. More. Setbacks. You hear me?

Rosie: Loud and Clear.

Dear Alex,

When will you stop giving me the silent treatment? You must understand that I can't make decisions to suit myself. I've Katie to think about too. It is important for her to get to know Brian. You of all people should know how it is to want and need to be there for your child. Brian has finally realised that he wants to be here for Katie. It's better late than never, as you always say. Some things are.

I think I've stressed my apologies to you on your answering machine but now I'm writing to thank you. To thank you for being there for me as you always have been over the years. For making all those arrangements for me when I couldn't even think clearly. That week, my world was turned upside down and everything that was once secure and solid was uprooted and came toppling down on top of me. Let's not allow your disapproval of my decision to stay to affect our friendship.

Perhaps sometime, someday we can be reunited in the way we planned when we were seven years old. I'm lucky to have a friend like you, Alex Stewart; you really are my moonbeam – guiding the way for me all the time. I don't know how unrealistic the promise we made to each other as children was, to stay together side by side for ever, but we have remained friends from across the seas for over twenty years, and that, I'm sure, is some feat.

I've been job hunting all week. My aim was to try and get

255

a job in a hotel, surprise, surprise, but it seems that as the summer has already begun students and immigrants only too willing to be underpaid have already taken everything for the next few months. The money for these jobs really isn't enough to help me and Katie get back on our feet anyway. I will join in with the insufferable moans of twenty-first-century Ireland in a chorus of 'everything is so expensive these days'. I'm waiting to hear from the council about getting a house but I've been here before and the waiting list is so long.

Unfortunately, my position at the Two Lakes Hotel has been filled. Brian has offered to pay child support but I don't want his money. I managed before without him; I certainly don't need his help now. He can give Katie whatever pocket money his heart desires but his money is neither requested nor required by me.

There hasn't been a peep out of whatshisname lately. That man is too afraid of his own shadow, never mind of me. I filed for a divorce last week; I need him out of my life for good. I gave him enough love and enough chances but he threw it all back in my face. I would be a fool to stay around pinning hopes on him again. It's not healthy for me or Katie. I'll dance around the streets naked when the divorce is final.

Did you hear that Stephanie is pregnant? She's due in November so all the family are naturally thrilled. Mum and Dad are in great form, always asking for you and Josh, and they're very much enjoying their retirement together. They're actually talking about selling their house and moving down to the country where it's cheaper so they can use the extra money to travel the world together for the rest of their years. I think it's a great idea. They don't need all these empty rooms in the house (apart from when I come home crying to them) and neither of them has any need to be living in the city. But it also means I have to hurry up and find a job so I can move out with Katie. They're not rushing me but they want to put the house on the market so it will sell quickly during the summer. I'll be the only family member living in Dublin then, which I imagine will be rather lonely. Kevin is in Kilkenny, Steph's in France and Mum and Dad will be off on their travels. It'll just be me and Katie. And Brian the Whine.

My friend Ruby is taking her son, Gary, to salsa lessons from this week, which should be funny. You've met Gary, and I'm sure you'd agree he's not the most expressive or emotive person in the world. But it's a good idea, I suppose. Katie and I should do something together. She gets to go out for the day with her father but we never spend any time like that together. We're always just at home biting each other's heads off. I'll think of something good she'll like, maybe bring her to a concert. With Greg in the house I was always the cool mum that came to the rescue, but now with Brian here, he's the cool new dad who runs the trendy nightclub and I'm the boring mum who makes her clean her room. Of course, knowing that Brian has a nightclub has only strengthened Katie's desire to become a DJ. I don't know what we've created at all. Her music just gets louder and louder. Mum and Dad have been so used to silence in the house for the last few years, I think Dad's going to blow his top if Katie blasts her music any more.

Anyway, that's all my news. I'm getting through each day slowly, taking each day as it comes and all those clichés. Please return my calls. The last thing on this earth that I would want to happen is to lose my best friend. Even if he is a man.

All my love,
Rosie

Phil: So you're pissed off because she's not moving to Boston now, because the father of her child, who she hasn't seen for over thirteen years, has come back and wants to get to know Katie?

257

Alex: Yes.
Phil: Jesus Christ. Who writes your scripts?

Dear Rosie,

I'm sorry, Rosie. I know these have been the worst few weeks of your life and I should have kept in contact. Sometimes I just get so frustrated watching your life but I no I can't control it for you. You have to make the decisions. I wasn't angry at you at all; I was just disappointed for you. I want to see you happy all the time and I new that whatshisname wasn't making you happy. I could see it for years. As crap as it feels right now, not being with him is a blessing in disguise. Anyway, I'll speak more about this over the phone during the week because I could rant about whatshisname for ever.

If I can help you out financially, just let me no, but I'm sure you're just skipping past that line and fuming I've even offered. Still, the offer is there. Business has been going really well lately. Thanks to the diets and lifestyles of the modern world, heart surgery is really in demand. OK, that's not funny.

Speak soon, Buttercup. I no you'll be OK.

Alex

From   Rosie
To   Alex
Subject Re: Messages

Alex Stewart, you KNOW I'll be OK.

From   Alex
To   Katie
Subject Catching-up

It's your beloved godfather here. I'm just emailing you to see how you are and to find out how things are going with your dad. Keep in touch. Haven't heard much from you

258

lately and I gather things have been tough. Let me no how your music is going too. Still want to be a DJ?

From   Katie
To   Alex
Subject Re: Catching-up

SorE this is just a real quick email 2 say hi & that I'm fine tanx. In a rush cos I'm goin out wit Dad in a mo. He takin me to concert in the Point Theatre. He got free tickets cos he nos the band. Felt bad cos Mum already got tickets as surprise for me & her. Said me & her should do more 2gether. Whatever. Don't no wot she's talkin bout we c each other every day. NE way Dad got better tickets so I'm goin with him, and Mum bringin Ruby. They got some crappy tickets down the bak of theatre. Brian is cool. He told me u & him were friends at school & that u went 2 his 10th bday party & that he threw goin away party 4 u b4 u moved to USA. But he said that u & Mum disappeared after first 10 mins. That was a bit rude!

Mum laughed when he reminded her. She wouldn't tell me where u and her went. Where did u go?

Oh here he is now – have 2 go.

Katie: Cool isn't he, Toby?
Toby: Yeah.
Katie: When I finish school I'll be able to move over to Ibiza and work as a DJ in his club. It's so perfect. It all fits in with my master plan.
Toby: Did he say you could work in his club?
Katie: No, but he's hardly gonna say no, is he?
Toby: Dunno. What's his club called?
Katie: Dyma Nite Club. Cool, isn't it?
Toby: Yeah.

Katie: You can come too if you want.

Toby: Thanks. Would you want to live in Ibiza?

Katie: To start off with I would, yeah. First I'd get the experience in his club and then I could travel the world and work in loads of different clubs in each country. Imagine being able to play and listen to music for a living? It sounds like heaven.

Toby: You need to get decks then, don't you?

Katie: Yeah. My dad said he'd get them for me. He's got loads of friends who are DJs and they can get all the best gear for cheaper than the shops. Cool, isn't it?

Toby: Yeah. It's weird – you calling him Dad.

Katie: Yeah, I no. I don't really say it to him, though, just to other people. It feels odd. I expect I'll get used to it.

Toby: Yeah, I suppose. Have you heard from Greg?

Katie: No. Why?

Toby: Don't tell your mum, but me and my mum and dad went out for a Chinese last night and he was there with some woman. He got all embarrassed when he saw me and tried to be all nice and friendly by calling me over to the table and stuff.

Katie: Oh my God. What did you say to him?

Toby: Nothing. I ignored him. I walked straight past their table.

Katie: Good. Serves him right. Did your mum and dad go mental?

Toby: No, Mum winked at me and Dad pretended he didn't see Greg.

Katie: Who was he with?

Toby: Who, my dad?

Katie: No, you stupid. Whatshisname.

Toby: Some blonde. Don't tell your mum though. Has she got a job yet?

Katie: No, but she's been going to interviews every day.

She's been in the worst moods EVER lately, banging
around the house like the Antichrist. Granddad says
that's the way I'm supposed to be now that I'm thirteen.
She's such a grump.
Toby: Are you going to the orthodontist guy soon?
Katie: Yeah, Granddad is taking me tomorrow. My brace
broke again. Why?
Toby: Can I go with you?
Katie: Why do you always want to come? I've got blisters
all on the inside of my mouth and he hacks away at me
while you sit there sucking lollipops.
Toby: I like going. I bet you had cornflakes for breakfast
this morning.
Katie: What are you, psychic?
Toby: No, it's all stuck in your braces.
Katie: Oh, get a life, Toby.
Toby: I have one. So can I go tomorrow?
Katie: What is your obsession with braces, you weirdo?
Toby: They're just interesting.
Katie: Yeah, about as interesting as this geography test. So
come on, what's the answer for number 5? Is the capital
of Australia Sydney?
Toby: Yeah, Katie, it is.

Dear Ms Rosie Dunne,
    We are pleased to offer you the position you recently applied
for. We would expect you to start in August. Please reply to
us as soon as possible with your decision and contact Jessica
at the phone number below.

Chapter 34

You have an instant message from: RUBY.

Ruby: Praise the Lord for he is a miracle worker! I love my son, he is perfect, an absolute genius!

Rosie: There's a turn-up for the books!

Ruby: Well, you would agree if, like me, you had just witnessed the rebirth of Fred Astaire. Not only am I in a great deal of pain from dancing like I have never danced before but I am shocked to the very core! As soon as the music started, magic happened!

I mean, Ricardo didn't exactly go easy on Gary, even though it was his first day. He said, 'Rub-ee, zis is ze advanceda classa, Gar-ee vill just have to try to keep up.' And, my Lord, my Gary kept up so much I almost passed out. Ricardo even put on '1, 2, 3 Maria' by Azuquita and you know, Rosie – it's fast, so fast that it had you and me in a slump on the floor halfway through, watching cartoon stars and birdies circle our heads. The way Gary moved was incredible. He looked so graceful, spinning and twirling around the floor with his sweat glistening like a . . . solar system. Ricardo said Gary was a star in the making and that he and I made a great team.

Teddy wasn't too impressed when I shared the good news. Well, I was so excited when I got home that I just blurted it out but I didn't realise that Teddy's fellow truck-driving friends were in the TV room and they were all equally unimpressed. Teddy went even redder in the face than usual and ranted and raved about all male dancers being gay and that I shouldn't be influencing Gary to fancy boys. I told him I was trying to help him come out of his shell a bit, not to literally 'come out'. But the lads wouldn't understand. They think crashing beer cans against their heads, farting (then sniffing the air and laughing), screaming at the football players on TV (as if they would do any better themselves if they got on that pitch), commenting on all the overweight women on TV (like they don't have big beer bellies and haven't let themselves go ten years ago), calling me every ten minutes to serve them more cans of beer (of the fifty-cent-per-dozen variety) and then having the audacity to *lecture* me on what makes a *real* man, the lazy selfish bastards—

Rosie: Whoa, whoa, Ruby, we seem to have gotten a bit sidetracked here. How did poor Gary feel when Teddy and co. had a go at him?

Ruby: Well, the poor lad was so embarrassed that he stormed out of the room, stomped up the stairs and slammed his bedroom door shut.

Rosie: Oh dear, poor Gary. I hope Teddy apologised.

Ruby: Are you demented? Of course he didn't. Gary's display only further showed how 'gay' he was becoming by pulling a 'woman's strop'. But I soon found solace in six delicate fairy cakes with pretty pink icing. So move over Fred Astaire and Ginger Rogers, Ruby and Gary Minnelli are coming through!

Rosie: Minnelli??

Ruby: OK, so I changed my name to something far more

superstar-like. Ricardo said he could train us both for competitions. We could even get to travel the world if we're good enough. For someone that considers walking to the end of her garden an adventure, being able to travel would be a real dream. That's *if* we're good enough, of course.

Rosie: Ruby, that's terrific news. What will Miss Behave say when she finds out she has been replaced?

Ruby: I'm worried about that; you know how jealous she gets when I even look at other men, but regardless of what she thinks, I'm bringing Gary all the way with me to the World Salsa Dancing Championships in Miami. You know you need to look beyond the four walls of St Patrick's school hall. *See* the possibilities, *smell* the success in the air, *taste* the rewards.

Rosie: Have you been watching Oprah again?

Ruby: Yeah, that 'Remembering your spirit' part gets to me every time. Maybe Gary and I can be on it someday, talking about how we came from nothing to salsa dancing millionaires just by *believing*.

Rosie: Oh, don't talk to me about remembering my spirit. All I can think of is the vodka I knocked back last night.

Ruby: Not that kind of spirit, you fool . . . Any word on the job front?

Rosie: Well, yes, I received a job offer in the post yesterday.

Ruby: Terrific! It's about time. Is it the one you wanted or the one you didn't want?

Rosie: You've known me all these years and you even had to *ask* that question? Actually it was neither, it's the one I really, really, really didn't want and would only accept if it was the last job in Dublin, if I was being thrown out of Mum and Dad's house on my bum and if Katie and I were so desperate for food we had to lick stamps.

Dear Mr and Mrs Dunne,

Hyland & Moore Auctioneers received your request and we would be more than pleased to act on your behalf for the sale of your home. Thank you for choosing Hyland & Moore to represent you.

Yours sincerely,
Thomas Hyland

You have received an instant message from: ROSIE.

Rosie: Hi, it's me.

Rosie: Helloooo?

Rosie: I know you're there. I can see that you've logged online.

Alex: Who is this?

Rosie: Oh, ha ha, you're so funny. What is this? Let's annoy Rosie day?! Tough luck, I am spilling the beans and sharing the sob story of my miserable little life with you whether you like it or not. OK here I go.

I was offered a job. But I turned it down because I didn't think I was desperate enough to have to accept it. It turns out I was wrong. Suddenly Mum and Dad tell me that they're putting the house on the market *the very next day*, and before my brain has a chance to register what they're saying, people start trampling in and out of the house, nosying through my bedroom, complaining about the interiors, laughing at the wallpaper, turning their noses up at the carpets, talking about which walls they'd knock down, which wardrobes they'd rip out and which of my cuddly childhood teddies they would like to burn in a bonfire in the back garden while they danced around it hollering, with stripes of animal blood on their faces (OK so they didn't say *that*). So then a couple put in an offer of full asking price, can you believe, after only seeing it once! Mum and Dad thought about it for approximately twenty seconds and then said yes!

Alex: No!

Rosie: Yes! Apparently the woman is eight months pregnant and they're living in a very small flat and they need to move house really quickly before the baby is born and has to bathe in the sink and play on the balcony.

Alex: No!

Rosie: Yes! Mum and Dad were really apologetic and everything, but I don't blame them because it's their life after all, and frankly they should have had to stop worrying about me the minute I first moved out. So all within a matter of days they've sold the house, everything has been boxed up, they bought a house for practically next to nothing in Connemara. The furniture is being auctioned off tomorrow (apart from the pieces I managed to grab), the rest of the stuff is being delivered to the house tomorrow (which is hours away). Mum and Dad have already bought tickets to go on a cruise for two months and they're leaving on Monday.

Alex: No!

Rosie: Yes! This means that I had to call back the people who offered me the job that I already turned down – not too politely, I might add. I had to apologise profusely and try to convince them that I really wanted the job after all. They were really pissed off and said they didn't need me until August. So today Katie spent the day with Brian while I went emergency house hunting.

Alex: No!

Rosie: Yes! Everywhere that was in any way affordable was absolutely disgusting. The apartments were still either too expensive, too small or too far from my job and Katie's school. So Mum and Dad were discussing my personal problems (as they generally do) with the young sickeningly happy couple who are about to embark on blissful family life while butchering my

266

childhood home. And because Mum and Dad had been so speedy and understanding about the whole 'moving out in a few days' scenario, they suggested that I move *into* the flat they just moved *out* of and had decided to rent out.

Alex: No!

Rosie: Yes! But the only thing is that they have already rented the place out for a few weeks to a group of male students so I have to wait until they move out. By which time it will no doubt be disgustingly smelly and dirty.

Alex: No!

Rosie: Yes! So who do I stay with while I wait, I hear you ask. Well, let's see, Mum and Dad have moved to Connemara, as you now know. Kev lives in the staff quarters of the Two Lakes Hotel in Kilkenny, Steph lives in France, Ruby has only two bedrooms and no space for me and Katie, and you're in Boston, which isn't convenient commuting for me. So who is the only other human being in Dublin that I know right now (and don't even think of whatshisname)?

None other than Brian the Whine.

Alex: No!

Rosie: Yes! I am afraid so. I am emailing you from the storeroom of Brian the Whine's rented flat, where I have to stay for a few weeks. How much lower can I go? And that's not even my worst news. I haven't even told you who my new boss is. None other than Miss Big Nose Smelly Breath Casey.

Alex: No!

Rosie: Yes! I am now secretary to the woman we most hated while growing up, the woman who made my daughter's life hell while in school and who is now principal of St Patrick's Primary School, and my boss. Why on earth Miss Big Nose Smelly Breath Casey even hired me is completely beyond me, but she has, and until I find another job in a hotel I won't complain or ask questions. Perhaps she just wants to make my life a misery well into my adult life and until I'm an elderly woman. And speaking of the elderly, she was old when I was *five years old*, for Christsake, and she's still old. The woman has nine lives.

So what do you think of all that? Any messages you want me to pass on to your favourite teacher?

Rosie: Hello, Alex?

Rosie: Alex?

Alex: Em . . . sorry, Alex isn't actually online.

Rosie: Oh, ha ha. Well then, how is his name on my screen and I am typing to him?

Alex: You're not. I logged on using his home computer. I guess his name automatically comes up on your system. I've never come across this little system, it's fun. Sorry, I didn't know you were looking for him.

Rosie: What?? You think I just rant about my private life to all strangers on the computer??? Who is this?

Alex: Bethany.

Rosie: Bethany?

Alex: Bethany Williams? Remember me?

Rosie: What the hell are you doing on Alex's home computer?!

Alex: Oh, I'm sorry, it all makes sense now. Alex didn't tell you, did he? I thought you two told each other everything. I'll be sure to pass on all your little messages to him, though. They were very amusing. Good luck with the new job, Rosie; I'll let Alex explain this one to you. By the way, Alex is working with my father now. He's making good money, doing very well for himself. Perhaps if you're that stuck for money he could give you a loan.

Rosie has logged off.

Chapter 35

Welcome to the Relieved Divorced Dubliners' internet chat room. There are currently five people chatting.
Buttercup has joined the room.
Divorced_1: Screw him, screw'm, screw'm, screw'm!
Buttercup: Hello, everyone.
Wildflower: Wahooooo! You tell her Divorced_1!
UnsureOne: I know, Divorced_1, but that's the problem now, isn't it? I can't 'screw him' any more; he's gone. I should never have let him leave. Oh, it's all my fault.
Buttercup: Em . . . hello, everyone. Is this working? Can you all read what I'm writing?
Divorced_1: Oh, shut up, UnsureOne. I'm sick of listening to you moaning night after night. How is it your fault? Did you drag him into the car and drive him to the hotel room? Did you pull his pants down around his ankles and push him on top of her on the bed?
UnsureOne: Please stop, Divorced_1! Stop! Stop! Stop! No I didn't!
LonelyLady: Oh, leave her alone. There's no need to be so graphic.
Divorced_1: Look, I'm only trying to help. If you didn't do all those things then how on earth is it your fault?

269

Buttercup: I'm not sure this is working. Hello? Hello? Hello? Stupid bloody computer. Can anyone answer me?

UnsureOne: Well, maybe I inadvertently put him under pressure to do better at his job. You know how things are so expensive these days and the kids always want more, more, more. They were going back to school and the uniforms and books are always so expensive and I kept telling him we needed more money because it was tight and I'm not sure but maybe it *was* my fault, you know?

LonelyLady: Oh, please, Unsure . . .

Wildflower: Oh, I have heard quite enough for one night.

Divorced_1: Look, just forget about him. He's a bastard and that's all there is to it. Screw him.

Buttercup: Well, not that anyone cares, but there was only one kind of job your husband was thinking of that night and it didn't involve a day at the office.

Wildflower: Wahoooo! Welcome, Buttercup!

Divorced_1: You're right, Buttercup, screw him.

UnsureOne: Are you sure, Buttercup?

LonelyLady: I tend to agree with the others, UnsureOne. Welcome, Buttercup. You want to chat?

Wildflower: Please, LonelyLady, every time you ask one of our visitors if they want to chat you scare them away. You sound like you want to talk dirty or something.

LonelyLady: I'm sorry, you know I don't mean to. I just have this horrible habit of driving everyone away.

Wildflower: What are your stats, Buttercup?

Buttercup: My what?

Divorced_1: Oh, everyone look, a chat-room virgin.

Wildflower: Your stats, cupcake – age, sex, that sort of thing.

Buttercup: Well, I'm thirty-two, I'm female, I have a thirteen-year-old daughter and I'm happily divorced.

Wildflower: Wahoooo!

Divorced_1: Congratulations, cupcake. Screw him – that's what I say.

UnsureOne: Buttercup, whose fault was the marriage break-up? Yours or his?

Wildflower: Ignore her, Buttercup. She's riding the 'blame' wave.

Buttercup: That's OK, I don't mind. It was one hundred per cent *his* fault.

Divorced_1: *Quelle surprise.*

LonelyLady: At least you have a daughter, Buttercup, and you weren't left all alone. My husband – well, my ex-husband – left me before we even had a chance to start a family. I don't think it would have been so hard if we'd had children. Then at least I wouldn't feel so—

Divorced_1: Alone, yeah, yeah. Well, trust me it's harder *with* kids. Unfortunately my rugrats are the spit of my husband and when I look at them I just want to strangle the little bastards. Do your kids look like your ex, UnsureOne?

UnsureOne: Yes and no. Some people say they do and others say they don't. I'm not too sure really . . .

Wildflower: Let's not be rude, guys, and introduce ourselves to Buttercup. I'm sixty-two years old, I've five kids and my husband left me last year.

Buttercup: Oh, how awful. I'm sorry.

Divorced_1: HA! No need to be sorry, cupcake. The man had good reason to leave her; she was sleeping with their gardener.

Buttercup: Oh!

Wildflower: Oh, *please*, like you lot never thought of ever doing the same thing.

UnsureOne: Well, my gardener was a woman.

Wildflower: I didn't mean *that*.

LonelyLady: I never would have done something like that to my Tommy. Never.

Divorced_1: Hi, Buttercup. I'm forty-nine years old, have four kids and my ex-husband was screwing his secretary. Bastard.

Buttercup: LonelyLady, what about you?

LonelyLady: I'm twenty-seven, I just got married last year but my Tommy left me. He just couldn't take married life, he said. One day he just left me . . . all alone.

Buttercup: UnsureOne, what about you?

UnsureOne: I'm thirty-six, have three children and I'm not technically divorced *per se*. We still live together . . . what about you, Buttercup, how did you and your husband split?

Buttercup: Oh, he was seeing a number of different women quite regularly and I was oblivious to it all.

Divorced_1: Bastard.

Wildflower: Well, I believe that we're all put on this earth to have as many sexual playmates as we want.

Divorced_1: Do shut up, you new-age hippy.

Wildflower: There's no harm in expressing my personal view. I don't recall ever attacking your opinions.

Divorced_1: That's because my opinions are always right. So, Buttercup, did you get the house?

Buttercup: No, I got the hell out of there. That was good enough for me.

Divorced_1: I was screwed in the divorce settlement. My ex got the holiday home and I got custody of the kids. What I would give to swap for a few months of peace and quiet in the sun.

LonelyLady: I got to keep the house and it just meant I had to stay here all on my own with rooms full of memories.

Divorced_1: Oh, drop it, Lonely. You sound like a broken record today.

LonelyLady: What? I would stay with Tommy even if he was a shit. I wouldn't care, I just want him.

Wildflower: Ignore her. Her balance is all wrong. The best way to get over one man is to get under another. We all know that.

UnsureOne: I'm not sure that's the correct attitude to have. I certainly have no intentions of sharing a bed with anyone other than my husband.

Buttercup: I don't understand, UnsureOne. You're still married?

UnsureOne: We're not technically divorced. He sleeps in our bedroom and I sleep in the spare room.

Wildflower: UnsureOne, you let him kick *you* into the *spare room* when *he* was the one messing around?

UnsureOne: Oh, is that wrong? I'm not too sure. This is all new to me . . .

LonelyLady: I wouldn't care if Tommy and I couldn't even stay in the same bed. I just want him home with me.

Divorced_1: Sweet Lord, have I taught you ladies nothing at all . . . ? Anyway, Buttercup, where are you living now if shit-for-brains kept the house?

Buttercup: Oh, this may seem a bit bizarre but I'm currently living with my daughter's father.

UnsureOne: The way it should be, I think.

LonelyLady: Oooh, what a wonderful love story!

Buttercup: Oh, no, no, no. Don't get me wrong, there's absolutely no love involved in this story. In fact, I hate him.

Wildflower: Thou doth protest too much.

Buttercup: Yes, I do, and if you met him you would too.

Divorced_1: I wouldn't be sure of that. Ever since this woman hit sixty she's been eating men for breakfast.

Buttercup: Not this one, I assure you, unless you mistake his head for a hard-boiled egg.

UnsureOne: Buttercup, why did you choose that name?

Buttercup: Oh, it's just a nickname my best friend calls me. When we were six we were in a school play and I was

Princess Buttercup and he was Prince Moonbeam. He's been calling me that name ever since.

Divorced_1: You're still in contact after twenty-six years??

Buttercup: Yep, we're still best friends.

Divorced_1: You're best friends with a man? Did you ever sleep with him?

Buttercup: Only when we had sleepovers in the non-sexual kind of way.

Divorced_1: Is he gay?

Buttercup: No he's not.

UnsureOne: Well, I think that's beautiful. I mean, I lost contact with my school friends as soon as I left and got married. Leonard hated me having any male friends.

LonelyLady: When I moved from Belfast to Dublin with Tommy I left all my family and friends behind and now with Tommy gone, my friends are all up north and I'm—

Divorced_1: All alone, yeah, yeah, we get the message. Buttercup, is your friend single, what does he do, where does he live and finally is he looking for a hot forty-nine-year-old with four kids? He can take or leave the kids, I'm not bothered.

Buttercup: No, unfortunately he's not single.

Wildflower: Why 'unfortunately'?

Buttercup: Because she's a real bitch. She's his first love from when he was sixteen. I hated her then and I still hate her now. Anyway, he ended up working with her dad in Boston, of all places, and I suppose their love was rekindled.

Divorced_1: And you're jealous.

Buttercup: I am not.

Divorced_1: Yes you are. I can hear it in your tone.

Buttercup: You cannot hear me; we're typing to each other!

Wildflower: What she means is that she *senses* it and, I must admit, I agree.

UnsureOne: But *surely* if you've been friends since you were six and you're now thirty-two, you've both been married once and are now living with other people in different *countries*, then if it hasn't happened by now, it won't be happening at all.

Wildflower: Oh, Unsure, don't be so pessimistic. Soul mates have a knack of finding their way to one another.

LonelyLady: Does that mean that my Tommy will come back to me?

Wildflower: No.

SingleSam has entered the room.

Divorced_1: Sam!

Wildflower: Wahoooo! Sam!

LonelyLady: Hi, Sam, welcome. How are you?

UnsureOne: Hello, Sam.

SingleSam: Hello, ladies, good to see you all here again tonight.

Divorced_1: Sam, meet Buttercup. She's thirty-two, has a thirteen-year-old daughter and her husband was cheating on her. Cupcake, meet Sam, he's fifty-four, has two daughters and his ex-wife's a lesbian.

SingleSam: Nice to meet you, Buttercup.

Buttercup: Nice to meet you too, Sam.

UnsureOne: So what's new, Sam? Are you happy or sad today?

SingleSam: Oh, today has been a bad day for me.

Wildflower: Oh please! This is supposed to be the *Relieved* Divorced Dubliners' chat room not the Depressed Divorced Dubliners. I'm heading to bed.

Buttercup: I better head off to bed too. It was nice to meet you all.

Divorced_1: See you same time tomorrow night, Buttercup.

UnsureOne: I better put the kids to bed.

LonelyLady: I think I'll watch the wedding video one more time before I go to bed.

Buttercup has left the room.
LonelyLady has left the room.
UnsureOne has left the room.
Wildflower has left the room.
Divorced_1: Well, Sam, it looks like it's just you and me.
    You put the music on and I'll light the candles.
Click on the icon to the left to print this page.

From   Stephanie
To   Rosie
Subject   Miss Casey!

I cannot *believe* you're going to be working with Miss Casey! Mum told me over the phone and I could barely understand her through all her laughing. She's wondering what her and Dad should do when they receive a letter from Miss Casey while they're in Australia, demanding to see them first thing Monday morning due to your behaviour at work!

    Whatever persuaded you to take this job? Have you gone nuts? I never had a problem with the woman personally, but I know that she drove you insane when you were a kid and then again when Katie had her for a teacher! What does Alex think about all this? I'm sure he's got some very interesting views on the subject!

Dear Stephanie,

    Well, you, of course, *never* had a problem with Miss Casey because you were Miss Goody Two-Shoes! She loved you and your neat copies and your finished and correct homework and your tidy uniform and politeness!

    I probably am nuts taking this job, but to be honest it's the best one with the most attractive pay packet by far. It's Monday to Friday 9 a.m. to 3.30 p.m. which is great, because

I had to work all hours and weekends with my last job. It's right beside Katie's secondary school, which means we can get the bus together every day. We're only a few minutes from the flat so I'll be able to escape home for lunch every day. With all of life's other complications these little things will really help me out a lot. I really don't intend working there for very long, just until a job in the hotel industry opens up.

But the main reason for me taking the job is the fact that I have very little choice. I have a week left here in purgatory (Brian's flat) before I can move into my own rented flat, which is a dump. I'm going to need all the spare cash I can get to fix the place up and make it feel like home. God knows, Katie's had so many of them so far. When the Rosie Dunne Hotel Chain buys Hilton Hotels, that's when I can rip up the budget.

Strange things have happened to Katie over the years, but none of them as bizarre as her mother and father living in the same house as one another. What may be a way of life for some children is something for Katie to laugh hysterically at. Actually, it's not as if Brian and I dislike each other, it's just that we know absolutely *nothing* about one another. We are two complete strangers who got together once in our lives (and only for a few minutes, trust me) in a moment I can barely even remember, to make the most incredible thing ever. How could two fools like us create something as great as Katie? When Katie comes home from school and starts to go off on one of her stand-up comedy routines about her day I look at her, I look at him, and think how did *him*, mixed with *me*, make *her*.

With neither me nor Brian working at all, I try to spend as little time as possible here. I stroll up and down Henry Street for most of the day just to stay out of his way. When I'm at the flat I stay in my room or lock myself into the store-room and send emails all day. You would think that we would share *some* sort of bond or friendship or have *some* kind of relationship. But we're complete strangers.

I still feel angry at him now, but it's a different kind of anger. Before I felt angry at him because he left *me*. *I* had to do everything. *My* social life was ruined, all *my* money was being spent, and *I* couldn't get a job. But now when I look at him joking around with Katie I just think what a waste. That's all he had to do while she was growing up – be there for her and she would have accepted him, as children do, no matter what he was like. I feel angry at him for not being there for *her*. I've finally lost that selfish part of me.

Once again, I don't quite know where I'm headed, Steph. It seems that every few years I'm shovelling up the pieces of my life and starting from scratch all over. No matter what I do or how hard I try I can't seem to reach the dizzy heights of happiness, success and security, like so many people do. And I'm not talking about becoming a millionaire and living happily ever after. I just mean reaching a point in my life that I can stop what I'm doing, take a look around me, breathe a sigh of relief and think: I'm where I want to be now.

I'm missing something, you know? That special 'sparkle' that life is supposed to bring. I have the job, the child, the family, the apartment and the friends, but I've lost the sparkle.

And in answer to your question about Alex, I don't know what he thinks of my new job because I haven't heard from him in a long time. He's so busy saving more valuable lives and attending charity functions that I couldn't possibly expect him to get in touch with a friend like me. He's far too busy hooking up with 'old' friends. Slutty ones at that.

Chapter 36

Bon Voyage!

I'll miss you both like crazy. Things won't be the same without you but I hope you have a brilliant time!

Love,

Rosie

To Grandma and Granddad

Have fun, send us loads of postcards.

Love,

Katie (your *favourite* granddaughter)

You have an instant message from: ALEX.

Alex: Hello.

Rosie: Oh, so he *is* still alive. Where have you been for the past few weeks?

Alex: Hiding.

Rosie: From whom?

Alex: You.

Rosie: Why?

Alex: Because I'm dating Bethany again and I was afraid to tell you because you hate her with a passion, and then you found out from *her* first, which made things even worse. So I was hiding from you.

Rosie: Why?

Alex: Because I thought you'd come over here and kill me.

Rosie: Why?

Alex: Because you think she's a slut and that she's no good for me.

Rosie: Why?

Alex: Because you're my overprotective best friend and you've always hated my girlfriends (and wife) and I've always hated your boyfriends (and husband).

Rosie: Why?

Alex: Well, because he had an affair, for one . . .

Rosie: Why?

Alex: Because he was an absolute fool and he didn't no how lucky he was. But let's not talk about him any more because he's gone and he's never coming back.

Rosie: Why?

Alex: Because I scared him off.

Rosie: Why?

Alex: Because I'm your best friend and I care about you.

Rosie: Why?

Alex: Because I've nothing better to do.

Rosie: Why?

Alex: Because it's the unfortunate way that my life turned out. Whatever happened made me care about you and yours. Anyway, it's great that I don't have to hide any more.

Rosie: Why?

Alex: Because I've apologised.

Rosie: Why?

Alex: Because I'm tired of not hearing from you and I miss you.

Rosie: Why?

Alex: Because (and I'm now saying this through incredibly

gritted teeth) You. Are. My. Best. Friend. But I have to warn you, I'm not going to listen to any of your bitchy remarks about her this time round.

Rosie: Why?

Alex: Because I really like her, Rosie, and she makes me happy. I feel like the little boy working in Dad's office again. And just think, if it wasn't for you getting so drunk on your sixteenth birthday that you had to get your stomach pumped, we never would have been caught, we wouldn't have been suspended and I wouldn't have been punished so severely by having to file every piece of paper in the world in Dad's office, where, I might add, I would never have met Bethany. So it's all down to you, my dear friend!

Rosie: OH, WHYYYYYY??? Dear God, why?

Alex: Ha ha. I'd better go now because I've got surgery in a few hours.

Rosie: Why?

Alex: Because I happen to be a cardiac surgeon and there's a poor man, called Mr Jackson, if you really must no, who needs aortic valve surgery.

Rosie: Why?

Alex: Because he has aortic stenosis.

Rosie: Why?

Alex: Well, the reasons behind aortic incompetence in general are rheumatic. But don't worry (because I no that you are), Mr Jackson will be fine.

Rosie: Why?

Alex: Because thankfully due to seventy-five years of studying I have learned an operation involving the ball valve prosthesis which will help him. Any more questions?

Rosie: The aorta, it's in, like, the heart, right?

Alex: Very funny. OK, I'm really going this time; I'm really glad we had this discussion and that we've cleared the whole Bethany thing right up. So I'm forgiven?

281

Rosie: No.
Alex: Great stuff, thanks. Speak to you soon.
Alex has logged off.
Rosie: Thanks for asking about my job, *Doctor*.

From   Rosie
To   Ruby
Subject   Help!

Help . . . help me . . . Oh dear, my head. My poor, poor head. My even poorer brain cells, they never even had a chance. They're gone. Dead. It's four o'clock in the afternoon and I am bedridden (not exactly half as much fun as it sounds) and bed is where I shall stay for the remainder of my years. Goodbye world, farewell all, thanks for the memories.

And of the ones remaining from last night I shall try to explain to you exactly what I got up to, although there seems to be a heavy mist working its way in from the edges of my brain towards the centre. I'll try to get it all out before I'm surrounded in fuzziness.

After a very frustrating meeting with my bank manager I returned to Brian the Whine's house feeling very deflated, angry and uncertain about my life. I really wasn't in the mood for conversation or company, but sitting in the living room were Brian's parents, who had flown over from Santa Ponsa to discuss meeting Katie and becoming a part of her life. I was already feeling weary and weak and the thought that Katie would have another set of grandparents – even more people in her life she could have known, yet didn't – just really got to me. And I became even angrier by the fact that all these years I knew who they were, they knew well who I was, they had passed me in the street on numerous occasions while I was pregnant, then again when Katie had been born, had heard the rumours that she was

Brian's child yet never bothered to make any sort of contact or give help of any kind. The last I had heard of them was that they had sold up and had moved to the sun to help heal Mrs Whine's arthritis.

The conversation was heated, didn't go that well. Let's just say, so I made my excuses and left.

Of course I had absolutely nowhere to go so I just wandered the streets for ages and pondered my life. After a while I decided I hated it and everyone in it (I know, I know – *again*), and seeing as Katie was away safe for the night and Brian the Whine had company, I made my way to the nearest pub and drowned my sorrows.

The bar was really awful actually, but because I was so upset I didn't care. All I saw was a friendly barman and two serial killers deep in discussion at the end of the bar. So the barman saw that I was really upset, and this is real film stuff, but he actually did ask me what was wrong and seemed genuinely concerned. I told him that Greg had ruined my life. (By process of elimination I reached the conclusion that it was entirely his fault.) It just all came spilling out of my mouth, Ruby, all about Alex missing the debs, Brian the Whine, having Katie, missing college, Alex getting married, meeting Greg, marrying Greg, Greg cheating on me, missing my job promotion, Greg cheating on me again . . . I told him about Greg having all those affairs while he said that he was away on conferences and because he was a bank manager I believed that he genuinely had to go to all that stuff.

So then the other two guys down the end of the bar were suddenly really interested in me, saw how upset I was and bought me loads of drinks. They were huge guys, Ruby, over six foot tall, muscles so big they looked like body builders, bald heads, one guy had a tattoo of a severed head on his forearm, but they were so nice! They were really concerned, asked me loads of questions, gave me tissues when I cried and told me I could do better than Greg. I was just really surprised, Ruby. They were kind enough to drive me home and make sure I got back safely because I was in absolutely no state to walk. I pointed out Greg's house as we passed and they seemed really interested and we all gave him the finger. Such nice guys. It just shows, you can never judge a book by its cover.

Anyway I have such a headache so I have to stop typing but last night proved to me that at least there are *some* caring men in the world and they're not just all out for themselves.

Bank Manager Attacked In His Home

A bank manager was badly beaten in a vicious attack and thousands of euro were stolen in a burglary yesterday morning. The victim was forty-two-year-old Greg Collins of AIB, Fairview, Dublin.

The savage raid took place when Collins was awaked in the early hours of the morning by intruders in his home on Abigail Road. The two masked men broke into the victim's home and demanded the bank manager open the bank and empty the safe. Terrified Collins put up a struggle but was punched viciously in the face by the thugs. His nose, which was healing from a previous injury, was further damaged.

A shaken Collins described how he was blindfolded and forced into their van in his pyjamas.

The thugs are believed to be over six foot tall and according to Collins had the appearance of body builders. Although he didn't see their faces he did notice a tattoo of a severed head on the arm of one thief.

The men stole €20,000 and sped off quickly, leaving Collins alone at the bank, beaten and dressed only in his nightwear. The gardaí arrived on the scene moments after the men had left, after the alarm had been triggered.

Collins is unsure of how they knew his address. 'I'm always careful to look out for anyone suspicious following me home each day but I didn't notice anyone that night. It was the worst night of my life – an absolute nightmare,' Collins said, visibly shaken. 'These thugs invaded my home and attacked me. I'm terrified.'

Collins was home alone at the time due to the recent break-up of his marriage. An investigation into the burglary was underway today but the Garda in charge says it is unlikely they will catch the culprits, due to a lack of leads.

If anyone has any information regarding this crime, gardaí ask that you come forward now.

Photo above: 42-year-old Greg Collins stands outside the bank and shows broken nose.

You have an instant message from: RUBY.
Ruby: You see the papers today?
Rosie: Nope. I've given up on my star signs.
Ruby: Well, may I suggest you purchase the *Daily Star* quickly and cast your mind back to Saturday night?
Rosie: Oh no, did the paparazzi snap me coming out of the pub? Ha ha.
Ruby: Not funny, Rosie. I'm referring to the men. Now quick, look at the paper.
Rosie: What? What men? What are you talking about?!
Ruby: Tabloid newspaper. Now. Quick. Go.
Rosie: OK.
Rosie has logged off.

From   Rosie
To   Alex
Subject Today's article

It's me, Rosie. Check your fax machine quick! I've sent you over an article that was in the paper today. While you're reading it bear in mind the story of my Saturday night out that I told you about.

Read the paper and tell me what you think. Quick! I need your advice.

From   Alex
To   Rosie
Subject Re: Today's article

Ha ha ha ha ha ha ha ha ha ha ha ha ha ha ha ha ha ha ha ha ha ha ha ha ha ha ha ha ha ha ha ha ha ha ha ha ha ha ha ha ha ha ha ha ha ha ha.

Chapter 37

You have received an instant message from: ROSIE.

Rosie: Oh. My. God. Alex.

Alex: Yes, Rosie?

Rosie: Are you free to chat or are you busy?

Alex: I'm just doing a bit of work but go ahead.

Rosie: My goodness, life-saving surgery on the internet? Is there no end to your talents, Doctor?

Alex: Apparently not. What's up?

Rosie: You will NOT believe what came through Brian the Whine's door this morning!

Alex: A brick.

Rosie: No!

Alex: A warrant for your arrest.

Rosie: No! Don't say that! Why would you say that?

Alex: Oh, no reason in particular. I was just wondering what the sentence is for people who hire other people to beat up and terrorise their ex-husbands.

Rosie: Alex Stewart, stop that talk right now! It's not safe to say things like that over the internet, you know, and I did *not* do that!

Alex: You're right, the gardaí are probably on a stakeout

right now across the road, watching your every move through a pair of binoculars.

Rosie: Stop, Alex, you're freaking me out. The only thing I'm guilty of is a bit of naïvety, that's all.

Alex: A bit? You think those 'serial killer-looking guys' are usually as friendly to lone women in pubs as they were to you?

Rosie: Look, I was drunk, my suspicions were at an all-time low and my guard was down. In fact, I had no guard. Stupid, I know, but I'm still alive so let's not keep telling me how foolish I was. Anyway, as it turns out they were caring guys. It just so happens that when I came downstairs this morning there was a brown package on the kitchen table with my name on it. Inside was €5,000, can you believe it?! And you said they weren't caring!

Alex: Was there a note inside, or a little thank-you card maybe?

Rosie: Alex, do you not take anything seriously? No, there wasn't any note so it may not even be from them.

Alex: Rosie, a brown package appeared on your kitchen table overnight with €5,000 inside. Unless the postman has a key to the flat I think we can presume it was them.

Rosie: So what will I tell the gardaí?

Alex: You're not keeping the money?

Rosie: Alex, I have a thirteen-year-old daughter, I do not think keeping knowledge of a bank robbery (as well as some of the money) is exactly the wisest thing to do. Plus, believe it or not I have a conscience.

Alex: Well, usually I would agree with the telling-the-truth theory and abiding by the rules but this time around I think you should keep your mouth shut. Firstly, those guys no you are the only person who nos anything about this, they no where you live and can enter your

288

home in the middle of the night without disturbing the neighbours or anyone else inside. I don't think they were giving you this money as a present for a wonderful start to your new life – they don't seem the type.

Rosie: Oh my God, I've shivers up my spine! This is crazy, like a movie or something. But I can't *not* tell the gardaí.

Alex: Do you want to die?

Rosie: Yes, eventually.

Alex: Rosie, I'm serious. Keep the money and say nothing. Give it to charity or something if it bothers you that much. You can make a donation to the Reginald Williams Foundation for Heart Disease if you want.

Rosie: Gag, gag, puke, puke. No, thanks. But the charity thing isn't a bad idea. I think I'll do that.

Alex: Which one will you donate it to?

Rosie: The Rosie Dunne Foundation for Women who haven't seen their Best Friends in America for ages.

Alex: Excellent idea. I'm sure the poor deprived woman will be delighted with your donation. When do you think she and her daughter will be visiting their doctor friend?

Rosie: I already booked them a flight for Friday week. They land at nine in the morning and they'll be staying a fortnight. You're right; giving makes me feel like such a better person.

Alex: Ha! You had this all planned. I'll be there to pick you up.

Rosie: Good. By the way, you *still* haven't said anything about my job.

Alex: Job? You got a job? When? Where? What are you doing?

Rosie: Alex, I've only left approximately 22,496 messages on your answering machine explaining this. Don't you listen to them?

Alex: Sorry. So what's the job?

Rosie: Promise not to laugh.

Alex: I promise.

Rosie: I'm starting in August as a secretary in St Patrick's Primary School.

Alex: You're going back . . . *there*? Hold on a minute . . . that means that you're going to be working with Miss Big Nose Smelly Breath Casey! Why?

Rosie: Because I need the money.

Alex: Wouldn't you rather starve? Why on earth did she hire you?

Rosie: I'm wondering the same thing.

Alex: Ha ha ha ha ha.

Rosie: You said you wouldn't laugh.

Alex: Ha ha ha ha ha.

Rosie: You promised!

Alex: Ha ha ha ha ha.

Rosie: Oh, bugger off.

Rosie has logged off.

Dear Rosie and Katie,

Greetings from Aruba!

Having a wonderful time here in paradise!

Hope all is well with you,

Lots of love,

Mum and Dad

You have received an instant message from: RUBY.

Ruby: Watch out, Ireland, here we come!

Rosie: Here who come?

Ruby: Gary and Ruby Minnelli.

Rosie: You're keeping the name, I see?! What are Gary and Ruby Minnelli up to now?

Ruby: Yes, we're keeping the name and Gary doesn't even mind because it means that he's in disguise and none of

290

his work colleagues or friends will recognise him. The All-Ireland Salsa Dancing Championships are on in a few months from now. A couple from each county goes forward and whoever wins becomes the Ireland champions, then there's the European Championship and the World Championship.

Rosie: So you're going for total world domination?

Ruby: Well, not quite the *world* but Gary and I are willing to take on Ireland.

Rosie: How does Teddy feel?

Ruby: He has no idea and that's the way it's going to stay. Anyway, we haven't even gotten through the Dublin heats so there's no point in causing mayhem and bloody murdering sprees until we get further into the competition. It's on in a few weeks – will you be there?

Rosie: I'm insulted you even had to ask!

Ruby: Thanks.

From   Stephanie
To   Rosie
Subject Visit

I hope you're keeping well. You're dealing with everything that has happened so brilliantly, I'm so proud of you. I know it's been a tough time and with me being all the way over here I feel like I haven't been there for you like I should have been. If it's OK with you I would love to come over and visit you. Maybe stay for a week or something. With Mum and Dad off gallivanting around the world, unfortunately the rest of us don't meet up like we should, and it must be very lonely for you. Maybe we should go to Kilkenny and visit Kevin. The three of us haven't been in the same room together since I don't know how long. (Don't worry, we won't go to the hotel. We can stand outside and throw eggs at the windows, if you like!)

To be really honest with you I need the rest as well. Jean-Louis is just too much for me right now. He's a bundle of energy and I'm simply not, so Pierre is taking the week off from the restaurant to mind him so that I can see you.

Also, I know that you're at Brian's so I'll stay with a friend – I certainly wouldn't want to upset the happy family! I haven't seen him since your school dance when he arrived at the house wearing his navy tux (I agree with you, it was definitely navy, not black). It'll be interesting to see how he's turned out and I'll give him a piece of my mind too. If you have other plans then feel free to let me know.

From   Rosie
To   Stephanie
Subject Re: Visit

Of course I would love you to come over. Next week is great; in fact it couldn't be more perfect. You see, Brian the Whine's parents have returned from the depths of hell (and are constantly complaining about the cold here, even though it's the middle of summer and everyone is wearing shorts. Every time I open a window they shiver and pull another blanket around them. Not what they're used to at their private *villa* at all, which just so happens to be a one-bedroom apartment in Santa Ponsa). Anyway, the traumatic thing is that they are staying in this very flat in a desperate attempt to get to know me and their 'granddaughter'. The only thing is, it's the summer holidays and all Katie wants to do is hang around outside with Toby, not inside with two shivering, shrivelled-up whinge-bags.

The flat feels even more cramped than usual with them being here and I feel so claustrophobic. Imagine, I actually can't wait to start my new job just so I can get out of the house. Toby is very funny: he keeps telling me and Katie to be nice to them so we can get to use the apartment whenever we want. So Katie and him keep making them cups of tea and bringing it to them while they're still in bed. I know the boy is only thirteen but he has a point, so recently I started putting biscuits on their saucers.

So you coming over, my dear sister, could not come at a better time. It is both a genius and life-saving idea. Plus I really miss you too! At least I'm going to have a great summer before I start the job in hell.

From   Rosie
To   Kevin
Subject   Steph's visit

Steph is over from France for the week. What days are you off so that we can come down and visit you? We can all go out for a meal or something. We haven't done that for a while.

From   Kevin
To   Rosie
Subject   Re: Steph's visit

That sounds like a good plan. I don't think the three of us have been in the same room together since Mum and Dad forced us to take baths together. I've got Tuesday off, so why don't you both come down on Monday and I'll treat you for dinner?

From   Rosie
To   Kevin
Subject   Re: Steph's visit

Going for dinner sounds good as long as we don't go to the hotel to eat. Knowing whatshisname was there with *her* is enough to put me off it for ever. Stephanie had the wonderfully juvenile idea of me throwing eggs at the hotel to release my anger. Stock up on those eggs, dear brother. We'll be down on Monday to celebrate your good news, see you then.

Invoice Number:	KIL000321	
Our Reference:	6444421	
		Fee Invoice
Fee for damage to dining-room windows of Kilkenny Two Lakes Hotel:		€6,232.00
VAT @ 21%		€1,308.72
		—————
Total		€7,540.72

Note to self:
Must always check that eggs are not hard-boiled before throwing.

From   Rosie
To   Alex
Subject Flight details

My flight is landing at 9 a.m. so don't forget!

Hello from Barbados!
We're having such a ball! The weather is fantastic and we've met lots of lovely people.
Love you both,
Mum and Dad

You have received an instant message from: ROSIE.
Rosie: I'm baaaaack!

Ruby: Oh, so you decided to come home! I'm surprised.

Rosie: Well, I almost didn't. If it wasn't for Brian the Whine and his parents wanting to be my new best friends and ruining all my plans.

Ruby: Imagine, having to think of other people. So how did it go?

Rosie: It was just so brilliant. That's all I can say. Pure heaven.

Ruby: You two get along well?

Rosie: Even better than usual.

Ruby: Did you—

Rosie: No!

Ruby: Did you tell him how you—

Rosie: No! Why on earth would I do that? There's no point. If I did that then I would lose him as a friend for ever and then it would all be a waste of time. He has never suggested to me that he has ever felt that way about me; remember it was me that kissed him the last time. That was embarrassing enough once, never mind having to do it a second time. Anyway, he is already with someone and even if it is Slutty Bethany I couldn't bring myself to do that. We had a really long chat about her, anyway. He took me out for dinner one night to a beautiful Italian restaurant that had wonderful murals of Venetian buildings painted across the walls. The restaurant had two levels, every table was in its own little alcove, and you could only get to them by walking under bridges and arches. It was supposed to have a gondola trip kind of vibe. There was running water tinkling in the background, which was really relaxing although it made me go to the bathroom about ten times. The restaurant was lit entirely by candles all held in big gothic-looking black holders – an insurance nightmare, I would imagine, but very romantic. I think he brought me there to talk about Slutty Bethany and to explain the situation.

It doesn't seem to be that serious a relationship. He said he's enjoying the company after being alone for so long and it's good that she understands his long working hours but they don't see that much of each other and he thinks she understands that it's a very casual relationship. It sounds like he's going to break up with her actually because he got really serious and I thought he was going to cry. It was weird; he said that she wasn't 'the one' for him.

Ruby: And then what?

Rosie: And then Josh rang the restaurant in a right panic, looking for us. He and Katie had been messing around, Katie had fallen and they were convinced she'd broken her wrist. We had to leave straight away but we had finished dessert and everything, so it was just as well. The conversation was finished.

Ruby: Or was just starting, by the sounds of things.

Rosie: What do you mean?

Ruby: God, you annoy me so much, Rosie. Can a human being really be this stupid?

Rosie: Look, Ruby, you weren't there. It's all very well you giving me this advice but I'm the one who physically has to go and do it. I'll tell him how I feel when it's the right moment.

Ruby: When will it *ever* be the right moment for you?

Rosie: When there's the silence again.

Ruby: What silence?

Rosie: It doesn't matter. Anyway, Katie's fine. It was only a sprain. She can't play basketball this week, though, so she's upset about that.

Ruby: Have you pencilled the Dublin Salsa Dancing Championships into your diary?

Rosie: Of course. Katie and Toby are coming too. Has Teddy had a change of heart yet?

Ruby: I can't tell him about the competition, Rosie. If I did he would probably march with his trucker mates to the Red Cow Hotel and protest against men dancing in glittery suits. It's far more enjoyable for myself and Gary if we don't think Teddy is about to barge into the reception hall looking like Homer Simpson on a mission. I'm proud of Gary. I don't want Teddy and his pure ignorance and lack of intelligence to ruin something that has taken years to achieve.

Rosie: Oh, I can't wait to see you two dancing together. I'll bring the camera, so if Teddy ever does have a change of heart he won't have missed the moment completely. So what are you going to wear while you're dancing?

Ruby: Well, that was proving to be a huge problem. I know all the other dancers competing will be baring flesh for all to see but the idea of my outfit will be to cover up as much as I can. Unfortunately, Upsizes don't make sexy salsa dresses, even for my size. Gary was having the same problem. So after Miss Behave got over being in a huff at being replaced, she offered to make us something. She said she's used to 'making women's clothes for people who haven't the natural figure of a woman'. Worryingly enough, she won't tell us what she's making. But I've told her to steer clear of pink, fluff and rubber.

Rosie: Look forward to it!

Ba'ax ka wa'alik from Mexico!

What an adventure this is taking us on. Hope you're both safe and happy.

Love Mum and Dad

Happy Fourteenth Birthday, Toby.

Hope you like the remote-control car I got you. The guy in the shop said the Rally ones are the best (and they're the most expensive too). I got it for you in the States so I don't think anyone else will have them here. Josh has one as well. That's what I tripped over and sprained my wrist on. They're really fast!

Anyway, here's to another year. Maybe ten years from now you'll be poking at people's teeth. Why you want to be a dentist is beyond me, but you were always weird. I heard Monica Doyle is going out with Sean. Tough luck, my friend.

Katie

From   Toby
To   Katie
Subject Re: Happy birthday

Thanks for the car. I'm gonna bring it to the crappy dance thing on Sunday. You girls can paint your nails and watch them dance while I drive my car out in the corridor.

Aloha from Hawaii!

I've sent photos of me, your dad and some people that we've met on the cruise. Having a ball. Heading to Samoa and Fiji next. Can't wait!

Love to you and Katie,
Mum and Dad xxx

Ruby and Gary Minnelli!

Good Luck!

I was going to say 'Break a leg' but I don't think it's quite appropriate for the occasion. You will both be brilliant and we'll all be cheering for you.

Love Rosie, Katie and Toby

You have received an instant message from: ROSIE.

Rosie: Congratulations, you Dancing Queen! I'm so proud of you! Are you still glowing from your win?

Ruby: I'm not too sure how I'm supposed to be feeling, to be honest. I really don't think that we should be the winners.

Rosie: Oh, don't be silly! The two of you danced brilliantly. Miss Behave did such a great job on your dress. I'm surprised it was so understated for one of her creations. Black with glittery sequins looked *très chic* compared to all the others. They looked like rainbows on E. Look, you won it fair and square – be proud.

Ruby: But we didn't even get through to the final round . . .

Rosie: Well, it's not your fault the couple who came first were practising out in the corridor. Anyone could have slipped on Toby's stupid remote-control car. It was their own fault. Anyway, her ankle will heal with time. She'll be back next year to reclaim her title.

Ruby: Yes, but technically we shouldn't have won at all, Rosie. Only the two couples who got to the final round were supposed to battle it out. The second couple who were in the final really should have won . . .

Rosie: Yes, but once again that wasn't your fault. It was the woman in purple who tripped over Toby's car (they're very fast, aren't they?), knocking the drink out of Katie's hand, causing the second woman in yellow to slip and land on her backside. That automatically put you through. It's not your fault. You should be delighted!!

Ruby: Well, I am in an odd kind of way. Me and Gary are performing our winning dance in Miss Behave's show in the George.

Rosie: That's fantastic! I'm delighted for you, Ruby. My friend the superstar!

Ruby: Oh, I wouldn't even be doing all this if you hadn't got me the vouchers for my fortieth birthday. Thanks so much, Rosie. And thanks for cheering for me so loudly. I heard you the whole way through the dance. And I'm really sorry you, Katie and Toby were asked to leave the dance hall . . .

Chapter 38

Rosie and Katie,

Magandang tanghali po from the Philippines!

Left the top end of Australia a few days ago. We were in Brisbane and Sydney – very beautiful. Here for a little while, then moving on to China for a few days.

Love you and miss you both,

Mum and Dad

From   Rosie
To   Alex
Subject   Slutty Bethany

So, Alex, did you dump her yet?

From   Alex
To   Rosie
Subject   Mind your own business

Rosie, stop! I'll tell you when I do!

Ni hao from China!

Sorry we're not there to help you with the move. We wish you luck in your new apartment. We're sure it will bring you lots of happiness.

Love, Mum and Dad xxx

Rosie: The place is disgusting, Ruby. Absolutely disgusting.

Ruby: Oh, stop. It can't be any worse than mine.

Rosie: Worse than yours multiplied by one hundred.

Ruby: Such a place exists? God bless you. What's so bad about it?

Rosie: Well, let's see, where should I start? Hmm . . . should I tell you about the fact that it's a second-floor apartment over a group of shops, among them a tattoo parlour and an Indian takeaway which has managed to leave the stench of tikka masala all over my clothes already?

Perhaps I should tell you about the *gorgeous* 1970s green and grey floral wallpaper which is just *dangling* off the walls, and I wouldn't want to forget the fact that there's matching curtains too.

Hmm . . . actually maybe I should start with the brown carpets, which have very curious-looking stains embedded in the pile, as well as cigarette burns and mysterious odours. I think it's been there for about thirty years and has never been vacuumed. The kitchen is so small that when two people stand in it, one person has to back out to let the other leave. But *at least* the water works and the toilet flushes.

No wonder the rent is so ridiculously cheap; no one in their right mind would want to live here.

Ruby: You are.

Rosie: Yes, well, I won't be here for long. I'm going to magically save loads of money and get us out of here.

Ruby: And open a hotel.

Rosie: Yes.

Ruby: And live in the penthouse.

Rosie: Yes.

Ruby: And Kevin can be the head chef.

Rosie: Yes.

Ruby: And Alex the in-house doctor so that he can save the lives of those you poison.

Rosie: Yes.

Ruby: And you'll be the owner and manager.

Rosie: Yes.

Ruby: So what can I be?

Rosie: You and Gary could be the evening entertainment. You can salsa till you drop.

Ruby: Sounds like heaven to me. Well, Rosie, you better get your ass in gear and get this hotel business off the ground before we're all old and grey.

Rosie: I'm working on it. So how's Teddy after the shock of you winning the salsa competition?

Ruby: Oh, he's taking each day as it comes. But seriously, Rosie, I'm finding his behaviour very hard to come to terms with. When he found out we had won the competition and that we were going to perform it in the George he hit the roof. But he must have banged his head or something because the other night he offered to drive us to dance classes, which almost made me drop dead, and he's coming to the gay club on Friday (he's either really proud of me and Gary or he's just tired of me refusing to iron his shirts). Although he's bringing a really large friend of his to make sure no one tries anything funny with him. As if any male or female would try *anything* with Teddy. Anyway, that's enough about me. What are your plans for the week?

Rosie: Well, I start work part time (with the work-experience kids) which consists of printing up the school letters explaining the return dates for the pupils next month, we put the letters in envelopes, stick stamps on them, lick them closed and post them. I don't know about you but I'm enthralled by that idea. But at least it's only for a few weeks and when the kids start back at school then I work full time.

Apart from that I'm trying to make this kip of a place look like a home. Brian the Whine has been very helpful, believe it or not. He's hired out a sander for the day and tomorrow we're going to rip up those smelly carpets and sand and varnish the floors in all the rooms. I'm frightened to think of what we'll find under them. Probably a few dead bodies.

Katie and Toby are having great fun tearing the wallpaper off the walls – well, what's left of it, anyway. We're going to paint the walls white, because even with a million-watt bulb the place still looks like a cave. It needs brightening up and I'm going for the minimalist look, not because I'm trendy and fashionable but because I don't really have that much furniture. I'm going to pull down the old curtains and burn them in a ritual.

My darling brother Kevin was only too delighted to come to Dublin and raid whatshisname's house for all my leftover belongings, which he gladly gave him, probably because he was so terrified of having his nose broken again. I even got the black leather couch which was in the house before I married him but, hey, I deserve it.

Ruby: It sounds like it's going to be lovely, Rosie. A real home.

Rosie: Yeah, now all I need to do is get rid of the smell of curry that's floating around and seeping through the walls of the entire building. It's turned me off Indian food for ever.

Ruby: Now *that's* the best diet I've ever heard of. Live over a restaurant and the smell will make you sick of food.

Rosie: I think you're on to something there.

Ei Je from Singapore!

Having such a wonderful time. We don't want to come home!

Good luck with your new job this week, love. We're thinking of you here as we lounge by the pool! (Just joking.)

Love,

Mum and Dad

You have received an instant message from: ALEX.

Alex: Have you a minute to chat?

Rosie: No, sorry, I'm busy licking stamps.

Alex: Oh, OK. Can I call you sometime later?

Rosie: I was only joking, Alex. Miss Big Nose Smelly Breath Casey has asked me to put together the year's first newsletter so I'm on the school website trying to figure out what happened or is happening that's worth writing about. I'm thinking of putting the fact that I'm working here as the main story.

Alex: How's the job?

Rosie: It's OK. I've been here a few weeks now so I've settled in and it's going OK. Nothing to write home about.

Alex: Sorry I wasn't in touch sooner. I hadn't realised it had been so long. Time has been flying by once again.

Rosie: It's OK. I assumed you were busy. I've moved into my apartment now and everything.

Alex: Oh, gosh, that's right. How is it?

Rosie: It's OK. It was absolutely dire when we first moved in, but Brian the Whine was a really good help. He fixed all that was broken and cleaned what was dirty. Just like a regular little slave.

Alex: So are you and he getting along then?

Rosie: Better. I only have the urge to strangle him ten times a day now.

Alex: Well, it's a start. Any romance?

Rosie: What? With Brian the Whine? You need your head examined. The man was created for scraping mould and sanding floors only.

Alex: Oh. Anyone else in your life?

Rosie: Yes, actually. A thirteen-year-old daughter, a new job and a drawer stuffed with bills. My hands are pretty full at the moment. Although my neighbour did ask me to go out on a date with him this weekend.

Alex: So are you going out with him?

Rosie: Let me tell you a little bit about him first and then maybe you can help me with the dilemma I'm faced with. His name is Sanjay, he's sixty years old, and he's married, lives with his wife and two sons, and owns and runs the Indian takeaway downstairs. Oh, and you'll never guess where he invited me out for dinner.

Alex: Where?

Rosie: His takeaway. He said he would pay.

Alex: So what's your dilemma?

Rosie: Very funny.

Alex: Well, at least you have friendly neighbours.

Rosie: He's not the nicest by far. Beside me there's the owner of the tattoo parlour (which is also below my flat). He's got tattoos covering his body from head to toe. He's got beautiful long black silky hair that he ties back in a plait, and a neatly trimmed goatee framing his mouth. He's over six feet tall, wears leather trousers, a leather waistcoat and big steel-toed biker boots every day. When he's not drilling away on somebody's skin downstairs he's blaring music from his flat beside mine.

Alex: Trust you to move in beside a heavy metal fan.

Rosie: That's where you're wrong. His name is Rupert; he's thirty-five years old, a graduate of the prestigious Trinity College, Dublin, where he got a degree in Irish History and a Masters in Irish Literature. James Joyce is his idol and across his chest is the quote, 'Mistakes are the portals of discovery.'

He's a huge fan of classical music and opera, and at 5 p.m. every evening when he's closing up and cashing up the till for the night he has Brahms' Piano Concerto Number 2 in B flat, Op. 83 blaring out. After that he heads up to his flat where he proceeds to cook the most savoury and delicious-smelling meals and settles down to read *Ullysses* for the billionth time while listening to the sounds of *The Best of Pavarotti* blasting out from his speakers (paying particular attention to 'Nessun dorma').

Katie and I practically know all the words to it by this stage and Toby stuffs a pillow up his shirt, stands up on the couch and mimes along to the music. At least Rupert is educating the children. Katie is going crazy about mixing 'Nessun dorma' into a dance song she's created on her new set of decks. Brian the Whine bought them for her, which made me really angry because I was planning on getting them for her as a Christmas present. But I've made her keep them in his rented flat so that she doesn't disturb my neighbours. Although, to be honest, I really don't know why I bothered caring, with all the other noises and smells going on around us. Oh yes, and did I mention that Joan of Arc is living across the hall from me?

Alex: Ha ha, no, you didn't.

Rosie: Well, this woman (her name is Joan, Mary or Brigid or something) is in her late twenties. She came over to say hello the day we first moved in and when she realised that it was just Katie and me, and that my singledom was not due to the tragic loss of my husband she left rather rudely and hasn't spoken to us since.

Alex: Well, at least she's quiet.

Rosie: Just because she ignores me, the sinner of the apartment block, it doesn't mean she's quiet. Every

Monday evening I noticed there seem to be a large herd of elephants making their way upstairs to our level and going into Joan of Arc's flat. After further investigation I noticed that the same twenty people visit every week, all bearing gifts of Bibles in their hands.

My further powers of investigation led me to believe that she was holding Bible-reading groups every week. Now she's put a sign up on the door saying, 'Ye shall walk after your LORD, and fear him, and keep his commandments, and obey his voice, and ye shall serve him, and cleave unto him.' I mean, what does 'cleave' mean? Whoever has heard of such a word?

Alex: Ha ha, Rosie. Oh, I really don't no!

Rosie: You mean KNOW, not NO. You will never learn, will you? Then down the hall from me is a family from Nigeria. Zareb and Malika and their four kids. And I thought the place was too small for just me and Katie.

Alex: How are your mum and dad?

Rosie: My multilingual mum and dad, you mean? Well, they're having the time of their lives away from all of us. Mum recently celebrated her sixtieth; she sent me a postcard saying, 'Zdravstvuite from Russia!' I can just imagine the two of them enjoying themselves like an old couple from *The Love Boat*. Speaking of the dreaded 'L' word, what was with all the personal questions about my love life?.

Alex: Because I want you to find someone, that's why. I want you to be happy.

Rosie: Alex, I've never found happiness with another human being and you know it. I'm separated from my husband; I'm not looking for another victim just yet. Possibly never.

Alex: *Never?*

Rosie: Possibly. Well, I'll never marry again, that's for sure. I'm getting used to my new life. I have a new apartment, a new job, a teenage daughter, I'm thirty-two years old and I'm entering a new phase of my life. I think I'm finally growing up. Anyway, there's nothing wrong with being single. Being single is the new black. You should know.

Alex: I'm not single.

Rosie: Not *yet*.

Alex: No, I'm not. I won't be.

Rosie: Why, have you changed your mind about breaking up with Slutty Bethany?

Alex: My mind was never made up in the first place to be changed, and please don't call her slutty. I never said I was going to end mine and Beth's relationship.

Rosie: Well, it sounded like that to me when we discussed it at dinner last month.

Alex: Yes, well, never mind that dinner. My head was elsewhere. So what I'm saying is that I want me to be happy with Bethany and you to be happy with someone and then we'll both be happy with people.

Rosie: I know what it is. You just don't want me to be single because I'm a distraction to you. If I'm with a man then you think that *perhaps* you just might be able to keep your hands off me. I know deep down that's what this is all about. I've sussed you out, Alex Stewart. You love me. You want me to have your babies. You can't stand another day without me.

Alex: I . . . don't no what to say . . .

Rosie: Relax, I'm joking. What happened to make you change your mind about Bethany?

Alex: Oh, not back to this again . . .

Rosie: Alex, I'm your best friend, I've known you since I was five. No one knows you better than I do. I'm asking this for the very last time and do not lie. What happened to make you change your mind about breaking up with Slutty Bethany?

Alex: She's pregnant.

Rosie: Oh dear God. Sometimes, because you're my best friend, I think that you're normal, like me. Then every now and again you remind me that you're a man.

Phil: Hold on a minute, Alex. A couple of years ago you were trying to *break up* Rosie's marriage and now you're telling me that you *want* her to meet somebody new?

Alex: Yes.

Phil: Just so that while you're with Bethany, you won't feel *tempted*?

Alex: No! That's not what I said!

Phil: Well, that's what it sounds like. At the rate you're going, I don't think the two of you deserve each other at all.

PART FOUR

Chapter 39

Welcome home, Mum and Dad! (Fáilte go h-Eirinn!)

Glad you arrived home safely and in one piece! Can't wait to hear all the stories of your adventures and see all the photographs.

See you at the weekend.

Love,

Rosie and Katie

Dear Stephanie and Pierre!

Congratulations on the arrival of your new baby girl!

We can't wait to meet little Sophia. In the meantime here are a few little outfits to keep her as trendy as her mother!

Lots of love,

Rosie and Katie

Happy 5th Birthday, Josh.

Lots of love,

Rosie and Katie

Hi, Katie,

Thanks for your card and present that you gave me fro my brithday. I guess my dad told you guys about Bethinny being pregnint. That means I'm gonna have a brother or sister.

Dad is sad because he said all the grils in his life are mad at him. Your mom is, my mom is and Bethinny is too. Bethinny is mad at him cos he won't marry her. Bethinny was crying and saying that dad didn't love her and he was saying that they needed to get to know more about each other before they got married. Bethinny said he knew everything there was to know about her and if he didn't marry her, her dad would be really angry and would fire him.

I think dad should marry her. I want a brother and dad really, really likes his job. I'll fill you and Toby in on more stuff as soon as I can. Cos I'm only here at weekends I miss all the good stuff.

Thank your mom fro my pressent.

Form Josh

PS. Bethinny wants a house in Marthas Vineyard. I've never met Martha and I don't know how she would feel about us moving onto her vineyard all of a sudden but dad didn't seem too happy about the idea. I think he hates grapes.

Dr Williams Rewarded

Reginald Williams was honoured last night at the National Health Awards in Boston. He was nominated through a highly selective process that recognises those who have made major contributions to the advancement of the medical sciences and public health.

This award is considered one of the highest honours in the fields of medicine and health. He was accompanied to the ceremony by his wife, Miranda, his daughter, Bethany, and her newly announced fiancé Dr Alex Stewart, cardio-surgeon at St Jude's Hospital in Boston.

See page four of the Health supplement for Wayne Gillespie's report.

You have received an instant message from: ROSIE.

Rosie: You wanted me to learn about this in the newspapers first?

Alex: I'm sorry, Rosie.

Rosie: You're sorry? You get engaged and you let me read about it in a newspaper? What the hell has happened to you these days?

Alex: Rosie, all I can say is sorry.

Rosie: I don't understand the way your mind works, Alex. You don't even love her.

Alex: I do.

Rosie: Well, that's convincing.

Alex: I shouldn't have to *convince* anyone.

Rosie: Only yourself. Alex, you told me you didn't love her. In fact a few months back you were planning on breaking up with her. Gee, I wonder what happened to make you change your mind all of a sudden.

Alex: You no what happened. There's a baby involved now.

Rosie: That's bullshit. The Alex I know wouldn't marry a woman he doesn't love for the sake of the baby. That's the worst thing you could do to the poor child – raise it in an environment where the parents don't even love each other. What's the point of that? You're not with Sally and things with Josh work out fine. It may not be the most desired position to be in – everyone wants to play happy families – but it doesn't always work out that way. This is ridiculous.

Alex: I'm a weekend dad to Josh; I don't want a repeat of that. It's not right.

Rosie: Marrying someone you don't love is not right.

Alex: I'm extremely fond of Bethany; we have a great relationship and get on well.

Rosie: Well, I'm glad you and your future wife 'get on well'. If you don't think this through properly, Bethany will be another Sally. Another failed marriage is not what you want.

Alex: This marriage won't fail.

Rosie: No, you'll just be miserable for the rest of your life, but that's great just as long as the tongues of disapproving people can't gossip about you.

Alex: Why should I take advice from you, Rosie? What on earth have you done in your life that makes you such an expert on telling me how to live mine? You lived with a man that cheated on you for years and you kept taking him back time and time again. What do you no about marriage?

Rosie: I know enough not to go racing up the aisle with someone else I barely know or love. I know enough to not allow my life choices to be influenced by my desire for money and power and prestige. I know enough not to marry a man so a bunch of rich people will smile at me and tell me how great I am. I wouldn't marry a man to get my picture in the paper, my name on an award trophy or for some dumb promotion at work.

Alex: Oh, Rosie, you make me laugh. You have no idea what you're talking about. You've obviously been spending too much time in your flat doing nothing but concocting conspiracy theories.

Rosie: Of course, because that's all I do. Sit around my council flat doing nothing, being the poor uneducated single mother that I am while you and your Harvard pals sit in your gentlemen's clubs, smoking cigars and patting each other on the back. We may live in very different worlds, Alex Stewart, but I know you and I'm sick of seeing who you've turned into.

So what would good old Reginald Williams have done if he had learned that his daughter was pregnant and that the fool who was responsible wouldn't marry her?

Oh, the shame that would bring on the family, how the people would talk.

But at least now she's got the ring on her finger, and you've got the job promotion, and we can all live happily ever after.

Alex: Not everybody walks away, Rosie. They might in your life, but not in mine.

Rosie: Alex, for Christsake! Not marrying Bethany isn't 'walking away'. As long as you're there for the child then you're not walking away. You don't have to *marry* her!

Alex: Look, I'm fed up with all this, Rosie, with you constantly checking up on me, me having to explain everything to you. You're not my wife or my mother, so give it a rest. Who says I have to run all my life decisions by you, anyway? I'm tired of you nagging at me and moaning at me about people I see and places I go. I can make decisions on my own, you no. I'm a grown man.

Rosie: Then for once in your life ACT LIKE ONE!

Alex: Who are you to insult *me* and lecture *me* when you haven't done a thing right in your life yourself? Just do me a favour and don't bother getting in touch until you have something decent to say.

Rosie: Fine! Well then, I think you'll find you'll be waiting a long, long time.

Rosie has logged off.

Alex: No change there then.

Phil: What are you doing?

Alex: You no what I'm doing.

Phil: Why are you marrying her?

Alex: *Her* name is Bethany.

Phil: Why are you marrying *Bethany*?

Alex: Because I love her.

Phil: Really? Because last time you stepped into the virtual confessional box, you told me you were planning on ending your relationship. Why do you feel you have to do this? Is her dad putting pressure on you?

Alex: No, no, no. There's no pressure. I want to do this.

Phil: Why?

Alex: Why the hell not? Why did you marry Margaret?

Phil: I married Margaret because I love every inch of the woman with all my heart and plan to be with her for the rest of my life, in sickness and in health, till death do us part. She is my best friend, we have five beautiful children and as much as they drive me up the walls sometimes, I couldn't live a day without them. I don't sense you have this with Bethany.

Alex: Not all relationships are like yours and Margaret's.

Phil: No, they're not but the intention should be there at the beginning. Was there the silence thing with Bethany?

Alex: Oh, shut up about the silence, Phil.

Phil: You're the one who's obsessed with it. So, come on, was there?

Alex: No.

Phil: Then you shouldn't marry her.

Alex: OK, I won't, just because you say so.

Phil: What does Rosie say about it?

Alex: Nothing. She's not talking to me.

Phil: How do you feel about that?

Alex: At this stage, I'm so mad at her, I don't care what she thinks. I'm moving on from her. Bethany and this new baby are my future. Can I leave the confessional box now?

Phil: Yeah. Say five Hail Marys and an Our Father, and God rest your messed-up little soul.

You have received an instant message from: KATIE.

Katie: You look very interested in learning about the female reproduction system.

318

Toby: I'm not. I'd rather figure it out for myself the practical way.

Katie: Oh, funny, but you'll be old and grey before anyone lets you get your hands on them.

Toby: My best friend is a comedienne. You had a salad roll for lunch, didn't you?

Katie: How do you no?

Toby: KNOW not NO. Because I can see the lettuce hanging out of your braces. So what do you want?

Katie: Well, not that you deserve to be asked, but I'm going to the orthodontist again later if you wanna come. You can ask him a million questions about everything he's doing, as always, and annoy the hell out of him. It's so funny the way that vein in his forehead pulsates when he sees you.

Toby: Yeah, I know. Sorry, I can't go. Monica is coming around to my house to watch the football.

Katie: Monica, Monica, Monica. I'm sick of hearing about stupid Monica Doyle. So why aren't I invited to your house?

Toby: Because you have to go to the dentist.

Katie: Yes, but you didn't no that until a second ago.

Toby: OK then, would you like to watch the football, the sport that you absolutely hate with a passion played by the two teams you hate even more, at my house today?

Katie: I can't. I'm busy.

Toby: You see? Now don't say I never ask you out anywhere.

Katie: How long have you known that I'm going to the dentist?

Toby: All of five minutes.

Katie: How long ago did you invite Monica Doyle to your house?

Toby: Last week.

Katie: My point exactly!

You have received an instant message from: KATIE.

Katie: Mum, I hate men.

Rosie: Congratulations, dear. Welcome to the club. Your membership is in the post. I'm so proud of this moment I wish I had a camera.

Katie: Please, Mum, I'm serious.

Rosie: And so am I. So what has Toby done this time?

Katie: He's invited Monica Doyle to his house to watch the football and he didn't invite me. Well, he did, but only after he new I was busy.

Rosie: Oh dear, he's caught the bug already. Is this moany Monica we're talking about? The little girl who cried all day at your tenth birthday party until her parents came to collect her because her false nail fell off?

Katie: Yes.

Rosie: Oh dear. I hate that child.

Katie: She's not a child any more, Mum. She's fourteen, got the biggest chest in the school, dyes her hair blonde, leaves the top buttons of her polo shirt open in PE and leans down so the boys can see down her top. She even flirts with Mr Simpson and pretends not to understand what he's talking about in computer class so he'll come up behind her and lean over her to show her what to do.

She hates talking about anything other than shopping so I don't no why she's going to even bother watching football. Well, actually I do no why.

Rosie: Sounds like she's got a case of the Slutty Bethanitis to me.

Katie: What? What do I do about Monica?

Rosie: Oh, that's simple. Assassinate her.

Katie: Please, Mum, for once in your life be serious.

Rosie: I am an incredibly serious woman. The only way to deal with this is to silence her. Because if not, she'll only end up coming back to haunt you when you're thirty-two years old. Death is the only thing for it.

320

Katie: Thanks, but I'm open to any other suggestions you may have.

Rosie: You said he invited you?

Katie: Yes, but only because he new I couldn't go.

Rosie: My dear sweet innocent daughter, an invitation is an invitation. It would be rude to turn him down. I suggest you turn up on his doorstep this evening, I'll give you the money for the bus to his house.

Katie: But, Mum, I can't go! You know I've got an appointment with the orthodontist.

Rosie: Well, the dentist can wait. I'll make another appointment for you. This is a very important football match, you know. I wouldn't want you to miss it just because of a silly little thing like getting your teeth fixed. Now get off the computer before Mr Simpson catches you and reports me to Miss Big Nose Smelly Breath Casey and gets me fired.

Katie: You wish, Mum. I don't no how you work with her every day.

Rosie: Actually, I'm surprised to admit it myself but she's not so bad. As far as bosses go she's been really, really pleasant. Her name is Julie. Can you believe it? She actually has a first name. And it's a nice, normal name too; I would have thought it was something more like Vladimir or Adolf.

Katie: Ha ha, me too. But is it not really awkward working with someone who used to give out to you every day?

Rosie: Things are a little awkward between us. It kind of feels like she's an ex-boyfriend of mine and we're meeting after years of separation. Every day conversation becomes a little longer, a little friendlier, a little less about work and a little more about life. We've spent so many years arguing with each other it feels odd to agree on things. But each day we talk more and more. Do you know that she thought Alex was your dad?!

Katie: Did she?!

Rosie: Anyway, I told her that Brian was your father and she couldn't stop laughing . . . Actually, perhaps this isn't a story to tell you.

Katie: Wait till Alex hears you saying that you like her. He'll drop dead with the shock.

Rosie: I'll let you tell him, so.

Katie: Oh, I forgot you two still aren't talking.

Rosie: Yes, well, it's a long story, honey.

Katie: People who say it's a long story mean it's a stupid short one that they're too embarrassed and couldn't be bothered to tell. Why don't you talk to him?

Rosie: Because I don't care about what he does any more. His life is his own to mess up as he chooses, and I have nothing to do with it now. Anyway, he doesn't want to hear what I have to say.

Katie: Our neighbour Rupert says, 'Mistakes are the portals of discovery.'

Rosie: Rupert doesn't say that. James Joyce did.

Katie: James who? Do I no him?

Rosie: He's dead.

Katie: Oh, sorry, did you no him well?

Rosie: What on earth are they teaching you at school?

Katie: At the moment it's sex education. It's boring as hell.

Rosie: I would have to agree with you on that one. Anyway, back to Alex: he has just changed as a person, love. He's not the man I used to know. He's different.

Katie: He'd bloody want to be. He was five years old and drooling when you first met him. If Toby is still acting like a fourteen-year-old when we're your age then I'll worry.

Rosie: Well then, as a warning from a woman who knows, be prepared to meet many thirty-two-year-old men who still think they're fourteen.

Katie: Yeah, yeah, yeah. I've heard all this before. Dad's coming home for Christmas, you no. He asked me to ask you if we would eat Christmas dinner with him and his parents. Seeing as it's only you and me this year anyway I thought it would be a great idea.

Rosie: Well, whoopdeedoo. Bring on Christmas Day.

Hi, love,

Hope all is well. It was great to see you at the weekend. Thanks for coming over to us in the west and joining us. I promise the house will be in better order next time you come to see us, but I'm finding it so difficult to settle down after travelling for months.

Settling into a new home, in a new village, in a new county is an adventure for us. Everybody is so friendly here and our Irish is gradually coming back to us. We don't have neighbours as exciting as you seem to have in your new apartment though.

You're my wonderful brave baby girl, Rosie, and your dad and I are so, so proud of you. I hope you know that. You are so strong, you never allow anything to knock you back and you're the best mother to Katie. She's a feisty young lady now, isn't she? She's definitely her mother's daughter. I'm sorry Dennis and I left you at such an important time of your life, it just broke my heart having to leave you and Katie when you were going through all that stuff with whatshis-name. But you're a tough cookie and what doesn't kill you only makes you stronger.

It would be such a shame for you to miss Alex's wedding. I was talking to Sandra earlier on and she was telling me that they're planning a very big Christmas wedding. They want to be married before the baby is born, and Bethany doesn't want to be showing too much in her dress. Sandra would love for you and Rosie to be there; they've watched you grow up over the years too. I get the impression she's not a huge fan of Bethany's herself, but she loves Alex and she wants to support him.

Sandra said that Dennis and I are invited but unfortunately we can't go because we are spending Christmas with Stephanie and Pierre in Paris, as you know. Christmas in Paris will be beautiful, no doubt, and I'm excited to meet granddaughter number two! It's such a shame that you and Katie can't come too, but I understand she wants to spend her first Christmas with her dad, and I know she wants to get to know her 'other' grandparents too. I can't help feeling jealous, though, that they'll be seeing my Katie on Christmas Day, and I won't!

Kevin has met a girl, would you believe, and he's spending Christmas with her and her parents in Donegal! It must be serious! I think she's a waitress in the same hotel as him or something, but I'm not too sure. You know Kevin: he's not too good at giving information out.

Your dad says hello. He's tucked up in bed with a nasty flu. He only got it the day you left so you're lucky you missed out on that. He's been very tired since we returned from the trip. I can't believe we're both in our sixties, Rosie. How time went by so fast I'll never know – make sure you savour each day. Anyway, I better go because he keeps calling me. Honestly, you would think he was on his deathbed by the way he's acting!

I'm so proud of my two girls in Dublin.

Love you.

Mum

Dr Reginald & Miranda Williams
invite **Katie Dunne** to join them in celebrating the
marriage of their beloved daughter
Bethany
to
Dr Alex Stewart
at
the Memorial Church of Harvard University
on 28th December at 2 o'clock
& a reception at
the Boston Harbor Hotel
RSVP Miranda Williams

Chapter 40

Welcome to the Relieved Divorced Dubliners' internet chat room. There are currently six people chatting.

Divorced_1: Oh, LonelyLady, just stop crying for one minute of your life and think about your situation. You should be angry, not sad. Repeat after me, I am a strong woman.

LonelyLady: I am a strong woman.

Divorced_1: I am in control of my life.

LonelyLady: I am in control of my life.

Divorced_1: It is *not* my fault that Tommy left.

LonelyLady: It is *not* my fault that Tommy left.

Divorced_1: And I don't care that he did because he is a bastard.

LonelyLady: I can't say that!

Divorced_1: Look, let me put your life into perspective for you. He walked out on you after only six months of marriage, took the furniture, the kitchenware, even the damn bathroom mat, and left you a *note*, for Christsake, so repeat after me, I don't care that he left me because he is a bastard!

LonelyLady: I don't care that he left me because he is a BASTARD!

Divorced_1: Screw him!

LonelyLady: Screw him!

Unsure One: Ladies, I'm not sure that this is a very healthy way to help LonelyLady.

Divorced_1: Oh, shut up, you're never sure of anything.

LonelyLady: Oh, shut up, you're never sure of anything!

Divorced_1: LonelyLady, I didn't mean for you to repeat *that*.

Wildflower: Ha ha ha ha.

UnsureOne: Gosh, I'm not sure anyone is ever allowed to have an opinion in here apart from you, Divorced_1.

Divorced_1: But you never *have* an opinion.

SingleSam: Look, everyone, calm down. Don't be silly, UnsureOne; of course we all want to hear your opinion. How did you deal with Leonard having an affair and leaving you?

Divorced_1: She cleverly moved into the spare room and stopped having a life.

SingleSam: Now, now, Divorced_1, give her a chance.

UnsureOne: Thank you, SingleSam, you're a gentleman. What I was going to say is that I don't believe in divorce. I follow the teachings of the Catholic Church and the Pope himself said that divorce is an 'evil' that is 'spreading like a plague' through society. I, for one, agree with him. The purpose of the family is to be together. And together we shall stay, no matter what happens.

Divorced_1: Well, the Pope was never married to my ex-husband, that's all I have to say to that.

UnsureOne: I'm not continuing this conversation. I don't like your tone.

Wildflower: The Catholic Church believes in annulments, UnsureOne, why don't you get one of those?

UnsureOne: No.

Wildflower: Why not? It's practically the same thing, only the Pope will give his, kind of, blessing to it.

UnsureOne: No.

Wildflower: But can't you at least explain why?

Divorced_1: Because she doesn't want to end her marriage, full stop.

UnsureOne: No, Divorced_1, I just don't think it would be right. For the children.

Divorced_1: What's so 'right for the children' about your husband taking the master bedroom with the TV and ensuite, forcing you to sleep in the spare room while you stay at home on the weekend and he goes out on dates? Your kids will all get married thinking they're supposed to have separate rooms and multiple partners.

LonelyLady: You let him go out on *dates*?

UnsureOne: Oh, they're not dates. Don't pay any attention to Divorced_1, she's in one of her moods tonight. He goes out on business dinners. I can't very well stop him from doing that, can I? And just because his boss is a woman I don't think I should worry. You wouldn't be at me about this if his boss was a man.

SingleSam: Yes, but, UnsureOne, it was his boss that he was having the affair with . . .

Wildflower: Ha ha ha ha.

LonelyLady: I can understand UnsureOne's reasoning. At least she gets to live with the man she loves, sees him every day, talks to him, knows where he is and what he's doing instead of being alone all day, every day. Who cares if he doesn't love her back?

UnsureOne: You should really work things out with Tommy, you know. Six months isn't enough time to make a marriage work.

Divorced_1: UnsureOne, Tommy *emptied* their bank account, *stole* her engagement ring, *swiped* the furniture, the TV, the CD player, all her CDs, clothes *and* personal possessions and *disappeared*. Why on earth should she want him back other than to point him out in a line-up?

UnsureOne: Because she loves him and marriage is for ever.

Divorced_1: But he is a *thief*. You ladies are nuts.

Wildflower: Well, you know they say love is blind.

Divorced_1: *And* deaf *and* dumb in this chat room.

Buttercup has joined the room.

Divorced_1: Oh good, here comes the voice of reason to sort you lot out.

Buttercup: He's a bloody bastard, you know that? He bloody well married her.

Divorced_1: Oh, well. Screw him.

SingleSam: Did he contact you yet?

Buttercup: No, haven't heard a thing from him since he told me not to contact him.

SingleSam: I thought maybe he would have sent a last-minute invitation.

Buttercup: Not a chance the selfish little—

UnsureOne: Well, you were very rude to him, Buttercup, accusing him of marrying that woman for all the wrong reasons.

LonelyLady: I wish my dad could give Tommy a job promotion. He'd definitely come back to me then.

Divorced_1: Yes, what a wonderful loving foundation to base your marriage on. Very healthy, LonelyLady.

Buttercup: Imagine inviting a thirteen-year-old girl to Boston all by herself. The man has gone insane. That's it; he is officially no longer my best friend.

LonelyLady: Can I be?

Divorced_1: You sad, sad woman.

LonelyLady: What *now*?

Wildflower: But would you have gone to the wedding had he invited you, Buttercup?

Buttercup: Not if he paid me.

LonelyLady: He probably just didn't bother printing up an invite because he knew you weren't going to attend. Invites are very expensive, you know. I remember

Tommy and me going through the wedding list together. We were so happy then.

Divorced_1: Probably because he knew he wasn't going to stick around long enough to meet half of the guests.

LonelyLady: That's unfair.

Buttercup: Well, these people are not short of money, believe me, and why else would he invite Katie and not me, if not but to rub it in my face? Smear it right in there like an exfoliating face pack that *scrapes* away at your skin . . . Anyway, I'm almost sure their wedded bliss will be short-lived. He'll be joining us on this chat room shortly because that woman is evil, I can sense it.

Divorced_1: No, divorce is evil, isn't that right, UnsureOne?

Wildflower: Ha ha ha ha.

UnsureOne: That's not funny.

Divorced_1: All she's done is laugh all night. I think Wildflower has been sampling the wild flower, if you know what I mean.

UnsureOne has left the room.

Wildflower: You're too hard on her, Divorced_1.

Divorced_1: Oh, don't be silly, she loves it. She comes back night after night, doesn't she? I think we're the only bit of adult conversation she has all day.

Buttercup: So did everyone enjoy their Christmas?

Wildflower: I haven't stopped partying all week. It's been great. I've never sat on so many Santa's laps in my life. Anyway, I have to go; I have to get ready for a fancy dress tonight. I'm going as a playboy bunny. Bye!

Wildflower has left the room.

Buttercup: What about everybody else?

Divorced_1: I think I put on about two stone.

LonelyLady: It was, you know, a quiet one.

SingleSam: Television was good this year, though.

Divorced_1: Yeah.

Buttercup: Yeah, I like the Christmas specials.

Divorced_1: Good for occupying the kids too.

Buttercup: Yeah.

SingleSam: Good documentaries too.

Buttercup: Mmm.

Divorced_1: Watched that one on polar bears last night.

Buttercup: I saw that one too . . .

SingleSam: I hadn't realised that all polar bears are left-handed.

Buttercup: Yes, that was interesting . . . and the snails . . .

Divorced_1: They're left-handed too?

SingleSam: No, but they can sleep for three years apparently.

Buttercup: Lucky buggers . . .

Divorced_1: Yes, TV is good at Christmas alright . . .

SingleSam: It's kind of nice to be alone at Christmas, to have a bit of peace and quiet.

LonelyLady: *Total* peace and quiet.

Buttercup: Yes, it's *very* quiet . . .

SingleSam: You know, myself and my ex, we used to have big parties every Christmas, busy all the time, out every night or entertaining whenever we were home. We hardly had any time to ourselves. But this is quite different. No one around. No parties, no guests this year . . .

Buttercup: Same with me.

Divorced_1: Oh, who are we kidding? It's awful; this is the worst Christmas I've ever had.

Buttercup: Me too.

SingleSam: Me too.

LonelyLady: Me too.

Click on this icon to print the conversation.

331

From   Julie Casey
To   Rosie
Subject Fax for you

Don't want to disturb you while you're so 'busy' working
(how is Ruby?), but a fax just arrived in my office a few
minutes ago. It wasn't addressed to you but on reading it I
discovered that it could *only* be for you, as which of my
other employees would give out *my* fax number for *their*
own personal use? I think I can just about make out a
'Form Josh' signed at the bottom. Come into my office and
collect it. Oh, and while you're at it, divert all your calls
to my office; bring two cups of coffee and a packet of
cigarettes in with you.

'Social Lives' by Eloise Parkinson

For those of us who were lucky enough to attend the
wedding of the year (or surely, *at least*, the wedding of
the week) we have lived to tell the tale of extravagance,
sophistication and splendor that was displayed for the
lucky three hundred guests of Dr and Mrs Reginald
Williams at the marriage of their daughter, Bethany, to
Dr Alex Stewart.

No expense was spared at the wedding ceremony,
which took place at the Memorial Church of Harvard
University, where vibrant displays of red roses and red
candles lined the aisle, like lights illuminating a runway
for the exquisite couple to take off to their future life of
happiness together.

Bethany, 34, was looking flawlessly stunning, as
always, in an elegant white dress designed especially for
her by the famous friend-of-the-stars (and mine) Jeremy
Durkin. The boned bodice was embellished in ten thousand pearls (and disguised that pregnancy everybody is
whispering about). The ballerina-style full skirt, made

332

up of layers and layers of soft tulle, swished as she floated up the aisle on the arm of her proud father, prominent surgeon Dr Reginald Williams.

Miranda Williams looked every bit the perfect mother of the bride in her scarlet red Armani trouser suit, teamed with a fabulous Philip Treacy hat that almost stole the spotlight from her daughter. Catwalk models (and *very* new friends of Bethany's) Sara Smythe and Hayley Broadbank acted as Bethany's two bridesmaids and wore sexy red silk spaghetti-strapped dresses that clung to their barely there curves, half a dozen roses resting between their French manicured fingers. The bride's bouquet was made up of half a dozen red roses and half a dozen white roses (and was caught by none other than *moi*). Her usually flowing long blonde hair was tied back tightly in a French bun that sat low on her head and helped the mother-to-be look every inch the perfect bride.

At the top of the aisle a confident-looking Prince Charming looked down on his princess proudly, dressed in a classic black three-button cut-away coat with white wing collar and red tie, accompanied by a single red rose in his lapel. Everything was certainly 'rosie' on this day.

The extravagant reception was held at the Boston Harbor Hotel where the finest speech by far was made by the best man, five-year-old Josh Stewart, son of the groom from a previous marriage to college sweetheart Sally Gruber.

The day lived up to the expectation (and standards) of 'Social Lives' and it was clear to all who witnessed the newlyweds dancing for the first time as husband and wife that this marriage was for ever. May they live a long, happy, rich and fashionable married life together. As for me, your favorite wedding columnist, I'm off with my bouquet, to find myself a beau.

333

Rosie,
    Happy Birthday, friend.
    Another year – here we go again.
    Ruby

From   Stephanie
To   Rosie
Subject   Your visit

Can't wait for you to come over and meet Sophia next month. She's excited to meet you too and Jean-Louis is as hyper as always.
    Happy thirty-third, sis. No doubt you and Ruby will be out until the early hours.

Dear Alex and Bethany,
    Congratulations on the birth of your baby boy.
    We wish you every happiness for the future and are delighted that Josh has the brother he wished for!
    Rosie and Katie

Happy fourteenth, my little angel.
    Have a good night at the disco tonight and remember no drinking, no sex, and no drugs.
    Lots of love,
    Mum

You have an instant message from: ROSIE.
Rosie: Who is this boy I heard you were kissing and slow dancing with on Friday night, Katie Dunne?
Katie: Can't talk, Mum. Mr Simpson is teaching something extremely important for the end-of-year exams, and it's vital that I listen.
Rosie: Liar.

Katie: I'm not lying. I'm sure it is important, whatever it is.

Rosie: Come on, spill the beans. Who was the boy?

Toby: Hi, Rosie.

Rosie: Oh, Toby, good timing. I was just quizzing my daughter on the mystery man at the disco on Friday night.

Toby: Oh, ha ha. News travels fast.

Katie: Don't tell her, Toby.

Rosie: So it's true?

Toby: Yep.

Katie: Yeah, and Toby was snogging the face off Monica all night as well.

Rosie: Oh no, Toby, not moany Monica.

Toby: Why do you two always call her that? She's not a moan when she's with me.

Rosie: That's because we don't kiss her in front of everyone at school discos. So come on, darling daughter, bond with me and share details of this budding romance.

Katie: His name is John McKenna, he's fifteen, he's in the year ahead of me and he's really nice.

Rosie: Ooooh, an older man.

Katie: I know, Mum. I've got taste.

Rosie: What do you think of him, Toby?

Toby: He's OK; he's on the school football team. He's good.

Rosie: You'll have to keep an eye on him for me, won't you?

Katie: Mum! Now he'll never shut up!

Rosie: Did you have sex with him?

Katie: Mum! I'm fourteen!

Rosie: I see fourteen-year-old girls on the TV who are pregnant these days.

Katie: Well not me!

Rosie: Good. Did you take any drugs?

Katie: Mum! Stop! Where the hell would I get drugs from??!

Rosie: I don't know, but you see fourteen-year-old pregnant girls on TV who are on drugs these days.

Katie: Well not me!

Rosie: Good. Did you drink alcohol?

Katie: Mum! Toby's mum drove us to the school and collected us – when would we have had time to drink?

Rosie: I don't know. You see drunken pregnant fourteen-year-olds who are on drugs on the TV these days.

Katie: Well that's definitely not me!

Toby: What TV programmes are you watching?

Rosie: Mainly the news.

Katie: Well, don't worry; you've lectured me enough to know that it's stupid to do all of those things. OK?

Rosie: OK, but remember, kisses are nice but that's as far as it should go. OK?

Katie: Mum! That's all I want!!

Rosie: Good, now you two get back to your work. I expect you to get As in this subject!

Katie: We won't if you keep bothering us!

Ruby: So what are you going to do for the next two months now that the kids are off school? You're so lucky, getting such long holidays. Randy Andy told me I'd used up all my holidays already, which is ridiculous because all those days were supposed to be sick days. He said there's no way someone could have been sick for sixty-five days of the working year and still be alive.

Rosie: So you can't take any holidays at all? I was hoping we could go over to England on the boat for the weekend. To Blackpool or something.

Ruby: I can now. I told him that if he'll give me two weeks off that I'd mention Randy Andy's Paperclip Company when Oprah invites me on her show to talk

about me and Gary wining the World Salsa
Championship. What are you going to do?

Rosie: I'm not too sure. Julie mentioned something about
being able to do adult courses at the school. She says I
should take a course in hotel management like I always
wanted to do. Like it's that simple.

Ruby: Why *can't* it be that simple? Look, Rosie, you don't
know until you try. Ever since I met you you've been
going on about working in a hotel. You're obsessed with
them; your home is like a tribute to hotel merchandise.
You can barely open the bathroom door for all the
stolen mats in the way. I can't claim to understand your
fascination with them but I know that working in one is
an absolute dream for you.

Rosie: Julie said that if I don't take the course she'll fire
me. And she said that when I finish the course she's
firing me anyway.

Ruby: You need to listen to her; she's been a good teacher
to you over the years.

Rosie: But, Ruby, it takes two years to get a diploma, and
it's expensive, and I'll have to work by day and study by
night. It'll be tough.

Ruby: Oh, but, but, but, Rosie Dunne. What's the
problem? Have you got anything better planned for the
next three years of your life?

Dear Rosie,

Apologies for the delay in getting back to you. The past
few months have been very busy for Alex and me indeed.
Adjusting to married life and a new-born baby all in a matter
of months is hard work.

We were delighted to receive your little card and we hope
you and Katie are keeping well over in Ireland.

Best wishes,

Bethany (and Alex, Theo, and Josh too)

337

You have received a message from: ROSIE.

Rosie: You're right, Ruby, it doesn't look like I'll be getting up to all that much for the next two years of my life. Why not educate myself?

Chapter 41

Hi, Mum.

Winter *again*. It's scary how the months fly by so fast. They turn into years without me even noticing. Katie is like my calendar, watching her grow and change. She is growing up so fast, learning to have opinions of her own, learning that I don't have the answers to everything. And the moment a child begins to understand that, you know you're in trouble.

I'm still on my journey, Mum, still caught in that in-between stage of life where I've just arrived from somewhere, have left it well and truly behind and I'm now working my way towards something new. I suppose what I'm trying to say is that my mind isn't settled yet. Still. I mean, you and Dad have done nothing but travel for the past year – you haven't been in one country for more than a few weeks at a time – but you are both more settled than me, and I haven't left for the past year. You both know where you want to be. I suppose that's because you have each other and anywhere Dad is feels like home to you.

I've learned that home isn't a place, it's a feeling. I can make the flat look as pretty as I can, put as many flower boxes on the windowsills as I want, put a welcome mat outside the front door, hang a 'Home Sweet Home' sign over the fireplace and take to wearing aprons and baking cookies, but the truth is that I know I don't want to stay here for ever.

It's like I'm waiting at the train station, busking to make a few quid, just enough to catch the next train out of here. And, of course, the most important thing to me is Katie. Everywhere I am with her should feel like home, but it doesn't because it's up to *me* to make the home for her. I know that Katie is going to leave in a few years and she won't need me like she does now.

I have to set up my own life for when Katie goes. I *need* to do that because I don't see any Prince Charmings coming along to rescue me. Fairy tales are such evil little stories for young children. Every time I'm in a mess I expect a long-haired posh-speaking man to come trotting into my life (on a horse, of course, not literally trotting himself). Then I realise I don't want a man trotting into my life because men are the ones who put me in the bloody mess in the first place.

I'm like Katie's coach right now, gearing her up for the big fight that is adult life. She's hardly thinking of life after me. Sure, she has her dreams of travelling the world and DJ-ing for a living *without me*, but the *without me* part hasn't hit her yet. And so it shouldn't – she's only fourteen. Anyway, she is not up to making her own decisions yet, and I've put my foot down on the quitting school idea.

Although lately I haven't had to force her out of bed in the mornings because of John, this new boyfriend of hers. The pair of them are inseparable; they go to discos every Friday night at the GAA club near where he lives. He's a real GAA man and plays hurling for the Dublin minors. In fact, we're all going to Croke Park this Sunday to see Dublin v. Tipperary, very excited. Anyway, it's tricky for me because I obviously don't drive so I sometimes put Ruby on driving duties. She calls it Driving Ms Lazy. John's mother is a very nice lady, though, and she's kind enough to collect Katie and drop her home some weeks.

I haven't seen or heard much of Toby lately, but I saw his mother at the school when she was dropping off her youngest and she told me he was acting more or less the same as Katie with his new girlfriend, Monica.

I never dated when I was fourteen. The youth of today are really growing up fast . . . (I sounded SO OLD there!) OK, OK, Mum, I can hear you fuming from here. I did become pregnant at the age of eighteen without having a job or education or man, and almost gave you a nervous break-down, but in some countries of the world that's old, so you should thank your lucky stars that I didn't get started even sooner.

Kevin called up for the weekend; he brought his girlfriend with him. She was very sweet but I've no idea what she sees in him. Did you know that they've been going out for a year now? Honestly, that brother of mine is so secretive; you prac-tically have to beat the information out of him! You never know, there could be more wedding bells in the air for the Dunne family! Tell Dad to get that dirty old tuxedo out of the attic and to brush the cobwebs and mothballs off in preparation. He'll be happy to know he won't have to walk down the aisle this time. (Honestly, he had *me* nervous at my wedding!)

As for my North Strand palace, we might as well have no glass in the windows here at all for all the wind they let in. It's so cold and windy tonight, the rain is pelting off the windows. That lamppost from outside shines directly into this flat. If only it could be moved a bit to the right then it could annoy Rupert instead. Although it does save me money on the electricity. I'm half-expecting Gene Kelly to be outside dancing around with his umbrella. Why is it movies can make everything – even rain – look fun?

Every morning I rise when it is pitch-black outside (and,

you know, it's not natural to be up at a time when even the sun can't be bothered to rise), the flat is freezing, I hop from the shower to my bedroom, shivering like hell, I make my way outside where I have to walk ten minutes to the bus stop, invariably in the wind and rain. My ears ache and my hair is normally in wet strings around my head, so I may as well not wash and blow-dry it at all. My mascara is running down my face, my umbrella has blown inside out and I look like a dishevelled Mary Poppins. Then the bus is late. Or too full to stop. And I end up late for work, looking like a drowned rat, having had at least one fight with a bus driver, while everyone else has their make-up, clothes and hair all perfect because they all got out of bed an hour later than me, hopped into their cars, drove to work, arrived at the school fifteen minutes before classes started in time to have a cup of coffee as a relaxing start to their day.

Singing in the rain, my bum.

Notice I'm writing to you today and not emailing and that's due to the guy in the internet café downstairs catching me one too many times staring at him. His face is so scrumptious I feel like taking a bite out of him. I think he's on to me so I decided to stay home tonight. The other reason for me writing is that I'm pretending right now that I'm studying. We both have Christmas exams coming up and I told Katie she needed to take them more seriously. Well, I walked myself straight into that one. So here we both are, crammed at the kitchen table with our books, folders, papers and pens, pretending to look intellectual.

I have so much study to catch up on that I haven't been able to cook dinner all week. So it's been downstairs' delights for the past few days. Luckily Sanjay is giving us forty per cent off our takeaway meals and he's even created a new dish called Rosie Chicken Curry. He sent it up free last night with our order. We tasted it and sent it back down. Just joking. It's basically chicken and curry. All he did was add the Rosie.

342

I'm flattered all the same at the sight of my name on an Indian menu, and it's interesting late at night to hear my name being yelled by drunken men in deep slurred voices. I keep thinking that my Romeo is standing on the pavement below my window, calling me and throwing stones up to awaken me from my slumber. Then I remember that it's Saturday night, one o'clock in the morning, the pub has just closed, drunken men are shouting their special order over the counter and the stones against my window is the rain. But a girl can always dream.

Every time I pass by Sanjay's wife she rolls her eyes and tuts. He's still asking me out on dates, he even asks me when she's standing right beside him. So I say very loudly that what he is asking me is wrong, considering his marital status, that he needs to have more respect for his wife and that even if he wasn't married I would say no. I say it loudly so that she can hear but yet she stills tuts and Sanjay smiles at me and throws a few poppadoms in the bag for me for free. The man is insane.

Rupert (my other neighbour) asked me if I want to go to the National Concert Hall at the weekend. Apparently the National Symphony Orchestra is playing Brahms Piano Concerto Number 2 in B flat, Op. 83, which is his absolute favourite. It's not a date or anything. I think Rupert is completely asexual and that he just wants some company. That suits me just fine. Plus, the 'I Love Mother' tattoo on his arm would be a real turn-off. That quote by James Joyce on his chest really upsets me too, because Rupert is so tall that when I look straight ahead I'm constantly forced to read 'Mistakes are the portals of discovery.' It's like a sign or something, like Rupert was put in the flat beside me to make me understand the error of my ways. Only I wish the message made more sense than that. Mistakes are more like the potholes of discovery. It's a bloody long bumpy road to discovery, strewn with obstacles and danger. I wish it said, 'Chocolate is good' instead.

Speaking of mistakes, I still haven't spoken to Alex and it's been over a year now. I think this is really it this time. All we've been doing is sending stupid cards back and forth to each other. It's like we're having a staring competition and neither of us wants to be the first to blink. I miss him like crazy. There are so many things that happen to me, silly little everyday things that I itch to tell him. Like the postman this morning was delivering across the road and that stupid little Jack Russell dog called Jack Russell was attacking him again. So I looked out the window and I saw the postman shaking the dog off his leg as he does every morning but this time he kicked the dog in the stomach by mistake and the dog fell over and didn't move for ages. Then the owner came outside and I watched as the postman pretended that Jack Russell was like that when he got there. The owner believed him and there was pandemonium as they tried to help the dog. Eventually Jack Russell got up and when he took one look at the postman he whimpered and ran away into the house. It was so funny. The postman just shrugged and walked off. He was whistling by the time he got to my door. Things like that would have really made Alex laugh, especially as I had told him all about the wretched dog keeping me awake all night barking, and always stealing my post from the poor postman.

Hang on a sec, Katie is trying to sneak a peek off my page . . .

MASLOW'S THEORY OF HIERARCHY.

Ha ha, that'll put her off the scent. OK, I better go now and actually do some work. See you both soon. Tell Dad I said hello and that I love him.

Oh, by the way, Ruby has set me up on a blind date on Saturday night. I nearly killed her but I can't cancel it. Cross your fingers for me that he's not some sort of serial killer.

Lots of love,
Rosie

You have received an instant message from: ROSIE.

Rosie: Hi, Julie. I've signed you up to be one of my instant message buddies. Whenever I see that you're online I can send you messages.

Julie: Not if I block your name from my list.

Rosie: You wouldn't dare.

Julie: Why would you set up an instant messaging service with me when I am in the next room?

Rosie: It's what I do. It means I can multi-task. I can speak to people on the phone and also do business with you online. Anyway, what is it that you actually do, Miss Casey? All I see you doing is terrorising innocent children and having meetings with pissed-off parents.

Julie: That's about all I do, Rosie, you're right. Believe me, you were one of the worst kids to teach and one of the worst parents to meet with. I hated calling you in.

Rosie: I hated coming in.

Julie: And now you've added me to your messaging list. How times change. By the way, I'm having a little get-together for my birthday next week and I was wondering if you would like to come.

Rosie: Who else is going?

Julie: Oh, just some other kids that I used to scare the hell out of twenty years ago. We love to gather and reminisce about the days gone by.

Rosie: Seriously?

Julie: No, just a few friends, a few members of my family for a few drinks and a few nibbles for a few minutes to mark the occasion, and then you can all leave me alone.

Rosie: What age will you be? I only ask so I can buy you a birthday card with a number on it. Maybe get a badge for you too.

Julie: You do and you're fired. I'm going to be fifty-three.

Rosie: You're only twenty years older than me. I used to think you were ancient!

Julie: Funny, isn't it? Imagine, I was only about your age by the time you left this school. The kids must feel that you're ancient now too.

Rosie: I feel ancient.

Julie: Ancient people don't go on romantic blind dates. Come on, spill the beans, what was he like?

Rosie: His name is Adam and he is a very, very attractive man. All evening he was polite, a terrific conversationalist and very funny. He paid for the meal, the taxi, drinks, absolutely everything, and wouldn't let me open my purse (not that there was any money in it to spend, given the slave wages I'm paid, ahem . . .). He was tall, dark and handsome, dressed impeccably. Plucked eyebrows, straight teeth and not a nose hair in sight.

Julie: What does he do for a living?

Rosie: He's an engineer.

Julie: So he was polite, handsome and had a great job. He sounds too good to be true. Are you meeting again?

Rosie: Well, after the meal we went back to his penthouse apartment. He lives along Sir John Rogerson's Quay – the place was fabulous. We kissed, I stayed over, he asked me out again and I said no.

Julie: Are you crazy?

Rosie: Probably. He was such a good man but there was just nothing there – no sparkle.

Julie: But it was only your first date. You can never really tell these things by a first date. What did you want, fireworks?

Rosie: No, actually, quite the opposite. I want silence, a perfect moment of quietness.

Julie: Silence?

Rosie: Oh, it's a long story. But last night only proves that you can put me with a guy who's perfect in every way and I'm still not ready. Everyone needs to stop pressurising me – I'll find someone when I'm good and ready.

Julie: OK, OK, I promise I'll stop trying to set you up until you give me your permission to. How's the studying going, by the way?

Rosie: It's tough working, studying and being a mother all at the same time. I end up staying up till all hours of the night, pondering life, the universe and all that's in it, i.e., not doing any work.

Julie: Don't worry, we've all had those days and believe me, by the time you get to my age you stop caring. Is there anything I can do to help?

Rosie: Yes, actually. A pay rise would be a terrific help.

Julie: No chance. How's the saving going?

Rosie: It would be going fine if I didn't have to feed, clothe, educate my child as well as pour rent money into the shoe box I'm living in.

Julie: That always seems to get in the way of things, that whole looking-after-your-child part. Have you spoken to Alex yet?

Rosie: No.

Julie: Oh, Rosie, you are both being ridiculous. I spent my life trying to separate you two from each other but now the fun is over for me. Tell him Miss Big Nose Smelly Breath Casey has given you both permission to sit beside each other again.

Rosie: That'll never work; he never listened to you anyway. And it's not like we're not in contact at all. Katie emails all the time and I send cards for every occasion under the sun and he does the same back. Every few months I get a postcard from a different exotic country with boring weather reports from him, and when he's not holidaying he's working all hours. So we're not completely ignoring each other. It's a very civilised kind of argument we're having.

Julie: Yes, apart from the fact that you don't talk. Your best friend has a six-month-old baby that you haven't even met. All I'm saying is that if you let this carry on much longer, the years will multiply and before you know it it'll just be too late.

Chapter 42

Dear Rosie and Katie Dunne,

Season's Greetings from St Jude's Hospital.

My wife, two sons and I hope that the year ahead brings you and your loved ones good health and happiness.

Merry Christmas and a Happy New Year from the Stewarts.

Dr Alex Stewart MD

To Dr Alex Stewart

May the coming year be filled with health, wealth and happiness for you and your family.

Best wishes,

Rosie Dunne

You have received an instant message from: ALEX.

Alex: Your card arrived this morning.

Rosie: Oooh, talking to me now, are you?

Alex: It's been long enough. One of us should be adult enough to make contact. Remember I'm not the one who started this in the first place.

Rosie: Yes you did.

Alex: Rosie, no I didn't.

Rosie: Yes you did!

Alex: Oh, *please*! Last year I told you Bethany was pregnant, at which point you went crazy. And, for your information, I proposed to her one night before we went to an award ceremony. Bethany said yes, and naturally being excited, she told her parents at the table (as any normal person would do). Her father was presented with his award and during his speech he announced that his daughter had just gotten engaged (as a normal proud father would on just learning that his daughter was to be married).

The press were there; they went back to their desks and reported on the evening in time to make the next day's papers. I went out and celebrated my engagement with my fiancée and her family. I got home to bed and woke up the next day to phone call after phone call from my family wanting to no why the hell I hadn't told them I was getting married. My in-box was full of emails from confused friends and I was just about to deal with them when I got an instant message from you.

So I sent you and Katie wedding invites anyway, thinking that even though you disapproved of my choice of wife and concocted pathetic stories about why I was marrying her, you might still have behaved like the friend you claim to be by attending my wedding and being supportive.

So I apologise for the last card you received, your name was on my mailing list, but this particular card was intended for my patients and not you.

Rosie: Wait a minute, I didn't receive any wedding invite!

Alex: What?

Rosie: I got no invitation to your wedding. There was one for Katie alright, but none for me. And Katie couldn't very well go because she was only thirteen and where would she stay? And I couldn't bring her over because frankly I couldn't afford to—

Alex: Stop! Now let me think about this for a moment. You didn't receive a wedding invite?

Rosie: No. Just one for Katie.

Alex: What about your parents?

Rosie: Yeah, they received one but they couldn't go because they were visiting Steph in Paris and—

Alex: OK! Yours wasn't sent there by mistake?

Rosie: No.

Alex: But my parents – didn't they tell you?

Rosie: They said they would love me to go but they don't control the invites, Alex. You never asked me to go.

Alex: But you were on the list. I even *saw* your invite on the kitchen table.

Rosie: Oh.

Alex: So what happened?

Rosie: Don't ask me! I didn't even know there was an invite for me! Who posted them?

Alex: Bethany and the wedding planner.

Rosie: Hmm . . . OK so somewhere between Bethany walking to the post box and the invite actually going in the slot, something happened to my invite.

Alex: Oh, don't start, Rosie. It wasn't Bethany. She's got much better things to be doing with her time than hatching plans to get rid of you.

Rosie: Like doing lunch with the ladies?

Alex: Stop.

Rosie: Well, I'm in shock.

Alex: So you thought all this time that I didn't want you at my wedding?

Rosie: Yes.

Alex: But why didn't you say something? An entire year and you didn't say anything? If you didn't invite me to your wedding I would at least *say* something!

Rosie: Excuse me, why didn't you ask me why I wasn't there? If I invited you to my wedding and I noticed

351

that you hadn't turned up, I think I would at least *say*
something.

Alex: I was angry.

Rosie: Me too.

Alex: I'm still angry about the things you said.

Rosie: Answer me this, Alex. Did you or did you not tell
me only months previously that Bethany was not 'the
one' for you and that you didn't love her?

Alex: Yes, but—

Rosie: And were you or were you not going to break up
with her just before she announced she was pregnant?

Alex: Yes, but—

Rosie: And were you or were you not worried about your
job when you refused to marry Bethany?

Alex: Yes, but—

Rosie: And were you or were you not—

Alex: Stop, Rosie. All of that may be true but it was
coupled with the fact that I wanted to be a part of Theo
and Bethany's life.

Rosie: So if you *did* invite me to your wedding and I was
partly correct on what I said, why did we spend the
entire year not speaking?

Alex: Right now what I want to no is where the hell your
wedding invite went to. The wedding planner had
everything arranged. Unless it was . . .

Rosie: Who?

Alex: Not *who* but *what* . . .

Rosie: *What*, then?

Alex: Jack Russell the Jack Russell. Next time I see him
I'm going to wring his neck.

Rosie: Oh, you can't do that.

Alex: I can do whatever the hell I want to that post-
nicking little—

Rosie: He's dead. The postman kicked him in the stomach
a few mornings in a row completely by mistake (I'm a

witness) and one morning he did it, Jack just stopped moving.

Alex: I'm not sorry to hear that.

Rosie: I'm sorry though, Alex.

Alex: Me too. Friends again?

Rosie: I never stopped being your friend.

Alex: Me neither. Well, unfortunately I have to go because my baby is pouring his breakfast on his head and massaging it into his scalp with a look of pure concentration on his face. I fear it may be nappy-changing time again.

For our beautiful daughter

We love you with all our hearts. Here's to a new year. Happy Birthday, Rosie!

Good luck with your exams in June. We have our fingers crossed for you.

Lots of love,

Mum and Dad

For my sister

You're finally catching up on me, Rosie, which I'm glad of because I don't want to be the only one nearing forty! Best of luck with your exams. You have two months to learn it all – you can get it done. I'm sure you'll fly through them!

Happy Birthday.

Love,

Stephanie, Pierre, Jean-Louis, Sophia

Happy Birthday, Mum.

Hope you like your present. If it doesn't fit you, I'll have it!

Love,

Katie

To a special friend

Happy 35th Birthday, Rosie. I'm working on a new experiment to slow down time. Fancy joining in with me?

Enjoy your day and I hope to see you soon!

Alex

To Rosie,

Happy Birthday again. After this celebration there will be no more distractions. You have to pass these exams with straight As. You can do it and you're my only hope of getting out of here. I'm still dreaming of that job as an entertainer at that fine hotel of yours.

Love, Ruby

You have received an instant message from: ROSIE.

Rosie: Sixteen. My little angel sixteen! What the hell am I supposed to do now? Where's the rule book?

Ruby: It's not like only yesterday she was two years old, you know. You did have a total of let's see, sixteen years' preparation. This shouldn't come as a shock to you.

Rosie: Ruby, you unsentimental witch, do you not feel anything? Are you numb to all emotions? How did you feel when your Gary turned sixteen?

Ruby: I just don't look at things like you do. I don't think much of ages or birthdays – they're just another day to me. They don't symbolise anything but a bunch of definitions and generalisations people have created to make conversation, debates and media discussions. For example, Katie is not going to go off the rails because suddenly she wakes up one morning and she's sixteen. People do whatever the hell they want to do at any age they fancy. Last month you were thirty-five. That means you're five years from forty. Do you think that the day you reach forty you will be any different than you were at thirty-nine or forty-one for that matter? People create little ideas about ages so they can write silly self-help books, stick stupid comments in birthday cards, create names for internet chat rooms and look for excuses for crises that are happening in their life.

For example, the man's so-called 'mid-life crisis' is just a bunch of hype. Age is not the problem; it's the male brain that's the problem. Men have been cheating since they were apes (insert your own joke there), since cavemen times (and again there) all the way up to now, the age of what is supposed to be the civilised man. This is simply the way they were made. Age is not the issue.

Your baby will remain your baby past the point when she has her own little baby. Don't worry about that.

Rosie: I don't want my baby to have a baby until she's grown up, married and rich. I mean, when I think of the things I did on my sixteenth birthday . . . actually, I can't remember exactly what I did.

Ruby: Why not?

Rosie: Because I was being incredibly juvenile and stupid.

Ruby: What did you do?

Rosie: Me and Alex forged our mums' signatures and wrote notes to school saying we would both be absent for the day.

Ruby: Coincidentally.

Rosie: Exactly. We went to some old man's pub in town where ID wasn't a necessity and we drank all day. Unfortunately it was ruined by the fact that I fell and hit my head, had to be raced to hospital in an ambulance where I received seven stitches and my stomach was pumped. The parents were none too pleased.

Ruby: I bet they weren't. How did you fall? Were you doing some of your funky moves on the dance floor again?

Rosie: Actually, no. I was only sitting on my stool.

Ruby: Ha ha. *Only you* could fall on the floor while you were sitting down.

Rosie: I know, that's weird, isn't it? I wonder how it happened!

Ruby: Well, you should ask Alex. I'm surprised it's never occurred to you to ask him before.

Rosie: Good idea! Ooh, he's online now so I'll ask.

Ruby: It's not that bloody important, but any old excuse to talk to him, I suppose. I'll hold on here and try to make myself look busy while you ask. I'm intrigued . . .

You have received an instant message from: ROSIE.

Rosie: Hi, Alex.

Alex: Hi, there. Do you ever do any work? Every time I log on you're on too!

Rosie: I'm just chatting to Ruby. It's cheaper this way. We don't have to answer questions at work about the telephone bill. Internet use is unlimited if you pay a monthly charge and, besides, typing makes us look like we're busy. Anyway, I just wanted to ask you a quick question.

Alex: Fire ahead.

Rosie: Remember on my sixteenth birthday, I fell and hit my head?

Alex: Ha ha, how could I forget? Are you thinking of this because Katie's birthday is coming up? Because if she's anything like you, you should be afraid, be very, very afraid. What should I get for her anyway, a sick bucket?

Rosie: Age is only a number, not a state of mind or a reason for any type of particular behaviour.

Alex: O . . . K then. What's your question?

Rosie: How on earth did I fall and hit my head on the floor while I was sitting down?

Alex: Oh my Lord. The question. *The* Question.

Rosie: What's wrong with my question??

Alex: Rosie Dunne, I have been waiting nearly twenty

356

years for you to ask me that question and I thought you never would.

Rosie: What??

Alex: Why you never asked is beyond me, but you woke up the next day and claimed to have no knowledge of what had happened. I didn't want to bring it up; you had brought enough up the night before!

Rosie: You didn't want to bring what up? Alex, *tell me*! How did I fall off my stool??

Alex: I don't think you're ready to no.

Rosie: Oh, shut up. I'm Rosie Dunne, after all; I was born to be ready for anything.

Alex: OK then, if you're so sure of yourself . . .

Rosie: I am! Now tell me!

Alex: We were kissing.

Rosie: We were *what*??

Alex: Yep. You were leaning across on your high stool, kissing me; the stool was very wobbly and lodged unsafely between the cracks of a very old uneven tiled pub floor. And you fell.

Rosie: WHAT??

Alex: Oh, the sweet nothings you whispered into my ear that night, Rosie Dunne. And I was gutted the next day when you woke up and forgot. After me holding your hand while you puked all night.

Rosie: *Alex!*

Alex: What?

Rosie: *Why didn't you tell me?!*

Alex: Because we weren't allowed to see each other for a while and I didn't want to tell you in a note. And then you said you wanted to forget everything that had happened that night so I thought that maybe you vaguely remembered and you just regretted it.

Rosie: You should have told me.

Alex: Why, what would you have said?

Rosie: Em . . . that's really putting me on the spot, Alex.

Alex: Yeah, sorry.

Rosie: I can't believe it. Because I fell, we got caught and I had to stay home for a week while your punishment was to start work in your dad's office, where you met Bethany. The girl you said you were going to marry . . .

Alex: That's right, I said that!

Rosie: Yeah, you did . . .

Alex: Well, I actually said that just to test you but as you didn't seem to care too much I went out with her anyway. That's funny. I had forgotten I had said that! Bethany would love to hear that! Thanks for reminding me.

Rosie: No no, thank *you* for reminding *me* . . .

You have an instant message from: RUBY.

Ruby: Come on, Ms Bumps, I need to look like I'm busy here. You find out what happened yet?

Rosie: Yes, I found out I'm the biggest idiot in the *whole entire world.* Aaaaaaaah!

Ruby: I waited around for *that*? I could have told you that *ages* ago.

Dear Katie,
    Happy sweet sixteenth!
    Love, Mum xxx

For our granddaughter,
    Happy sweet sixteenth birthday!
    Lots of love,
    Grandma and Granddad

For my girlfriend
    Happy Sweet 16!
    Lots of love,
    John

To Katie

Happy birthday, you pain in the ass. Another few months and those braces will be off. Then I won't be able to tell what you've eaten for dinner.

Toby

For my daughter

Congratulations, Katie. Happy sweet sixteen!
I hope John doesn't try to kiss you!
Love, Dad

Dear Mum and Dad,

I'm never speaking to Rupert again. *Sweet* sixteen my *arse*.

Katie demanded that I give her the money that I would have spent on her present, so that she could go into town and pick her own clothes, which suited me fine because then I didn't have to bother spending sleepless nights trying to think of the 'perfect' gift that she would inevitably hate and hide under her bed. Anyway, she walked into the flat, hand in hand with the big friendly giant (John), beaming from ear to ear so I immediately knew something suspicious was going on. She lifted her top, lowered her trousers an inch and there it was.

The tattoo from hell.

An awful-dirty-disgusting-very-ugly-I've-just-realised-I'm-beginning-to-sound-like-you-mother kind of tattoo. It sat there on her hipbone, sticking its tongue out at me.

Mum, it's ugly. Mind you, it was bleeding and beginning to grow a scab by the time I saw it. Apparently Rupert said his clients only needed to be sixteen to get a tattoo, which I strongly disagree with so I came downstairs to check the internet. It turns out he's right, but if I could just find some sort of loophole that would allow me to kick his ass . . .

Cute internet café guy asked me if I was OK and he looked

really concerned, which I thought was possibly the beginning of something new for the both of us. But then I realised I was thumping the keyboard with my fists so he was probably only concerned about his computer. I have no time for selfish men like that in my life so I've decided there's no chance of a steamy love affair occurring between us after hours on the computer desks. Purely my decision, though.

What makes it even worse is that I was trying to study for my *final* exams and the drilling coming from the tattoo parlour downstairs was really distracting me. What I didn't realise was that I was listening to the mutilation of my own daughter's body.

It was kind of difficult giving Rupert a piece of my mind because I couldn't express my hatred of tattoos without offending him, seeing as he is an actual walking tattoo. It would be like slagging one of his family members.

But the tattoo is the least of my worries. She also got her tongue pierced. Rupert threw that part in for free. She sounds like she's got hot potatoes in her mouth when she speaks. So no wonder I got such a shock when she walked in with a scary look on her face and said, 'Aah, uck at I aa-oo,' and then proceeded to lift up her top. John got one as well but he got a tattoo of a hurley stick and a hurling ball on his hipbone. You don't even want to know what that picture resembles. Rupert drilled the ball too close and on the wrong end of the stick, if you know what I mean.

I suppose it could be worse: they could have gotten tattooed with each other's names. And there are worse tattoos Katie could get than a tiny little strawberry the size of my thumbnail.

Perhaps I'm overreacting?

How on earth must you and Dad have felt when I told you I was *pregnant*?

Now that I think of it, perhaps I should give Katie some sort of award? Anyway, I ought to go back upstairs and face the (very loud, banging) music, plus I need to continue with my studies. I can't believe I've reached my final year. Two years flew by and while it was virtually impossible studying by night, working by day and trying to be a mother at both those times, I'm glad I didn't pack it in the hundred times a day that I said I would. Imagine, I'll have a graduation ceremony! You and Dad will finally be able to sit in the crowd while I collect my diploma in my unflattering robe and hat. It's only fourteen years later than originally planned, but I suppose it's better late than never.

However I won't get to the graduation ceremony if I don't pass my exams so, *no more distractions*. I am going to study!

Love,

Rosie

From   Rosie
To   Alex
Subject Dad

Something awful has happened. People at work said you were in surgery but, please, as soon as you get my messages and this email, can you ring me?

Mum called me just a minute ago in tears; Dad has had a massive heart attack and has been rushed to hospital. She's in huge shock but she told me not to travel over to her because my first exam is starting tomorrow. I don't know what to do. I don't know how serious it is, the doctors won't tell us anything yet. Can you maybe ring the hospital and see what's going on? You understand all that stuff. I don't know what to do. Please get this email on time. I don't know who else to call.

I don't want to leave Mum on her own, although Kevin is going over to her now. I don't want Dad to be alone either. Oh, this is so confusing.

Oh God, Alex, please help. I don't want to lose my dad.

From   Alex
To   Rosie
Subject Re: Dad

I tried calling you but you must be on the phone. Just stay calm. I rang the hospital and had a word with Dr Flannery there. He's the doctor looking after your dad and he explained Dennis's condition to me.

What I suggest you do is pack a bag for a few days and get on the earliest bus you can to Galway. Do you understand what I mean?

Forget about your exam, this is more important. Keep calm, Rosie, and just be there for your mum and dad. Tell Stephanie to come home too, if she can. Keep in touch with me during the night.

Chapter 43

Dear Alex,

Coffin sizes can be no wider than 76 cm; can be made of chipboard with approved veneers and plastics for cremation purposes. Did you know that? Ferrous screws are acceptable in small numbers and wood braces will give extra strength but must *only* be placed in the inside of the coffin.

The coffin must have the full name of the deceased on the lid. Wouldn't want to get anyone mixed up, I suppose. The thing that I really wished I hadn't learned was that the coffin should be lined with a substance known as 'Cremfilm', or use absorbent cloth or cotton padding because apparently fluid can leak from a body.

I didn't know any of this.

There were forms. Lots and lots of forms. Forms A, B, C, F and all the medical forms. No one mentioned anything about D and E. I didn't know you needed so much proof to show you were dead. I thought the fact you've stopped living and breathing was a huge giveaway. Apparently not.

I suppose it's like going away to live in another country. Dad just had to get his papers ready, get dressed in his Sunday best, arrange his mode of transport and off he went to his final destination, wherever that may be. Oh, how much Mum would have loved to have gone on this particular trip with him, but she knows she can't.

She just kept repeating to everyone at the funeral, 'He just didn't wake up. I called him and called him, but he wouldn't wake up.' She hasn't stopped shaking since it happened and she looks like she's aged twenty years. Yet she seems younger. Like a lost little child who looks around her and doesn't know where to go, like suddenly she's in a whole new place and she doesn't know the way.

I suppose she is. I suppose we all are.

I've never been here before. I'm thirty-five years old and I've never lost anyone close to me. I've been to ten funerals in my life and they were of distant relatives, friends of friends and family of friends whom my life is none the worse off without.

But Dad going? God, that's a big one.

He was only sixty-five years old. Not old at all. And he was healthy. What causes a healthy sixty-five-year-old man to fall asleep and never wake up? I can only comfort myself with thoughts that he saw something so beautiful that he just had to go. That's the kind of thing Dad would do.

There's something completely unnerving about seeing your parents upset. I suppose it's because they're supposed to be the strong ones, but that's not just it. When people are kids they use their parents as some sort of measurement for how bad a situation is. When you fall on the ground really hard and you can't figure out whether it hurts or not you look to your parents. If they look worried and rush towards you, you cry. If they laugh and smack the ground saying, 'Bold ground,' then you pick yourself up and get on with it.

When you find out you're pregnant and feel numb of all emotions you look at their expressions. When both your Mum and Dad hug you and tell you it's going to be OK and that they'll support you, you know it's not the end of the world. But depending on the parents, it could have been pretty damn close.

Parents are the barometers of emotions for children and it has a domino effect. I have never seen my mum cry so much in all of my life, which scared me and made me cry, which scared Katie and made her cry. We all cried together.

As for Dad, he was supposed to live for ever. The one who could open all the jar lids nobody else could, who fixed whatever was broken, was supposed to do that for ever. The man who let me sit on his shoulders, climb on his back, chase me around while making monster noises, throw me in the air and catch me, spin me around so much that I felt dizzy and fell over laughing.

And in the end without being able to say thank you and a proper goodbye, my final memories of him turn into coffin sizes and medical forms.

I'm still over in Galway with Mum. In the wild, wild west. But it's a beautiful summer and it doesn't feel quite right. The atmosphere doesn't suit the mood, there's the sound of children's laughter floating up from the beach down below, there are birds singing and dancing around the sky, swooping low and catching their fresh meals from the sea. It doesn't feel right to love the world and see such brightness when something so awful has happened.

It's like hearing gurgling babies echoing in the church at the funeral. There's nothing more uplifting than to hear the sound of an innocent child being so happy in a place that people are sad. It reminds you that life goes on and on and on, just not for the one you're saying goodbye to. People come and people go and we know this happens, yet we get such a shock when it does. To use that old cliché, the only certainty in life is death. It's a certainty, it's the one condition of living that we're given but we often let it tear us apart.

I don't know what to do or say to Mum to make her feel

better; I don't suppose there really is anything that would accomplish that, but watching her crying to herself all day tears me apart. I can hear her pain in her tears. Maybe she'll just run out of tears.

Alex, you're a heart doctor. You know the heart literally inside and out – what is there you can do when someone's heart has broken? Have you any cures for that?

Thanks for coming over to the funeral. It was so good to see you. It was just a shame that it was under these circumstances. It was good of your parents to come as well. Mum really did appreciate it. Thanks for getting rid of whatshisname too; I really wasn't in the mood to have any discussions with him at the church. It was good of him to come but if Dad had seen him he would have leaped out of that coffin and thrown him in in his place.

Stephanie and Kevin headed home a few days ago but I'm going to stay on for a little while longer. I just can't leave Mum alone. The neighbours are being so good to her. I know she will be in good hands when I do finally leave. I've missed all my exams and by the sounds of things I'll have to repeat the entire year if I do want to complete the course. I don't think I could be bothered doing it all over again.

Anyway, I'll have to go home in a few days as no doubt the bills have been piling up in my letter box since the day I left. I really need to get back before they cut everything off and evict me.

Thanks for being there for me once again, Alex. Isn't it typical of us that it's a tragedy that gets us together?

Love,
Rosie

From   Rosie
To   Alex
Subject Dad

I just returned home from Connemara to be greeted by an overflowing mailbox. Among a pile of bills was the following letter. It was posted the day before Dad died.

Dear Rosie,

Your mum and I are still laughing from your last letter about Katie's tattoo. I do love it when you write to us! I hope you're over the trauma of your daughter becoming a fully fledged teen. I remember the day that happened with you. I think it hit you before Stephanie! You were always eager to try new things and go new places, my fearless Rosie. I thought that when you finished school you were going to set off around the world and we would never see you again. I'm glad that didn't happen. You were always a delight to have around the house. You *and* Katie. I'm only sorry we had to leave you when you needed us both. Your mum and I questioned our actions time and time again. I hope we did the right thing.

I know you always felt that you were in the way or that you were letting us down, but that's far from the truth. It just meant that I got to see my little girl grow. Grow from being a baby to an adult and grow as a mother. You and Katie are a great team and she is a fine example of the good parenting she received. A bit of ink on her skin doesn't tarnish the goodness or dim the brightness that shines from her. A tribute to her mother.

Life deals each of us a different set of cards and out of all of us there's no doubt that you received the toughest hand of all. But you shone through the tough times. You are a strong girl and you grew even stronger when that idiot of a man (whatshisname, your mother told me to say) let you down. You picked yourself up, dusted yourself off and started

367

all over again, set up home with Katie, found yourself a new job, provided for your daughter and did your dad proud once more.

And now you're only days away from your exams. After all you went through you'll now have a diploma. I'll be proud watching you accept that scroll, Rosie; I'll be the proudest dad in the world.

Love,
Dad

From   Rosie
To   Alex
Subject Diploma

There's no way I'm giving this college course up now. In the wise words of Johnny Logan, what's another year? I'm going to do these exams and I'm going to get this diploma in Hotel Management. Dad wouldn't want himself to be the reason for me missing out.

It's the goodbye I needed, Alex. What a wonderful, wonderful gift to be given.

From   Julie
To   Rosie
Subject Staying with me?

So you're staying with me another year then?

I'll allow you, but after that, once you have your diploma, I'm serious when I say I'm firing you. I'm fifty-five years old; I don't have much longer at this job to be waiting for you to fulfil your dreams.

This year the courses will be a breeze, first because you've done it before and second and more important because you have the good wishes and pride of your father behind you. That's the best motivation a person could get.

Do you mind me asking what is it about these hotels that you love so much?

From   Rosie
To   Julie
Subject   Why I love hotels!

I just get this feeling when I walk into really nice hotels. For me they represent everything in life that's luxurious and full of splendour. I love that people pamper you and look after you. Everything is so clean and pristine, so completely perfect. So unlike home – well, my home anyway.

I love that people go to enjoy themselves; it's not so much a place of work as being a host in paradise.

I get excited by the sparkling bathrooms, the big fluffy robes, the slippers and the décor. Where else would you find chocolate on your pillow? It's like the tooth fairy and Santa Claus all at once. There's twenty-four-hour room service and bouncy padded carpets, turned-down beds and mini-bars, bowls of fruit and free shampoo. I feel like I'm Charlie in the Chocolate Factory. Everything you want is at your disposal. All you have to do is pick up the phone and press the magic number and the people on the other end of the phone are only too delighted to help.

To stay in one is the ultimate treat; to work in one would be an everyday pleasure. When I finish this course I'm automatically placed in a hotel as a temporary manager in training so I just know that there's a job for me at the end of the rainbow.

You have received an instant message from: RUBY.
Ruby: Hello, stranger.
Rosie: Oh, hi, Ruby, sorry it's been so long; I've had a lot on lately.

Ruby: No apologies needed, you know that. How's your
mum?

Rosie: Not great. That tear reservoir still hasn't dried up.
She's coming to stay with me for a little while.

Ruby: In the flat?

Rosie: Yes.

Ruby: How's that going to work? You don't have any
spare rooms.

Rosie: Oh, gosh, it has been ages since I spoke to you.
After many days of deliberations with Brian the Whine I
eventually gave in and have decided to allow Katie to
stay with him in Ibiza for the summer. I must be crazy
because no matter how much Brian the Whine assures
me that he's a responsible father who will keep an eye
on his daughter, I can't stop thinking of the fact that he
ran off when he found out I was pregnant and only
returned when she was thirteen. I'm not too keen on his
definition of responsible. Plus he will be working nights
so I don't know how he'll know what she's up to.

Ruby: The good thing about Brian being her father is that
he's the owner of a seedy nightclub on the part of an
island where he's used to seeing what exactly sixteen-
year-olds get up to. He will not want his daughter
joining in with that kind of fun. Trust me. Anyway,
she'll be on her own, and how much partying can a girl
do on her own?

Rosie: You really want the answer to that question?
Anyway, John is going to join her for a few weeks and
Toby and Monica are going over for a holiday too. But I
can't put up too much of a fight because Brian the
Whine is good enough to spend most of the year here
for Katie and he needs to be over there during the
summer. There has to be a bit of give and take, and
Katie has never actually seen her own father's home.
Also, Brian said he would make sure she gets a bit of

experience DJ-ing while she's there, which would be brilliant for her.

Ruby: Have you convinced yourself enough yet?

Rosie: God, does it really sound like that?

Ruby: Yep.

Rosie: Well, without wanting to sound like a complete moan (because we all know I'm not one to moan), this summer is going to be really lonely for me. Even Mum is only staying with me a short while before she's off again. A few people Mum and Dad met while they were on their cruise got in touch with Mum. They're planning a trip to South Africa and they're going to stay for a month. That was the next place Dad wanted to go to. He always used to watch National Geographic and swear he would one day go on a safari. Well, he's going now because Mum is taking his ashes and scattering them with the tigers and elephants. She's really happy with the idea so I'm not going to get in her way. Kevin is a bit upset about it – he wants to have a place for Dad that we can all visit – but Mum insists this is what Dad would want. I don't know why Kev is causing such a fuss. He barely visited Dad when he was alive. I can't imagine him visiting his cremation site every day. Come to think of it, maybe that's what his problem is.

Anyway, Mum doesn't want to stay in Connemara a moment longer on her own, so she's coming to stay with me for two weeks before she heads off. But after that, everyone is gone. Mum, Dad, Katie, Steph, Kev and Alex. I'm all alone and because it's the summer and the school is closed, all I have to do is to study.

Ruby: You think that maybe this is a sign to meet more people?

Rosie: I know, I know. I'm alone by my own choosing. When I was eighteen everyone my age wanted to talk about boys, not babies; at twenty-two they wanted to

371

talk about college not toddlers, at thirty-two they wanted to talk about marriage not divorce, and now when I'm thirty-five and finally willing to talk about men and college, all people want to do is talk about babies. I tried all these coffee morning things; I tried chatting to other mothers as we waited at the school gates for our children. It didn't work. Nobody understands me like you do, Ruby.

Ruby: And even I have trouble with that. You're unique, Rosie Dunne, you're definitely unique. But I'm here for you, and unless me and Gary miraculously become Ireland's Salsa Champions and are whisked off to Madrid for the European Championship, I ain't going nowhere.

Rosie: Thanks.

Ruby: No problem. But continuing with this 'meeting new people' theme, when are you going to start dating again? It's been a few years since you've been in action!

Rosie: Excuse me, did I not go out on a date with Adam, whom you set me up with? Anyway, apart from that enjoyable night with Adam, it's not like dating was ever that brilliant that I miss it.

Ruby: Really?

Rosie: Oh, please, sex with whatshisname was so mechanical. He used to move in time to the bloody bedside alarm clock that ticked so loudly it would keep me awake (at night, of course, not during sex). Sex with Brian the Whine was a mere drunken fumble in the dark so I can't even remember that. I suppose the night with Adam was special, he was different from the other two but I don't think I'll ever meet my Don Juan. I don't really care either. What you don't know, you don't miss.

Ruby: But doesn't what you don't know make you even the teeny tiniest bit curious?

Rosie: No. I have a shit job with shit pay, a shit flat with shit rent. I have no time for shit sex with a shit man.

Ruby: Rosie!

Rosie: What? I'm serious.

Ruby: I just cannot believe my ears. I'm flabbergasted by this news. OK, I'm taking you out clubbing at the weekend.

Rosie: Clubbing? Do you really think bringing me to a place where I am ten years older than everyone is really going to make me feel better? You think young hot-blooded males are interested in thirty-five-year-old, out-of-shape single mothers these days? I don't think so. I think they're interested in women with breasts resting *above* their belly buttons.

Ruby: Oh, don't exaggerate. You're *thirty-five* not *ninety-five*! I met my Teddy in a nightclub, and he may not be Brad Pitt but what he lacks in looks he makes up for in the bedroom department.

Rosie: Really? You mean to tell me that sex is *good* with Teddy?

Ruby: Well, I'm not with the man for conversation, am I?

Rosie: Of course not. But sex was the last thing on my mind.

Ruby: Well, all that's going to change now, so come on, let's go out and have a good time.

Rosie: Honestly, Ruby, thanks but no thanks. I really have no interest in meeting anyone. And if I did what would I do, bring him home to meet my grieving mother sleeping in the room next door?

Ruby: I suppose you have a point, but sooner or later you're going to have to start enjoying yourself again. You recognise that word, Rosie? *Enjoy*. To have fun.

Rosie: Never heard of it.

Ruby: Fine then, we'll go to the cinema again this weekend, but after that I'm putting you back on the market.

Rosie: OK, but trust me when I say I'm only going for the

full asking price. And if no one's interested in buying I'm not taking on any renters.

Ruby: What about squatters?

Rosie: Ha ha ha. All trespassers will be prosecuted.

Ruby: I can just picture you standing there with a shotgun in your hand, ordering men off your land.

Rosie: Now you're getting the picture.

Chapter 44

Dear Mum,

Sorry I didn't write sooner but I've been so busy ever since I landed that I haven't had the chance to pick up a pen. It's really hot here at the moment so I'm trying to work on my tan before John comes over. I want to meet him at the airport looking like a complete beach babe!

Dad collected me from the airport, which was a weird experience. Weird to see him dressed up, or I should say dressed *down* in shorts and flip-flops. I didn't know he had legs. You would have laughed if you'd seen him. He was wearing this navy-blue Hawaiian-style shirt with yellow flowers splattered all over it, although he insisted it was black (by the way, I believe you now about his debs suit being navy; he is completely colour blind).

He has an electric-blue convertible, which is pretty cool (he thinks it's black) as I've never been in a convertible before. The island is so beautiful. He lives in a really nice complex just outside the busy part of town and there are about ten white-painted villas that share a swimming pool. There's a really cute guy that lives straight across from Dad, who just swims and sunbathes all day. He's so brown and muscly and such a babe so I spend the entire day by the pool drooling.

Dad is freaking out and keeps telling him to put his shirt on. He pretends he's trying to be funny but he looks too angry when he says it.

Toby and Monica are coming over next week, which should be good fun as long as Monica keeps her gob shut. They're both staying in a hotel in town and there's loads of cool clubs around them. But before you go ape shit let me tell you that the day I arrived, Dad brought me up and down the street of bars and clubs and introduced me to all the bouncers and managers. I thought he was doing it so that they'd recognise me and let me in, but when I tried the bars last week not one of them let me in. Not *one*. I thought maybe they hated Dad and were trying to piss him off or something, but yesterday a bouncer from the club down the road came up to Dad's club with his fifteen-year-old son who was staying with him for the summer too, and introduced him to Dad and all the head doormen. Then I heard Dad tell the guys at the door to remember the boy's face and not to let him in.

So I've just been going to Dad's club most nights. Last night I was allowed to stand in the DJ box all night just watching the DJ work. It's crazy over here. Dad's club is really cool. It's packed every night and you can barely move on the dance floor. No one cares, though; it seems the more packed and stuffy a place is, the more popular it is.

The resident DJ is DJ Sugar (He. Is. Gorgeous!) and he was showing me what to do all night and he even let me take over for a few minutes. The entire point was for the crowd not to notice because I wanted to sound as good and professional as Sugar, but I looked up and everyone was staring at me because Dad had a massive camera in his hand and was trying to get people to pose for the camera in front of the DJ box. It was so embarrassing.

I also met Dad's girlfriend. She's twenty-eight, her name's Lisa and she's a dancer in the club. She dances on a podium that's about ten feet off the ground in the centre of the club, and inside a ring of fire in a tiger-print piece of material that she wraps around her body (I wouldn't call it a dress). She's from Bristol and she moved over here to become a dancer when she was my age. She said she worked in a club down the road (which I'm presuming is the strip club) and she met Dad and he offered her a job (I don't want to know *how* or *where* they met!).

She's talking about bringing a snake into her act next because she bought a new snakeskin costume and she thinks it'll look cool. I told her to dance with Dad. (I think you possessed my body for a minute.) Anyway, Dad thinks she's crazy and refuses to get her a snake and they've been arguing about it all week. I didn't have the heart to tell her that everyone is so drunk in the club I don't think they'd notice if Lisa was dancing with an elephant, never mind a snake. She says she wants to do it so she can put it in her CV. Dad asked her if she was planning on applying for a job with the circus. They're funny to listen to.

I've just realised that you and I have never been on a proper holiday together. In fact, apart from visiting Steph and Alex have you ever been *away* away? You and me can go away next year when I've finally finished school and I'm enjoying my freedom. You'll have finished your diploma by then too so the two of us can celebrate! I hope your studying is going well. At least you don't have me there distracting you from your work. If Rupert blares his music too loud just bang on the floor and he'll turn it down. That's what I do.

I'll write again soon. I miss you!

Love,

Katie

Dear Rosie,

I'm writing to you from Cape Town in South Africa, which is so stunning. The rest of the group are taking good care of me so don't you worry about that. And because they all knew

Dennis from the cruise it's nice to be able to talk to them about him and remember the funny times we had. There's another lady here who has also lost her husband and this is her first holiday alone, so we both tend to get teary-eyed together at times. I'm glad she's here because we both understand each other and what we're going through.

I miss Dennis very much. He would have loved this holiday. But in a way he is here with me. I don't care how nuts Kevin thinks I am, I've scattered your father's ashes. Some into the air, some into the water and some into the ground. He's all around me now. I know this is what he would have wanted. He told me not to let him rot away six feet under or remain in an urn on the mantelpiece. This way he's floating through the air all around the world. Seeing more of it than me now. His final adventure.

Some days are very difficult and I just want to phone you up and have a good cry, but being here is a nice distraction. Not only that, it's a nice place to grieve if you have to. Kevin doesn't understand me at all. He thinks I should be wearing black and visiting a graveside every day like a miserable old soul. But I won't do it. Honestly, I don't know where he gets his way of thinking at all. We have three weeks left and already the gang are talking about travelling some more after! They have a lot of contacts in the travel world so we could get some really terrific deals. I may as well keep spending my savings because it's no good wherever I'm going next.

I hope Katie is getting on well in Ibiza and that Brian is taking good care of her. He seems to have turned into a decent, hard-working man so I wouldn't worry, my dear Rosie. Could you please pass on the enclosed letter for Katie? I wasn't sure of her address.

I expect you're delighted to have a bit of peace and quiet while you're studying. I hope Ruby is leaving you well alone, and not dragging you out for too many nights on the town!

Good luck with the studying, love.
I love you and miss you.
Mum

From   Ruby
To   Rosie
Subject Bye!

Hi, Rosie, just a quick email to let you know the great news! Teddy and I got a cheap last-minute holiday to Croatia today. €199 each for a fortnight, including accommodation and flights. How cheap is that! The reason for the price is because the flight is leaving tonight! So I'm throwing all my clothes into my case at the same time as typing this (multi-talented, I know). Do you think it's too late for me to get the perfect beach bod? Maybe I won't eat the food on the plane and we'll see what difference that'll make. Maybe I'll fit into that thong after all, ha ha.

Just wanted to wish you farewell, my friend. I'm sure you'll be delighted I'm gone as you'll finally have a bit of peace to study now. I hope you've fun when Alex and co. come over on their hols, but remember he's a married man now so don't do anything I wouldn't do!!

Take care.
Ruby

Rosie,

Greetings from Hawaii!

As you can see, there was a change of plan! My crazy wife decided that Hawaii would be a far nicer resort than Ireland, why on earth I have no idea!!

The weather is fantastic, the hotel a dream. (I've taken the liberty of stealing a few things for you from my room, which should be enclosed in the package. A shower cap and bath gel all the way from Hawaii! I hope the cap fits.) Restaurants are great too.

You're probably delighted we're not coming over as now you finally get a bit of peace and quiet to study. I hope Kevin leaves you alone and stops annoying you about your mum. I think she's right.

Lots of love,

Alex, Josh, Theo (and, dare I say, Bethany)

Rosie,

Hello from Cyprus.

Weather nice. Hotel nice. Food nice. Beach nice.

Hope you're enjoying your summer of silence and study. (If Steph and the rest of the troop don't invade your home. By the way, we need to talk about Mum scattering Dad's ashes.)

Kevin

Hello from Euro Disney!

Hi, sis, having a brill time. Feel like I'm ten years old! Met Mickey Mouse yesterday and we all had to get a photo with him (as you can see I look slightly star struck. Pierre was a little worried about me). The kids are in heaven. There's so many things for them to look at I think they're going to make themselves dizzy! There's so much to do here that we decided to stay an extra few days so unfortunately we won't be able to go to Dublin at the weekend.

Hope the studying is going well and that you're enjoying your peace and quiet. Don't let Rupert from next door drag you to the National Concert Hall any more. Just tell him you need to study.

Lots of love,

Steph, Pierre, Jean-Louis and Sophia

Hi, Rosie,

I called around earlier but you weren't here so I thought I'd leave you this note. I'm going away for a few weeks with the choir I sing in. We're going to sing for the people of Kazakhstan. We're touring the country and I'm really looking forward to it.

I'm closing the shop, so you'll be pleased to know that there won't be any noise coming from either the shop or the flat while I'm gone. You should be able to study now that we're all away. I've left my key with you in case there are any emergencies.

Good luck with the studying, enjoy your peace and quiet, and I'll see you when I get back. Maybe by the time I'm back you'll have asked that internet guy from downstairs out on a date. I think he likes you – he keeps asking after you.

Rupert

Rosie Dunne,

You have an outstanding bill of €6.20 owed from the last time you were here to use the internet. Please pay it immediately or we will take legal action.

Ross (from the internet café downstairs)

You have entered the Relieved Divorced Dubliners' internet chat room. There are currently no people chatting.
Buttercup has entered the room.
Buttercup: Where the hell *is* everyone?

Chapter 45

You have received an instant message from: TOBY.

Toby: I bet you had a salad sandwich for lunch again.

Katie: How do you no?

Toby: It's KNOW not NO. I can see the lettuce hanging out of your braces again. I'm surprised you haven't taken to eating mashed foods by now, or at least something you could suck through a straw. Solids are a bit of a no-no.

Katie: This time next week you won't be able to slag me any more. For the end of an era has come. The braces are coming off. After three and a half years behind bars, my teeth, my now *straight* teeth, may I add, will be free.

Toby: Well, it's about time. I can't wait to see how they come off. I *need* to see how they come off.

Katie: You don't actually *need* to no everything *before* you study it at college, Toby. The general idea is to learn it there.

Toby: Well, I haven't been accepted yet, have I? I could screw up in my exams and not get enough points for the course.

Katie: You'll get in, Toby.

Toby: We'll see. Have you figured out what course you're

going to do yet? You better decide soon because we need to fill out our CAO forms soon.

Katie: The stress of it all. How the hell are we expected at the age of sixteen (and seventeen, in your case) to decide what we want to do for the rest of our lives? Right now all I want to do is get *out* of school, not start planning to get into another one. You're lucky you've always known what you want to do.

Toby: Only thanks to you and your manky teeth. Anyway, you've known what you wanted to do for longer than I have. Be a DJ.

Katie: I can't study that in college, though, can I?

Toby: Who says you have to go to college?

Katie: Everyone. The career guidance teacher. My mum. My dad. All the teachers. God, Rupert, even Sanjay from downstairs said I should go and that he will take care of Mum for me.

Toby: Well, I wouldn't listen to Sanjay because he's got (scary) ulterior motives. I wouldn't listen to the career guidance teacher either, because his job is to take you for a half an hour every week and discuss college courses to his heart's content. Do you think he really cares what you do? Who cares what Rupert thinks, your dad is only agreeing with your mum, and your mum is only saying you should go because she thinks you want to. And don't mind God – as your mum always says, he's only having a laugh.

Katie: But Mum has worked so hard to finally get round to studying what she wants and it's been such a struggle for her. She wanted this opportunity so much at my age and I kind of got in the way and now it's my turn and I've nothing in the way. I think Mum thinks I should be jumping for joy at the idea but it feels more like a prison sentence. Dad said that I could go over to him for the summer again and work in the club behind the bar for a few nights a week. Sugar will train me in on the other nights. He says if I really want to do it I might as well start taking it seriously.

Toby: He's right.

Katie: Well, you don't sound like you're going to miss me too much!

Toby: Of course I won't. If you don't go, then I'm the one who has to listen to you moan for the rest of my life. Look, if your mum knew you really wanted to DJ, seriously, then she'd tell you to go for it.

Katie: I never thought of it like that. Who new we would ever get to our final year, Toby? After all those days of detention, I will finally never have to wear another tie again. For you, dear Toby, your tie-wearing days are just beginning.

Toby: No more double computer class on a Monday morning and I can assure you that if I get into college I will not be wearing ties.

Katie: Brown cords and long hair then, and you can listen to Bob Dylan all day while you're flaked out on the grass, man. I'm actually beginning to think that double computer class on a Monday morning could actually be easy compared to moving away from Mum and Grandma. Oh my God, what about John?

Toby: John has legs. He'll be able to walk on to a plane, sit down, fly to Ibiza or wherever you may be, get off the plane and see you. I noticed you didn't mention me there. Will life be that easy without me?

Katie: Yes, of course it will. No but honestly, aren't there any dentistry colleges in Ibiza?

Toby: Not where you're going, unless you include extracting people's teeth using your fist.

Katie: Well then, I guess it's Ibiza for just me and Dad then.

To Katie and Rosie

Good luck to the both of you in your exams. I'm praying for my girls.

Love Mum/Grandma

To Rosie and Katie

Good luck!

Love, Steph, Pierre, JeAN-LOuiS and Sophia

To Rosie and Katie

My best friend and goddaughter, best of luck in your exams. You will both excel as you always do. Let me no how the first one goes.

Love,

Alex

To Rosie

After these exams can you start going out again? You're becoming an awful bore, and an intelligent bore at that, which is even worse. The quality of conversation with Teddy and Gary is declining week by week, and the other day I was forced to listen to hours and hours of 'discussion' about whether the Aston Martin DB7 is as good or as fast as a Ferrari 575. Oh yes, my family likes to get down to the nitty-gritty and discuss the important things in life.

I know I encouraged you to go for this diploma but if you fail these exams this year and have to repeat I'm giving you the official warning that I have the firm intention of making a new friend. One that won't be so ambitious.

So absolutely no pressure there. Good luck!

Ruby

To Mum
　Here we go. In a fortnight we'll both be free.
　Best of luck.
　Katie

To Katie
Good luck, honey. Thanks for being my study partner. No matter how you do, I'm proud of you.
　Love,
　Mum

Exam results: Rosie Dunne.
Student number: 4553901-L
Course: Diploma in Hotel Business Management
Recognised by Irish Hotel & Catering Institute (MIMCI)
& Catering Managers Association of Ireland (MCMA)

Subject	Grade
Accounting	B
Computer Applications and Data Summary	B
Economics	B
Hospitality Ethical and Legal Studies	B
Financial Control and Marketing	B
Human Resource Management	A
Enterprise Development	A
Languages (Irish)	A
Tourism and Hospitality Industry Studies	A

Graduates qualify for membership of a period of professional internship in the hospitality industry.

YES! YES! YES! YES! YEEEEEESSSSSS! ALEX I DID IT! I FINALLY DID IT!!

Rosie I'm so happy 4 u! Congratulations!

From   Rosie
To   Ruby
Subject   Let's celebrate!

Now we can definitely go out! By the way, Katie is coming out with us too so get your dancing shoes on (of course in your case I don't mean that literally. No one wants to see those scary-looking salsa shoes in a nightclub). She did well in her exams and got accepted to a few college business courses but she's going to stick to her original idea of trying out DJ-ing. Toby got enough points for Dentistry in Trinity College, which is wonderful news so over all everyone is happy, happy, happy!

You know when I was eighteen I missed out on going to Boston and I thought my world had ended. While all my friends were partying and studying I was cleaning dirty nappies. I thought my dream was lost. Never in a million years did I think that I would be able to share this special moment with my teenage daughter.

Everything does happen for a reason. I'll just be so sad to see my baby go away. The day I've been preparing for has finally arrived, Katie is spreading her wings and moving on and I must do the same. I think I might be close to gathering enough money to buy that train ticket out of here.

Rosie Dunne is leaving the station and moving on. *Finally.*

Dear Rosie,

On behalf of all of us here at St Patrick's Primary School I congratulate you on your recent exam results. You have proved yourself to be a true achiever and should feel proud.

Keeping my promise, I am delighted to inform you that your services are no longer required. Your contract with us will not be up for renewal in August.

We are sorry to see you go but you have to. My retirement was one year later than planned but it was worth hanging around to see you succeed. Rosie Dunne, you have been the longest project of my life, my eldest and longest-serving student, and although we may have had a rocky start and an even rockier middle, I am so glad to see you succeed at the end.

Your hard work and dedication is an inspiration to us all and I wish you the very best for the future. I do hope you keep in touch and I would love to see you attend my retirement party, for which you will receive an invitation shortly. I ask that you forward on an invitation to Alex Stewart too.

After years of separating the two of you it would be nice to see you both in the same room again after so many years. I do hope that he can make it.

Congratulations again.

Keep in touch.

Julie (Big Nose Smelly Breath) Casey

Katie,

My baby girl is moving away! I'm so proud of you, love. You are so brave to be doing this. Make sure your dad doesn't forget to feed and clothe you.

I'll miss you so much. I loved having you here with me but I hope I'm welcome to visit you lots!

If you need me, just call and I'll come running.

Lots of love,

Mum

Dear Brian,

This is a huge responsibility. Please take care of Katie and don't let her get up to anything stupid over there. You know what eighteen-year-old males are like – you yourself were one. Keep her away from them as best you can. She's over there to learn, not party and make babies.

Let me know *everything* that's going on with her. Even the stuff she's afraid to tell me. A mother needs to know. Please listen to her and be there for her all the time. If you even sense that something is wrong and she won't confide in you, just let me know and I'll subtly find out.

And last but not least, thank you so much for giving my baby, *our* baby, her dream.

Best wishes,

Rosie

Dear Rosie Dunne,

Congratulations on completing your Diploma in Hotel Business Management.

We are pleased to inform you that your professional internship in the hospitality industry will be undertaken at the beginning of August. Each graduate's employment has been randomly selected and chosen by a computer without discrimination or prejudice. Once a placement has been made the graduate cannot change.

The contract of twelve months is for the position of assistant manager and is to be held at the Grand Tower Hotel in Dublin's city centre. You are to begin on Monday, 1 August at 9 a.m. For more information regarding your placement please contact Cronin Ui Cheallaigh, manager and owner of the Grand Tower Hotel. The phone number, details and map of directions to the hotel are provided overleaf.

We wish you luck in your new venture and hope it brings you success in the future.

Yours sincerely,

Keith Richards

Hotel Business Management Course Director, St Patrick's Primary School Night Courses

Alex: Very impressive, Rosie. The Grand Tower Hotel? Sounds amazing.

Rosie: Oooh, I know! That's what I thought! I'm not familiar with the hotel, though, are you?

Alex: Oh, you're asking the wrong person, Rosie. Every time I'm back in Dublin some new building, office block or apartment block has popped up where there was nothing. I don't no where anything is any more. You should go down and take a look yourself.

Rosie: Yeah, maybe. After we hung up the other night, I was thinking, and do you know you're losing your accent?

Alex: Rosie, I have been here twenty years. I've spent more years here than in Ireland. My kids are American; I have to keep up with the lingo (Irish expression added entirely for you)! Of course I'm going to lose an accent.

Rosie: Well, you're not so much losing an accent as gaining an accent. But twenty years . . . how did that happen?

Alex: I no, time flies when you're having fun.

Rosie: If you call the last twenty years fun, then I don't want to know how fast time goes by when you're really enjoying yourself.

Alex: It hasn't been so bad for you, has it, Rosie?

Rosie: Define bad.

Alex: Oh, come on . . .

Rosie: No it hasn't, but I wouldn't complain if it became a whole lot better.

Alex: Well, none of us would . . . the job must be exciting for you.

Rosie: It really, really is. I feel like a kid on Christmas Eve! I haven't felt like that for a long, long time. I know the job is temporary and that I'm only in training but I've waited a long time for this opportunity.

Alex: You've waited too long for it. I of all people no how

much you've wanted this. I used to hate it when you
made me play Hotel.

Rosie: Ha ha, I remember that. I was always the person in
charge and you had to be the customer!

Alex: I hated being the customer because you would never
leave me alone. You kept fluffing my pillows and lifting
my feet up on stools 'for the customer's comfort'.

Rosie: My God, I'd forgotten all about that! I used to try
to be like the guy on *Fantasy Island* who looked after
his guests so much he would use magic to give them
their dreams.

Alex: I don't call forcing me to go to bed at two in the
day, tucking me in so tight that I could hardly breathe,
a comfort/dream-providing service! I don't no what
type of manager you were trying to be but if you
behave like that with your real customers then a few of
them will have restraining orders taken out against
you.

Rosie: Well, at least it was better than playing Hospital.
All that game consisted of was you tripping me up on
concrete and then tending to me. Mum and Dad used to
wonder where all my cuts and bruises were coming
from.

Alex: Yeah, that was fun, wasn't it?

Rosie: Well, you have a distorted idea of what fun is. Like
the last twenty years, for example.

Alex: Obviously not *all* fun for either of us.

Rosie: No . . .

Alex: Hotels and hospitals. Sounds like some sort of dodgy
porn movie.

Rosie: You wish!

Alex: I do wish. I have a three-year-old son who likes to
sleep in between me and Beth.

Rosie: Well, I could join the nunnery and I don't think it
would bother me in the slightest.

Alex: Oh, I disagree!

Rosie: No really, trust me, Alex. After the men I've been with, celibacy would be like a *gift*.

Alex: It wasn't the celibacy I was referring to; it was the vow of silence that would kill you.

Rosie: Funny. Well, believe me, Alex, there are certain kinds of silences that make you walk on air. And on that note, I'll leave you.

Rosie has logged off.

Alex: Those silences I no.

Chapter 46

Hi, Mum,

Just a quick note to wish you luck (not that you need it) on your first day of work tomorrow. I'm sure you'll knock 'em all dead!

Best of luck,

Love,

Katie

You have an instant message from: RUBY.

Ruby: Well, Ms Assistant Manager, tell me all about it. How's work going?

Rosie: Very, very sl o o o o o wly.

Ruby: Should I ask why?

Rosie: Are you ready for a rant? Because if you're not I'm giving you the opportunity now to get out of this conversation while you can.

Ruby: Believe it or not I came into this conversation prepared. Fire ahead.

Rosie: OK, so I arrived on the road the hotel was situated on nice and early and proceeded to walk up and down the street for three-quarters of an hour trying to find the very beautiful and *Grand* Tower Hotel. I asked shop owners and stall owners but none of them had any idea where this hotel was.

After ringing the course director almost in tears and in a complete panic over the fact that I was late for my first day of work, I also succeeded in accusing him of giving me the wrong address. He kept on repeating the same address over and over again, which I told him couldn't be possible because the building in question was completely derelict.

Eventually he said he'd ring the hotel owner and double-check the directions with him so I sat down on the filthy front steps of the derelict building (dirtying the bum of my new suit) and tried not to cry about how late I was and what a bad impression this was making. Suddenly the door of the building behind me opened with a very loud farting noise at the hinges and this *thing* looked out at me. The thing spoke in a very strong Dublin accent, introduced himself as Cronin Ui Cheallaigh, the owner of the building, and insisted I call him Beanie.

At first I was confused by his nickname but as the day wore on it all became very clear. The hinges of the front door were not what made a farting sound; it was indeed the gaseous behind of Beanie.

He brought me inside to the ancient, damp building and showed me around the few rooms on the ground level. He then asked me if I had any questions and I, of course, wanted to know why I was in this particular building and when was I going to see the hotel. To which he replied proudly, 'Dis is de bleedin' hotel. Nice, wha'?'

He then asked me if I had any ideas on how to improve the hotel after my first impression and I suggested displaying the actual name of the hotel on the actual building so as to make it easier for the guests (although not doing so was also a good marketing ploy).

I also suggested spreading the word of its existence among the surrounding businesses so they could help advertise the hotel (or at least be able to help give directions to completely lost tourists).

He studied my face very hard to see if I was being smart. Which, by the way, I absolutely wasn't. I'm currently waiting on a sign for the front of the hotel to arrive.

He then gave me a name tag which he insisted I wear. His reason for me having to wear this was so that if customers needed to complain, they would know who to blame. A very positive-thinking man, as you can see. The problem with the name tag (other than having to wear it) was that he appeared to have misheard the spelling of my name over the phone.

I have been walking around the entire week as 'Rosie Bumme'. Something that Beanie seems to find incredibly humorous. Although after he had gotten over his laughing fit he was slightly disappointed. That alone is an example of his level of maturity and the seriousness with which he takes his job and general running of the so-called hotel.

How it has remained open up until now is beyond me. It is one of those beautiful houses that in its time would have been extremely grand but that has been left to rot away. It's probably decaying underneath the floorboards with whatever else is causing the smell.

It was once red-bricked but is now dirty brown. It has four levels and on the underground level, I have now learned, is a lap-dancing club also owned by Beanie. As you enter the ground level of the hotel, you are greeted by a tiny little desk made of dark mahogany wood (as is all the wood in the building). Behind it is a messy collection of former guests' hats, umbrellas and coats that are currently collecting dust.

The walls are wood-panelled from the floor to halfway up the wall, which is a nice feature, and the walls, which were probably once a rich olive-green colour are now more a mouldy green. Small lantern-like lights adorn the walls and throw out absolutely no light at all. The place is like a dungeon. The carpets look like they were laid in the seventies. They're dirty and smelly and have cigarette burns, black patches of stuck-on chewing gum and other stains the origins of which I don't wish to know.

A long corridor leads down to a large bar area, which contains the same dirty smelly carpet, dark wood, paisley-covered stools and chairs and when the sun shines through the tiny, paint-flaking window all you can see is the air thick with wisps of smoke, probably still there from the old man who used to sit with his pipe two hundred years ago.

The dining area has twenty tables and a limited menu. It has the same carpet, but with the added feature of food stains. There are brown velvet curtains, and net blinds; the tables are covered in what were once white but are now yellow lace tablecloths with rusty, food-stained cutlery. The glasses are misty, the walls are white, which makes it the only light room, but no matter how much the heat is turned up it feels cold.

But the *smell*! It's like somebody died and was left to decay. It has since been absorbed into the furniture, the walls and into my clothes. There are sixty rooms. Twenty on each floor. Beanie proudly announced that half of them are ensuite. You could imagine how happy I was to hear that – *some* bedrooms have bathrooms!

Two wonderful women, Betty and Joyce, each about one hundred years old, clean the rooms three times a week, which frankly I find rather disgusting. And given how slowly they move, I'd be surprised if they cleaned each room even that often.

I was also beginning to wonder what kind of customers a hotel like this would attract but it all became clear to me as I worked the late shift one night. As the lap-dancing club finished downstairs, the party continued upstairs. This gave me all the more reason to employ more chambermaids.

The only way someone would find a chocolate on their pillow is if the previous guest had spit it out. The only reason someone would wear the shower cap would be to protect their head from the yellow water that runs through the pipes (though probably safe, I'm sticking to my bottled water).

Last week a radio station rang up to ask if the hotel could be part of a competition they're running – they must have got desperate, or been fooled by the hotel's much swankier-sounding name. I couldn't think of a good enough excuse to say no. People had to write in and explain why they deserved a weekend of pampering in Dublin. They would be treated to a night at the theatre, a meal, a day out shopping and two nights' bed-and-breakfast at a central hotel, all expenses paid. It was great for the hotel as we were advertised all week on the radio and we got a good few guests as a result. Not that any of them knew what they'd let themselves in for.

The people who won had a story so touching that I was nearly crying listening to it on the radio. So I had the honeymoon suite (completely the same as all the other rooms but I told Beanie to put a sign on the door to make the winners feel special. He ended up stencilling it on himself and spent an hour with a black marker in his hand with his tongue hanging out in concentration) filled with beautiful flowers and left a complimentary bottle of champagne for them. I really tried my best with the room, squeezing enough money out of the budget for new bedlinen, etc., but there was only so much the meagre profits could get me.

Anyway, when they found out they'd won, they were so excited they kept ringing the hotel every day before they got here, asking questions and making sure everything was still OK. They walked in the door, took one look at the place and left within fifteen minutes.

Ruby, those people had lost their *home*, the husband had lost his *job*, broken *both* his legs, lost their *car* and had to leave their village. They had been given an all-expenses-paid weekend and could stay in the hotel absolutely *free* and *still* they didn't want to stay. That's how *bad* this hotel is.

Rosie: Ruby?

Rosie: Ruby, are you there?

Rosie: Hello? Ruby, did you get all that?

Ruby: Zzzzzzzzzzzzzzzzzzzzz

Rosie: Ruby!!

Ruby: Oh, what?! Did I miss something? Sorry, I must have nodded off about an *hour* ago when you *started* telling me about your job.

Rosie: I'm sorry, Ruby, but I warned you.

Ruby: Don't worry, I managed to wander off and make myself a cup of coffee and came back when you were talking about olive-green walls and decomposing bodies.

Rosie: Sorry, it's been one of those months.

Ruby: Not all jobs turn out to be what you think they're going to be. Anyway, would you rather be a secretary at Randy Andy Paperclip Co. or assistant manager of the Grand Tower Hotel?

Rosie: Oooh, definitely assistant manager of the Grand Tower Hotel.

Ruby: Well, there you go, Rosie Bumme. Life could be worse then, couldn't it?

Rosie: I guess so. But I do have one other slight problem.

Ruby: Can you tell me what it is in less than one thousand words?

Rosie: I'll try! Alex is coming over for Julie Casey's retirement party in a few weeks and he's bringing Bethany, and they've booked themselves into the hotel for the weekend. You see, I kind of told him that it was really nice . . . and they specifically requested a room with a view. At this stage I'm hard pushed to find a room with a *window* (OK, not *really*) but under the circumstances, we at the Grand Tower Hotel consider a special request to be a room with a *bathroom*. I mean, view-wise, which do you think they'd prefer, a view of a butcher's or a view of a scrapyard?

Ruby: Oh dear . . .

You have an instant message from: ALEX.

Alex: Hi, Rosie, you're up late.

Rosie: So are you.

Alex: I'm five hours behind, remember.

Rosie: Katie's debs ball is on tonight. She's there right now, in fact.

Alex: Oh, I see. Can't you sleep?

Rosie: Are you mad? Of course I can't sleep. I helped shop for the dress, helped her get ready with her make-up and hair, took photographs of her being so excited on her special night. The night when she will see friends she probably won't see again for years, or never again, despite promises of keeping in touch. It was like turning the clock back to me and Mum twenty years ago.

I know she's not me, she's her own person with her own mind, but I couldn't help but see myself walking out that door. Arm in arm with a man in a tuxedo, excited about the night, excited about the future. Excited, excited, excited. I was so bloody young. Of course, I didn't think I was at the time. I had a million plans. I knew what I was going to do. I had the next few years of my life all figured out.

But what I didn't know was that within a few hours all those plans would change. Ms Know-it-all didn't quite know so much then.

I just hope Katie comes home tonight when she should.

Alex: She's wise, Rosie, and if you've raised her the way I think you have, then you have nothing to worry about.

Rosie: I can't fool myself. She's been with her boyfriend for over three years now so I don't exactly think they've been holding hands all this time. But for tonight at least, on the night that changed my life, I wish her home early.

Alex: Well then, I'll just have to distract you until she comes home, won't I?

Rosie: If you wouldn't mind.

Alex: So how is our hotel room set for when we're over? I certainly hope the manager can arrange the very best for us!

Rosie: I'm actually only the *assistant* manager, remember, and the hotel isn't exactly . . .

Alex: Isn't exactly what?

Rosie: As snazzy as the ones you're used to when you travel.

Alex: This one will be extra special because my best friend is running it.

Rosie: I wouldn't want to take much credit for the general running of the hotel . . .

Alex: Oh, don't be silly. You never give yourself enough credit for what you do.

Rosie: No, *really*, Alex. I wouldn't want to accept any responsibility for this hotel *at all*. You know, I'm only there a few months. I haven't had a chance to put my stamp on it. I only follow orders . . .

Alex: Nonsense. I can't wait to see it. How funny would it be if someone was poisoned in the restaurant and I had to be the in-house doctor that saved the day? Remember that was our plan when we were kids?

Rosie: I remember alright, and it may not be too far off a possibility. Wouldn't you and Bethany like to eat *out* that night? There are so many beautiful restaurants you haven't been to in Dublin.

Alex: We might. I tried looking the hotel up on the internet but nothing came up.

Rosie: Eh, yeah, the site is being updated right now. I'll let you know when you can see it.

Alex: Great. It'll be weird seeing Miss Big Nose Smelly Breath Casey again. It's about time she retired. The children of the world need a break from her.

Rosie: Her name is Julie, remember that, and do *not* call her by the other name. And she has been very good to me over the past few years so please be good to her.

Alex: I will, I will. Don't worry, I have been out of the house before; I do no how to deal with people.

Rosie: Of course you have, Mr Socialite Surgeon extraordinaire.

Alex: Whatever image you have in your head of me right now, please get rid of it.

Rosie: What? The naked one? You can't tell me to get rid of that.

Alex: Well, whatever image that is, increase the size by ten.

Rosie: Jesus, ten inches, Alex?

Alex: Oh, shut up! So how's your mum these days? Any word back from the hospital about those tests?

Rosie: No, not yet. She's away with Stephanie right now, taking a break from it all, and when she comes back the results should be ready. They really don't seem to know what's wrong with her. I'm really worried. I looked at her the other day and it was as though I hadn't seen her properly for years. Without even noticing it, my mum has gotten old.

401

Alex: She's only sixty-five. She's still young.

Rosie: I know that, but I had an image of her in my mind and that image was of her years ago. Somehow, since I was young, I've continued to see her like that. But the other day when I looked at her in the hospital bed, she looked old. It was a shock. Anyway, I just hope they find out what it is and fix it. She's really not feeling well at all.

Alex: As soon as you find out, let me know.

Rosie: I will. It's tough having to travel to Galway on my days off. As much as I love Mum, it's a bit of a trek for me. Between working incredibly unsociable hours, travelling to Mum, helping her, I haven't had any real days off for the past few weeks and I am tireder than tired.

Alex: Where is Kevin in all this? Can't he help out, for once in his life?

Rosie: Good question. Well, in all fairness to Kev, he's just bought a house and is in the process of moving in with his girlfriend. If he had more time I'm *almost* sure he would help out.

Alex: Kevin has decided to commit? That's a shock. You should have a talk to him about all this, try to get him to help out a bit more. You can't be expected to do everything.

Rosie: Well, I'm not exactly doing *everything*. Steph is looking after Mum for the week and she's got two kids so it's not exactly easy for her either. (*Looking after* Mum doesn't sound right, does it?) And I don't mind because I want to be there for Mum. She's all alone and I know how that feels.

Alex: You asking for help from Kevin doesn't mean you don't love and want to help Alice. Kev should be told. And he shouldn't *have* to be told.

Rosie: Well, I'll wait until he's settled into his new house, and when that's done, and if he *still* hasn't pulled the finger out, then I'm not holding back. He didn't visit Dad half as much as he should have and I know he's paying for that now. I've never entirely understood Kevin. He likes to keep himself to himself. He came and went from the house and never filled anyone in on what he was doing. Then when Dad died he suddenly thought he could take control of all the plans. Now with Mum being sick he's backed off again. Steph and I have tried to talk to him about it on numerous occasions but there's just no getting through to him. He's selfish, simple as that. Hold on, a coach pulled up outside. Wait while I run to the window and check.

Alex: Is Katie in it?

Rosie: No.

Alex: Oh. She'll be—

Rosie: Oh, *thank God*, there she is. I'd better switch off the computer and dive into bed. I don't want her thinking I was waiting up. Oh, thank you, God, for bringing my baby home. Night, Alex.

Alex: Night, Rosie.

Chapter 47

Mother dearest,

Thanks for last week. It was so good to be home again with you. I missed our late night chats! I bring good news with this letter! Tony Spencer, an English bloke who owns Club Insomnia down the road, was here in Dad's club last night when I was doing my set, and he was so impressed he asked if I'd like to work for him! How cool is that?! He also organises some summer dance festivals so I'll be off around Europe during the summer, playing at those. I'm really excited!

Club Insomnia is a really popular place, and it goes on till about six or seven in the morning. I'll only be on the decks from about 10 p.m. till midnight, just to get started. Tony pays really well, though, and as soon as I get my first decent cheque, I'll send some home to you. I've met a really cool crowd of people over here, who are also just out of school a short while and are doing bar work. Me and three other girls, Jennifer, Lucy and Sara, are talking about renting an apartment together.

I don't no when John is coming over. Ever since he started college in September he's been out all night every night with a bunch of people I've never heard of. He keeps bumping against his phone and accidentally ringing me when he's out, and all I can ever hear are loads of drunken people screaming in the background. It's just been really weird with the two of us. Only more so every time we meet up after weeks apart. It's not the same at all and I don't like it. I thought I'd be with him for ever but the rate we're going I can barely imagine being with him until the end of the summer.

Meanwhile, I haven't heard from Toby in a long, long time. It's entirely my fault because he rang me loads of times at the beginning when I moved over here and I just didn't get round to calling him back. Time just ran away. I keep on saying I'll call him tomorrow but it's been months and now I'm embarrassed. The last time I spoke to him he was having a great time at college, making friends with lots of teeth, no doubt. I'll call him tomorrow, promise I will.

I hope everything at work is OK. I can't believe you got your contract extended. I thought you hated the place. Let me no what's going on there, I'm confused.

Alex wrote to me a while back and told me what happened when he and Bethany stayed in the hotel when they were over for Miss Big Nose Smelly Breath Casey's retirement party. How funny! Didn't you no it was going to be the lap-dancing club's Christmas party? I don't think Alex seemed too disturbed by the sight of red-and-white-fluffy-bikini-clad Mary Clauses dancing around the bar. I can't believe Bethany refused to stay the night. That woman really doesn't have a sense of humour. I don't no what Alex sees in her. I've only met her a few times but she's so uptight and he's so laidback I really don't see them lasting together for much longer. I can't believe Alex had to tend to one of the guests in the restaurant – was the man poisoned? What kind of food is your restaurant serving?! Just as well there was a doctor in the house.

Anyway, I better go and figure out what tracks I'm doing tonight. Dad's giving me a two-hour set just to prepare me for Insomnia. Lisa keeps trying to persuade me to play eighties music so she can do her flash-dance routine. If it's not snakes she wants it's something worse, like shoulder pads and perms.

When Grandma gets better, you and she should come over to me for a few weeks. There are loads of nice relaxing areas to go to with lovely beaches and scenery; it's not all pubs and clubs. Think about it. Maybe a break would be good for Grandma.

I miss you so much but whenever I'm lonely I just look at the photos of you and Alex in my locket. You're both close to my heart. Always.

Love,
Katie

You have received an instant message from: RUBY.

Ruby: I've been dumped.

Rosie: *What?* By Teddy?

Ruby: No! Don't be silly, that man doesn't know how to put the bins out, never mind dump me. No, the culprit is in fact my adoring son. He has informed me that my salsa services are no longer required and he's traded me in for a younger model.

Rosie: Oh no, Ruby, I'm so sorry. Who's the other woman?

Ruby: Actually, I pretend to be mad but I'm not really. Well, that's a lie. At first I was *really* angry and ate an entire chocolate cake myself – Gary's favourite cake that I had bought for him, coincidentally. Halfway through it I was just angry and then while I was spooning the last mouthful into my mouth I began to think rationally (that's what it does to me, you see). So I devised a plan whereby I was going to invite this 'other woman' into my home for dinner so that I could poison her.

I needed to find out who she was, why on earth Gary left me for her. As it turns out she's only in her late twenties, is from Spain, teaches Spanish at the school (that's where Gary met her, where he works as a custodial engineer), she's thin, pretty and is a very beautiful person.

Rosie: She's everything you would usually hate, right?

Ruby: *Usually*, yes. But this time it's different because she and my Gary have found love.

Rosie: Ooooh!

Ruby: I know! Isn't it great? So I had no problem stepping aside and hanging up my dancing shoes. To tell the truth, I was thinking of parting with Gary soon anyway. I'm not far off fifty now, I need to dance with someone more my own age, who won't have the energy to be flinging me across the other side of the room. I'm not up to it any more. I'm just happy Gary has finally found someone. Maybe Maria will make him move out of my house and in with her.

Rosie: Would you be upset by that?

Ruby: As upset as I would be if I found a million euro under my bed. The boy needs to realise he is a grown man now and move out. I can't cook him his dinners and clean his clothes for ever. Anyway, enough about me, how's your mum?

Rosie: Not great. It just seems that bit by bit everything is failing on her. Her arthritis has gotten so bad now that she's almost crippled. It wasn't so much of a problem when she and Dad were travelling because then they had the hot weather. Now, though, I don't think cold Connemara is really the best place for her what with the winters there. But she won't move from there. I'm worried for her. She's in and out of hospital with infections and problems with parts of her body that I didn't even know existed. It's as if, when Dad died, her body just gave up.

Ruby: She's a toughie, though, Rosie. She'll pull through.

Rosie: Let's hope.

Ruby: How are things at Fawlty Towers?

Rosie: Ha! Well, I won't have to put up with the place for

much longer because I'm leaving at the end of the month.

Ruby: You say that every month and you never do. You might as well just wait until your contract is up next year and then leave. Anyway, unless you actually *look* for another job you're not going anywhere.

Rosie: Between working all hours and travelling back and forth to Mum, I just don't have *time*. I mean, when's the last time I even saw you?

Ruby: Yesterday.

Rosie: Well, apart from when you drove by me at the bus stop, beeping and waving. Thanks for speeding up, driving through the puddle on the side of the road and saturating me, by the way.

Ruby: We were going in different directions and you looked like you could do with a shower.

Rosie: Whatever. Anyway, it's been at least a month since I've been out properly. It's ridiculous. I have no life. I really want to go visit Katie, and Alex has invited me over to him lots of times but I can't do any of those things because of Mum – not that I'm blaming her, of course.

Ruby: When your mother gets better everything will be a lot easier.

Rosie: She's not *going* to get better, Ruby. She doesn't want to get better. She's just waiting now. She's practically wheelchair-bound at this stage and she's only sixty-six.

Ruby: Get lazy Kevin to help.

Rosie: What would Kevin do? He wouldn't know where to start and I know Mum feels more comfortable with me helping her. Anyway, we'll just have to keep on going.

To Josh
  Happy 10th birthday.
  Lots of love,
  Rosie

To Rosie

Thanks so much for my present and card. It's really cool. Wherever Katie is tell her I said hi. She sends me postcards all the time from different countries and she sounds real happy. She's got the coolest job! I never hear about her old friend Toby any more. I guess they lost touch or something. Anyway, thanks again for the present. I'll be able to buy a new computer game with it.

See you soon,

Form Josh

To Mum

Hello! I'm in Amsterdam. Met a gorgeous guy who picks strawberries for a living. Doesn't speak English but we get along just fine.

Everything here is great. Got loads of gigs and the cafés are nice too!

Love,

Katie

To Rosie

Happy thirty-eighth!

How scary is it that we're so close to forty?! Have a drink for me.

Love,

Alex

Rosie, if you think thirty-eight is bad, just imagine how I must feel, pushing fifty. Aaaah! We'll have a *huge* party. Just you and me invited.

Happy birthday again.

Ruby

Hi, Mum,

I'm in Andorra. Met this gorgeous guy who's my ski

instructor, who's trying to teach me how not to break my neck. He doesn't speak a word of English but we get along just fine. Everything is great here. You and I should go skiing some time. You'd love it! The winter festival is going really well, got a few small gigs to do. I'll be home for Christmas so we can catch up on all the gossip! Can't wait to see you!

Love,

Katie

Hi, Mum,

Do you want to stay with me for Christmas? Katie is coming home and it can be the three of us. I think it would be really nice, you can have Katie's room and I'll set up a sofa bed for her. I'm so excited about the idea. Beanie has given me Christmas Day off so please say yes!

Rosie

Rosie,

I'd love to come over, honey. Thanks for the invite. Can't wait to see little Katie. Not so little any more, I suppose!

Love,

Mum

From   Katie
To   Mum
Subject   Coming home

Thanks so much for Christmas dinner. It was absolutely yummy, as always. It was good for us three to be together again. Just the girls!

Grandma has changed a lot since the last time I saw her and you look tired. I was thinking of coming home for a few weeks and helping out. Maybe I could get a job around Dublin for a short while? I want to help out. (Plus there's the added bonus of meeting up with that guy I met while I was there!)

Let me no.

From   Rosie
To   Katie
Subject Re: Coming home

Do *not* come home! That is an order! Everything is just fine here. You need to live your life too so you can continue on with your travels, work hard and enjoy yourself! Don't worry about your grandma and me. We're absolutely fine!

I'm really enjoying the job and I don't mind the long hours. It's also nice to be able to go away every week to breathe the fresh air of Connemara. I do have one favour to ask, however. Ruby and I would love to go over to you for a week sometime in February if you could fit us into your schedule. Ruby said she wants to go to a foam party and win a wet T-shirt competition before she's fifty!

Let me know when a good week is for you.

From   Rosie
To   Steph
Subject Mum

I've a favour to ask. Do you think you might be able to take Mum for another week in February? I'm sorry, I know you're really busy too, but Beanie has finally given me a week off and I really wanted to get over to Katie to check out how she's living these days. I want to meet her friends and see where she's working; you know, annoying things that mothers do.

If you can't then I understand. Perhaps I could twist

411

Kevin's arm into caring about someone else for a change.

Give my love to the family.

From   Steph
To   Rosie
Subject   Re: Mum

Of course I'll take Mum. In fact, I'll go one better and take the family over to Connemara for the week. Pierre dragged me to his mother and father's for Christmas dinner so I think I'm entitled to have my turn!

You deserve a break, Rosie. I'm so sorry you're stuck doing everything. Sometimes I feel like going over there and giving Kev a good kick. I intend to have a serious talk with him when I'm there, and perhaps he may even want to see his niece and nephew for a change.

Have fun with Katie. I can't believe how grown up she is now, and so much like you! When she stayed with us a few months back I felt like I was talking to you. Enjoy the week with Ruby. I need to spend some quality time with Mum anyway.

From   Alex
To   Katie
Subject   Surprise 40th

I don't no where you are in the world right now, but I hope you're still checking your emails! Seeing as your mum is going to be forty next month and you are going to be twenty-one, I thought it would be a good idea to have a double birthday party. But I was hoping that we could fly you home and surprise your mum with a party?

You can invite all your friends and we can organise all of Rosie's friends too. Perhaps we can bring Ruby in on this too for help? I think she would love it.

Let me no if you think it's a good idea.

Rosie: I'm forty in a few days, Ruby. *Forty.* The big 4–0.
Ruby: So?
Rosie: So it's *old.*
Ruby: Then what does that make me, ancient?
Rosie: Oh sorry, you know what I mean. We're not exactly twenty years old, are we?
Ruby: No, thank God for that, because then I would have to go through a shit marriage and a divorce all over again. We would have to go out and look for jobs, be all uncertain about our lives, care about dating and how we look and what car we're driving, what music we're playing in it, what we wear, whether we'll get into certain clubs or not, blah blah blah. What's so good about being twenty? I call them the materialistic years. The years we get distracted by all the bullshit. Then we cop on when we hit our thirties and spend those years trying to make up for the twenties. But your forties? Those years are for enjoying it.
Rosie: Hmm, good point. What are the fifties for?
Ruby: Fixing what you fucked up on in your forties.
Rosie: Great. Looking forward to it.
Ruby: Oh, don't worry, Rosie. You don't need to make a song and dance about the fact the world has spun around the sun one more time. We should just take it as a given by now. So what do you want to do for your fortieth?
Rosie: Nothing?
Ruby: Good plan. Why don't we go down to my local on Friday night for one too many?
Rosie: Sounds perfect.
Ruby: Oh, hold on, though. It's Teddy's brother's birthday that night too, and we're all gathering in the Berkeley Court Hotel.

Rosie: Oh, very snazzy! I love that hotel!

Ruby: I know, I think he's on the fiddle again. Honestly, you would think he'd know the gardaí are watching him after he's just got out of prison. Some people never learn.

Rosie: Oh well, would you rather change it to Saturday night then?

Ruby: No! Will you collect me from the hotel and we can head to the pub together?

Rosie: OK, but I don't want to get stuck talking to Teddy's brother. The last time I met him he tried to put his hand up my skirt.

Ruby: He had only been out of prison a few days, though, Rosie; you can understand how he was feeling.

Rosie: Whatever. So what time should I pick you up at?

Ruby: 8 p.m.

Rosie: Are you joking?! What time does it start at?

Ruby: 7.30 p.m.

Rosie: Ruby! You'll have to stay a lot longer than that! I'm not arriving to take you away after only a half an hour; everyone will think I'm so rude! I'll come at 9.30 p.m. At least that way you'll have two hours.

Ruby: No! You *have* to come at eight!

Rosie: Why?

Ruby: Well, for one thing the party is in the *penthouse suite* of the Berkeley Court Hotel.

Rosie: Oh my God, why didn't you just say so? I'll be there at 7.30 p.m.

Ruby: No! You can't!

Rosie: What is wrong with you? Why can't I?

Ruby: Because you're not invited and they'll think you've a cheek just turning up like that. If you come at eight then you can quickly see the place and then leave.

Rosie: But I want to stay at the penthouse. Have you any idea how much that would mean to me?

Ruby: Yes I do . . . but I'm sorry, you can't stay. Anyway, once you meet the rest of Teddy's family you'll want to leave straight away.

Rosie: OK, but I hope you know that you're breaking my heart – and I don't care what you say, anything in the bathrooms that isn't nailed down is going in my handbag. Actually I think I'll bring my camera!

Ruby: Rosie, it's a birthday party. I'm sure lots of people will have cameras.

Rosie: Yes, I know, but I'll take some photos for Katie too. She'd love to see what it looks like. I was hoping she would be able to come over but she can't. It's her twenty-first birthday a few weeks after my birthday and I was hoping we could celebrate it together but unfortunately it's not to be. Mum is going over to stay with Stephanie again so she'll miss it as well. I was a bit upset about that but she's been so ill lately I didn't want to cause a fuss. I was just glad she said she wanted to go somewhere, even if it was on my birthday.

So it will just be you and me once again, but at least this year I'll get to sneak a peek at the penthouse suite! I'll steal a few ideas for my own hotel. What a treat!

Ruby: Looking forward to seeing your face, Rosie. See you at 8 p.m., room 440.

Penthouse Suite
440

SURPRISE, ROSIE!
HAPPY BIRTHDAY, ROSIE & KATIE!!

Happy fortieth, Rosie.

I had a wonderful weekend at your party, we really did surprise you, didn't we?! It broke my heart pretending to you that I was staying with Stephanie but it was worth it to see

415

the look on your face (and the tears in your eyes). Alex arranged the entire thing. He's a lovely, lovely man, Rosie. Shame about the wife, though! Do you know, I always thought you and he would get together when you were children. Silly, isn't it?

Anyway, thank you, thank you, *thank you* for being a wonderful daughter and for all of your help over the past few years. Your father would be proud of you. I'll be sure to tell him all about you when I see him!

You are a beautiful young woman, Rosie Dunne. Your father and I did well!

Lots of love, Mum

Chapter 48

Happy seventieth, Mum!

You made it to the big 7–0 and you look as beautiful as ever! We'll have you out of hospital as quick as we can; in the meantime here are some grapes to make you feel *really* sick!

Love you always and for ever, Mum,
Rosie

Hi, Kev, Steph here. Texting as can't get you on the phone. You might want to come to Connemara now. It's time.

Hi, love, get in touch with ur dad asap. He's booked u a flight home 2morrow. I no it's short notice but grandma asking 4 u. Kev will collect u from airport & bring u here. C u 2morrow. Love, Mum

> Dunne (née O'Sullivan) (Connemara, Co. Galway and formerly Dundrum, Dublin 10) – Alice, beloved wife of Dennis and loving mother of Stephanie, Rosie and Kevin; will be missed by her grandchildren Katie, Jean-Louis and Sophia, son-in-law Pierre, brother Patrick and sister-in-law Sandra. Removal at 4.45 p.m. today from

Stafford's funeral home to Oughterard Church, Connemara. May she rest in peace.

'Ar dheis lamh De go raibh a anam uasal.'

THIS IS THE LAST WILL, dated the 10 day of September 2000, of ALICE DUNNE

Of

HEREBY REVOKING all former Wills and Testamentary Dispositions made by Alice Dunne.

If my husband survives me by thirty days **I GIVE DEVISE AND BEQUEATH** the whole of my estate to him and appoint him my executor. If my husband does not survive me by thirty days the following provisions shall apply:

1. **I APPOINT** Rosie Dunne (hereinafter called 'my Trustee') to be executor and trustee and appoint her trustee for the purposes of the Settled Land Acts, Conveyancing Acts and Section 57 of the Succession Act.
2. **I GIVE, DEVISE AND BEQUEATH** to my Trustee the whole of my estate upon trust to sell the same (with power to postpone such sale in whole or in part for such time as they shall think fit) and to hold the same or the proceeds of sale thereof on the following trusts ...

You have received an instant message from: STEPH.

Steph: How's my baby sister holding up?

Rosie: Oh, hi, Steph. I'm not sure. There's an eerie silence in my world these days. I find myself switching on the TV and the radio just to fill the background. Katie had to head back to work; people have stopped ringing and calling around to offer their sympathies. Everything is calming down now and I'm left with this silence.

I'm not quite sure what to do with myself on my days

418

off. I'm so used to hopping on the bus and travelling over to Mum. Life is strange now. Before even when she lay in bed looking frail and weak she still managed to make me feel safe. Mothers do that, don't they? Their very presence can help. And even if I ended up mothering her in the final days, she still was taking care of me. I miss her.

Steph: I do too, and at the oddest times. It's only when you get back to the normal routine of life that you really feel it. I keep on having to remind myself that when the phone rings it's not her. Or when I get a free moment in the day I pick up the phone to call her and then I remember that she's not there to call. It's such an odd feeling.

Rosie: Kevin is still in a huff with me.

Steph: Ignore Kevin; he's in a huff with the entire world.

Rosie: Maybe he's right, though, Steph. Mum has put me in such an awkward position by leaving me the house. Perhaps I should sell it and split the profits three ways. It's fairer.

Steph: Rosie Dunne, you will not sell that house for me and Kev. She left it for you for a reason. Kev and I are both financially secure – we both have houses. We really don't need the Connemara house. Mum knew that so she left the house to you. You work harder than the two of us put together and you still can't get out of that flat. Obviously I didn't tell you, but Mum discussed it with me before and I agreed with her. This is the best way. Don't listen to Kev.

Rosie: I don't know, Steph; I'm not hugely comfortable with it . . .

Steph: Rosie, trust me, if I needed the money so badly I would tell you and we could work something out. But I don't. Neither does Kevin. It's not like we were forgotten about in the will. We're both fine, honestly. The house

in Connemara belongs to you. You do with it whatever
you wish.

Rosie: Thanks, Steph.

Steph: No problem. So what are you going to do over
there on your own, Rosie? I hate you being all alone.
Do you want to come over here for a while?

Rosie: No thanks, Steph. I really have to work. I'm going
to throw myself into this job and make it the best damn
hotel in the world.

Grand Tower Hotel
Tower Road,
Dublin 1

Dear Mr Cronin Ui Cheallaigh,

Following our visit to the Grand Tower Hotel we at the
Department of Public Works are sending you an emergency
order due to an imminent and substantial hazard to the life,
health and safety of occupants.

After their visit last week, the Department of Building
Inspection listed more than 100 code violations including missing
smoke detectors, water damage and inadequate lighting.

The bathrooms are noted as being unsanitary, and during
our visit rodents were spotted in the kitchens.

According to our records you have received many warnings
over the years to improve the maintenance of the building and
you were advised to make the necessary improvements in order
to keep the building acting as a hotel. These warnings were
ignored and we have no choice but to shut you down.

The business on the ground level may remain open.

Please be in touch with our offices as soon as you receive
this letter. Details of the Health and Safety Act are overleaf.

Yours sincerely,

Adam Delaney

Office of Public Works

I'm so sorry to hear about you losing your job. I no you hated it, but still, it's never nice to have to leave when it's not your own decision. I couldn't reach you on the phone – you've either been on the phone all day or they've cut you off. Either way, I thought I'd email you instead. I completely forgot to tell you that when we returned to Dublin after the funeral, whatshisname called round to the flat to see you.

I didn't want to call you because you were upset enough as it was, so I took a message. He dropped in some post that had been delivered to his house for you and said that he hoped that they would be some sort of help to you now that your mum and dad are gone. He said he understood how you felt, as his mum died last year and he didn't want to be the cause of your loneliness.

He seemed sincere, but who can ever tell with him? It was odd seeing him after so many years. He's really aged. Anyway, I hope whatever is in the envelopes isn't too important but let me no what they are all the same. I left the two envelopes in the bottom drawer of the living-room cabinet.

Dr Reginald & Miranda Williams
invite **Rosie Dunne** to join them in celebrating the
marriage of their beloved daughter
Bethany
to
Dr Alex Stewart
at
the Memorial Church of Harvard University
on 28 December at 2 o'clock
& a reception at
the Boston Harbor Hotel

Rosie,

I'm returning to Boston tomorrow but before I go I wanted to write this letter to you. All the thoughts and feelings that have been bubbling up inside me are finally overflowing from this pen and I'm leaving this letter for you so that you don't feel that I'm putting you under any great pressure. I understand that you will need to take your time trying to decide on what I am about to say.

I no what's going on, Rosie. You're my best friend and I can see the sadness in your eyes. I no that Greg isn't away working for the weekend. You never could lie to me; you were always terrible at it. Your eyes betray you time and time again. Don't pretend that everything is perfect because I *see* it isn't. I see that Greg is a selfish man who has absolutely no idea just how lucky he is and it makes me sick.

He is the luckiest man in the world to have you, Rosie, but he doesn't deserve you and *you* deserve far better. You deserve someone who loves you with every single beat of his heart, someone who thinks about you constantly, someone who spends every minute of every day just wondering what you're doing, where you are, who you're with and if you're OK. You need someone who can help you reach your dreams and who can protect you from your fears. You need someone who will treat you with respect, and love every part of you, *especially* your flaws. You should be with someone who can make you happy, really happy, *dancing-on-air* happy. Someone who should have taken the chance to be with you years ago instead of becoming scared and being too afraid to try.

I'm not scared any more, Rosie. I am not afraid to try. I no what that feeling was at your wedding – it *was* jealousy. My heart broke when I saw the woman I love turning away from me to walk down the aisle with another man, a man she planned to spend the rest of her life with. It was like a prison sentence for me – years stretching ahead without me being able to tell you how I feel or hold you how I wanted to.

Twice we've stood beside each other at the altar, Rosie. *Twice*. And twice we got it wrong. I needed you to be there for my wedding day but I was too stupid to see that I needed you to be the *reason* for my wedding day.

I should never have let your lips leave mine all those years ago in Boston. I should never have pulled away. I should never have panicked. I should never have wasted all those years without you. Give me a chance to make them up to you. I love you, Rosie, and I want to be with you and Katie and Josh. Always.

Please think about it. Don't waste your time on Greg. This is *our* opportunity. Let's stop being afraid and take the chance. I promise I'll make you happy.

All my love,

Alex

Chapter 49

From   Ruby
To   Rosie
Subject Are you OK?

I haven't heard from you in almost two weeks – that has to be the longest time we've ever spent incommunicado. Is everything OK? I called round to see you at the flat but Rupert told me you had gone to Galway. You just packed up and left without saying goodbye – something must be up. How long are you planning on staying there and why didn't you tell anyone?

Your mother's phone has obviously been disconnected so I didn't know how else to reach you. I understand that you probably just need some time to yourself. Losing parents is really difficult. As much as I complain about how mine were, it was still tough dealing with their loss. I know I joke around a lot but I'm seriously here for you, Rosie, if you need someone to talk to, a shoulder to cry on or even someone to scream at.

I would say I'm sorry that you lost your job at the hotel but I'm not sorry at all. You were better than that hotel; you had bigger dreams that extended far beyond those crumbling walls. Now the world is – once again – your oyster.

Please just let me know you're OK or I'm coming down there myself to check up on you and that's not a threat, it's a promise.

Welcome to the Relieved Divorced Dubliners' internet chat
    room. There are currently three people chatting.
LonelyLady: The guy from my reading group asked me out
    yesterday. To go out on a date, like. This weekend. Just
    me and him. But I just don't know . . .
Wildflower: You don't know what?
LonelyLady: Well, I don't know if I should start dating
    again. I mean I don't know if I'm ready, being so soon
    after Tommy and all . . .
Wildflower: So soon? *So soon?* In case you haven't noticed
    it's been *ten years* since Tommy left you.
LonelyLady: Oh. It doesn't *feel* like ten years.
Wildflower: Well, if you ever stopped whinging and
    moaning about how lonely you were, you would be able
    to think rationally about your life. Which guy in your
    reading group are you dating?
LonelyLady: The *only* guy in the reading group.
Wildflower: I bet the ladies will drop out like flies now.
    The all-important question for you is, does he have a
    criminal record?
LonelyLady: No, I checked.
Wildflower: God, I was only joking! But at least you know
    your TV won't go walkabout when you go to the toilet.
LonelyLady: A luxury which most women don't appreciate.
SureOne has entered the room.
Wildflower: Well, he sounds perfect for you then. I see no
    reason why you shouldn't go out with him. Good luck
    with the date.

SureOne: LonelyLady, are you going out on a *date*?

LonelyLady: You say it like it's a disease.

Wildflower: Well, it could turn into one, I suppose.

SureOne: No, I'm just shocked! But in a good way! Congratulations!

LonelyLady: Thank you! Hey, you changed your name!

SureOne: I know. I was granted my annulment. See, I told you the Church had sense. They agree that Leonard is a complete prick.

Wildflower: SureOne! Well, it's a change to hear that come from you! I'm not quite sure the Church thinks exactly *that* but it's a start . . .

Buttercup: Congratulations, SureOne.

SureOne: Thanks, girls! We haven't heard from you in a while, Buttercup. Where have you been lately?

Buttercup: I've been staying in the house in Connemara for the past few weeks. I've had a lot of thinking to do.

Wildflower: Is everything OK?

Buttercup: No, not really.

SureOne: Do you want to tell us about it? Maybe we can help.

Buttercup: Well, my mother died, I lost my job and I'm afraid to say the words of the 'something else' in case it validates it and causes me to have a nervous breakdown. Because if it becomes true, then it would officially declare the past ten years of my life to be utterly useless and a waste of time.

LonelyLady: But we're all experts on that subject. You know by now that what goes on in this room, stays in this room, maybe we can shed some light on it for you.

Buttercup: Thanks. OK then, here goes . . . I came across a letter that was written just after my thirtieth birthday. A letter that was meant for me but that never made it into my hands. It was from Alex.

LonelyLady: Oooh, what did he say in the letter?

426

Buttercup: Here's the tough part. He said he loved me.

Wildflower: Whooooah!

SureOne: Oh. My. God.

LonelyLady: No! So where did you find the letter?

Buttercup: Whatshisname returned it to me. He 'didn't want to be the cause of my loneliness any more', he said.

LonelyLady: He had kept it all these years?

Buttercup: Why he would keep it all these years I have no idea. I haven't quite figured that out yet. Although I never truly figured him out at all while I was married to him. I can't really think anything now, I'm in so much shock.

Wildflower: So have you spoken to Alex?

Buttercup: How can I speak to him, Wildflower? Knowing what I know, how can I even *think* of him?

Wildflower: Very easily, I would imagine. He's just told you that he loves you!

Buttercup: No, Wildflower, he told me over *ten* years ago that he loved me. *Before* he got married, *before* he had Theo. I just couldn't bring myself to talk to him. He's been writing and phoning but the thought of that missed opportunity makes me so sick to the stomach that I can't respond to his messages.

LonelyLady: But you have to tell him you know!

Buttercup: I was going to. I was half fearful, half excited. I was going to ring him on the phone and say it to him casually at first to test the waters and see how he felt and then go a bit further. But that morning his annual Christmas card arrived in the post box. With the photo of his wife and two sons on the cover of the card, all wearing colourful knitted Christmas jumpers – Theo with his two front teeth gone, Josh with his beaming smile just like his dad, Bethany hand in hand with Alex. And I couldn't tell him. What would he care now

427

anyway? He's married. He's happy. He's over me, and even if he's not, I wouldn't expect him to jump out of that perfect Christmas photo for me. The possibility of me and Alex being together has faded, just like those old photos of us in Katie's locket.

SureOne: Take it from me, Buttercup, you're right to leave the family alone.

Wildflower: But she *loves* him! And he loves her! And everyone airbrushes their photos these days!

SureOne: What age are you now, Buttercup, forty-two?

Buttercup: Yes.

SureOne: Right. He wrote that letter twelve years ago, before he got married. It's not right to bring it up now. She could break too many little hearts by telling him.

Wildflower: Oh, don't listen to her, Buttercup. You hop on a plane and go to Alex and tell the man that you love him.

Buttercup: But what if he doesn't feel that way about me any more? I've never ever picked up on any vibes from him over the past ten years.

SureOne: Because he's *married*. He's a good man, Buttercup. He follows the rules.

Wildflower: Oh, rules were made to be broken!

SureOne: Not when people get hurt, Wildflower.

Wildflower: Don't let people walk all over you, Buttercup. It's your life. If you want something, you need to get out there and grab it by the horns because no one is going to give you what you want on a plate. Good girls always come second.

SureOne: Good girls have a conscience and that way they can live with themselves. And anyway, we haven't even thought about the fact that Alex's feelings may have diminished for Buttercup over time.

Wildflower: Oh, why don't we just slit her wrists *for* her, SureOne?

Buttercup: She's right, Wildflower. I need to cover all angles before I jump into this head first. God, I feel sick. OK, so what happens if I tell Alex that I received his letter and his feelings have changed? What do I do then? Things between us could never get back to normal ever again and I would lose my very best friend and I don't think I could cope with that.

Wildflower: Yes, but then what if when you tell him how you feel, he grabs you passionately, relieved you finally know his true feelings and the two of you live happily ever after?

SureOne: Yeah sure, in between one messy divorce, child custody court fights, a heartbroken ex-wife . . .

Wildflower: And a partridge in a pear tree.

SureOne: If you can live with yourself by doing that, then by all means go ahead, but I for one couldn't.

Wildflower: But she can't pretend nothing happened.

SureOne: Your friendship will remain strong with Alex and the happiness in his life will also remain intact, just as it did when Alex heard no reply from you all those years ago. He kept on as normal, as though nothing had ever happened.

Buttercup: Why did he keep on as normal? I remember him asking about a letter and I told him I didn't get it. Why didn't he just tell me then?

Wildflower: He could have chickened out.

SureOne: Or he saw that you were in love with your husband.

Buttercup: This is all very confusing. LonelyLady, you've been very quiet. What do you think?

LonelyLady: Well, I of all people know what it's like to feel all alone and there were times that I thought I would do just about anything to find love, *but* SureOne has put it into perspective. Knowing the hurt she has gone through, I wouldn't look for my own happiness at

429

the expense of others. I would carry on as normal, as though nothing had happened.

Wildflower: You three are unbelievable. Learn to live a little. Do unto others as others have done to you. You have all been screwed with by people.

Buttercup: Yes, we have, and as much as I don't like Bethany she has never done anything to hurt me.

Wildflower: Apart from marrying Alex.

Buttercup: I don't *own* Alex.

Wildflower: But you could.

Buttercup: People can never *own* people but whether I can be with him or not right now, the answer is no. Not now. Maybe in another time.

FatherMichael has entered the room.

Wildflower: Ah, don't tell me you're through a divorce yourself, Father?

SureOne: Don't be silly, Wildflower; have a bit of respect! He's here for the ceremony.

Wildflower: I know that. I was just trying to lighten the atmosphere.

FatherMichael: So have the loving couple arrived yet?

SureOne: No, but it's customary for the bride to be late.

FatherMichael: Well, is the groom here?

SingleSam has entered the room.

Wildflower: Here he is now. Hello there, SingleSam. I think this is the first time ever that both the bride and groom will have to change their names.

SingleSam: Hello, all.

Buttercup: Where's the bride?

SingleSam: She's right here on the laptop beside me. She's just having problems with her password logging in.

SureOne: Doomed from the start.

Divorced_1 has entered the room.

Wildflower: Wahoo! Here comes the bride, all dressed in . . . ?

SingleSam: Black.

Wildflower: How charming.

Buttercup: She's right to wear black.

Divorced_1: What's wrong with misery guts today?

LonelyLady: She found a letter from Alex that was written twelve years ago, proclaiming his love for her, and she doesn't know what to do.

Divorced_1: Here's a word of advice. *Get over it*, he's married. Now let's focus the attention on me for a change.

SoOverHim has entered the room.

FatherMichael: OK, let's begin. We are gathered here online today to witness the marriage of SingleSam (soon to be 'Sam') and Divorced_1 (soon to be 'Married_1')

SoOverHim: WHAT?? WHAT THE HELL IS GOING ON HERE? THIS IS A *MARRIAGE CEREMONY* IN A *DIVORCED PEOPLE'S CHAT ROOM*??

Wildflower: Uh-oh, looks like we've got ourselves a gate-crasher here. Excuse me, can we see your wedding invite, please?

Divorced_1: Ha ha.

SoOverHim: YOU THINK THIS IS *FUNNY*? YOU PEOPLE MAKE ME SICK, COMING IN HERE AND TRYING TO UPSET OTHERS WHO ARE GENUINELY TROUBLED.

Buttercup: Oh, we are genuinely troubled, alright. And could you please STOP SHOUTING?

LonelyLady: You see, SoOverHim, this is where SingleSam and Divorced_1 met for the first time.

SoOverHim: OH, I HAVE SEEN IT ALL NOW!

Buttercup: Sshh!

SoOverHim: Sorry. Mind if I stick around?

Divorced_1: Sure, grab a pew; just don't trip over my train.

Wildflower: Ha ha.

FatherMichael: OK, we should get on with this; I don't
    want to be late for my two o'clock. First I have to ask,
    is there anyone in here who thinks there is any reason
    why these two should not be married?
LonelyLady: Yes.
SureOne: I could give more than one reason.
Buttercup: *Hell*, yes.
SoOverHim: DON'T DO IT!
FatherMichael: Well, I'm afraid this has put me in a very
    tricky predicament.
Divorced_1: Father, we are in a divorced people's chat room –
    of course they all object to marriage. Can we get on with it?
FatherMichael: Certainly. Do you Sam take Penelope to be
    your lawful wedded wife?
SingleSam: I do.
FatherMichael: Do you Penelope take Sam to be your
    lawful wedded husband?
Divorced_1: I do (yeah, yeah my name is Penelope).
FatherMichael: You have already emailed your vows to
    me so by the online power vested in me, I now
    pronounce you husband and wife. You may kiss the
    bride. Now if the witnesses could click on the icon to
    the right of the screen they will find a form to type
    their names, addresses and phone numbers. Once that's
    filled in just email it to me. I'll be off now.
    Congratulations again.
FatherMichael has left the room.
Wildflower: Congrats, Sam and Penelope!
Divorced_1: Thanks, girls, for being here.
SoOverHim: Freaks.
SoOverHim has left the room.
Wildflower: Ah, just call me Jane. Right, you love birds,
    I'm off. Enjoy your honeymoon and I expect to never
    see you in here again. LonelyLady, good luck with that
    date. SureOne, enjoy the start of the rest of your life

and, Buttercup, or should I call you Rosie Dunne, what *are* you going to do?

Ruby: *What do you mean* you're moving to Co. Galway?

Rosie: I mean exactly that. I'm leaving that horrible flat in Dublin once and for all and I'm moving to Connemara for good.

Ruby: But *why*?

Rosie: Ruby, there's nothing there for me in Dublin. Apart from you, of course. I have had a string of unsatisfactory jobs, have no family there, had my heart broken twice there, have no money and no man. I don't see a reason why I should stay.

Ruby: Well, forgive me for being the bearer of bad news but you have no family and no man in Galway, and no job.

Rosie: I may not have all those things but I have a *house*.

Ruby: Have you gone nuts, Rosie?

Rosie: Probably! But think about it. I have a great big modern four-bedroom house right on the coast in Connemara.

Ruby: Exactly! What are you going to do all on your own with no job, in a four-bedroom house, hanging off the cliff in Connemara?

Rosie: You could be close to guessing!

Ruby: Well, I was thinking very much of you committing suicide so I hope I'm not.

Rosie: No, silly! I'm opening up a bed and breakfast! And I know I've always said I hate B&Bs, but I'm planning on turning the house more into my own mini hotel. And I am going to be manager/owner extraordinaire!

Ruby: Wow.

Rosie: What do you think?

Ruby: I think that . . . wow. I can't think of anything sarcastic to say, actually. I think that's a great idea. Are you sure you want to do this?

433

Rosie: Ruby, I've never been surer in my life! I've done my
research. With my inheritance from Mum and Dad I can
afford the insurance. I've asked all the B&Bs around and
the place is *crawling* with tourists.

The area is beautiful, the coastline is dramatic and
rugged, the boglands have a foggy mysteriousness to
them, the sea crashes and whips against the cliffs and I
love it. It's just nature and all the elements at their best
– who wouldn't want to come here? Who wouldn't want
to live here?

Ruby: Well, *I* wouldn't, but I appreciate what you're
saying. I think it's a great idea, Rosie.
Congratulations, you little genius. I hope that whatever it was that sent you packing isn't going to chase
you away any further.

Rosie Dunne will be your hostess in Buttercup House. The
building is a modern four-bedroom home approved by Bord
Failte, the Irish Tourist Board. All of the rooms are ensuite,
centrally heated, and also have telephones. Double, twin and
family rooms are all available.

Buttercup House is the ideal location to explore Connemara,
and enjoy hill walking, mile-long sandy beaches, sea angling,
and fishing in Lough Corrib, Ireland's largest natural inland
water mass, a favourite with fishermen for salmon and brown
trout. Scuba diving, sailing and surfing are accessible along
the coastline.

Connemara National Park is a 2,000 hectare state-owned
conservation centre, with mountains, bogs, grasslands and
spectacular wildlife. Traces of ancient settlements can be seen,
including 4,000-year-old megalithic tombs. There are golf
courses aplenty, with rocky hills and ocean inlets providing
the ultimate challenge for the keen golfer. Walking, horse-
riding and cycling are wonderful ways to explore the terrain,
and mountaineering is also popular.

The television lounge is comfortably furnished, with log fire, board games and plenty of books for our guests to relax with after their active days. Traditional Irish breakfast is served in the dining room and the conservatory, which offer panoramic views of the mountains and Atlantic Ocean.

Rates are €35 per person per night.

Contact Rosie Dunne to make your reservation.

From   Katie
To   Mum
Subject Wow!

Wow, Mum, that looks fantastic! The photographs are beautiful. You've really done so much to the place. You are finally Rosie Dunne, general manager and owner of Buttercup House! I'll come over next week and help with all that's left to do, and we can go shopping for more things to fill this big house! Grandma and Granddad would be so proud of you using the house like this. They always said it was such a waste of space only having the two of them there.

Well done! See you next week.

Dear Rosie,

I just wanted to no if everything between us is OK? You've been sounding a little, well, odd on the phone lately. Have I done something to upset you in any way? I can't think of anything that I may have said to piss you off but do tell me. It seems I have to do nothing these days in order to succeed in upsetting the women in my life. Bethany starts a fight with me if I even look at her. If I have unintentionally done the same to you, Rosie, please let me no.

Bethany is going crazy about organising Theo's tenth birthday party next week. She has invited more of her own friends than Theo's, and Josh keeps stealing my car and driving it around all night with his new girlfriend. She's a sweet girl but I don't no what she sees in my son, that's for sure. He's a mad man. I can't seem to get him to settle down and study (I sounded like my own dad just then). He's supposed to be starting college next September but considering the fact he hasn't applied for anywhere and can't figure out what he wants to do other than drive my car, I'm presuming that he'll be taking a year out before he heads off to educate himself further.

Luckily Theo thinks Josh is nuts. He's actually afraid of him. So we're hoping that Theo can be the son that we can talk about and admit to having. That, of course, is a joke.

Things at the hospital are going well. I'm still doing the same old thing but my life has been made massively easier, due to the retirement of Reginald Williams. I can breathe now without having to explain it. Working with your father-in-law is as advisable as living with his daughter. Joking once again, *of course*. Well, kind of, but we won't go into that.

I have to go now but I wanted to make sure things were OK between us. The brochure for the B&B looks fantastic! I wish you well with it, Rosie. You deserve the best!

Love,

Alex

From   Rosie
To   Alex
Subject Sorry

I apologise for sounding off with you on the phone. I was a little distracted by a few things that popped up from the past in my life that I was previously unaware of. They were holding me back for a little while, but they've let go of me now and I'm back on course.

I'm ready to move on and spend the next ten years of my life tending to my quest for greatness and happiness.

You are more than welcome to stay with me *whenever* you are ready to.

From   Alex
To   Rosie
Subject Thank you

Thank you very much for that generous offer, Rosie. I'll be sure to take you up on that whenever my wife isn't looking.

From   Rosie
To   Alex
Subject Flirt

Now, now, are you flirting with me, Alex Stewart?

From   Alex
To   Rosie
Subject Re: Flirt

Why, Rosie Dunne, I do believe I am. Get in touch with me in ten years' time when your quest for greatness has reached its pinnacle.

PART FIVE

Chapter 50

You have received an instant message from: KATIE.

Katie: Happy Birthday, Mum! How does it feel to be fifty?

Rosie: Hot.

Katie: Are you having another flush?

Rosie: Yes. How does it feel to be almost thirty-one? Any sign of my only daughter settling down, getting a decent job and giving me grandchildren?

Katie: Hmm . . . I'm not sure, although there was a little baby boy playing on the beach making sandcastles this morning and for the first time ever I thought it was cute. It's possible that I'm coming round to the rest of the world's way of thinking.

Rosie: Well, that sounds hopeful. I thought those dreams would have to die, but you've given me hope. Perhaps I can start telling people I actually have a daughter now.

Katie: Funny. How's the B&B going?

Rosie: Busy, thank God. I was just in the middle of updating the website when you messaged me. Buttercup House now has *seven* ensuite bedrooms.

Katie: I no, the place looks terrific.

Rosie: It's KNOW, not NO.

Katie: Sorry, us DJs don't need to be able to spell. OH MY

GOD, I almost forgot to tell you! I can't believe this isn't the first thing I said to you! You'll *never* guess who I met in the club last night!

Rosie: Well, if I'll never guess I don't think I want to play this game.

Katie: Toby Flynn!!

Rosie: Never heard of him. Is he an old boyfriend?

Katie: *Mum!* Toby Flynn! *Toby!*

Rosie: I don't see how repeating his name is going to help.

Katie: My best friend from school! *Toby!*

Rosie: Oh my lord! Toby! How is the little pet?

Katie: He's fine! He's working as a dentist in Dublin just like he wanted, and he's over here in Ibiza for a holiday for two weeks. It was so weird, seeing him after ten years, but he hasn't changed a bit!

Rosie: Oh, that's fabulous. Tell him I was asking for him, will you?

Katie: I will. He had lots of lovely things to say about you. Actually I'll be seeing him again tonight. We're going out for dinner.

Rosie: Is it a date?

Katie: No! I couldn't date Toby. It's Toby! We're just going to catch up.

Rosie: Whatever you say, Katie dear.

Katie: Honestly, Mum! I couldn't date Toby – he used to be my best friend. It would be too odd.

Rosie: I don't see anything wrong with dating your best friend.

Katie: Mum, it would be like *you* dating *Alex*!

Rosie: Well, I would think that would be perfectly normal too.

Katie: Mum!

Rosie: What? I don't see the big deal. Anyway, have you been speaking to Alex lately?

Katie: Yeah, just yesterday. He's on the couch again, so to

speak. Bethany is tormenting him again. Honestly, I think they're both stupid to wait until Theo heads off to college.

Rosie: Well, they were both stupid for getting married in the first place. You know what Theo is like, though, Katie – he's such a softie. His parents splitting up would break his little heart. But he's going to have to deal with it from Paris at art college, so I'm not quite sure why they feel that will be better for him.

Katie: Well, the sooner the better. They're a match made in hell, I've said it all along. Josh says he can't wait for Alex and her to split up. He can't stand her.

Rosie: Still, they lasted longer than anyone thought they would. Tell Josh I said hi.

Katie: Will do. I better go and tell Alex about Toby. He'll never believe it! Don't work too hard on your birthday, Mum!

You have received an instant message from: KATIE.

Katie: Hi, Alex.

Alex: Hello, my wonderful goddaughter. How are you and what do you want?

Katie: I'm fine and I don't want anything!

Alex: You women always want something.

Katie: That's not true and you no it!

Alex: How's my son? I hope he's working hard over there.

Katie: Still alive at least.

Alex: Good. Tell him to phone me a bit more often. As good as it is hearing from you and all, it would be nice to hear about his life from him.

Katie: I understand; I'll pass it on. Anyway, the reason why I'm messaging you is because you'll never guess who I met in the club last night!

Alex: If I'll never guess then I don't want to play this game.

Katie: That's exactly what Mum said! Anyway, I met Toby Flynn!!!

Alex: Is he an ex-boyfriend or someone famous? Give me a clue.

Katie: Alex! Honestly, you and Mum are getting forgetful in your old age. Toby is my best friend from school!

Alex: Oh, that Toby! Wow, there's a blast from the past. How is he?

Katie: He's fine. He's working as a dentist in Dublin and he's just over in Ibiza for a few weeks' holiday. He was asking about you.

Alex: Great, well, if you see him again give him my regards. He was a good guy.

Katie: Yeah, I will. I'll actually be seeing him again tonight; we're going out for dinner.

Alex: Is it a date?

Katie: Honestly, what is it with you and Mum? He used to be my best friend. I couldn't go out with him.

Alex: Oh, don't be stupid. There's nothing wrong with dating a best friend.

Katie: That's what Mum said too!

Alex: She did?

Katie: Yeah, so I tried to put it into perspective for her by explaining that would be like *her* dating *you*.

Alex: And what did she say to that?

Katie: I don't think she was particularly put off by the idea. So you see, Alex, whenever you get your lazy behind out of that house of yours, you no that there's one woman at least who'll have you. Ha ha.

Alex: I see . . .

Katie: Jesus, Alex, lighten up. OK, I gotta go and get ready for dinner.

You have received an instant message from: ROSIE.

Rosie: Hello, old woman, what are you up to?

Ruby: Sitting in my rocking chair, knitting. What else? No, Gary, Maria and the kids just left and I'm knackered. I can't run after them like I used to.

Rosie: Do you really want to anyway?

Ruby: No, and stiff muscles are a great excuse for not having to play hide and seek 24/7. What are you up to?

Rosie: I'm just taking a break from clearing away all the dust from the builders. Honestly, have they ever heard of the words 'vacuum cleaner'?

Ruby: No, and neither have I. Is it a new invention? How is the new wing looking?

Rosie: Oh, it's great, Ruby, I'll have so much more privacy now. I can stick to my side of the house and the guests can have theirs. I've decorated a room just the way you like it so it can be yours when you stay. Let me know when you can come over. I'm heading off out with Sean tonight.

Ruby: Again? Well, this is really becoming a regular occurrence indeed.

Rosie: He's a lovely man and I really enjoy his company. Even though the house is always full of strangers, I can still feel alone so it's nice to be able to meet up with him once in a while.

Ruby: I know what you mean. He seems a real gentleman alright.

Rosie: He is.

Ruby: I heard that Alex's marriage had ended.

Rosie: Ruby, his marriage barely even started, never mind ended. Unfortunately for him.

Ruby: How do you feel about it?

Rosie: Sad for him. Happy for him.

Ruby: Now you can tell me the truth. How do you *really* feel?

From   Katie
To   Rosie
Subject Oh, Mum

Oh, Mum.

Oh my God, Mum.

The most bizarre thing has happened.

I've never felt so . . . *odd* in my whole entire life.

Last night was the weirdest night of my life. I met up
with Toby and we went to dinner at Raul's restaurant in
the old part of town. In order to get there we had to walk
up a really steep cobbled stone hill, passing by the local
women dressed in black from head to toe, who were just
sitting on wooden chairs outside their houses, enjoying the
warmth and silence.

The place had only a few tables and as we were the only
tourists there I almost felt bad for intruding but they were
so friendly and there was such a good atmosphere. It's not
a part of the island that my job allows me to see very
often, unfortunately.

The manager of Toby's hotel suggested the restaurant
and it was such a good choice because it sat high on a
mountain top overlooking the island on one side and the
sea on the other. The air was warm, the stars were
twinkling, a man played on the violin in the corner. It was
like something out of a movie only it was so much better
because it felt real and it was happening to me.

We chatted and chatted and chatted for hours until well
after we had finished eating and eventually we were asked
to leave at 2.00 a.m. I don't think I've ever laughed so
much in my life. We continued talking as we strolled along
the beach and the air felt so magical! We talked about old
times and caught up on new times.

Mum, I don't no if it was the wine, or the heat, the
food or just my hormones but there were some forces in

motion last night. Toby touched my arm and I felt all . . .
zingy from head to toe. I'm almost thirty-one years old and
I've never felt that before. And then there was this silence.
This really weird silence. We stared at each other as
though we were seeing each other for the very first time. It
was like the world stopped turning just for us. An odd
magical silence.

Then he *kissed* me. *Toby* kissed me. And it was the best
kiss I have ever had in all my thirty years. And as our lips
pulled apart my eyelids opened slowly to see him staring at
me, looking as though he was going to say something. And
in true Toby form he said, 'I bet there was pepperoni in
your dinner.'

How embarrassing.

Immediately my hands flew to my teeth, remembering
how he used to always tease me about the food stuck in
my braces. But he grabbed my hands and pulled them
gently away from my mouth and said, 'No, this time I
could taste it.'

My legs nearly buckled from underneath me. It felt so
odd that it was Toby that I was kissing but in another way
it felt completely natural and I think that's what the odd
thing was about it, if you no what I mean.

We spent all day together again today and my stomach
is doing somersaults at the thought of seeing him again
tonight. My heart is beating so hard the vibrations are
practically causing my locket to bang against my chest. I
now no what all my friends were talking about when they
tried to describe this feeling. It's so good it's indescribable.
Dad kept teasing me for walking around with a silly grin
on my face all day.

Toby asked me to move back to Dublin, Mum! Not to
live with him, of course, but just so that we could be
closer. And I think I'm going to. Why the hell not? I'll
throw caution to the wind and leap into the darkness and

all those clichés, and we'll see where I land. Because if I don't follow this feeling right now who nos where I will be twenty years on from now?

How crazy does all this seem? What a twenty-four hours it's been!

From   Rosie
To   Katie
Subject   Yes!

Oh, it's not crazy at all, Katie! It's really not crazy at all! Enjoy it, love. Enjoy every second of it.

From   Katie
To   Alex
Subject   In love!

So Mum was right, Alex! You *can* fall in love with your best friend! I've packed everything up and I'm heading home to Dublin with my heart filled with love and hope, and my head filled with dreams! Mum told me about the silence she experienced years ago. She kept telling me when I felt that silence with someone, it meant they were 'the one'. I was beginning to think she made it up but she didn't! This magical silence exists!

You have received an instant message from: ALEX.
Alex: Phil, she felt the silence too.
Phil: Who, what, where, when?
Alex: Rosie. She felt that silence too, all those years ago.
Phil: Oh, the dreaded silence thing is back to haunt us, is
   it? I haven't heard you talk about that for years.
Alex: I new I wasn't imagining it, Phil!
Phil: Well then, what are you doing talking to me? Get off

the internet, you fool, and pick up the phone. Or the pen.

Alex has logged off.

My dear Rosie,

Unbeknownst to you I took this chance before, many, many years ago. You never received that letter and I'm glad because my feelings since then have changed dramatically. They have intensified with every passing day.

I'll get straight to the point because if I don't say what I have to say now, I fear it will never be said. And I *need* to say it.

Today I love you more than ever; tomorrow I will love you even more. I *need* you more than ever; I *want* you more than ever. I'm a man of fifty years of age coming to you, feeling like a teenager in love, asking you to give me a chance and love me back.

Rosie Dunne, I love you with all my heart. I have always loved you, even when I was seven years old and lied about falling asleep on Santa watch, when I was ten years old and didn't invite you to my birthday party, when I was eighteen and had to move away, even on my wedding days, on your wedding day, on christenings, birthdays and when we fought. I loved you through it all. Make me the happiest man on this earth by being with me.

Please reply to me.

All my love,

Alex

Epilogue

Rosie read the letter for what seemed like the millionth time in her life, folded it into four neat squares and slid it back into the envelope. Her eyes panned across her collection of letters, greeting cards, email print-outs, chat-room print-outs, faxes and scribbled notes from her schooldays. There were hundreds of them spread across the floor, each telling its own tale of triumph or sadness, each letter representing a phase in her life.

She had kept them all.

She sat on the sheepskin rug in front of her fire in her bedroom in Connemara, and continued to take in the array of words spread out before her. Her life in ink. She had spent the entire night reading back over them, and her back ached from stooping and her eyes stung. Stung from the tiredness and tears.

People she had loved had so vividly come alive in her head during those hours as she read their fears, emotions and thoughts, which had once been so real but which were now gone from her life. Friends that had come and gone, work-mates, schoolmates, lovers and family members. She had relived her life all over again that night in a matter of hours.

Without her even noticing, the sun had risen, the seagulls

were dancing around the sky, calling with excitement as their meals were thrown around by the angry sea. The waves crashed against the rocks, threatening to come further. Grey clouds hung like smoke rings outside her window still left behind despite the early morning rainfall.

The delicate shades of a newly formed rainbow rose from the sleeping village, stretched across the wakening sky and fell into the field opposite Buttercup House. A vibrant vision of candy-apple red, buttermilk, apricot, avocado, jasmine, oyster-pink and midnight blue against the grey sky. So close Rosie wanted to hold her hand out to touch it.

The bell from the front desk downstairs rang loudly. Rosie tutted and glanced at her watch: 6.15.

A guest had arrived.

She rose to her feet slowly, wincing at the pain of being crouched in the same position for hours. She held on to her bed post and pulled herself up to her feet. She slowly straightened her back.

The bell rang again.

Her knees cracked.

'Ouch, coming!' she called, trying to hide the irritation in her voice.

She had been so stupid to stay up all night reading those letters. Today was a busy day and she couldn't afford to be tired. She had five guests leaving and four more arriving not long after them. Their bedrooms needed to be cleaned, their sheets washed and replaced for the next arrivals and she hadn't even started making breakfast yet.

She carefully tiptoed between the mess of letters scattered around the rug, trying not to step on the important papers she had saved all her life.

The bell rang again.

She rolled her eyes and cursed under her breath. She was not in the mood for impatient guests today. Not when she hadn't had a second's sleep.

'Just a *minute*,' she called cheerfully, holding on to the banister and rushing down the stairs. She felt her toe hit against the luggage that had stupidly been placed by the end stair. She felt herself falling forward and then a hand grabbed her firmly by the arm to steady her.

'I'm *so* sorry,' the man apologised, and Rosie's head shot up. She took in the man that stood before her, nearly six foot in height, with dark hair that had greyed along the sides. His skin was tired and wrinkled around the eyes and mouth. His eyes looked tired, as would anybody's who had just spent four hours in a car to Connemara after a five-hour flight. But those eyes sparkled and they glistened as the moisture inside them began to well up.

Rosie's eyes filled up also. The grip on her arm tightened.

It was him. Finally it was him. The man who had written the final letter she had read that morning, begging her for an answer.

Of course, after she had received it, it hadn't taken her long to reply at all. And as the magical silence once again embraced them, after fifty years, all they could do was look at each other. And smile.

THE END